BECOMING BUDDHA

BY: COREY CROFT

FLY PELICAN PRESS

Published by: Fly Pelican Press

Vancouver BC, Canada V6E 1N9

www.flypelicanpress.com

Registration number: 1157856

ISBN E-BOOK: 978-1-9990730-6-0

ISBN PAPERBACK: 978-1-9990730-5-3

First edition

Cover illustrations: Spencer Croft

Photograph: Alex Parmar

Cover and interior design: Indie Publishing Group

Editing: Sydney Triggs

In Memory of Michael (Papa) Bryan

The original Papa

I killed him the day you died.

The world is lucky I had you.

I miss you.

He said only true niggas will advance
I'm becoming a Buddha, but for now I'm still man

-Bronze Nazareth

EDITOR'S NOTE

Editing Becoming Buddha was a wild ride, and I'm sure reading it will be a similar experience.

The story will suck you in, shake you around, and spit you back out. In other words, it's sure to challenge you. I would encourage you, however, to stick with the characters and see what they can teach you about yourself.

You see, many of Buddha's characters have experiences that are familiar to so many of us. We work jobs that we feel are below us. We wonder if we've made the right decisions in our lives. We have existential crises. We suffer from depression and anxiety. We're complete idiots when it comes to romantic relationships. We compare ourselves to the people around us and feel inferior. We make decisions that we know are wrong, but we make them anyways because we're looking for a little excitement. We fall under the influence of the wrong people. We have sex. We smoke. We drink. We black out. And so on, and so forth.

Becoming Buddha's characters don't deal with these experiences perfectly. Far from it, in fact. Sometimes they deal with them appallingly. They do, however, deal with them honestly. That's another important truth to keep in mind about this story. *Sometimes honesty makes us uncomfortable.*

Some characters, one in particular, will say things that shock you. Ask yourself this, however. *'Is this shocking because it's offensive, or is it shocking because*

it contains at least a grain of truth that I'm too ashamed to admit I agree with?'
Other characters will put up with situations that will make you want to tear
your hair from your scalp. Ask yourself this, however. *'Would I deal with that
situation any differently if I was in it?'*

All in all, it will be hard to get through this story without a good degree of
reflection. I suggest that you lean into that reflection. You know, just like all
those self-improvements fanatics suggest nowadays.

Enjoy the ride, just don't call it a coming of age novel.

It's an anti-coming of age novel.

And Without further ado...

Becoming Buddha

PROLOGUE

How do I start this?

I SUPPOSE THAT I must've lost track of time, staring at myself. Anywhere between five minutes and five hours might have passed. I can't recall my last thought, or even how I ended up here, like walking up a staircase where each preceding step devours itself. My jaw is slack and my cheeks are tense; my skin is loose and the muscles underneath it are stiff. My face feels like the toes of a jerk-off sock. My breathing is baseline and my lungs are on autopilot. My thirsty eyes are begging me to blink. A lovely sting. The pleasant stretch after a long flight. Strange. With all my senses coming back to life, I'm becoming acutely aware that my body hasn't stirred. Not the slightest movement. A waking coma. A gargoyle fighting out of its stone-casing to stretch its hideous, bat-like wingspan and growl at the surrounding scenery. *How many kings died the curse last?*

I barely recognize the man in the toothpaste-speckled mirror. *I can't believe that I've let it get so dirty.* What would my mother think? She *should* be proud that I've cared for my pearls with such vigor that I've earned receding gums, evidenced by the smattering of fluoride and baking soda on the mirror. *They do look nice.* Not bragging, but you'd never guess that I've been a smoker for my entire adult life. They do look a *tad* yellow, although that could be due to the effect of the cheap lighting and old paint in the bathroom, so it's a wash. *The sink looks better.* The toothpaste and soap don't show up as clearly against the off-white basin, though the knobs are hard to clean; the grout and muck have set up shop beneath the taps.

Fuck them. I've used spray cleaners that are supposed to remove all stains and bacteria, I've folded my cleaning rags at the slenderest of angles, and even sacrificed some brave veteran toothbrushes to the task. Unfortunately, they're stubborn tenants that I haven't been able to evict.

I'm surprised at how much weight this unassuming sink can take! I'm not a heavy man, but the lion's share of my upper body weight has been resting on this thing for a while. I guess the nauseating echoes of the older generation's voices ring true. *'They don't make things like they used to.'*

Ugh. My mouth feels stale. Not altogether swampy, but not freshly brushed. My lips are dry. Of course, this is all testament to the duration of my suspended animation, perched like a regal bird, supported by the rim of this mighty sink. It smells like shower in here, but that smell can last for an entire day due to a lack of windows and defunct ventilation.

I might as well open that embarrassing Pollockian mirror and get going. I have a strange affection for medicine cabinets that tuck themselves behind mirrors, likely owing to Rockwell era pictures of fine gentlemen and conscripts shaving in sterile yet homely scenes of vintage Americana. It could also be due to the fact that these sneaky cabinets make tiny bathrooms feel less asphyxiating. Optimal utilization of space, especially where there's little, gives me a utilitarian hard on. The cabinet's hinges are rusted; it must be opened in two stages to avoid spilling all of its contents.

If I were to drop dead, and the police or my sparse loved ones were to comb through my apartment, they'd open the medicine cabinet and probably spill everything into the sink and onto the floor, unaware of the two-step opening process. I hope they'd come to the conclusion that I was someone for whom hygiene was paramount. I have a wood-handled, charcoal-bristled toothbrush with fibres that are soft yet punishing: meek accountant-types turned dominatrixes by sundown. My skincare products consist of an exfoliator and two skin creams; one for daytime, one for bedtime. The exfoliator is all-natural and uses coffee grounds, coconut oil, and sprigs of rosemary to eradicate blackheads and whiteheads, while the creams expel the toxins that try to invade my pores living in a big, filthy city. All-natural, odourless body lotion. Dental tape. Aftershave bottles, beard balms, tinctures of beard oil, pomades, talcum powder, pomades, and waxes… You get the idea.

I also have a straight razor. It's beautiful: wood-handled, inlayed with stainless steel, and equipped with a blade sharp enough to treat brick like butter. It's 5/8 of American steel and crafted with the nuance and attention to detail that only a bladesmith born in a country that wouldn't dream of being invaded could fashion. The wedge and pivot pin match the iridescent shimmer of the imperial blade. *Conqueror of Miscreant Hair. Creator of Symmetry. The Evener.* The rounded point and slickness of the hinge work symbiotically with my thumb. It takes a millisecond for the heel to join the toe. *Snikt*: it pops out. *Snikt*: it retracts. Its movement is nearly soundless, as fluid as oil heated in a skillet. The handle strikes a perfect balance between glossy sophistication and rustic charm; a restrained starburst erupting over a deep mahogany grain. Smooth, with enough tactile resistance to avoid slippage or dropping. Of any object that I've owned, it's the most elegant and masculine to ever come into my mitts; both cosmopolitan and bucolic. Learning to use it, then relearning how to use it correctly, then refining those skills to perfection, has led me to incorporate this piece of metal, screws, and wood as a symbol of my identity. If I could, I'd carry it around in my pocket like a reiki stone, soothingly thumbing its spine and deriving life force from it as a conduit of energy-medicine. However, that's highly illegal and reiki stones are stupid quackery. Besides, a quality stropping and whetting of a barber's notch, so it doesn't bite, is a form of therapy that no spiritual guide or voodoo witchdoctor could ever offer.

The razor was a gift from the best, and only, friend that I made when I moved to the city some while ago. A good friend is very much like a good razor: with proper maintenance and care, its dependability is price-less. Both offer a sense of familiarity and renewal when you stray from yourself. Most objects break, are lost, are given away, are discarded, or are forgotten about. Some become so used and worn that they dissolve in your hands. Some objects are rediscovered hiding in a box or tucked away in the overlooked corner of a loved one's attic, preserved until nostalgia strikes. A pair of boots, for instance, oiled and massaged regularly, can be a useful companion for a lifetime, especially if the sole is revamped. Then, they may outlive the feet they protect.

People that hoard objects are bizarre to me. Cubes upon cubes of cardboard crammed with clothes, books, kitchen equipment, textiles, and media in a variety of formats. The irony is that these people most likely use perhaps three items in their quotidian life.

Not me. I've always been someone who has few irreplaceable items in their catalogue, and a proud detachment from other *things*. My razor is the best example of a personal object that'll last longer than my physical husk, possibly along with my leather boots and jacket, and a solid oak box that's housed everything from photographs to marijuana and its many accessories, in my younger days. Everything else is superfluous. Dollar stores are abundant and sell cheap, expendable cutlery and dishware. Bookcases and beds flower like freckles in the spring, easily picked off street corners at no charge or investment.

When I arrived here two years ago, I purchased the necessities that made my apartment a home, and found further pieces on their secondary run that were inexpensive and just as useful. Still, it's impossible to prevent the casting of world-ending plastics and other faux-materials; the shit's born to break. In a perfect world, we'd need one fork, one knife, and one plate and the like for the rest of our lives. This isn't the ranting of an altruistic global citizen, however. I'm the piece of shit behind you in the queue at the dollar store trying to replace yet another broken spatula.

I don't care much for people. Hate is a strong word, but so is love. So are like and dislike. Perhaps the way I feel towards people is neutral, though that doesn't seem strong enough in any particular direction.

I've had a handful, at most, of close friends, alongside a few girlfriends and lovers, a slew of acquaintances, some strategic partnerships, people with whom I shake hands with upon encountering, and social-media-milestone-wishers. This is probably due to my generally reserved nature, as I've never been an extrovert. This condition isn't out of want, need, or choice, if the latter is even possible. My introversion was procured in childhood and never outgrown. Still, I wouldn't use the term shy in the first dozen or so words used to describe myself. It could be a confidence issue. I've never felt my inner dialogue as some kind of cheerleader *ra-ra-ing* for my mental and physical attributes, which are neither poor nor exceptional. Very normal, rather. Blame it on a malaise that sprouts from a condition I'd refer to as *super average*: an underwhelming malady, which is as hollow and guiltless as its sufferer. Perhaps my greatest strength is having a third-eye insight that acknowledges the satisfactory normalcy that is 'me,' and the fact that I humbly accept that I'll likely spend my life residing on the median. The problem with knowingly inhabiting the realm of *super averageness* is similar to that of someone who's diagnosed with bi-polar disorder, minus the mood swings. Hopes are raised and dashed with the reckless monotony of ocean churn and the unbearable dread of impending sameness; nominal victories only exist to regain the pitiful centre.

I'm not sure what remedy is out there, but enduring such a condition is Sisyphean. Self-confidence is a boomerang, and depression is alienating. Grinning and bearing it works in segments, but consistently devolves into spite. While I don't like people in a big picture sense, I couldn't have always hated them. *Could I?* The regrettable truth is that I'd like them more if I didn't *need* them, and knowing that lies at the core of my hate. As you enter the baptism of fire that is adulthood, or 'real life', you discover how badly you *need* people. Words like *network* and *affiliation* become synonymous with success and opportunity. I never learned how to superficially bond with people, perhaps because I never cared much about getting to know them, save for a select few, and now find it irksome to forge such fortuitous relationships. You can call it a love-hate relationship, if you want to call it anything.

I feel as though I'm painting a rather bleak and unappetizing picture of myself at this point. A misanthropic rambling somewhere between nihilism and petulance. I suppose that's what happens when you let the mind go for a stroll. *A prisoner's walk in the yard.*

This razor, as well as the man who gave it to me, are era-defining entities that have saturated my memories and will forever remain like scars. I can see him now as I close the medicine cabinet, staring back at me through wisps of black-brown hair, not yet flung from his smooth forehead, never wrinkled with stress or surprise. I can see his beautiful eyes, both sincere and stern due to their shape, looking deeply into mine. Even through the chalky white flecks, those bottomless brown irises stare at me and the similarly-coloured handle of my razor fixedly. How about that? I never noticed until now. *Snikt.*

For the average man to call another man beautiful is a majestic submission to a higher form of power. Beauty is a characteristic that we give to things we cherish like women and babies and sunsets and sunrises and star showers in the desert and serene lakeshores and one-handed football catches and bespoke suit stitching and turtle-waxed Corvettes and puppies *and, and, and.* Women serve as the most renowned and deserving subjects for the label. They're built from the same flesh and bone as men, but are sculpted to arrest all admiration and meaning away from life itself. The word itself was created for them. There's no art without woman and there's no life without art. *Her* beauty is what sustains the prolonging of our species and the inspiration of our greatest and most languishing artists: poets, musicians, and me. A beautiful woman elicits corporeal sensations that only being beaten half-dead, swallowing a tapeworm, and tripping on LSD can yield. That's how they make me feel, at least. Women own the word beautiful, or at least hijacked and appropriated it. They've taken it as their possession and share it with only the most highly valued and sought after phenomena, which the cosmos work in vain to try and rival. I'd take a beautiful woman over a Hubble-shot Andromeda galaxy any day. Men, whether or not there's a homophobia that curtails the usage of beautiful in a masculine sense, have their own words: handsome, dashing, proper, dapper, and striking.

Look at him. Beautiful. Anomalously so. He became my closest friend at a time when I needed just that. He became as influential as the air that floats my lung sacks.

I can say with pure honesty that I've never had a friend like Alex. I doubt that I ever will again. But will I ever need another one like him? No. I *have* changed since I met him… for the better? For the worse? All I can say for sure is that I'm not the same person I was when I left home, and I owe that all to him, that beautiful man. Not beautiful like a woman, but beautiful like a man. Sitting there, watching me. He's always watching me, just as God would.

What does our friendship mean to me? That's a good question. I've never really thought about it. I'm too busy living and trying to practice what he preached. We had some ups and downs, laughs and yells. You know, a couple of chums palling around Paris. It makes me wonder if he was my first *real* friend, ever. How did we get here? Who was looking for who? Who needed who? I think I was searching for something. I had been for a while, and his beautiful eyes were always on the lookout.

I can't say which aspect of Alex was the most intriguing: his inhuman beauty, his confidence, his poise, the assertiveness of his voice and eye contact, his imposing largesse, or the minutiae of his peculiar idiosyncrasies.

Leading up to this precise moment, a question lingers: *Why?* Maybe I could ask him. Or, let it be a mystery. Locked in a chest and buried at sea. A final symphony that died in the cancer-infested brain of its composer. What good is an answer when it's the question that motivates you? The destination signals the end of the journey. If we journey forever, we're never lost.

Whether it was due to boredom, loneliness, or just a readiness to be accepted by another shipwrecked wolf, Alex's tender of friendship came at a time when I was hopeless and bottomed-out on the shores of depression. The move had been hard because I'd never been the type to leap out the window and beg for friendship. I'd only allowed people to sniff the back of my hand or maybe place their head on my lap, but always with tepid anxiety. *Pourquoi?* There are many reasons. The human species has taken a step back from the clan life, where survival hinged on a tribal gregariousness. Did we outgrow the *need?* The *want?* We're without the synchronized hive minds of ants or bees. Still, we *must* entertain partnerships to ensure our progress, unlike sharks and crocodiles. Humans are the only apex predators who struggle with morality and moral incertitude. We may be a social species by nature, but it's the *forced* nature of having to develop an aptitude for conviviality that places *me* at odds with being a social butterfly. I admit, however, that I couldn't live exclusively in a cocoon-state. Caterpillars are prey to damn-near everything.

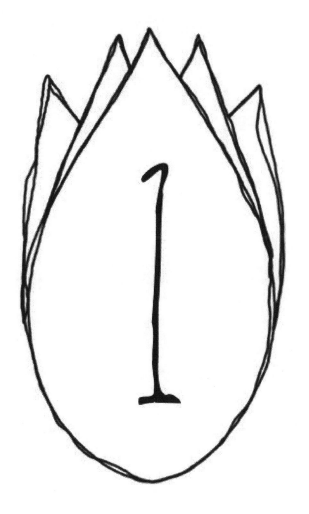

1.

As a young child, I was quiet, agreeable, and obedient. The crystalline depiction of ordinary in school, I seemed destined to grow up to be an average man. My easily-sparked imagination often rewarded me with complimentary adjectives like *sharp*, *bright*, and *quick*, which I now see are the equivalent of giving a dog a biscuit simply for being what he has no other option to be: a tongue-wagging imbecile.

I was never fully aware of this as a child. I was only confused by the output of my grades, which weren't terrible, yet certainly not the grades of an elite student. This confusion begot further confusion as to why I was confused and what I was confused about. I was unable to capture the significance of discovering that the world was *not* my oyster, and that I might *not* become whatever I wanted to be. It befuddled me that, if I was so *bright*, I couldn't retain information without eliminating all other post-school activities like the other gifted, socially awkward kids. If I was *quick*, then why were maths and sciences, the yardsticks for prodigious students, unobtainable? It took me until the academic apathies of secondary school to dismiss these reflections, by which point I'd found other interests in drugs and girls. Imagine that, a crisis of role and identity at so young an age that I was too puerile to grasp that I'd already been shown my rank.

My friends consisted of schoolmates, teammates from local sports troops, and some of my parents' friends' children. Friendships with the kids in my school was necessary to avoid boredom and getting picked on. I was normal enough to be rewarded with invitations to birthdays and for kids to accept being the recipients of mine. I did all the formative activities that those who miss out on harbour within them: bike rides, stealing candy from the corner stores, playing doctor, and getting tattled on. Truthfully, however, I mostly grew up by myself. I was more concerned with the apocalypse, the wars overseas spilling back home, or my mom dying than bad grades or bullies. You know, normal childhood fears. With the exception of such and such student that can draw very well, run very fast, or sing in falsetto, young children are almost all the same until puberty tilts the playing field. Of course, the medial lines of talent and ability become more distinct throughout the teens and into adulthood. Though I don't talk to any of the kids I went to school with, I'm positive that most are still comfortable with repetition, order, and a perfunctory annual rise in status and salary. I, on the other hand, have seemed to refuse to allow my lack of remarkability in intelligence or speed or cunning or strength to hold me back. *If only I could see me now…*

My dearth of meaningful friendships or bonds forged in blood didn't surprise me as a child, and fails to arouse any intense feeling in me today. I was close with my mother, who worked from home and raised my younger siblings and I. My father worked long hours. I always thought he hated being with us, despite having the primitive love that the king lion has for his pride. He was a machinist and enjoyed disassembling anything with moving parts, only to put them back together again. He thought I was a momma's boy, which I suppose I was, considering that she was the only one who was always around and listened to my feelings. I also had no interest in mechanics or even how things worked and why. I had an *'if it ain't broke'* kind of attitude. And, twist my arm, I was kind of lazy. My father would show me manly things as if it was a chore, performing tasks and showing me finished products, expecting praise and acclaim. My lack of interest usually resulted in my being sent to help my mother, where we'd read, talk, and discuss the alienation I felt from my classmates.

I don't think I was weird. Perhaps it was a gift to be so self-aware and self-admonishing at a young age. As I mused, it could've been the genesis of a strange virtuosity. My mother had a way of broaching my feelings with sincerity. What a nice lady. It was as though she could untangle the choking fog that obscured my psyche and make it seem as though my torrential thoughts of loathing and persecution weren't silly or singular, but normal and false. I don't know if she was simply mitigating any damage possibly caused by drinking or smoking during pregnancy, or if she really believed it, but she made me believe it, too. My poor little kid mind was wrought with complex brooding and advanced placement stress. I wasn't sure how many of the other kids thought like I did, but I didn't trust them enough to tell them anything… especially when they questioned me on why I liked to be alone. Like they never needed some time away from themselves.

2.

I saw three dead bodies before the age of 15. I'm not saying that this sets a child up for failure, but I'm sure it has some effect.

We lived in a landlocked town roughly twenty miles from the big city. We had a house with a room each for myself, my parents, and my two siblings. Here's to you, Levittown. We had a driveway full of cracks, and I used to make miniature bouquets for my mom out of the mighty sprouts that caused them. We also had a backyard that was fenced from a large drainage field that was used to soak up heavy rains and contained a succession of massive, buzzing electric towers. The towers buzzed like an old guy with bad knees, worse when it rained. I sometimes felt a slight, dull stinging in my mercury fillings on humid days.

When I was around 5 years old, I was playing catch with a tennis ball, bouncing it off of the wooden, cyan blue-scabbed fence. It must've been summer, as I remember the yard only dried completely in the longest and most arid days of July, and only then could you play in the yard and not worry about muddying up your shoes, accompanied by a chewing out from Mom about not knowing how to take care of your clothes. I was forbidden to go in the field because the grass, only cut twice a year, was at its peak height, which created fertile hunting grounds for coyotes, pedophiles, and other malefactors that wished for nothing more than the ruddy flesh of a young boy. While trying to find out how close to the top of the fence I could throw the often-used, less-than-woolly tennis ball, making it pop up and obscure the sun like a real pop-fly, I lobbed it into the restricted zone. While retrieving the ball from the forbidden badlands of the drainage field, I came across the limp, still-rosy body of a teenage boy. I remember being startled at first, then staring for a moment before trying to shake his shoulders and knees to wake him up. I stared at his docile face and milky features. He looked peaceful in his play clothes, like he was napping on the couch at his family home. Meanwhile, my mother had lost sight of her baby boy, entered the field, shrieked, picked me up, and rushed inside as fast as she could. She called the authorities, and within twenty minutes our yard was full of police officers, emergency medical specialists, and the frantic parents of the dead kid. They said that he'd been climbing the scaffolding of one of the electrical towers with his friends, fell thirty feet, and broke his neck. I never got my ball back.

The second time was very different. Being a few years older, I was defiant against the proscription of venturing out into the field and threw caution to the wind with our dog to search for treasure: frogs, balls, quarters, shoes, anything that a tramp or an older kid might've dropped. The Husky-Labrador mix, with his beige-gray coat and simple-minded breathing, led me to a tower deep in the field. We didn't find any profitable rewards, but a teenage girl hanging by her neck from the lowest rung. She didn't look docile or at peace. She was purpled and distended. Her face was chubby and sullen to a degree that seemed to evince her personality. She wore a blue hoodie and gray jeans with black skateboard shoes that had extra-large laces to avoid tying them every time they were slipped on. Her hair was blond, greasy, and cinched into a pony tail. I remember it was an overcast autumn day and the invisible sun cast all objects, living and man-made, with a dismal ashen paste. If I were forced to guess, the girl was lucky to have jumped with the appropriate strand count and fathom of rope for her death drop. The knot even withstood the impact, though her head was propped up, and she more than likely choked to death rather than snapping her neck. It would've been time consuming and painful, rather than a quick break, then hanging lifeless until the dog and myself journeyed upon her.

The third instance was when I was walking along the catwalk to get some nickel candies with my friend while he got a pack of cigarettes for his mother with a note, which was a pretty common thing for the area back then. His parents were lazy alcoholics and real pieces of shit. On the return trip, we decided that we'd conceal ourselves in the spikes of tall grass and infiltrate manhood using the soothing kiss of filtered menthol tobacco sticks. I was paranoid and ever-fearing of my mother's wrath, and to a lesser extent, pinching a dart from my friend's folks, who did little parenting other than beating the piss out of him when he irritated them. We inched further and further into the adult-height blades of slightly dampened spring grass. The post-winter bloom was in full effect. Cotton flitted above our heads like fallen clouds, too heavy for the sky to hold. Dandelions with thick stems were abound. The yellow ones refused to be extinguished underfoot, were beheaded, and then used as a natural jaundice on our arms and legs as camouflage. The white ones, on the other hand, were used to launch their gossamer paratroopers for colonial expansion. Pockets of purple and pink wildflowers were lifting their faces towards the sun for breakfast. We lit one cigarette and passed it back and forth. It was dry and mouth-watering at the same time, which had a calming effect over my body that felt both bold and comforting. My friend became increasingly nervous, though the whole thing was his idea, and we couldn't get far away enough to finish the cigarette. The agitated grass spit dew on us as we waded deeper into the make-believe Vietnamese jungle. I wondered how my friend was going to explain the missing cigarette to his mother, but once we were to part ways, that would no longer be my concern. His ass-kicking was to be his, and his alone. We patrolled the field and soon spied upon some depressed grass twenty or so paces to the east. We decided to explore, as there could've been a stolen bicycle or, if luck was so kind, a motor bike that someone was hiding for future reclamation. Instead, we found a man. He was face up with what appeared to be shovel-handle-sized holes in his chest, and maggots covered one side of his head. It was grotesque. His blood was like raspberry jam: dried on the corners of his mouth, crusted underneath his nostril, temple, and streaked in his wavy black hair. His mouth was twisted agape and his eyes were half-open. His pupils were fixed with a vacant glance, looking through his left eyebrow. Flies were dancing melodically over his teal sport coat, which covered a dress shirt, now more brown-red than white. The smell was pungent, a unique and off-putting odor: the tangy bitterness of sour milk and the sinus-pummeling force of sulphur, with a pinch of human excrement left for a day or two, then halved directly in front of your nose. And, ammonia. My friend was appalled and beside himself. I finished the whole cigarette while he vomited and cried.

These experiences didn't result in me talking to a shrink. Even if I did want to, it was never offered, at least not once the afterglow of each event had faded. I gave the police my account every time, which seemed like enough. It *did* initiate and reinforce the pattern of me liking to be alone. Solitude refreshed me. I found luxury in withdrawal, contented with only my thoughts. People judge you based on your experiences and how you handle them, but how many experiences happen on purpose? Was seeing dead bodies *my* choice? It didn't matter. When I met people, I was the kid who kept finding dead people. Some found it interesting, others assumed I was ruined.

So then, how many experiences *are* engineered by *choice*? And, how many experiences are due to the unseen hand of chance rolling dice on your behalf? In any case, I continued to occupy the middle of the road with regards to my development. I played the sports, did the homework, lost the virginity, tried the drugs, muscled through the puberty, and completed the high school with no idea what I was supposed to do next.

3.

I've distinguished a few characteristics about myself at that time. While not the best, I was a decent athlete, who, thanks to my parents' unprotected sex after a The Cure concert, combined genes that gave me a frame that was able to grow muscle and strength at a respectable rate. I also discovered that I loved women. They became the impetus to almost all my industry. I was still reserved, something I couldn't fight, but I became apt with a well-timed blandishment, thigh caress, and tongue to the ear.

I enjoyed drugs, recreationally, at least the ones that didn't warp my connection with reality too gravely. Pessimism, paranoia, and worry, my *Athos, Porthos*, and *Aramis*, were congenital and inexorable personality traits. This meant that psychedelics weighed too heavy for my simple, cherubic head and didn't provide the most relaxing or mentally propitious trips. Marijuana, alcohol, and cigarettes were always great comrades. Depressants as they might be, I still had coffee.

As for education, I've never been able to grasp anything beyond a rudimentary understanding of maths and sciences. Registering how highly they were valued, ear-marked by scholars as touchstones for intellect, I understood my erudition had limitations. I *was* proficient in languages, and used my electives to learn more. By the time I left high school, I was capable in Spanish and fluent in French.

After graduation, I didn't have a problem packing up my meagre possessions and taking my talents to the newer, less-than-prestigious university-college situated some dozen highway exits further inland. This was not, of course, the ambitious student or enthusiastic parent's first choice for higher learning, but one that offered a longer landing strip to steady the speed wobbles heading into the *real world.*

My folks were proud, as neither they, nor any of my aunts or uncles, had entered college, opting instead to take the route often-traveled of saddling up with a company until Gold Watch Day. They were happy that one of their cubs had left, meaning only two more to go before they could get a divorce and become a slice of what people call *happy*. They may not have known it, but you could smell their mutual distaste for the propinquity they shared. As parents often do, they used us kids as a suture to try and keep the crevasse that was growing between them from becoming a canyon. I didn't really care whether they stayed together or got divorced. I thought it would probably benefit my relationship with each of them if they broke up. I'd gotten them into the situation, I'd lead the offensive to get them out. My imminent crowning some three decades ago had coerced the two lustful parties into a holy matrimony, which must've seemed like a good idea at the time. I can't dispute that they'd once loved each other profusely, but the routine and sequential forward movement in opposite directions really just begged for a mercy kill to liberate two otherwise fine people who would get on just as fine after the axe dropped.

The college life, different from the metropolitan life of the more prestigious university located in the center of the big city, was idle and quaint, just like the high school life I'd left. The college itself was nothing like the top-drawer university campuses, with their prestigious grand halls named after slave owners that had illustrious backstories and columns of graduation pictures with nearly all-white faces. Newly furnished satellite outposts were freckled strategically in historically significant areas throughout the city, all of which had classrooms that contained exposed brick and reclaimed wood and were taught in by haughty pedants with tenure and sycophantic lackeys and a salient distaste for the class time that funded their laboratory renovations.

Our humble, little university-college was of a newer design, built of that smooth and esoteric material that looks like wood and stone but feels like plastic. Many of the professors had second or third jobs in town as insurance clerks or beat writers. It was also connected to a strip mall by a parking lot. Basically, it was built for the city's average kids with lazy or uninterested hands that had dropped out of school and were unfit for trade school. The college and mall were key cogs in the city's promotional video package to entice new residents and enterprises, a bolt-on attachment meant to fuel a sprawling suburban city funded by a consortium of local businesses. Those business owners were eager to see their future employees not stray too far from the hive.

The school was an arm of these businesses, and the classes matched. Students had to transfer to a better institution if they wished to train for a career in medicine or law. However, we didn't have homeless people like the mid-gentrification metropolitan university, performing tricks like circus seals to earn some money for heroin in the foreground of a legally sanctioned piece of graffiti. We had about an acre of parking lot with a clumpy-handed, middle-aged woman that left citations on your windshield if your ticket expired. We didn't have vibrant sandwich shops with exuberant shop owners or pretentiously independent coffee shops with frail baristas measuring pour-overs with nautical tattoos and septum piercings. We had corporate sponsorships that brought in underpaid, foreign workers to usurp student jobs at chain-operated food counters around campus, with two-ton trucks delivering *freshly baked* bagels and *freshly squeezed* fruit juices at 7am every morning from some warehouse.

People did seem to have more open minds than the kids in high school and my neighbourhood, although this varied depending on one's private life and incumbent experiences. All the *'college kid'* tropes were present: the sheltered kids racing to get herpes, the determined and quiet students, those with clear goals and objectives, striving to make a difference in their community or transfer to the big university to receive a *different* piece of paper with *different* Latin writing and *different* signatures from *different* professors, who out-professed our professors, and the big-talking, small-school athletes who tore their ACLs or MCLs while playing third division ball. They never had a fucking chance, did they?

Then, there was me: a few hook-ups, solid attendance, painfully gleaned participation marks, side job in a restaurant, and eventually a French language major. Regarding the last point, the money that I borrowed and am paying back wasn't a complete waste.

4.

The program afforded my year of studying abroad in Nantes, France, the capital city of the beautiful coastal region of Normandy. Other than the year in Europe, I had what I'd call a fairly uneventful undergraduate career. I'd already tried most drugs in high school, as well as sex. Overall, friends in college were a different flavour of bland. Friends in high school offered a linear quality of consistency, with some wavering of identity and attitude due to teenage hormones and adolescence. Friends in college, however, were fickle as fuck. I'm a natural listener, but the volatility of people's sensibilities tested my patience. It's almost cute, in a pitiful way, to hold a newly discovered belief with the same juvenile indulgence as a child would a new toy. Beliefs that contradict my own, as most do, have never bothered me. There's no reason that someone acting on their own behalf should cause injury to me in any way, unless that's their intent. It was the flip-flopping and hasty galvanization of newfound ideologies, however, that kept me at a distance from my peers. While some used literature and statistics from their lectures to fortify their perspectives, others were like fleas hopping from host to host, but in this case from Marx to Nietzsche to whoever.

This is the nature of thinking critically for the first time, whether empowering or damning. These overgrown children were momentarily visiting the dungeon that my mind had long lived in: the fear of the future's uncertainty and the disturbing realization of being a small nothing in a large, vast nothingness. These ideas were training wheels to a veteran like myself. My identity, as it was, barely shifted beyond wearing better fitting clothes and growing a poet's beard. I liked having facial hair. Once you get past the awkward phase of patchy bristles and uneven, stubbly growth, you develop a kindred connection with your beard, gaining a wiser look that younger women find attractive.

The struggle of identity that people went through in university caused me to lose respect for many, but I *still* needed them. Women, that is. One girl stands out. We dated for the final two years of school. The depth of her subtle yet constant personality changes were difficult. I met her as a sultry freshman. She was relaxed and witty, with a particular knack for pop culture references and funny voices. She had an appreciation for dry humour and was kind of fucked up from an abusive father. Soon, we were having the best sex of our lives. We fucked at any time of day, with mouth and hand detail when time was a bastard. She was hot. Not beautiful, if only because of the way she chose to doll herself with arguably heavy doses of makeup in order to make it appear as though she was using very little. She wore clothes that were hyper-stylish, but lacked a certain subtlety and sought only to publicize her thin stomach with its muted ab-muscles and swell her round ass. It might've been a confidence thing, or a deep-seated lack thereof. Hot, not beautiful, but visually searing. A broken-neck-causing head turner. She made me feel the blood pumping through my body and become aware of the veins tightening in all of my extremities; the savage lust of wanting to ground another person and attack them with unrelenting ferocity until orgasm, a spiritual horniness that extends beyond the physical.

My relationship with her was the closest I'd ever been with someone. Her optimism complimented my dryness, her cutesy humour and my dark humour wove together nicely, and my lack of confidence in my intellectual capacities was equal to hers with her tits. While being gifted a naturally svelte and toned body and a compact, perkily-uplifted ass, her breasts were virtually just nipples. This didn't register as notable to me because I'm an ass man. It didn't take away one ounce of my attraction to her. She'd cover her chest with her little hands for the first several months of our intimacy. I learned how important and empowering a good pair of breasts can be to a lady. She always said that she wanted to get breast implants one day.

Then, the changes started. She started to become more involved in women's issues, then civil rights, and finally, anything that was the slightest bit derogatory towards anybody, anytime, and anywhere. It was confusing on a sliding scale. I was still attracted to her physically, and her me, but we were becoming different people from when we'd first met. I like to think that I maintained a straight course; as always, as forever. She, however, had a Californian attitude one day and a militant disgust for men the next. As the new traits of her identity started to solidify, she ceased eating meat, though she hadn't eaten anything but fish and occasionally chicken before, refused to look at unnatural or mass-produced hygienic products, and refrained from shaving her pubic or underarm hair. None of this bothered me. In fact, I now have a fetish for a big bush on an otherwise smooth woman. She was turning into a hippie, albeit one that still enjoyed dressing in expensive designer clothes and having her eyebrows and nails done, as well as rarely being caught without makeup. It was all very strange. She'd received a women-only scholarship by her third year, several thousand dollars, which she eventually used for breast augmentation surgery. Don't get me wrong, they looked great. They gave her the confidence to ride on top with the surety of Hannibal on elephant back. The sex, amazingly, got better. Puddles had to be covered with a towel on the bed, and my beard was consistently drenched in her fluid, which I always hoped wasn't piss. However, her militancy for the rights of marginalized insert-vulnerable-demographic-here began to outweigh the counterbalance of her previously laid back, sex-hungry persona. As my graduation approached, we rarely saw each other, and when we did, sex was infrequent. I believe we both lost respect for one another. She couldn't face her comrades while dating someone so redolent of the enemy, while I couldn't rationalize the contradiction between her ethos and her physical appearance. By the end, I'd make misogynistic comments, as well as racial and sexist remarks to jab for a reaction and to hammer home the distance between us, further pushing her away. I'm sure that this was subconscious, but it may have also been a way to tempt her back into her old mindset, or a defense mechanism against barbs that I felt were unfairly slung my way every time she rolled her eyes and bemoaned men. Sometimes I wonder what I did that was so wrong. I still miss that little bitch.

5.

In France, I felt at home. I thought it was the place where I was meant to serve my lifetime sentence of personhood, on the cobblestone streets with steel grating that allows the musty smell of sewage to blend with the unidentified meat of kebab hugged between compressed Panini cheeks. I loved the feeling of speaking another language at length, learning argot, and apprenticing slang. It was like being a fully-grown child with a fully-formed libido and spirit of humour. I was experiencing new thoughts, feelings, and fears almost every day. It was the first time I felt totally at peace with being nervous and alone. It also felt refreshing to be different. I can't think of a more eloquent word for it, but it was a difference that I could chalk up to being exotic, foreign, or simply *not French*.

Important note: the French are an incredibly sardonic nation. While they're genuine and soul-baring, they're very much the same people that weaponized the word *ennui* and founded the school of Existentialism. I found the students in my *fac* authentic in their passionate views on life, politics, media, literature, and human beings. Their commitment to their roles, whether hippie, academic, athlete, or any other sub-group of university stereotype, was performed with ubiquity. There were no watery affiliates or indecisive undergrads like home. The French, and Europeans by extension, manage their ideologies and the embodiment of those beliefs with candor and fire.

The women in France are as symbolic as their vineyards, cheese, and arrogance. Two get stronger with age, one stronger in poverty. Guess which is which.

Women have long since replaced men as the *de facto* leaders of France. It must be that after centuries of being fawned over and idolized in poetry, they came to the realization that they were *indeed* superior beings. French men are decidedly emotional, prone to caprice, and hubristic to cartoonish lengths. They haven't achieved a balance between refined and rugged, always maintaining an inclination towards violence as long as the liquor provides enough bumptiousness for the battle. The women struck me as dominant, aggressive, direct, and navigated by logical thought. At the same time, they stand in a figurative clam shell, flanked by roseate angel babes with albatross wings, holding scimitars in their left hands and top-knots of their *amoureux* in their right. They're not the least bit insecure of their sexuality, and will tell a man within a minute if they want to have sex with him or not. Other than the rise of wearing pants beneath dresses, which was a trend during my exchange, the women understood the subtleties of their own femininity: fashion, *maquillage*, and hygiene. The natural quality of their beauty is the personification of the phrase, '*Brevity is the charm of elegance.*' The most make up I saw was on street walkers in *Pigalle* or on tourists. French women are angular yet soft, with a prominent darkness to their eyes and lips that magnifies their prominent chins and cheekbones, with lips that are not too large nor too thin, and noses that tie their faces together with unassuming bridges and nostrils not given to excess. All these features are bordered by hair that's just as succulent straight out of the salon or left for the wind to breathe life into. This all culminates into sexually confident and competent human beings that I missed when I had to return home to complete my degree. I wanted a French woman: well-read and dirty-minded, petite and prodigiously strong, a little nympho with pert, palm-fitting tits, and a great ass. Still, I didn't understand that whole pants-under-skirt phenomenon. Seemed excessive.

Pardon me while I stray from my story for a moment and talk about sex.

My favourite kind of sex happens when I feel little to no respect for the other person. There can be care and love, but respect should be thrown to the floor with the condom wrapper. It's about connection and chemistry. Rare have been the times where bombshells were the most frenetic in bed, the same with brilliant or even very smart women, with exceptions in both cases.

Some of my greatest sexual matches have been cute women, bright and athletic enough, with some kind of unwholesome upbringing or an abnormal trigger event. In most cases, otherwise 'average' women have been those with whom I have the most in common with. We both have the same lost hopes and faltering aspirations that culminate in a wandering sense of inward vacancy and confusion that escapes in various forms of sublimated misery. Others may lie to themselves, but we know. What we're doing is punishing each other for what we despise, fear, or lament in ourselves. There's no pity, nor remorse. I don't care to psychoanalyse the deeper meaning of rough and rewarding sex, and truthfully, I'm unconcerned about capturing an iota of Freudian psychology. All I can say for certain is that when two underachieving adults tacitly agree to consensual, self-deprecating sex, the chances of a great experience are limitless.

Race, height, age, whatever... none of that matters. I *do* have a thing for noses, however: big, long, wide, bumpy, or anything awry. Being in my thirties, my greatest sexual chemistries have been obvious from a glance or a nice talk. After introductions, with smoldering loins, we launch explosive salvos at one another, resulting in drenched sheets and sticky orgasms. With some people, sex gets better as time goes on; with others, the opposite. It's all about getting to a level of passion where true personality emerges. I enjoy being carried away with another who has the same veiled animalism punching at the ceiling within them. I love the choking abrasions, blue-brown welts, bite marks, handprints, thumb bruises, and the scalar degrees of shared trauma that force neighbours to hammer their fists onto shared walls with no concern but jealousy as their copies of self-help literature flap to the ground. I love the instant connection of legs and arms wrapping around each other while lips and tongues press greedily at the other's neck and mouth and entire body. I love the freed strands of hair that last longer than the sex itself, torn from a head being pushed away or pulled closer.

It's all topped off by casually laying in the damp steam until being carried to the wash tubs like hedonists, wincing at the sharp water and sting of soap. The entire performance is reminiscent of two veteran carnival wrestlers, never having met one another until the moment of action. Each is so familiar and comfortable with their skills and experience that creating a strong performance is intrinsic. Clothes are shredded to the floor, and the back and forth of positional superiority begins. Reciprocal oral harkens back to the early egalitarian days of agrarian-based human civilization when we all ate plants, wore fig leaves, and worked as one.

Sex and women. I've never been able to classify sex, whether as a hobby, distraction, or necessity... I just know that it's proof that we're still primal, simple-celled creatures. I've often used and been used as a diversion, maybe even as a drug. Women consume time, more than anything, forcing decision-making and some degree of temporal planning. Sex, on the other hand, can be done conveniently, relative to the time you have. It can take the form of anything from a quick bang in a public stall to a weekend fuck fest in some picturesque mountain town. Women are an investment; a beautiful flower that may die, even with diligent attention. Sex is had and cumming follows.

Does that mean it's all about cumming? I've masturbated every day since I was 13. No work day is too long or any thought too macabre to stop me from cranking one out before hitting the sack. 9/11, dead relative, bad breakup, caught in the act of jerking-off... it makes no difference. I'll cum. This might be considered an addiction to cumming, a calming cousin of nicotine and alcohol that quells anxiety and eases self-doubt. Women,

men, and other humans are all fine vessels in which to release the pent-up daily struggles that sag the boxers and the spirit.

You can feel and taste the difference when women are fucking out of frustration, sadness, happiness, or sport. Women masturbate more than men; their recharge time is staggering. They're also very fond of letting you know, acknowledging that you're not presently fucking them, and that they're taking care of business handily, without you. Whether you're in their good books or the opposite, they let you know how much they wish you were, or weren't, helping them make puddles and spider webs between their fingers.

Thank you for your time.

6.

Graduating university, while an accomplishment for my family, presented another period full of destabilization and doubt. I didn't leave higher learning with a direct route to a job, or even an idea of what I might want to pursue as a career. I was able to keep the wick a-flicker on top of the candle that earned me the designation of *bright* as a youth, but for all the brightness of a collapsed, solar-system-flattening star, I couldn't mobilize *them smarts* into a career.

I was still acutely self-aware and prepared to start at the bottom, as older generations say like an incantation. What they won't admit is that they have a stranglehold on the job market in most places, past their prime and stunting opportunities for fresh graduates with underwhelming majors, like French. You can *almost* see the banana-stroking of middle to late-aged men as they bluster about the nobilities of *climbing the ladder* and *corporate loyalty*. Any mention of the perilously aging workforce, or gender and racial inequalities, pre-empts a petulant diatribe about effort and meritocracy. Their bombastic tones turn pettish, and previous grandiloquence gives way to a sour and churlish reticence. A generation of overfed, spoiled, puny, and chalk-skinned men.

To say that I was anxious when I graduated only explains half the state of mind that I had packed in a box with my graduation cap and textbooks. I had a clean slate. No longer would I have face melting sex with an alluring but unfortunately transmuting girlfriend. No more studying in every solitary moment, when I wasn't sleeping or working a night job to stay afloat. I was free to make money and begin paying back my regrettable, but unavoidable, student loan.

The newly freed time at one's disposal directly after college can have a sliding range of effects on a person, depending on their post-graduation journey. Do they have a clearly delineated pathway, or a muddy swamp of a trudge to their next landing spot? There were networking events and job fairs, places where students could create professional relationships with teachers, university staff, and representatives from local and international businesses looking to enlist a few cadets for their future ranks. That is, once the 50-plus crowd starts to ease their nut-clench on the job market. I always found these events to be kind of a wank. Most recruiters were looking for accountants, marketing and business majors, or local drones to be cubby-holed as packets of energy to power the machines. I grew exceptionally passive and found the sensation I got from networking and dick-sucking to be wholly distasteful, even dispiriting. While not being enrolled in a program that led directly to a vocation, for which I take full blame, I felt rudderless. I knew that I wanted to work abroad, make money, meet women, and be challenged and fulfilled. Pretty simple, or so I thought at the time. What makes me smile is that there was still some optimism in that scruffy, plucky baccalaureate.

I kept up my job at the restaurant, taking a full-time role and expecting to be either travelling or laying the first cornerstone of my career within 6 months. The restaurant and hospitality industries require a special kind of monster for prolonged servitude. Former industry folk often recount their years served like ex-convicts.

From what I've seen, there are three main types of people who are lured into the restaurant industry for more than a summer's cup of tea. First, people who aspire to own or operate a restaurant: cocksure and greasy with unbuttoned, light-reflecting shirts. Second, actors and musicians: eyes-to-the-sky optimism of mentally-handicapped children's school photographs, looking at something creative and glorious that us average plebs can't see. Third, people who may have at one time had something that they were working towards, something grand or precise that gave them hope during the long hours, dealing with personality after personality, when they were probably not spiritually cleared for such attrition. They have an aura of begrudging perseverance, haggard and soul-torn, like hunchbacked shadows, and display curtained, manic talents for shielding rage and mechanically going from expressionless to jubilant by instinct. Individuals in each of these groups can be spotted with so much as a cursory glance.

I was in the third group.

The third group dismisses the idea of progressing in the restaurant industry. They abhor the status of *restauranteur*, having observed the pitfalls and failures that seem to await three-quarters of those that try their hand at the onerous and volatile venture. Still, something like hope still resides; an unfulfilled pledge repeated into the mirror of the staff bathroom every day, which echoes in moments of pause like a self-deluding mantra. Alcohol quiets the voice, but becomes the petrol for habitual querulousness and escapism. The third group are pigs who feel too good for the pen, but aren't above eating theirs.

7.

The industry is by no means a wicked place. The flexibility of the schedule and the ability to make a glut of non-taxable *dinero* is seductive and consistent. My issues weren't money based. I was making enough loot to pay rent, repay my loans, save for a trip, and *still* drink myself to sleep. Dealing with people on a continuous basis was eating me from the soul outwards. There are certainly enjoyable aspects to any job of this nature, even while being in the disenfranchised curmudgeon category. The constant stream of attractive coworkers is the foremost benefit, which still doesn't make up for the lack of *actual* health benefits. Nevertheless, anyone who wants to sharpen their sexual spade and punch holes in their belt should work in a bar. Freshly minted and age permissive rookies begin their stopovers as barmen and maidens, waiters and waitresses, garcons and wenches. They're impressionable, buoyant, and inexperienced in life, having just entered the formative years of their social and sexual development. Eventually, even the best feel a sense of self-imposed yet intractable captivity; manumission featuring 15-20% minus tip-out at a time. Unless they're tourists.

The restaurant worker earns a stipend salary compared to any other occupation, meaning that the stacks of banknotes are undisclosed to the taxman, but susceptible to frivolous expenditure. The opiate of the serving class has to be the groupthink and unspoken affirmation that they're perfect examples of average people, working under other average people, who have spent more time perfecting their ability to perform the humdrum status quo than others. While remaining a fast-paced environment with catastrophe and chaos looming within every hungover cook and short-skirted, dim-witted hostess, it's a boilerplate life. Each new day is one of many, synthetically carved out with pre- and post-shifts and 6-7 day workweeks. Each one has enough imperfections to never be diarized as a unanimous victory, but indistinguishable milling makes it indiscernible from the next, or any other.

Such is how I spent the *five (!)* years that followed my graduation. I became a member of countless internet-based agencies dedicated to placing eager employees into careers that suited their analytical and interpersonal skills. I made appointments with counselors from the college, attached curriculum vitae with headshots for European and Asian companies, and tailored cover letters and mission statements to fit desired employers with fresh dates of creation in the corner and personalized salutations. I set up coffee sessions and Q & A's with firms and enterprises. These only produced the often-heard rhetoric of, *'Keep plugging away'* or, *'We don't need anybody with an academic level of reading and writing in French.'* I had, however, received my fair share of offers to floor-manage rival restaurants, as well as constant offers to have my very own set of janglers to the restaurant where I worked. Each offer was handled with gracious negation, eroding further into internalized vexation.

Growing up with modest access to money through summer jobs and parents that kept a tuber famine-like sense of thrift, I didn't spend my ducats before they had a chance to sniff my wallet's lining like so many of my cohorts. My problem rested more on the side of ego, and feeling as though I *may not* deserve a superior marketplace status. I had money, but was unfulfilled. I kept whiskey glasses for each denomination of banknote, a couple of gin bottles that held vast quantities of jingling money, and my parsimonious way of life begged little beyond bank deposits on the 14th and 27th of each month through polite yet direct interactions with automatic banking machines. I still felt the humanity being drained through my pores, becoming aware that it was largely noticeable to my coworkers, patrons, and bosses.

I wanted to feel delight at the prosperity of my longer-termed colleagues being promoted out of the holding cell industry, and verily shook hands, squeezed torsos, and parted my mouth for congratulatory smiles and genial *'Best of luck to ye's.'* I felt like the last child at the orphanage, overlooked and getting older, cognisant of the slimming chances that a pair of frigid, sweater-wearing suburbanites would take this gawky, bespectacled teenager with buck teeth and knock knees home, probably with some rare illness like *lumbago* or *spina bifida*. The staff meals were long-redundant and the once promising inauguration of new employees pushed this gray beard further into his cave. Just when my voice started to growl with a less than savoury huskiness from the anxiety-smoking I was filling my spare time with, something happened.

8.

An indentured servant becomes quasi-familial with the patrons that frequent their favourite or most convenient local establishment. Personally, I tried to keep a regulated demeanour towards my guests. I allowed them to talk my ear off at the wood as I carried on robotically polishing Riedel stemware or stirring swizzled bar spoons in a mixing glass for some cocktail or another. I shouldn't act as though I was some kind of pre-coded cyborg with a programmed set of instructions and gestures meant to convey baseline sentience... Well, maybe when I really stopped giving a shit towards the end.

I was incentivized by the opportunity to squeeze out a little more gratuity, especially from first timers and out of towners. Regulars are consistent, down to their obligatory percentage. Attention to detail, for example, remembering small particulars about Joe Blow's favourite lager or Jill Kill's job title and place of business, is an arrow in the quiver.

I honed my ability to provide an anecdote, make a recommendation for activities to do while on a date, shake my head from side to side contritely while casting my eyes downwards, nod sympathetically, and lift one hand steeped in exaggeration paired with a gasp and a '*Well, what are you gonna do?*'

I never offered advice. I believe that a bar isn't a place to seek therapy, and people who ask for advice, especially from relative strangers, will never take it. I didn't share personal information beyond topical narratives when convenient to further develop a conversation. I couldn't think of anything more unnerving and weird than having intimacy with people that were at opposite points of their work day. I can't think of many other jobs where people pretend to give a shit about someone's grandma's liver cancer or father's gay lover that tore apart his marriage. Before you say shrinks, they *have to care* and *make moolah*. Conveniently, I didn't associate with regular customers outside the walls of my establishment, see above. Some coworkers engaged in pseudo-familiar relationships with their guests, and it seemed bizarre. If you want to fuck, just fuck.

The ability to network while humping out booze and grub didn't really cross my mind. My goal-oriented program consisted of: make the drink, take the order, clean the bar, take the money, go to sleep, and repeat, all punctuated with enough charm to balance out the sweat. Many of our guests were after-work specials, suits outwaiting the traffic for their suburban-bound commutes. When I speak of guests who appreciate the mental recording of their favourite beverage and amplitude for small talk or silence, all with rigid consistency in their tipping and habits, these are the people.

One guest, a certain man named Ward, was usually quiet and pensive, staring at the television, watching rope after rope of sports highlights while scrolling through his phone and soundlessly sipping on beer: chestnut-coloured ales in the colder seasons, Munsell yellow pilsners in the drier months. He was a thin, sharp-featured chap with receding red hair, an alert visage that was accentuated by dark, little eyes, a slender nose that came to a point like a Chelsea boot, and a small, pink-lipped mouth, which was often met by his thumb sitting atop his tightly wound fist. I liked him. He was quiet without being sombre, stoic without being rude, and aside from having a beer poured or plate of food ordered, cared for himself like a latchkey kid. He would nod to other suited gentlemen at the bar, and didn't seem to be one for small talk. I always took this as a desire to decompress, a possible escape from the tumult or prickling silence that awaited him at home. I didn't know what Ward did, and I couldn't have cared any less. He was as consistent as they came, and seemed to want to keep our spheres untangled. He spoke with a firm friendliness, and was a far cry from trying to obtain any degree of familiarity with the staff.

On a day like any other, yet different because I'm mentioning it here, there was a distinctly different expression on Ward's face. He had the read-ied look of a man who wanted to ask a question: head slightly raised, brows scrunched, jaw relaxed, and teeth slightly visible though lips that were soft-ened and ready to speak. He had his hands folded, clean and average, dec-orated with a golden wedding band and a handsome, brown leather watch with silver casing, a conservative, white face, and black notches. He wore a blue-checkered shirt, and his cobalt blazer was hanging neatly over the high-backed, wooden barstool. I picked up his first empty pint glass, still a little cold with traces of foam sliding down the sides. I grabbed the glass while rotating my hand sideways, lifting one finger towards the ceiling and punching out the sentence *Another one, bud?* while placing the glass into the rotating glass washer.

Allowing 1.5 male fingers of head, as per the preferred method of execution bemoaned by the owner via the general manager via the floor manager, I swung the fresh pint over to Ward and introduced the glass to his cocktail napkin like an often-repeated memory. As I was turning, I heard him thank me and begin anew.

"Thanks man... Hey, do you mind if I ask you a question?" he said in a direct and controlled tone.

"Not at all, Ward. Fire away."

"Do you enjoy your job?"

"Not at all, Ward. Fuck no."

9.

I suppose that I'd delivered my response with a certain sparkle in the eye that happy people exhibit and desperate people learn. Ward looked at me through his dark, plastic glasses and tightened his gaze, staring at the back of my head through my eyes. After a few more seconds of trying to gauge the level, if any, of sarcasm in my tone, I curled my lips inwards, eased my brow, nodded nonchalantly with my palms raised skyward, and said:

"*What are you gonna do?*"

"Wait," he began, ironing the deliberation out of his face. "I'm guessing you're being serious. You're so frank about it, it's kind of funny."

"I'm glad I could give you a laugh then, big guy. You hungry?" I retorted in the same measured tone, with the correct syllables inflected and stressed to avoid sounding too phlegmatic.

"I'm good," he replied, raising his thumb to his bottom lip, never ceasing to stare up at me with the same questioning face. "I only ask, because you do a very good job here. I've been your bar fly for a few years now. We don't talk often, and I appreciate that. I usually just want to unwind for a couple mugs while the traffic simmers down and the kids become a little less hyper. I've listened to you deal with tons of different characters, and I like your style." He paused, tilting his head and nodding subtly with a complaisant air. "You seem to have a good read on people, and, I don't know if you're courteous or funny or serious, but you're very professional and never stop prepping or polishing or doing something, ever."

I was intrigued that a guy who'd been a prominent fixture at my wood had broken character and seemed to be driving towards something. "Thank you sir, I just try and do a good job... put myself in the owner or manager's boots, you know. Plus, keeping busy makes the time go faster," I responded to Ward, not unlike a fatigued athlete who's just had a press-stamped journalist shove a microphone in his face while trudging off the field. It always feels strange to receive commendation for satisfactorily performing the perfunctory chores of one's monotonous daily duty. It most likely wasn't the intended effect, but it felt like a patronizing sermon from a member of the echelon whose footsteps you hear from above while working on the stitching floor of a sweatshop. There was something of a head-pat-tail-wag sensation that left me chagrinned. Also, I felt a modicum of anxiety that this consistently readable and easy-to-manage guest was possibly altering our dynamic, which had been so convenient. He *was* here a lot, and I had had no time to prepare for this strange new direction.

While trailing off to a less and less audible stammer, I was fishing for a way to either continue or end the conversation in the least awkward way possible, while seeming polite yet firm. I really didn't want to offend the guy, but also didn't want to start a dialogical relationship after all this time.

"I've seen you put up with some shit, man, from the customers, your friends, and the managers. You seem consistent. I like that."

That makes two of us, I thought. I responded a little more earnestly and with a slight tone of self-glorification. "Thank you very much, sir. It's more or less what I set out to do. Only, you're not customers, you're *guests*. You don't want me to catch a beating, do you?"

Ward laughed, genuinely, and continued: "Ha, where's this guy been? It's interesting that you say that. We flay people for calling our *members* customers or clients."

"I suppose I should ask. What do you do, Ward?"

"I was in a financial advisory role for years and loved it. The hours were a little crazy and the schmoozing can take you all over the place for God knows how long. I took a management position at a credit union a couple of years ago, when the family life started to demand a little more 9-5. You know what I mean?"

"No idea man," I crossed my arms. "But, as long as you enjoy what you do, it's all good."

"What about you? You just told me that you hate your job. Are you in school? I always figured you were, but you've been here for so long. Are you becoming a doctor or something?"

"Honestly, I'm just tired of it. I'm sick of the people and the setting. You can form your own opinions as to why, but I'm not happy in the hospitality industry. It was never something that I wanted to do for this long anyways." I stopped myself, fearing that I was getting a little too liberal with my tongue and thoughts to a relative stranger, paying me to serve him. "I'm done university, and not really in a place where I have any med-school aspirations. Surgery and clinical studies waved me goodbye when I almost had to repeat math and science at age 6."

"Interesting. What did you take in university? I was never any good at math or science either, to be honest."

"French."

"Oh," he said as he looked down and away.

"Yeah." After that response, the weight of my contempt, self and situational, and the lack of options I had to escape from it, began to encumber my crown, shoulders, and back. I smoothed out my shirt with my hands and nodded back at him, not in total command of my facial expression.

I didn't feel shame when I told Ward what I'd devoted my four-year enrolment towards, it was a sword that was harmful no matter which way it was flourished. I was harbouring an ever-growing chip on my shoulder, realizing that my lack of career might have had to do with my scholastic choices. The past five years had been nothing but steam boiled from a pot of plain water. There'd been no mirepoix, bouillon cubes, or even a pinch of rock salt to provide any substantial flavour.

"I didn't mean to take the piss. Are you planning to be a teacher or something like that? My sister did a Spanish concentration and teaches at a high school. She gets to travel around and do guest teaching in South America, Spain, and wherever else. Is that what you're planning on doing?" Ward said, giving me a perfectly feasibly alternate route to save some dignity.

"Honestly man, I don't think I'd be very good with the kiddies. I mean, I like kids, but I think if I had to deal with them on a daily basis… I wouldn't have the same degree of tolerance that I have now. As for high school, I remember the kids being dicks, even to the nice teachers, and language classes were a total joke. I really liked language classes, and I speak some *Español* as well, but most of the kids just ripped on each other, doodled, skipped the class, or went purely to drive the staff up the wall." I was being honest with the man. I mean, he did cause me to engage with what felt like a burgeoning existential crisis, which would really kick in during the loneliness of bar close and cash out. "I've applied to hundreds, if not thousands of jobs online and whatnot. It's kind of soul-crushing, but this job pays the bills and lets me save up some mattress money."

"Any idea what you want to do?" Ward seemed legitimately curious.

"Nothing in particular. I have a lot of interests, too many maybe, so I haven't been able to narrow one thing down. I was thinking about going back to school, but I've kind of boxed myself in with the whole French thing. I'd like to believe that it wasn't a complete waste, but I'm starting to think that it was four years of fees that I'm starting from scratch to pay off."

"Bah, I'm sure you had some experiences! You're young, and assuming you didn't just go to party, you probably learned study habits, organization, and other lessons that will come in handy in any career!"

"You sound like my parents," I answered. "It's true. I got good marks, great marks when I was really enthused, but I get bored easily when I feel like I've mastered something…"

"Can anything really be fully mastered?" Ward interrupted, with a hint of guile.

"Well, *sensei*, it depends. I could probably further explore the structural framework of my taps, the engineering components and hydraulics that make the soda shoot from my fountain gun and the beers flow. I could even build a serious sommelier standard of knowledge on our draughts and wines. Furthermore, there's an entire operations side to the restaurant that could take a lifetime to unearth, review, and enhance, whether through a LEAN methodology or an A3 problem solving schemata to improve the modality and discipline of the restaurant, and then patent it to help perfect the orientation and superstructure of the hospitality industry at large."

This felt very much like an out-of-body, stream of consciousness situation. It was a recital that flowed naturally and only paused momentarily for emphasis. I didn't know where all that jargon and operational effectiveness had been plucked from in my memory, but I suddenly regained my senses, cockily leaning on the bar like a Latin lover. '*Well, what are you gonna do?*' I raised my hand, then let it fall. Ward maintained his lukewarm stare with his fist clenched and thumb pressed against his narrow lower lip and said:

"So, you want a job?"

10.

Gone were the insane jealousies of the restaurant dating game. Gone were the ridiculous secrets and gossiping about who banged who. Gone were the all-black pants and shirt combos, the fatigues of barmen and Johnny Cash, who must've also not liked to show dirt and stains. Gone was the seasonal turnover of acquaintances moving on to bigger and better things, occasionally visiting to regale their former colleagues about life on the other side of the gulag's razor wire.

Finally, I got to be one of those assholes that came in and covered up the lugubriousness of wearing a suit, 9-5, Monday to Friday and some Saturdays, meal prepping on Sundays, paying $5 for cake on Stephanie or Joel's birthday, and sitting at a computer with a mouse pad complete with a jelly-filled bubble for the wrist because Jane's a pussy.

I still wanted folding money on weekends, though.

Ward went on to ask me why I didn't offer my ideas to the management team at the restaurant. I shrugged at the question and said that neither side cared enough to invest any time in their employees. Both groups were happy with using minimal effort for maximum gain. I didn't want to admit that those had just been feverish ramblings rifled out in my best salesman voice to cover up any kind of significant nerve that he might've been probing at.

It turns out, as Ward would later explain to me once I'd been welcomed on board at the credit union, that he'd long admired my hustle and social skills. He said that he'd look up from his phone or down from the sports highlights and catch me doing multiple duties in succession, while at the same time dealing with nagging co-workers and guests at the bar. He'd wanted to offer me a job, or at least a sit-down with one of his resident financial advisors, though he'd been unsure if my lifestyle allowed me to save what money I made. Since he'd been given *carte-blanche* to hire at his discretion, the lengthy and unplanned monologue that I'd dropped on him pushed his opinion over the wall. He admired that I was looking for an entry-level job in a role that I could sculpt and tweak into a rewarding future. He figured that I'd be a boon for the sales team when the appropriate spot opened at the appropriate time. The branch wasn't clamoring or even short-staffed in most departments, but two employees were on long-term disability. At a credit union, I remind you. There were pregnancies, cancer battles in the family, and South East Asia trips in order to find oneself going on. The ability to climb the corporate ladder and peer out over the valley of high-level jobs wasn't only tenable, it was damn-near promised.

The hospitality industry is very much like a drug. Not a loaded spike of H or a chestful of PCP, but a casual bump of cocaine from the scaphoid. One long night's worth of white outs can be equal to a few days' worth of squeaks from the wheel of a rolling chair at the credit union. Not to mention the sudden arrival of new and beautiful women, to whom I wouldn't be a sulky, disgruntled geezer, but a carefree and affable weekend guy.

The credit union wasn't what I'd anticipated. It was reminiscent of the hospitality industry except for the significant inclusion of people's financial livelihoods and sensitive information at your fingertips, along with the constant reminder that security monitored the work of newly-minted employees like a pack of black-backed jackals. Fun fact: Anubis, the Egyptian God commonly associated with the afterlife, had the head of a jackal. I researched that during banking hours.

I started as a teller. Even with the feeling of having been rescued, drowning, from the center of a vocational ocean, my ego was still being rocked by surface waves. Whatever. I got to dress in three piece suits, have a timely lunch break and two fifteen-minute cigarette sabbaticals, an e-mail account, eventual access to health and dental benefits, and a regular schedule.

The first thing that caught my attention was that people kept calling me a '*male bank teller*'. You see, some occupations become gender-themed to the point where the speaker has to let the listener know the sex of the person with the job: male flight attendant, lady cop, man nurse, female fire fighter, male librarian, or female postal worker: *fe-male-mail-lady*. I didn't think of myself as dainty or effeminate. Plus, I don't really see how a job says anything about the person doing it these days. There aren't enough well-paying jobs with benefits to really pick and choose based on your inborn traits.

My fellow tellers were all women, middle-aged for the most part, and both sickly and complacent. I wasn't just new, I was a *contemporary* if not *cutting edge* new hire. Ward insisted that this was the best way to work my way up. He'd started off as a teller, quickly moved over to account openings, climbed to account management, did courses on mortgages and high-end loans, and eventually figured out that he wanted to be a full on financial planner before taking the managerial route to accommodate his growing nest. He said that his path had rounded out his ability to make calculated choices while attaining more responsibility. He'd acquired wisdom through experience, as if there were any other way to become wiser.

I was coming in totally green with no banking experience or image of the industry as a whole.

The entire setting was, as the Thai say: *'Same, same, but different.'* While the roster was smaller and more static, there were still trivial complaints from fellow employees that swarmed around my head at all hours. I'd hoped that the archetypal pissing and moaning of the restaurant worker regarding scheduling conflicts, too few or too many hours and how they were doled out, the questionable existence of breaks, promiscuity backlashes, talking behind peoples' backs, and the casual venting of any discrepancy that popped into a server's mind as they hummed and waited idly for the stir or shake of a cocktail, were gone. The tellers never ceased wagging their gums at each other, members, and especially the fresh blood of an inert, new human-wailing-wall. In the first weeks alone, after shaking hands and being spuriously smiled at and welcomed, I was given the dirt sheet on each person by every other person wo-manning a wicket. The level of physical disparagement regarding style of dress (too pomp or too casual), weight (too fat or too skinny), and other ways to conventionally diminish another person were explained to me. *So and so* did this, or *so and so*'s husband only makes this much money. I didn't know if this was normal, if this was how grown-ups were supposed to behave: smile at someone's face, then whisper that their ass is fat when they turn around. I didn't respond, usually extending my chin and tightening my lips while looking up and away with my *'Well, what are you gonna do?'* shrug, which I'd luckily already perfected. I'd also been told that I wouldn't be there for the long term, just to test the waters before diving into the lake.

One lady was obese. She had a litter of runts and had gained, I was told, in the neighbourhood of 60 pounds. She was out indefinitely when I arrived. Another lady, who was also absent when I arrived, had developed a sensitive disposition to both neon lighting and carpet fibres, and was showing symptoms of lethargy. Another wasn't diagnosed, but was able to take weeks of paid injury leave for something she explained as feeling similar to carpal tunnel syndrome. Although her claim was never officially ratified, the company found it to be in their best interests to allow her time to rehabilitate, return, and reinjure. This is by no means a female proclivity. It was evidently clear to me as a disease of laziness, especially one endured in a soft, languid workplace with a fear of lawsuits. Other people, men and women, complained of the slightest introduction of a bug or illness that threatened to cause them discomfort in Puerto Vallarta or leave them in bed on Saturday morning. One lady always discouraged anybody with a sniffle or sneeze from coming too close, blaming whichever avian, swine, or murine flu that was airborne for threatening her chances at conception. One guy was always cold and wore a scarf, while another was constantly sweating due to his hairy limbs. They'd passively quarrel over the red triangle that controlled the thermostat. I prayed that, someday, they'd have a knife fight.

Perhaps the worst of all was the senior customer representative associate supervisor, Jane. If that job title sounds made up, it's because it is. The gentlelady in question had been with the company for four decades, a feat that recent generations, including my own, will probably never strive towards or have the wherewithal to emulate. She'd apparently served out her sentence and was given a nice send-off party, tropical vacation and suitable allowance with which to enjoy the amenities of the resort, a necklace and earring set with a matching watch, a plaque, a certificate of gratitude with modestly regal lettering, *and* a retirement fund with a bonus. Within a year, she was hounding both Ward and the bank director, threatening to squeal afoul that she'd been forced to retire due to her age and against her wishes. She'd returned as she'd left: a cannonball shaped woman, stocky yet somehow frail, like a potato with preternatural sprouts that became legs and arms. She took immediate issue with me. Perhaps it was my sense of humour, or our inability to find any similar interests or views on any topic whatsoever. I wanted nothing more to do with her than she with me, however, her newly created position left her without a computer monitor or any clear sense of purpose. She'd natter constantly that '*things weren't like they used to be,*' wistfully glancing at the other tellers, wishing that they could reassemble the *lady line*. I had one person to vouch for me on the actual line: Eleanor. She was something of a mother figure, a good listener with a complex personal life of her own. I'd hear her raise her voice in dissonance from the hushed tones Jane posed her questions in, ensuring that I heard and was aware that I was being complained about. I respected her, and I respected that move.

I even asked Jane if she had a problem with me one day, on a personal or professional level, or if she just didn't like my face. I approached her with an intended air of humility, with body language that urged non-intimidation. I kept an open posture with my hands visibly uncrossed and out of my pockets and decreased the inherent seriousness of my face in the most endearing way possible. She returned my question with: *'Of course I don't, sweetie,'* in a shrill manner that only wicked stepmothers can emulate. She went on to say that it'd been different in her day, her day being at most three years prior, and that she was just partially jealous that I got to command a teller's wicket and wasn't used to dealing with *men like me.* She of a 40-year husband, four male children, and some grandchildren, of course.

"If you're sure, Jane. I just want to be the best I can be and see how far I can go in this company. I'm learning a lot, and I thank you all for the opportunity and guidance that you've given me thus far. I feel as though I'm really coming along!" said *Ol' Johnny-fight-for-what's-right* to try and pacify, and maybe even win over the tentacled snake.

Eleanor told me that Jane had sneered down at her papers and side-eyed my unsuspecting ass all the way back to my station, where I removed my *'Please See Next Teller'* sign and welcomed the next member. A week or so later, I had my performance review with her, Ward, and the fake-titted manager who always had a Starbucks cup, Linette. I was deemed unsatisfactory and placed on probation. The cause: a threatening attitude.

While I fully embraced the *'We have members, not clients'* ethos that had replaced the *'We serve guests, not customers'* ethos to which I was already acclimated, I tried to keep my head low. I had coffee sessions with Ward who insisted that I, though always capable of better, was still doing great. He wasn't totally sure what Jane had against me. He advised me to meet with all the departments in the company, read all the material, take all the courses, and nibble on the ears of all directors, planners, and executives. I accepted and looked up to him as a mentor of sorts; one that loved dick jokes, as long as they weren't about his own. The director, Linette, was another story entirely. I saw her maybe once a week. Her schedule was inaccessible, except via her personal assistant, who was equally absent. I found out that she'd recently been divorced and surgically enhanced, with pellucid blue eyes and a black bob hair cut like Cleopatra. She had a sharp pterodactyl beak and miniature Doberman-Pinscher legs that were always tensed in masochistic high heels and above the knee skirts. She was quite handsome, though I couldn't say her age, somewhere between 40 and 50, which is a tremendous jump. I wasn't aware if she even knew my name for the first year, even less about my goals in her branch. She would end every conversation with a brittle '...*that's nice.*'

After feeling like I was competent at my job, I wanted to apply for another position, whether branch or head office, to challenge myself and no longer be a *male teller*. Big banks are still a homespun offspring of the martini drinking, cocaine cutting, predatory setting that they've always been. Men are pit vipers charged with winning accounts, earning promotions, and netting higher salaries. Women, whether because it's been historically harder to advance, or because only lionesses are endowed with foot claws for hunting, become even more intense and macho in such an environment. Credit unions, however, feel dopey at best. They've distinguished themselves as more humane and socially conscious, therefore a safer route for members and staff. The marketing and promotional material always proffered how credit unions differed from banks, how they were the understanding and morally aware choice versus the cutthroat rates and competition-slamming branding of banks. My team was playing because they enjoyed the sport, but had no desires of competing in the Olympics or pumping steroids to be the number one slugger.

11.

I don't know if it was just our branch, but the repetition of daily duties, punctual break times, and small talk amongst staff and members was making the new car smell fade fast. I was hiding my agitation beneath efforts to find a more challenging and engaging job. Ward was coaching me on how to go about impressing the right people and booking *rendez-vous* with the heads of different departments to see where my interests might lie. I continued to maintain a degree of error-free excellence and top notch sales in my position on the front line. Sales, though not demanded with the vigor I'd heard in banks, were still important to drive branch statistics, hit goals, and win paltry sales-related prizes like pizza or doughnuts. A year seemed like a good amount of time for me to have delivered phenomenal customer service, completed all the necessary tests and workbooks through the company's private, employee-only website, and show steady progression in my sales.

I applied for a job at another branch, as well as my own, and organized interviews at the headquarters with executives responsible for marketing, securities, commercial banking, and investments. These activities effectively spanned about six months, bringing me past my anniversary with the credit union. I was trying to show my worth and build my portfolio. My meetings with department heads were often rescheduled by their secretaries, who continually informed me that they were very busy and often called out of the office with little time to spare. Copy and paste answers for a control-C, control-V life.

Growth within my own branch was inaccessible due to Jane's constant punching down and an absence of necessity. The positions held by variously-termed disabled weaklings and dotards always seemed to be conveniently filled, not requiring a new candidate. It was a synchronized ballet. One person would succumb to illness or get knocked up, and another person would magically return from an absence to take their place. One job in account openings was posted on the formal 'employees only' job board. I'd figured I'd be a shoe-in for the job because of nepotism, pure and simple, and I was ready for some of that sweet trickledown of institutionalized favouritism and corruption. On the day that they announced that the position had been filled, it went to Jane's niece, who was looking for part-time work to balance with university. She was actually very nice, toothsome with a cute bum, and spent most of the day photocopying and gliding about with crisp cheerfulness.

Applications at other branches seemed a little more promising, though they yielded no nectarines in my basket. I wasn't attached to anyone at my branch besides Ward and Eleanor. This isn't to say that I didn't enjoy the company of some of them: we worked together and on occasion had pizza and doughnuts purchased for us. Additionally, Jane wanted to see me out to clear the way for some enfeebled hag eyeing a return to the teller line, so she now had reason not to stymie my attempts. Most of the other branches seemed to be a little more contemporary, enlisting younger staff and designed in a way that seemed to evoke words like *streamlined, modern,* and *open concept.* These branches almost exclusively promoted from within their own ranks, favouring in-house talent nurtured from seed to sapling to evergreen. I couldn't really argue with that. They could see my sales figures, run a report to check my service errors, and prompt my superiors to offer their honest appraisals, but in their position, I'd do the same thing.

It was disheartening, sure, but I was already a wily veteran of failure. Ward seemed stunned after I let him know about the follow ups with other managers and directors. I guess he thought I'd been fit to steal one or two of those jobs, at which point he'd say something like *'You'll get them next time,'* or *'For now, at least we still have you, big guy.'*

Eleanor left the branch, which was a fairly large knock to my ability of not wanting to strangle everyone in my direct vicinity. She'd earned a nice promotion to be the administrative assistant to one of the bob-hair-styled, sharp-cheeked ladies at the head office. I was happy for her and wished her the best. She was replaced by a surly woman whose name I honestly can't recall. She was the one whose sensitivities to light and air resulted in her staying at home for however long she needed. She was best friends with Jane in and out of work, barked like a hen, and was equally dismissive towards me.

The interviews with higher-ups were exactly what I feared they'd be: less an informational session developed for the purpose of exploring the potential room for learning and growth within a company than it was older, white men masturbating their accomplishments. The sessions, booked for an hour each, usually lasted 15 to 30 minutes and involved me asking very basic questions:

"How would you define your department and what it does?"

"What do you look for in prospective employees?"

"Where do you see the company going in the next 5-10 years?"

Some of the men required fluffing in order to pry more than terse answers out, like stubborn toddlers. They were the worst. If they chose to elaborate, they lorded as though they were standing in the spotlight accepting a Nobel Prize. They explained how they'd slaved away through school, worked their way up, and now played huge parts in the direction of the company. They also informed me that the department was a close-knit group that was already overstaffed, that they were lucky to have dug themselves out a niche, and that they could only imagine the difficulty of breaking into the world of gainful and rewarding employment in this day and age. I'd leave feeling like a cum rag, tossed short of the hamper every time it mercifully concluded; watching the mens' eyes roll back and chins point to the ceiling as they pontificated their own achievements, climaxing when they told me that there were too few seats at the table. Without fail, every information session was the same, which I tried to see as anything but infuriating and depressing. There were occasions when I shared ideas for the future, for expansion and attracting different demographics. I was always shot down promptly.

Some of my ideas were later used without any recognition of where they'd come from. Of course, they'd come from a discarded, sperm-soaked kerchief, rung for its seed of the empire and chucked neglectfully, dried and gnarled, time again.

I was determined not to let any of these dead ends and idea robberies pull my spirit down. I tempered my expectation levels after returning from job interviews. I forbid myself to become excitable, a character flaw that wasn't beneficial. Such is the restless existence of the anxious, I suppose.

I was trying to remain positive after two years plus of routine humbling, though it'd been insinuated that I'd only be working my entry-level job for a season, maybe a solstice to an equinox. Two summers had now passed, and I was entering the part of fall where hues had already crimsoned. I was so fucking humble.

12.

I had begun to casually, very casually, in fact, date a new hire at the restaurant. Having a curtailed schedule made my coworkers in the restaurant seem more palatable. It never occurred to me, but was often pointed out, that our age difference was nearly a decade. It never came up between us, though. We were simply two people who enjoyed each other's company, found each other attractive, and were in an equal state of trying to ignore the complacent nature of our lives by distracting ourselves. Her name was Jaclyn, and it all began while engaging in small talk at work.

"How's the bank?" she asked.

"It's not a bank, it's a credit union."

"Oh, that's fascinating!"

"Trust me, it isn't."

"What are the differences between the two?"

"Do you really care?"

"Eh, no, not especially. Just making conversation while waiting for my Paloma."

"Sorry, I didn't see the chit. I was wrapped inside your voice, like baby Moses in his blankie and basin floating down the Nile. Glad I'm not one of your tables, or I'd never be able to order."

"Actually, it's pronounced *bay-sin*, not *bah-sin*. *Bay. Bay-sin.*"

"That's bullshit. Who told you that? You a witch?"

"Everybody knows that, you freak. Plus, I was thinking about taking classes to become a doula."

"Like a chambermaid or a wet nurse or something?"

"No… a chambermaid is someone who empties chamber pots. A wet nurse, like, breastfeeds other people's children. I don't think any babies would want to suck my beestings."

"Can I?"

"Umm…" she blushed and fought a smile. "*As I was saying*, a doula helps out with the actual birthing. They're like a source of information, emotional support, and advice. And technical support, I guess."

"Yup. Sorcery. You're a sorceress."

"Hey! A lot of people are using more natural birthing methods these days."

"Yeah, because the one thing we haven't done better since the Dark Ages is our health and medical innovations. You like Penicillin? A pharmacist would've cut your foot off for a rash in those days."

"It's not like that! They have a lot of different technical ways of doing it. It's a mentally, physically, and spiritually connective experience that lots of women say is a better alternative."

"Well, I'm never suspect when the word technical is used along with a '*mentally, physically, and spiritually connective experience.*' I'm going to need to see some statistics here. I may not be a lady, but I do know that when someone says '*lots of women say*,' regardless of what you piss with, if you can't produce any numbers or raw figures, the argument is specious. I'm a sabre-toothed tiger for data in an argument, and I… *Midwife!* That's the word I was thinking of!"

"Yes, a doula is similar to a midwife, but is more of a guide, whereas midwives can do more specialized procedures. They take different courses in college."

"Oh, right on. So, either way, they both make sure the ten fingers come out before the ten toes, and that the mama is safe and sound."

"Exactly that. You get a star!"

"*Bah-sin*. It's a French word."

"Are you French?"

"No. Would it matter if I was?"

"No, I think you're cute anyways."

"You're a babe. *Bay-*be. *Bay-sin.*"

"You got it!" Her cheeks lifted like they were attached by strings pulled by angels. She placed her drink and a beverage napkin on her tray and walked on.

She was petite, tiny but not skinny, like a miniature version of a normal-sized thing, scaled down with all proportions maintained. When she walked away, my eyes always followed the tight, black lycra skirt hugging her God-given ass. She turned around to make sure that I was looking, sticking out her tongue with a sassy grin, throwing extra hip into her slinky stride. She had a royally proud posture like a show pony, likely involuntary as her diminutive torso and stovepipe legs were bound together by a congenitally round and firm posterior like a linchpin. She had what'd be best described as a cute personality: laid back, effervescent, and somewhat silly. She had an incredibly varied sense of humour. Not dark, though she didn't put up any barriers regarding subject matter and was often dragged into the most ribald depths of a joke. She was a cool chick and we spent a lot of time together, mainly at my apartment, as she still lived with her parents. We were usually doing some kind of time-squeezing activity like watching a movie or just walking around being an pair of oddballs. If she was anything at this time, Jackie was a convenient way for me to stay busy after work and not let my spirits become too deflated. While we'd never decided on explicit monogamy, little time was left to spend apart from each other outside of our jobs, her school, and other auxiliary activities. I liked having her around. She had a strong sexual appetite, and despite not having the amount of confidence in herself that she should've had, she didn't require fawning and praising. She didn't speak negatively about herself, and tried to forbid me from taking pot shots against my own career and intellect. She was very young, both in age and the intangible nature of her soul. Most importantly, she was feral in the sheets and could roll a mean joint.

13.

Around the two-and-a-half-year mark of my time in the financial services industry, I was summoned to Ward's office for what I figured would be a coaching or rib session, both of which usually progressed into the other, complete with dick jokes. I took my usual seat across from his desk, placed my elbows on the wooden armrest, clasped my fingers, and sunk into the fabric backing of the unmistakeably mass-produced office chair. His office was what I imagined every managers' office to look like worldwide: a faded gray wall, a desk and shelves in a slightly darker shade of *nuage*, pictures of work events (probably lame gifts from the director or colleagues) on the walls, and pictures of family and real friends on the desk facing the manager, to remind them of their life beyond the unmelodic non-white walls.

Ward looked the same as he had in the bar the day he'd poached me for the credit union. I was trying to reason whether that'd been an asset or a hindrance to him. He began to speak in a nervous, not quite giddy, yet in no way distressed, manner. He was unable to conceal some form of edginess.

"You're coming up on two and a half years here, big guy. Have you enjoyed your time so far?" I was slightly taken aback as Ward had to have already known my answer.

"Yeah, I mean, it hasn't been all that I thought it would be, but I've learned a lot, seen the other side of banking, got to... figure some things out about my career. It's been a wild ride, Ward," I ably stammered while trying to keep my cool.

Ward looked down at an empty space on the desk, took a deep breath, and calmly stated: "I'm leaving in just under two weeks to go back to investments, personal finance, mutual funds... the whole shebang, at a national bank."

"Oh... well is that what you want?" I asked him, somewhat perplexed. "I thought you loved the style of socially responsible banking, or whatever. And the time to be with your family."

"Well, I miss the rush of landing a fat, juicy account, and the equally filthy cheques that come with it. A friend of mine's been running the show over there for a while now, and made me an offer that I just can't refuse. The hours will be tailored to what I want, and the money's just *sick*." He elongated the *i* in *sick* a few extra beats for emphasis. "Honestly man, I've been with this place for a while. I've been to different branches, done almost every job, and I'm just done. We have a raptor-woman for a director... I'm not even sure what she does. I basically do all her work while she throat-bangs execs, all while I'm making far less money than I did when I was a planner with more responsibility and boring-ass paper work. Jobs for directors rarely open up, and head office is a weird place full of stale people working like ants for something they can't even grasp. My licensing is primo and I haven't lost a step. It's a total rush to sell to and grease people. Grease them hard."

More than a little surprised by the candid way in which Ward was airing his grievances, which sounded eerily familiar to some of mine, I was left wondering *where this guy had been*. He must've noticed my startled expression. My hands had slid down the armrests, my back was pushed into the chair, and my head was tilted back. He continued: "I wanted to apologize to you as well, man."

I huddled forward with an eyebrow-forehead configuration that wrinkled my hairline.

He released the same sigh that he had before. "I honestly thought things were going to be easier for you. It's not like me to promise things I can't deliver, but I feel that I most definitely let you down. I didn't fuck you, because I didn't say that you'd be someplace by some date, but I don't recall ever seeing someone with as bad of luck as you've had, young man. I've spent extra time coaching you and teaching you things that you have no other use for learning, if only to get a leg up. I'm stunned... floored...

that you haven't snagged anything yet. It's baffling. I don't want to make you feel bad, because now that I know you better, I can see that you're *sharp*. You're *bright*, a *quick* learner with some kind of ability to deal with people, even though you aren't a typical people-person. Look, I'll always be down to write you a letter of recommendation, be it a reference, or anything else you need, because I really do feel like this place let you down. Just… try not to get too down on yourself. You can do a lot of things in this world. Figure it out and go for it. I don't know if this job is for you, or even this sector. I'm not saying get out of here, but don't grow old, bitter, and resentful here, get trapped with some lady, have babies, and wish you were pushing up fucking daisies, kiddo."

It was a trip. My only flag waver was taking his ball to the enemy side.

"I don't know what to say. I don't think you need to apologize. I'm happy for you. You can go back to what you're more familiar with. It does sound like a pretty amazing opportunity. I don't think it's your fault that I haven't seen any action or lucked out with a new job yet. Postings aren't that frequent and people just aren't retiring, am I right?" I felt the need to retort with some form of flattery. I realised that my success didn't hinge whatsoever on the work of another person. It was comforting, however, to hear that he was as shocked as I was that I was still a goddamn teller. The golden shower to my jellyfish burn.

"No, maybe it's not my fault," he began with a renewed sense of stewardship over his loose tongue. "But, I've nonetheless hated watching you out there with those miserable women, day in and day out, eating shit and spitting out teeth."

"Damn, man. I mean, I don't think it's *that* bad," I said in a faintly exasperated tone, though was utterly in agreement.

"You are right though, no one's retiring. Everyone's either gun-shy about the future, or hasn't planned well enough in a financial sense… at a financial institution. Ironic. It's pretty crazy, if you ask me, that we work at a bank, or, credit union, and people can't see past the tip of their noses."

"Question. Do you believe in that whole credit union line you've been feeding me for the past couple?"

"I believe and will make my staff believe whatever company or business is paying me wants. Do I believe it while I'm here? *Of course!* Will I believe it in a couple months? Wholeheartedly irrelevant. When I was in your position back in the day, I figured out that the only way I was going to make it, anywhere really, was to drink a little piss punch and say it tastes delicious."

Naivety, despite its unattractive puerility, was still alive and well in me at the time. To hear that this man was a mercenary for the highest bidder startled the image of a family man that my mind had painted. Looking back, he was a protean talent, demonstrating the value of versatility in that moment.

"Here I thought you bled for the company, but I get it. It's enviable that you can wear that disguise."

"All good salesmen can. It's in our composition. You only sell your soul one time, and you can't have it back."

"Is that the advice you're currently giving me?"

"No," he stated, flatly and airlessly.

"No? You don't think that I can read a map and figure out what the x near the palm tree means?"

"Listen, don't quit your day job. There are two big differences between you and myself. The first is that I don't think you could keep up the act like I have. You're clever, but you don't have the same opportunities that were offered to me, and I worked with way fewer of those," he gestured out his blinds towards the murder of cackling middle-aged women. "A second very big difference, which I know you've noticed, is that when I was coming up, men had more of an edge. I got ripped on for starting off with a chick's job, but when I made it, it was even sweeter. The gentlemen's club was on its last legs at the branch level, but it still existed. In this pocket of the industry, we basically see sexism in reverse. Most of the directors and managers are women. Hell, most of the accounts people are women too. Head office is still pretty masculine, but lots of long-term employees are still resentful, and it's harder to get on as a guy."

"Well..." my face was tight, "...that sounds like an impossible thing to battle. Not that it can't be done, but it seems... fair. Unjust for me, but in the grand scheme of things, it does seem fair. I just picked the wrong time, maybe?" I was unable to fully communicate the fact that I understood the complexity of an enclave of female-dominated industry, surround by the male-colonized, larger-scale banking industry, all within an even more vastly masculine-coloured world. In short, I was in the unique, if not ironic, position of playing something of a sacrificial lamb. I was fucked. "So," I continued, looking to change the subject. "We have you for a little longer?"

"Well, I have vacation time that I haven't used up and..."

Ward would be gone by the end of the week. We kept in loose contact over my work e-mail and his new account at the big show. He would, with restraint, explain how he was happy to be oiling up potential investors again with a shiver of sea dogs, and how he had time to enjoy watching his kids reach all kinds of formative landmarks. It was nice to hear that he was happy, and I was as happy as someone can be for someone else whose life no longer has any impact on theirs. I told him that things on my end remained the same. Same job, same job postings and interviews, same weekend job, same girl that I was banging... probably more information than he'd known about me beforehand. Our correspondence gradually fizzled out, chumminess naturally diminishing with the absence of workplace commonalities. I'm sure he's doing just fine.

Big bank takes little bank.

14.

The replacement who was brought in to fill the empty manager's position was a lady named Mrs. Black. I can't scrounge up her first name, I only remember that unlike most contemporary adult humans, Mrs. Black seemed perfectly at ease, calmed, or even preened by someone addressing her with titular prestige. Strange, when everyone, including the director of the branch, wanted to be called by their first name. Mrs. Black didn't instruct me to refer to her by her family name *per se*, she simply never proffered me the alternative of calling her by her first name, usually so ubiquitous. Even the entirety of the head office executives and personnel that I'd met were quick to privilege me with the informality of a first name basis. She had a long, boring, and virtually unmoving face, even when speaking. She had the demeanour of sand and was equally as interesting to converse with or listen to. The only time I could really discern any deviation from her camel-like mug was an extra-glazed, drooping-eyed look of smug self-satisfaction that washed over her countenance after being called *Mrs. Black*.

It was within the first week that I knew Mrs. Black and myself would never be on any level comparable to that which I'd shared with her predecessor. Her inaugural speech sounded as though it came from a manual handed out to robots on their last day of human school. She always wore gray, olive, or beige pantsuits with restrained jewelry and watches to match. She was in a word: taupe. When I met her, I was impressed by the dullness of her character, that someone surrounded with so much stimuli and potential for human experience could have such an absence of vitality. Oh no, had she noticed that my eyes hadn't moved and that I was creating movies in my head while she spoke? What was she saying? Was she staring at me, and did I need to respond? Nod, smile, nod, and shrug: '*What are you gonna do?*'

I'd taken for granted that I'd genuinely liked my last boss. Small talk with Mrs. Black was a chore. She'd find any way possible to talk about her husband, Bert. I'd never met him, but the way she honked out his name still haunts me when I throw bread crumbs for swans. She was tight with the chorus of old crones from when she'd been a teller. In short, Mrs. Black thought that I was weird, and had an over-active imagination and bad sense of humour that dined largely on other people's expense. After the first conversations where we unsheathed our true characters, I knew that any attempts to curry her favour would be in vain. I ceased any meaningful ways of ingratiating myself to her, and spoke only when spoken to with brief answers.

With full use of the internet, I made the most of my 8-hour workdays by plugging away on job boards, company websites, business-centered social networking sites, employee and employer-oriented forums, and even the old black and white newspaper that was on our break room table. I stopped trying to conceal the fact that I was looking for a way to change my career path, whether a subtle nudge towards another company or area of the financial sector, or a diverging path that might hold manifold routes with opportunities squared, even cubed! Any optimism and enthusiasm rarely lasted long, however, before the more powerful negative swells struck with their turbid whitecaps. My workmates were ambivalent with my use of company time for my own business. Pretty much everyone was always gawking at vacation deals in French Polynesia or online boutiques anyways. Some of my truly sympathetic and closer companions sent me ideas and sites to check out. Jane lectured me about not being patient enough, and that this proved that I didn't have the dedication and level of professionalism to make it in the banking world.

I was looking to avoid feelings of discouragement at all costs, remembering the miserable piece of shit I'd felt like before getting this job. I tried to keep a cheery enough outward presentation. I guess I was growing up. I was supressing all my frustration, trying to keep my diminishing cool with members and colleagues, and avoiding releasing all the maelstrom of hidden, non-sexual rage on innocent Jackie.

I began to observe these symptoms becoming physical sensations, finding some kind of subconscious backroad to get out of town. I would get ulcer-like stomach pains, bewilderment, and anxiety-accompanying sweat on my palms, feet, and miscellaneous pits.

A sting on the back of my neck began. Each week, it became more noticeable and frequent. It was an unmarked, unbranded area teeming with physical irritation. Psychosomatically, I could feel that something was trying to burst through my layers of flesh. At first, I thought that my barber had planted the seed of an ingrown hair with shoddy technique, but time again, I couldn't find anything. I pinched. I squeezed. I tried to milk what felt like an alpine shaped infection and clawed at the area with my crude talons. Whenever I checked, however, there was nothing but the damage I'd inflicted on myself.

I was frequently boozing again. This became apparent when I walked into a bar that I thought I'd only fancied every so often for a pint of Guinness and a glass or two of Lagavulin after work. It was a snug Irish spot with some maritime decorations, low music, moody ambience, and one tiny television. When I entered, I was pointed to a stool by the bartender, a few years older than myself with tattoos and a bushman's beard. He said that *my spot* was open.

Upon Jackie's request, I, or rather *we*, socialized with our work-friend group more often. Some of the people had long since grown on me, and even those who I'd previously found insufferable were saints compared to the hags at my day job. I'd always thought that, although I could drink most under the table and out of their clothes, I was a gentleman and a scholar even when two or three sheets. These nights spent out boozing, and they happen frequently when everyone is in the bar industry, had been getting progressively more disorderly. Never one to start a fight or stir the pot, there was an emerging mean streak fermenting within me and given feet to walk further and further each time I boozed, becoming more harmful the more I imbibed. I'd wake up on a friend's couch, bed, or floor when that friend had needed to chaperone me about town and make sure that I didn't get rolled, or challenge an entire gang to a brawl. Other times, I'd wake up in my bed, being doused by overcast rays pissing through the blinds, allowing me to see Jackie's tiny arms supporting her tiny head with malevolent and despairing eyes, sometimes with trails of charcoal dried down her cheeks. She was waiting for me to wake up, tell me what an asshole I was, ask me if I remembered what I said or did while I was intoxicated, and wonder if I even liked her whatsoever. For all the time that we'd spent together, I'd never been aware of how long it'd been, nor how I felt about her. I liked her in a platonic way, like life-long companions of the same sex, but was attracted to her in a hyper-sexual, slamming each other against the wall by the throat, tearing shirts and sending buttons under sofas, kind of way. Truthfully, I'd never stopped to think about how she felt either. We'd just allowed whatever we had to bloom like perennials in a new house's old garden. We'd never had *the talk*. It was very unofficial and seemingly casual, or so I'd thought.

Jackie repeated the cycle of hectoring me about my previous evening's behaviour, causing me to chase her to the door as she was carrying out her miniature, doll-sized clothes. I would run my hand over her caramel shoulder and (re)iterate that I was an animal when I drank, that I shouldn't be a dick to the most supportive and caring person in my life, begin to win her back, lose her briefly, and then receive an eye-roll upon saying that she shouldn't let me get to the state of blacking out on a regular basis. I'd save the day by leaning in with a handful of chestnut hair and planting a passionate kiss on her mouth. It must've tasted awful. She'd drop her clothes, place both hands on my jaw or bare buttocks, and my dick would go from a subdued half-mast to an aggressive full salute. I knew that I'd won when she smiled, feeling my head nuzzle and push against the soft fabric of her panties. Her coquettish smile would grow and she'd send her tongue to waltz with mine, grind me, wrap her hand around my dick, and start jerking. At this point, any number of surfaces in any number of rooms would become the squared circle that we used to duke out the remaining resentment and penitence of our first-light fight. I'd defeat my hangover grog by taking her into my chest, moving her stringed panties to the side, sliding in, and pressing her against the wall, knocking the next-door neighbour's pictures from their hooks. Necessary means to obvious, necessary ends.

15.

My behaviour continued to be more erratic and damaging to the mousiness of my younger partner. Although the sex was blue ribbon, the repetitive fighting and guilt was another source of dread-filled anxiety and moral impertinence that was doing me no favours.

One night in particular we had, which I had to be informed of the following day, a cracking good episode that caused her to leave the bar we were at with our group. She took her leave with a couple girls and left me with some acquaintances, mostly newcomers to the restaurant. During the time that she went to a friend's nearby apartment, collected her bearings, and returned (still with the establishment's stamp on her wrist), I'd bolted. I didn't remember what'd happened, other than waking up naked with my dick pressed into the cracks of a half-Japanese, half-Scottish girl whose name is far from important. I picked up my cellphone to discover 42 missed calls and 37 text messages. The messages began in a worrisome tone, then furious, then panicked, then paroxysmal, then exhausted. I met up with her and explained what I'd been told second-hand. We had our first conversation that really touched on the aspects of responsibility that formalized couples have. It was a heavy and draining session that didn't end with sex, but with Jackie ruling that we'd been more than a mere item and what I'd done was stupid and hurtful. I could only agree as I got raked over the coals and thrown over a barrel. She left just enough rope dangling for me to pull an inch, then another inch, finally gathering enough to wrap my fist around to pull her back down with, not so much raising myself up.

I realise now that my emotional framework and ego make me grab the spiked-bat only when I have to. My fight emerges only when something that I've previously possessed is threatened to be taken away from me, like a selfish child. I hadn't put any thought into whether or not I loved or even liked this girl, which I did, but I was fighting like a cornered beast because I didn't want to lose something that I felt belonged to me. I started to resent her for showing me how weak I'd become and how immature I truly was when facing big decisions. I cared about her and wanted to protect her against any predator with the parental investment of an emperor penguin, yet felt animosity towards her prolonged indignation in response to my actions, especially when we hadn't established any rules for ourselves. An equal anger was directed at myself, because I knew that we should never have had to define ourselves given the current climate. I also had a gut churning fear that she could do the same thing to me, and I had no idea what my reaction would be. Her bitterness lessened, but that too irritated me. I'd harmed this beautiful woman and she either didn't have the spine to walk away, or cared for me deeply and had never told me, which made me feel duped.

I no longer wanted her around, but couldn't send her away. She was mine. I was mightily attracted to her, but felt sick at the sight of her smile and knifed at the sight of her grimace. I felt hollowed to the core, and couldn't figure out why at the time. I still cared for her, but I knew that my affection was no longer pure. It felt contrived when it'd never felt that way before. I knew it would probably never return to its original carefree state of amiable lust, which was most likely love. Pure love. Real, human love.

On the most average of days, a mid-autumnal humdrum with a tedious grayscale landscape, somewhere between an expropriated pagan holiday and a Hispania-inspired Saint's Day, I was sitting on my unlubricated rolling chair with stubborn plastic wheels emerging from their casters. I was using the swivel function to make the most impish little rotations, causing the bearings in the wheels and the central leg to chirp softly, almost noiselessly, though piercingly enough so that I could hear the early stages of an unhappy focus group coming together to brood collectively over the soft wheezing that my chair was emitting. I realized that I was in the same position that I'd been in 3, 4, and even 5 years earlier. I stopped twisting my trunk left and right in my cloth-backed seat to feel the production of sweat all over my body. A sharp tingling sensation was apparent on my neck, traveling down to my lower back. My face became flush with the heat of standing too close to a building in flames.

Mechanically locking out my monitor, I pushed myself away from my desk, instigating a quicker, shriller trill from my chair, drawing the heads of the offended in my direction. My entire back had been pressed against the back of the chair. When I stood up, my dress shirt was a much darker shade of blue than its original periwinkle.

I shuffled into the single-occupant staff bathroom and began to dry heave over the blueish-enameled toilet. I bent closer to the rim and felt another convulsion throw itself from my gut. There was no food or drink launching from my oesophagus. All that spilled was a watery saliva that coated the opening of my mouth before leaping towards the ceramic bowl in strands, like when I used to unsuccessfully mash my fingers down my throat as a child, not wanting to go to school. I was never able to vomit to avoid school, only tease the bowl with disappointment and failure. I prayed that I'd never ingest poison.

I had yet to check my face, but it felt magenta and I could tell that my eyes were bloodshot. I grabbed a piece of toilet paper and sat in the corner, sleeves rolled up with my hair and shirt dishevelled, placing my head in one hand while the other wiped the corners of my mouth and eyes.

"My fucking body's in mutiny," I whispered to myself. I drew a heavy sigh.

I grabbed the handicap rail next to the toilet and pulled myself to my feet, setting my hands on the sink, the same way I always did when dealing with heavy thoughts. I took a long look in the mirror. I looked like shit. I declined to recognize the face, turning to avoid it like a loathed acquaintance in public. He wasn't bad looking for all intents and purposes, and could probably clean up rather well with a fresh set of dress clothes and some pomade. Give him a wet wipe and a cup of coffee, and he could look like a prudent fellow with his entire life in front of him. Slowly, I became increasingly aware of who was staring back: someone whose emotions had run roughshod in his circuitry because he was either too weak, stupid, cowardly, shallow, narcissistic, or any combination thereof. I wouldn't call this moment a panic attack, but I was unwilling to observe myself with any positivity.

Under normal circumstances, I'd be angry, knowing that I'd given my all trying to merit a promotion or find another career that would keep me fulfilled. It's easy to curse the unseen force of the universe, having been sucked in, swirled around the mouth of chaos, and spat back out, dubious and dazed from the vague and unclear rules governing existence. I could've easily blamed coworkers, colleagues, former classmates, parents, priests, or pigeons, all the people in all the lands that I didn't know, who couldn't have been better than me by such a vast margin; punching their greedy straws through the Capri Sun-like ether, sucking up all the available luck and fortune. On this day, however, I put myself against the wall with no blindfold and locked eyes with the shooter.

After remedying my appearance, I decided to take a personal day and return home for the afternoon based on the reactions of my coworkers. I returned to the row of teller wickets and was met by Jane's trademarked snarl.

"You were gone for a while. Are you sick? If you're sick, I don't wanna catch anything. I have my grandkids coming out this weekend, and then Mexico in a couple more." Before I could respond, the other ladies chimed in with random insights about all-inclusive Mexican resort towns.

"Are you going to Puerta Vallarta? There's this boy named Julio there who makes the best Mojitos." Pronounced *mah-jee-tahs*.

"I've been to Playa del Carmen. They have a nice pool and some activities, but a cloudy day or two almost ruined the trip."

"Chuck and I did Playa twice last year and Cabo San Lucas once. We got a good deal on the Playa trips because Chuck's brother, Eddie, works for the airline and lets us know when the good deals are."

"How was Cabo? I did Mazatlán. Too hot!"

"Cabo wasn't good at all. It was spring break and I could barely get any sleep or privacy."

"Acapulco was the place to be in the 90s, but all those drug cartels ruined it. They'll cut your melon off and send it to your husband, or turn you into a drug mule! Sick, just sick."

"What about Cancun? The people are so friendly!"

"Oh my goodness gracious, aren't they? So friendly, almost everywhere. They're dirt poor, but love to make little crafts and sell them."

"So friendly. This one boy, Jose, taught me how to salsa! I gave him 2 dollars for a 3-hour lesson. They are so grateful!"

"*So* grateful. Any little thing. *So* friendly."

They finally returned their attention to me, and asked what my deal was.

"I've got a pain in me Gulliver." I said, upbeat as fuck with absolute sarcasm. The anger that washed over Jane's face was only tempered by her instinct to solve multiple problems with one easy stroke.

"Well, you might as well take off, kid. Only an hour or two left today, and honestly, it *is* slow season, so if you need to take tomorrow off…" she prattled out.

I wordlessly shook my head in agreement. "Thanks. I didn't want to infect anyone." I faked a lame cough.

"How considerate of you," Jane seethed with squinted eyes. I paused as I began to cash out for the day. I rotated my head 90 degrees, but she'd already lowered her head and begun scribbling something on a strip of paper.

16.

Jesus Christ, I thought. As I walked home, it occurred to me that this had been the first day I'd been out sick from work. I'd missed some days that were scheduled off for vacations, but this would be the first day that I'd been absent from work due to some kind of ailment in nearly three years. For all it's worth, my perfect, and no other word can describe my lack of any unscheduled absences from work, attendance record was an overlooked and unappreciated staple of my service to the company.

The little balls of hateful nausea started to loosen immediately as I began to walk away from the credit union grounds. A strange tunnel vision guided me home, similar to a blacked-out tramp inadvertently dodging or being dodged by vehicles, arriving to his usual bridge-covered resting place in one piece. A cyclone of thoughts was swirling around my dropped head. The world around me faded in and out of perception. I raised my eyes periodically, allowing me to discover how many blocks I'd covered and what streets I'd overlooked or missed compared to my usual walk homeward. Future-oriented and tactical patterns of thought were caught up in the whirlpool, too hazy and too slick to grasp for any useful length of time.

Some random shit crept in and earned a brief deliberation, for example, thinking about cereal, and how it'd been years since I'd filled a giant metal mixing bowl up and eaten it like a young prince. I wondered what my girlfriend from college and her fine ass were up to, and whether I'd missed out on any kinky threesomes with some half-shaved-headed, bisexual girl. Was the first human who discovered grapefruit pleased with their find or pissed off because they thought it was an orange and were totally bamboozled by the acridity of the fruit? A grapefruit tastes like an orange with a jaded ex. Why did some people like dogs and cats so much, more than other humans, and why did they think it was okay to go ahead and lay their mitts on another person's property without asking? This nonsense was a defense mechanism to stop me from doing some real soul-searching. I ended up sitting on a damp park bench not too far from my apartment, watching strangers approach a girl and her dog and petting it without asking.

I figured that I might as well light up a cigarette, the snare drum to the marching band of deep self-examination. I decided that I was a pretty poor excuse of a man for not verbally palm-facing Jane for her insolence as I'd staggered out the door. I remembered being casketed with sweat as I'd been leaving, but now felt a chill, prompting a more conservative buttoning of my pea coat. I inhaled a sedating chest-full of tobacco, and exhaled an expressive waft of warship-coloured smoke.

Alright, this is stupid. The crusade to regain my senses began. *What the hell's going on here?*

Trying to calm my eddying plethora of thoughts was like trying to dam a tsunami mid-wave. *For starters,* I told myself, trying to strategize, *I'm going to spend this weekend figuring some things out, because this is getting ridiculous.* With the first step settled, I alerted some coworkers about the availability of some much-prized weekend closing shifts, and was easily able to get them covered. *Secondly, I should figure this out alone,* deciding that the bizarreness between Jackie and I wasn't going to help. *Third, I should get my ass home, because it's late and dark out, though that's misleading this time of year. In the summer, people would still be shirtless on the beach. Nevertheless, I'm cold and starting to get hungry.* I caught myself speaking aloud and wondered if I'd been vocalising each bullet point. I took a quick look around, seeing only a few cherries lit on empty pathways underneath the argent street lamps.

17.

As I attempted to undertake deep, self-reflective study, I realized that I didn't know myself very well. I didn't know how to begin or what I was trying to accomplish.

The first night I had a strange dream…

An ivory horse with a sash reading *Boris*, transfixed by a brass pole through its torso and a sinister frozen face on a carousel, galloped jerkily to a dissonant loop of fanfare from what sounded like overgrown clock-radio speakers. I was holding onto the twisted brass bar that was impaling the horse, looking inward towards the carousel's mirrors to see the warped faces of cheery onlookers and some disfigured snouts of equine, a circus elephant with one broken tusk, and a two-seater buggy with a wheel that only steered in one's imagination. I was riding the horse with pride and the keen posture that comes with jockeying a ceramic beast in a predesignated oval. There were children of varying ages enjoying the ride to varying degrees. Up and down the lifeless animals went, in and out of focus, depending on their height and angle, as they circled around the pivot. There was a young lad, dressed smartly in beige English-style rain gear with a little newsy cap. He was aiming a horn molded to the shoulder of a gray seal that appeared to be frozen in mid-jump, shooting water at the backs of two other children. In fact, it was at two girls with pigtails and checkered-tablecloth dresses, one blue and white, the other red and white. I suddenly realized that I was a fully grown adult and how out of place I was. I looked down at the nape of the horse's neck, took hold of the brass bar with my fully-grown, adult mitts once more and started scrutinizing the ashen-coloured hair of the horse's mane and its paint-chipped body. I saw that my boots were untied and that I had a ketchup stain on the khaki-coloured pants covering my fully-grown adult genitalia. I became fraught with people thinking that I was a pedophile or mentally retarded. Looking around, I could see that the children had, somehow, already disembarked from the still-moving ride, collected into the arms of their loving parents, all holding cotton candy, caramel apples, and replicas of animals made with knotted balloons. The ride began to move faster and the music became more menacing and disorienting. The brass clanged with hostility, the percussion lost its metering, and the pace became frenetic and surly. After all the families had scuttled away, no one remained in the surrounding area. The carousel was rotating in an empty gravel lot, now lacking the usual sounds of carnival bedlam and the smells of sugar and grease from food stands and burger trucks. The twisted faces of the other galloping objects now seemed grotesque and cold. They were chasing me and my gallant steed, though making no ground. I turned my body towards the centre and found that the mirror showed no image of a rider. Boris' ivory frame just bounced up and down, unbothered by the weight of a fully-grown human, picking up speed with each revolution. His face turned more psychotic with each lap, the other animals becoming equally more disfigured as the ambience descended from a saturnine blur into nothing.

I woke up from an abbreviated sleep with only the faint recollection of a desolate merry-go-round scene. I didn't understand what it meant, but I found it amusing that the horse's sash had said Boris. Unusual name for a horse, is it not?

I've never been one to put much stake into dream analysis. Still, I thought about this dream in an innocent way, amused that I'd retained so much detail, most notably the realistic sentience I'd felt at the fairground. The next nights were spent in quieted darkness, silent and dreamless sleeps, with some turning and the odd mid-night urination. I've known people that savor in fermenting their dreamscapes with their conscious minds, and feel compelled to deduce what an image or moment might represent. Once I woke up in the morning to find that the woman sleeping by my side had a sudden prejudice against me, for something an imaginary actor, a fraudulent me, had done in the course of her dream: a false and entirely created reality. I rarely retain any crumbs from the cinema of my sleep. Maybe I fantasize enough during my waking hours, and the whole machine just needs to be turned off at night. Another peculiarity about that night was the sleep I'd had. Normally, I was a purposefully truncated sleeper, not wanting to discard any precious moment of night or morning with unneeded shut-eye. That night, however, I was toe-up at 9pm, and didn't rise until 11am. I was cleared-headed and felt detangled from the muddled viper's nest that was my mind and stomach the previous evening.

I was bothered by a sense of embarrassment due to my helplessness on my last day of work. Anxious energy had taken over my body with little deference as to whether it manifested itself in public or private. I doubted that anyone had noticed the manner in which I'd taken ill, but I'd embarrassed myself in front of my idealized self that couldn't tolerate such feebleness of mind and body. I peered into my mind, launching a self-inquiry to try and appraise what I wanted.

Who are you? Why do you find this so difficult? Where do you want to be? What's keeping you down? When did this start?

I took a quick look at my phone and noticed a bushel of missed calls from Jackie, hers being the only ones I responded to anyways. I could only imagine what kind of bawdiness she must have thought I was getting into. When I called, I was greeted by her voicemail and let her know that I wasn't feeling well and had had to take the weekend off. I explained that I'd be in touch, but was very weak and would be bedridden, at least in and out, for the foreseeable future. With the only human being that'd be likely to contact me informed of my absence, I could take up the mallet and chisel.

Pages and pages of yellow legal paper that I'd stockpiled from the credit union were covered with double-spaced doctor's handwriting, strewn like fallen October leaves all over the floor. Written on the sheets, in a variety of pens also absconded from the same place, were notes about what I didn't want to be doing, things that I didn't enjoy or ever see myself embracing, things that were obstructing my way, and ways in which I wasn't adequately prepared or educated. I was always telling myself that my failure wasn't due to a lack of effort, but I didn't know if I actually believed that. Sure, I spent lots of time surfing through sites and boards for employment, trying to meet with management teams to discuss their members and how to stroke them, but for what? A lifetime sentence as a male teller? University was the last time that I'd had any legitimate peers, and even with the smallest amount of visible opportunities available, I rarely compared notes or discussed my future with classmates. *A single tear in the bucket for failed or broken down networks.*

Whenever I started to become overwhelmed, or felt like blaming someone else, I reminded myself that aside from speaking an above-average level of French for someone not born in a Francophone county, I hadn't really accomplished anything to earn myself a float in the parade. The most blindly devout spouse or pathologically adoring mother would have a bitch of a time melting down my achievements. All that I'd really done thus far was equivalent to spending time in prison without any infractions or quarrels that would add sentence years or time in solitary confinement. At most, I'd earned the right to be listened to with dispirited consideration at an early parole hearing. *Two tears in the bucket for shinbone bruises from tripping on a low bar.*

I kept coming back to the compelling notion that I was *normal.* Always had been, and by this point, always would be. My lily pad occupied the perfect centre of the pond. Perfect, a word that I fear using for its literal implications, but perfect here means perfectly normal. *Averageness perfected.* I felt the stress and anxiety of someone whose greater purpose is determined by intellectual pursuits and solving Earth's aging process, rather than divertissement, cupidity, or sex, as it probably should. I was no genius; I'd just grown arrogant, or adopted it. Patience served me little in this context, because I knew I probably wouldn't be content with nominal increases in status and salary at my current job, or any job. All this in spite of acknowledging my medial destiny. Did I think that I should be running the place? My boss was a vacuous idiot, but it couldn't be possible that every boss at every branch in every company was a dullard of equal plasticity. How often, as of late, had *I* come to dominate my own thinking, both at times of strategizing and wandering, and pillow-like thoughts at night? This level of self-absorption made me feel embarrassed again. I'd let myself recoil so deeply into the fortress of my mind, and become so weak in the fearful face of failure, that I'd been hiding in the armory like a cowardly king. What was failure, at any rate? Was it worse to fail at something tremendous, falling towards the earth like a burning sycamore? Or, due to death from a million paper cuts, where bleeding out races against scabbing. In short, I was being a little bitch filling up the bucket with one or two tears at a time, which would eventually drown me if I kept being such an abhorrent twat.

Man, I concluded in what felt like a moment of clarity. *Who the fuck is this guy?*

I had to remind myself who I most certainly was: a magnum opus of normalcy. The creation of *Adam* or *Peer Gynt Suite Op. 23. The ordinary man,* orchestrated masterfully. The perfect construction of satisfactory. Things were just going to happen, and I might as well get used to not having a say in anyone's happiness, sadness, or survival but my own. This brought up one more issue.

18.

On Sunday evening, I went to Jackie's house. Her parents' house, to be more precise, though she had a separate entrance around the back to a basement suite that functioned with virtual autonomy, aside from the shared laundry machine in the adjacent room. I rapped my usual *'shave and a haircut'* with primate knuckles on the door and waited for about five seconds before *'two bits'* sounded through one of the four cutaway glass squares, shielded from view by a thick, doily-like curtain. Jackie opened the door with her hair in a tousled, ponytailed funnel-cloud that rose at least six inches above her scalp, bobbing in sync with her head movements. She had her favourite pair of dark, plastic-framed glasses on, which gave magnificence to her oaken irises, ringed by delinquent curlicues of baby hairs that didn't have the length or strength to make it into the elasticated hair tie. She greeted me with a thin, face-extending smile, throwing her little arms around me on ballerina toes. She felt freshly bathed and smelled faintly of skin creams, not overly sweet; a handsome, smoky vanilla, in a feminine sort of way. It was rich like bourbon, a hushed wind carrying soft-pedaled tobacco. I felt the musk in my pours. Every inhale made my insides simmer. The aroma carried masculine tones. In fact, I'd wear it myself. I wondered what would happen if another man smelled that way. Would it arouse me? Would their skin make it smell different? A voice inside of me asked if that would make me gay. Another inner conversation had begun.

I squeezed her tight and sniffed her repeatedly. I squeezed and sniffed for a while. I can only imagine what she was thinking, being snuffled-on like a toilet lid at a disco. I doubt she would've guessed that I was questioning my own heterosexuality.

"That tickles," she pushed away to force eye contact and moved her hands down to my hips.

"Sorry," I said. "Can I borrow it?" She laughed and kissed me on the jaw, neck, and earlobe. A moment later we'd crash-landed on her hunter green suede couch.

I hate the feeling of suede against my skin due to the simultaneousness of having one fabric feel two different ways, both of them being irritatingly grainy. The sensation was almost psychoacoustic, like chalkboard scraping on my flesh. Even worse, when the fabric gets wet. Yuck. I also hate touching wet knife blocks.

She kneeled motionlessly, wrapping herself around my waist, still penetrated, her head sideways on my shoulder and breathing in quick, soft puffs. She rose like a child on a living island as my chest expanded and retracted with large inhalations, unburdened by her slight frame. My hands hung down at my sides, my head resting on the wooden frame poking from behind a large velvet pillow. My erection began to recede, reminding her to flex her pussy and hurry to spill my cum into the toilet, lest the couch become further ruined.

She flushed and summoned me to her bedroom, preferring to stretch out on the smoother, cooler bedspread. I laid on my back and adjusted the pillow behind my head with my hands behind, partially sitting up against the headboard. She moved closer to my torso and nestled her head on my chest. She let her hand fall to my waist, gently rubbing my hip bone with her middle finger in a circle. This was how we'd arrived in what some people would call a relationship. A spirited orgasm contest followed by nervous bemusement.

I glanced down at her finger, tracing around and over the ridges and grooves of my thigh, trying to wriggle her glasses up the thin, well-built bridge of her nose. In spite of her efforts, the thick glasses latched onto her perspiration and kept sliding down the arch towards her nostrils. I leaned my right arm over and gently pressed the centre of the glasses, sliding them up as her eyes met mine while gleaning a smile that instantly made me feel sad. She thanked me in a fluttering tone as she resumed amusing herself with my leg.

I still can't explain the emotions I was feeling at the time, and trying to elaborate on them now seems complex and fruitless. My dilemma with Jackie was Cornelian. Here was a nubile and affable young lady, still apprenticing womanhood and shedding her layers of adolescence; still shaping her identity, and still flowering. I petted the rope-like strands of her damp, fragrant hair and entertained the fact that she'd one day grow to hate me. Perhaps she loved me. I didn't know. Equally important was whether I loved her, which I'd never allowed myself to meditate with any sincerity. I can say, now with a sober and perhaps too-nostalgic heart, that I had, afterwards, when it'd been too late. I'd loved her with a genuine heart, as I'm now sure she had too, which no doubt turned to hate or a form of disgruntlement built from the ashes of apathy like a phoenix, kicking up dust from time to time.

"Hey," was all that I could push out from my mouth in a plebeian drawl. It seemed to promise more substance, but ended with aimless inflection. Jackie merely turned her head and repeated my own greeting and tonality back at me. She sensed that I was disturbed or caged, easily observed from my countenance and body language. Easily observable by an outsider, let alone my closest cohort for two summers.

"Is something wrong?" she asked.

"Nah. Well. Kind of? It's hard to explain." I sputtered out, though prepared for her question. I was reluctant to force my thoughts into words and make them a reality. What's done can't be undone.

"I've been a little off lately. You may have been able to tell," I mumbled, to which she nodded, as one would in response to a fact. "I don't know what it is. Sometimes I think I'm crazy, sometimes I think I'm just depressed and being a whiny little bitch. A weak man who may never have been as strong as he thought, or even strong to begin with. Of mind, I mean. I can lift at least 10 pounds with my arms and 20 with my legs." I threw a little joke in there to see if it caught any traction. Her studious expression didn't change. I continued, overlooking my failed attempt at lightening the mood. "I guess what I'm trying to say is that I haven't been myself. I've been mad at myself and my life, or at least where my life is at compared to where I feel like it should be, where I want it to be. That means that I haven't been good to you. You've probably noticed that it's been impacting us. I've noticed, anyways. I care about you a lot, more than most people I've cared about, which speaks volumes because that might be one of the things that makes being a bastard to you so difficult. You're cool and beautiful and all the things anyone could ever ask for in another human being."

I could feel her little body tensing up as I finished. I think she expected me to start again, but I didn't know how to continue.

"Thanks," she said in a suspicious tone. "I do agree, but I forgave you for that... thing. Honestly, it's mostly been *you* acting different. I can tell that you're unhappy and mad at yourself for whatever reason. I don't like that I can't help you more than saying supportive things, and you're always so deep in your own head. You're weird that way, but I like your weirdness. I still don't know what we are, and I know it's not the time to talk about that, but after you slept with that *bitch*, I can only assume that we're on the same page in some ways." I took in her rebuttal, waiting for her to finish a big breath and slow blink. "I know you want better. You deserve better. You work hard, have good ideas, and are nice and funny and weird. I don't know what to tell you. I don't know how to help you. You scare me sometimes. You get so down on yourself, and most people don't beat themselves up the way you do. You just have to be more positive!"

Her prescription of positivity and riding out the tempests with an upbeat demeanour was expected. This time, however, I felt a trifled peevishness towards her. Perhaps I was irked that she was so nice at a time that I needed a gelid-veined ball-breaker. I wanted her to be mad that I fucked another girl and blast me with a heated beam of cathartic, volatile fury that would expunge all decision-making and give me a zero-option answer, for once. Her equivocality was what made her a dangerous pairing for a person currently controlled by the fluctuations of his own spirit. What if the Incredible Hulk downloaded the gamut of his blitzkrieg into Bruce Banner's conscience? Instead of a regrettable day after levelling Long Island, I was perpetually shamed for mistreating a beautiful young woman due to pointless reasons at best.

"What are you thinking?" she said, fracturing the silence of my lengthy rumination.

"I was just thinking that I need to do something different. Something brand new. Something outside my comfort zone," I replied, unblinking.

"Something big? Another job? You could volunteer or something to help people less fortunate," she said. I ignored her suggestion to not become agitated by such a stupid idea.

I found myself thinking aloud. "No, something more drastic. Something like a trip, or even a pick-up-and-go."

"What? *Really*? Where would you go?"

"I don't know, France? I liked France a lot, and they seem to have life figured out there."

"*France*," she said. "Well... France, huh?"

She seemed to take offence at my aspirations to leave, probably compounded by the distance of my desired port-of-call. I was glib at the indignation of her following line of questioning concerning money, lodgings, work, friends, and various other logistical issues. I gave thorough and complete answers, as though pre-rehearsed, although where they came from I'm not entirely sure. I was shooting from the hip. I suppose that I'd thought up my departure as a jailbird may nurse his sanity by plotting escape routes, combatting the prescription of fate while providing recreational diversion from the iron bars and concrete walls. I reflexively spat out a reasonable and persuasive sketch of what life would look like in the land of cheese and wine. Her brow was visibly searching for counter arguments with a pessimistic tenor, an approach as unnatural and unpleasant to her as it was normal for me. We seemed to have exchanged roles of belligerents: she, picking up a cutlass with a blade forged in fires of negativity, myself: a rapier with the tip having been soaked in an inkwell of optimism. Each gladiator produced their arguments, some slights were thrown (mostly by her when her attempts were parried). I deflected the attacks and lanced forwards against my adversary in a war that was becoming increasingly personal.

Jackie's rising rancor was adding heat to the conversation and threating to boil it over into a full-scale conflict. These kinds of fights always release long-silenced ghosts and repressed hostilities; the build-up of pebbles that create Gibraltar-like grievances. When these wraiths are shaken from their incubation pods to circle the room and flood the air, only then can they be vanquished by the two previously opposing armies, now recognizing a greater threat. Putting everything on the table is like Russian-roulette. The longer ill-will accumulates, the more bullets there are in the gun.

It wasn't the notion of moving far away that unleashed the Cerberus in Jackie, but the realization of her position as secondary in my life. I let her bleed all her pent-up animosities while gesticulating militaristically. We were still naked. She kept her tear sacs brimmed with saline, glistening on the verge of eruption, but never allowed one teardrop to slide down her cheek.

She didn't say anything about her feelings regarding me leaving, how she felt about me, or what I meant to her, now or before. Instead, her tactics were to tell me what *I was feeling*, how *I felt* about *myself*, how she felt that *I perceived her* and *me*, and what *I was* doing with all this France-talk gibberish. It was impressive, a virtual masterstroke in placing the burden all on me by using my own voice to incriminate myself. In reflection, I can't remember her stating her own opinion until she became exasperated and slumped over from releasing her final fusillade of emotionally-repressed shells. I was relieved and at the same time insulted, but not in an angry way. It had the refreshing sourness of what closure tastes like.

She began to whimper; her frenzy has dissipated. I had to marvel at how quickly she'd dug her heels in and machine-gunned my shortcomings and their impact on my behaviour. I ran my hand over my head and nodded with serene antipathy. "So, tell me how you really feel."

She snapped out of her mild daze and smiled as tears finally began to tumble from her long lash-blinking. "I'm sorry, I guess I've been building up a lot of stuff, a lot of feelings. I'm sorry. I care about you so much and you surprised me," she sniffled, mucus gurgled.

"Well, to be fair, it was the first thing that came to mind," I said. My unfocused eyes were looking at the ceiling.

"But, that means I wasn't," she replied dolefully. "And... I'd come with you if you asked me to."

"Look, I don't even know what I'm going to do," I said. At that exact moment, I realized that I did. "You know you have a special place in that ticker under my ribs."

"Your heart? I know. If you go, I'm going to miss you. I promise I'll come visit you."

Right then, I could've blown off my made-up plan with a shrug. I could've altered my course, starting anew with a scrubbed slate and Jackie to become a new me. I could be hand-in-hand with the first woman I'd ever opened up to, who was equally open with me and obviously cared for me. She'd follow me around the globe, and wanted me to be happy. *Us to be happy.* I could've used the failed relationships and the negative energies from my work life and dedicated my heart to starting a life with this woman who appealed to me in ways that previous women hadn't.

Jackie: great sex and good humour, the left-jab-right-uppercut to my soul. We could've been a mediocre couple that worked in a restaurant, making our 20-something-year-old co-workers shirk and shudder as my 60-year-old cock rubbed dryly against her 50-year-old ass, nibbling her earlobe in the pass. I'd regale them about my wife of 30 years and how we still had greasy sex and ask if there were any takes on a threesome. I could've said '*I love you*' to someone and felt good about it. I could've heard it back. As lovers, we could've *made love*: deep hipped-driving, wet-hands clasping, slow-tongue kissing, staring into each other's souls through our half-opened but fully engaged-eyed love-making.

"That'd be cool!" I said with vacant enthusiasm. "I'll miss you too... if I even end up going."

Jackie and I slept together a couple times after that. I was busy with preparations and she was using her time for wiser pursuits. Never underestimate the ability of a beautiful woman to get over a man. Any man. They're resilient and aware of how special their lot is. She seemed almost enthused when we said our final goodbye, in a *50 Ways to Leave Your Lover* kind of way. We spoke for some months after I touched down in Paris and set up the next act of my story. She pulled away gradually. Lustful and affectionate messages dried up and became the skull and bones of an ox bleaching in the desert sun, descending into bland, sterile communications. One of the last pieces of news I remember was that she was starting university. Women, more than men, earn a second, more cerebral puberty in their mid-twenties where their minds and hearts strengthen. Through lithesome alchemy, they mature based on their experiences from teens to early twenties. The process expunges the useless molecules and atoms from their composition to achieve their final, golden form. In my experience, if you meet a woman at too young an age, you'll be rinsed out of her system when she outgrows you. And, she will.

I still think about and miss Jackie, too.

[GREEK CHORUS]

The choice was made easy for me, which is what I'd wanted. I reluctantly accepted the fact that I'd become indecisive in character and pale in spirit. France was a knee-jerk machination, but a land to which I'd been pining to return.

My parents hosted me and my siblings for a nice turkey dinner when I told them about my plans, wanting to get the entire bloodline under one roof. If a natural disaster had occurred, our family tree would've been uprooted from the forest entirely. They reacted with surprise, which was lessened when it was made clear that we saw each other perhaps twice a year, to the point that hugging each other was clumsy. They wished me off and also said that they'd visit, although they'd never left their town, a town I'd been too busy to spend more than a night in for the previous decade. I took no offence and even felt sedated by their lack of sojourning. They'd have the interest of an illiterate in a library if they ever did come to France.

The credit union was just as easy. I returned the next Monday and gave myself 3 weeks to obtain all the necessary documents, tickets, and itineraries to better my luck in the old *tricolore*. My notice read as follows:

Dear Sirs and Madams of the Company,

To Whom It May Concern,

My Last Will and Testament,

It's with a heavy heart, hand, and head that I regrettably resign from the credit union after three of the most enthralling and passion-filled years of my life. Shout out to my suspenders for holding me up, and the crack fiends for not. I'd like to thank my many, many, many superiors for their expertise and tutelage that helped me ascend to the ranks of titan. Verily, I feel like Poseidon controlling the oceans and sea life with the wave of my triton. Better yet, I've been empowered to walk the boulevard and feel like Odin in the streets, known and feared by all when I wear my paisley tie on Wednesdays. Thank you for the memories, which I'll cherish in the brass-buckled treasure trove of my hippocampus, basal ganglia, and team of lobes to make sure that I never overlook the important lessons of hard work, meritocracy, keeping your chin held towards the hypnotic buzzing of the cancer-causing, fluorescent tube lights, the grinning and the bearing of the it, and the Shakespearian leitmotifs that've been the maestro to my symphony. I love each and every one of you like a mother with undiagnosed postpartum depression, which is what makes me so gut-wrenchingly sad that this decision is the irrevocable next footprint in the sand. As a book once said: 'Man is born free, and everywhere he is in chains.' I can't remember the next line, but I can only bet that it's a doozy. Another jaded pendragon roughly stated that God is dead, dead are all the former gods, to be replaced by the new man. I too wish to be a new man, and I hope that you wish me luck on my voyage to become the most uber of all menschen that ever lebte. Or don't, I'm done in 3 weeks anyways.

God bless,

He also giveth and taketh away,

He also doesn't exist.

XX

I dropped the letter on Ms. Waldorf's desk and put in for my two-week vacation. I'll give special thanks to Ward for that idea. I didn't have an ounce of desire to spend my time at the branch when I could make money at the restaurant flexibly for the last two weeks. The letter remained unopened until the final Thursday when Jane suddenly had the copy in her hand, with her clumpy, little, pork-coloured mitten shaking and crumpling the computer paper. I'd learned enough professionalism to use the most business-like approach, even when what I'm saying is slighting and maybe a little overtly offensive. Jane, a regular attendee to the Presbyterian Church and one of the many hard-right Christians that worked at the credit union had her eyes fixed on mine. The smarmiest of grins began to leak out of my face with a quarter chuckle and slight nod to let her know that she had my attention. Further crumpling the letter in her hammy fist, she walked around to the front of my wicket and put my 'See Next Teller' placard in the middle of my desk.

"You think this is funny? Were you going to tell us you just weren't coming back after your little two-week getaway?" she seethed the way a furnace kicks up, rattles, and hisses in the fall, after a summer of discontinuation. Her breath was hot and musty.

"I left the note on Madame Director's desk first thing two Mondays ago. If she didn't get to it until now, that says something about…"

"Look, you insolent little prick. No one's happier to see you gone than me."

I waited for her to continue her venting with an expectant look, but the longer she paused, the more I realized she was waiting for a retort. "Well…" I started, expecting her assault.

"Don't you start! You think this is funny? Marilyn had postpartum depression 15 years ago and it wasn't funny. God is dead? What in the blazes do you even mean by that?! I think this is pure, mean sarcasm."

I knew her plan was to cut me off every time I tried to speak. I began to smirk and try to ease my amusement out through my nostrils with puffs of breath. She paused again, waiting for me to pipe up so she could interrupt again. I sat there, beaming, nodding with my lips pursed, admiring her disgusted scrutinizing of my light demeanour.

"You're a hate-filled, angry young man, and you're lucky I don't call my husband and boys."

"Jane," I began, holding back laughter, trying to be serious now that she was, in her own way, threatening to have my hide tanned by her kinsfolk. "I'll fuck your husband *and* your sons up. Real ugly. Quick fast." I knocked on the table as if calling a game of poker.

She became alarmed and stormed into the break room, probably to cluck about the incident with her brood. No cheque big enough could've made me care. I didn't even need the following weeks' money. I felt liberated. I didn't see her for the rest of the day and came in the following morning to say goodbye to my coworkers, wish them luck, and receive their blessings in return. Several said they would love to come, and had been planning a vacation to France at some point. I never saw any of them again.

As I left, Jane played the wall near the exit and extended her sweaty, little clump of dough towards me. "Good luck, boy," she said derisively with her posse around her for protection... I assume?

I looked her lumpy little frame up and down with the disinterest of a rich man eyeing an ugly woman. "Go fuck yourselves," I said in a happy voice, with all the sincerity and gaiety of an innkeeper in rural Galway, while unbending my middle finger upward and making proportioned, meaningful eye contact with the others.

Pushing open the heavy, one-way exit door, I heard the ladies' keening. Burning bridges didn't matter shit to me. As long as I was on the other side of the river, all the beautiful bridges in New Hampshire and Vermont could've vanished in flames as far as I was concerned. As an aside, Ward had previously committed to providing me with a work reference whenever I needed it.

1.

The average person, notably of American heritage, has a preordained notion of what Paris should look like, matching the pastiche of novels and postcards in their minds. They know the Eiffel Tower, the Louvre, the Arc de Triomphe, the Notre Dame Cathedral, the Moulin Rouge and a mishmash of other images more in tune with fantasy than reality. Literature and cinema have spurred a romantic fascination with the one-time world capital that induces images of frolicsome days spent in a bright, warm, and colourful city that smells of potent espresso beans and freshly baked, buttery brioche. There, the citizens are well-crafted, svelte, if not overly-athletic creatures, who are knowledgeably conversant in worldly events and have a sophisticated, dialogic approach to posing and answering questions of identity and soul. It's a veritable Neo-Hellenism where urbane metropolitans take nightly perambulations to digest rich, gourmet meals with a minimum of five courses.

Having already visited the city, that wasn't my expectation. The scenario previously described is an inherited, unchallenged fantasy world where the most fluffed icons and visuals are turned up to their fullest potential, strangely accurate and inaccurate all at once.

In Paris, very little is located within a distance suitable for the average person to walk, especially with the gait of a visitor who'd be hyper-stimulated by the actual sounds of Paris. She's loud, dirty, touchy, and not very ladylike. She's the source of inspiration and lionization for even the most curmudgeon writers. She'll bring the poet and the brawler out of any long-term resident. She can be a mother and a harlot wearing the same *maquillage*, inviting you to her abode for some *pastis* or into an alley for a *poniard*. She's heaven in the cleanliness of the sun, and a sewer once the dusk is wholly swallowed by the teeth of night. She's a living and breathing organism that personifies the Homeric question: the living city exists purely for itself, a dichotomy that perpetuates its own contrasting existence of being equal parts folklore and reality.

The yolk that contains the arrondissements of *Centre-ville* contains almost exclusively what people think of when they picture the city in their minds. It contains the monuments, the must-see and must-eat restaurants, the museums with their indomitable queues, and the best chance of having your billfold plucked from your pocket or purse slashed and wallet pilfered with stunning quickness. Upon getting off the metro at *Gare du Nord*, I was harassed by Roma, Bosnians, Armenians, Albanians, North and Black Africans, various Slavs, and Eastern European beggars. I tried to placate them and explain that I had no pocket change, nor did I want to purchase any sex or bastard children. I wanted to explore, light up an entire pack of Gauloises, and get the key to my apartment. I'd negotiated renting an apartment within my price range in the *banlieue*. I told the landlord that I'd send him a message once I arrived so we could meet in person, sign any necessary papers, and exchange any other information.

The subway was an intricate network of nodes and pathways that intersected and wove together in a colour-coded honeycomb that fleshed the wolves out from the sheep. I entered the cramped metro with a big duffle backpack and suitcase, trying to find a position that was out of the way while simultaneously trying to keep vigilance at my four winds for any snakes creeping in the garden. The smell of the metro in general is unique and hard to describe. A smokiness and a sweetness share the same molecules, not unlike a mesquite. It's reminiscent of heavily-perfumed clothes worn to a bonfire that have sat in a crumpled heap for a day. It's neither malodorous nor pleasing, but redolent and fixed to the deepest receptors of the olfactory memory.

This maiden excursion was when I first encountered Alex. I suppose encountered is the incorrect word. It was the first time that Alex and I were placed in each other's presence. It happened that quickly upon my arrival in Paris. He may tell the story a little differently, but from what I gathered, he was riding out of the centre to take care of business, standing near the middle of the car and casually holding the pole. I'd noticed one side of the car's door had remained unopened for a few stops and dragged my baggage over to wedge it behind a seat. I figured my position could block it from potential thieves. I had a fairly long ride ahead of me, so I took out a used paperback, which I'd almost finished on the plane. I decided to try and complete it en route to the *banlieue*, looking up every so often to admire the stations and their individualized décor. Another thing that sets the newcomers apart is their scanning of people coming on and off the train. Residents get on and off, perhaps passing time with a phone, book, or music, but generally keep their eyes downcast and away from other passengers. The newly-arrived prick up their attention and gape at the slightest sign of movement or sound, especially if the person is travelling by themselves, which was my situation. During one of my obligatory scans, I happened upon Alex and my impression that everyone in Paris was statuesque and model-like was confirmed. Granted, I'd already seen numerous hunchbacked and damnable-looking creatures at the station as well as on the train, but he had the classic look and style that makes the average person feel bad about themselves.

He was staring out the window from the corner of his eyes. In hindsight, he was probably getting lost in his own reflection, something he did a lot. His eyes were perfectly inlayed by imposing cheekbones, thin cheeks, and a sharply-rounded jaw that allowed for no excess skin. His face still had a softness, not doughy, but a similar to that exuded from the sight of smooth, buttery leather. A light peppering of intentional dark stubble toughened his otherwise porcelain face, lightly dusted from his slightly cleft chin to his strewn-about, sumptuous, black-brown hair. His '*mother's lips*' were a feature that women seemed to be unable to resist exploring, moody and plum-like with a puckish upturn at the margins. He had a height that was impressive but not imposing, above average but in no way daunting. He was slender, but his proportions didn't seem at all ungainly, all clothed in a manner that accentuated the breadth of his shoulders and narrowness of his waist. He wore all-black from top coat to waxed alligator shoe, with a white dress shirt poking out of the collar of a black cashmere sweater. I shook my head as I resumed reading my book, deciding that he could have any woman, or man, that he chose, like the lead singer of a glam-rock band in 1984 pointing into a crowd and extracting whichever groupie he felt like taking for a turn. All of a sudden, a quick brake pump by the conductor launched my book from my hands, landing near this strange man's feet. Peeling his eyes away from the window, he knelt down and picked it up.

"This yours?" he began, holding it out towards me. "Any good?"

"How'd you know I speak English?" I responded.

"Well, it's in English," he stated.

"Ah. Well, it's pretty good. They're brothers, and one of them is a dick. So is the dad, I guess," I explained, responding to his original question.

"Hmm," he nodded. "You moving or something?"

"Yeah. Just landed here from over the pond, as they say."

"Really," he mused as the train pulled into a new station. He glanced out the door at the sign and became aware that we'd arrived at his stop. "Good luck to you, brother," he said as he sauntered off, possibly having intended to continue the conversation a few sentences longer. As he exited, two girls nearly snapped their vertebrae turning to catch a glimpse of him, reduced to chickadees in their coquetry, whispering and giggling. It'd be months before our paths would cross again. Once more, Alex would be the initiator, remembering me as an *oversized, nerdy nouvel-arrivant*. He thought I'd looked strange and out of place, like a puzzle with the pieces crammed in with no worry of fit, but at the same time was interesting and good conversation. I told him that I thought he was gay and was trying to pick me up.

2.

'Why would you come here?'

This was a phrase I commonly heard uttered with disparaged semi-curiosity while trying to make small talk with potential acquaintances in my new neighbourhood. There was never any purposeful causticity, but a genuine incredulity that sought to pinpoint my motivations with absolute, perspicuous clarity.

Two elements underscored the locals' abrupt and forthright line of inquiry, which had more or less become the *de facto* introduction that I'd shared with most clerical and service-type workers. The first is that I arrived in France at a time when university graduates were leaving in swelling numbers to America, Germany, Canada, the United Kingdom, or anywhere they could find steady work. One grizzled veteran from my neighbourhood cafe informed me that her niece, after receiving her baccalaureate in sociology, was working as a wedge jockey at a pizza by the slice joint in Vancouver. This was a common anecdote that more than a handful of jaded servers and barmen seemed comfortable enough to impress upon me, somehow intending to help guide my journey. I had to get my French up to snuff, so I tried to start conversations, usually with a question. My opener was often met with a vulgar head shake and squint that prefaced the 'Where are you from?' investigation, which would neatly rollover to the 'Why are you here?' query. Most 'conversations' led to personal story time accompanied by a sourness that only the sneer of a working-class French-man could relay. Their stories birthed tangents and bemoaning that desic-cated my desire to further engage in conversation.

The second important feature of their directness was related to geogra-phy. Chiefly, my *being* in the *banlieue*. Rarely did non-Francophones patrol or even spend a considerable amount of time in the massive ring of Paris's suburbs, at least not this far from the historic centre. The neighbourhood was a composition of blue-collar whites born in Paris and immigrants from Maghreb and French-speaking Africa. Books have been written about the racial, cultural, and economic climates of the various *banlieues*, including their social frameworks and the myriad of issues stitched within. There are, of course, some affluent suburbs and functional areas of art and letters; diversity happens wherever difference exists. These enclaves of prosperity were generally surrounded by areas of higher crime. My particular area wasn't destitute, but it didn't have an empowered self-identity or even much hope. My choice to live there said little about myself to the people of the area who felt trapped by the postal codes that were all too present on their identification cards, acting like barcodes stamped on their fore-arms. This invisible tattoo indicated to police and prospective employers in other parts of the city that they came from the wastelands and had scant means to mobilize socially. Why would a person from the land of milk and honey choose willingly to settle in an unpredictable tumor sprouting from a cancerous liver that'd poisoned itself from excess? Their outspokenness seemed like a way to advance-lunge outsiders, getting them off balance and testing their mettle. It could also very well have been that they were letting outsiders know they'd always be on the perimeter of their social bubble for another generation or two.

This outspoken nonplussing was a particularly European reaction to my invitation for conversation. For whatever financial or ancestral course that had led these people to the *banlieue*, perceived as a desperate and inescapable one, a staunch pride of name and country still resonated. They were still bathed in the previous conquests of kings and could become violently agitated if, an outsider for instance, assumed too comfortable a voice in denigrating their homeland. Far from laying lips on the chalice of white-privilege and superiority, a twinkle of hubristic nationalism cymballed their blood under invisible wounds. These were scars that pained the wearer in the mirror and turned supercilious in the face of the *other*.

The non-whites, which is only fair because of so many Algerians, Moroccans, Cote d'Ivoirians, Senegalese, Haitians, and others holding a passport, have their own take on the matter. No categorical neatness or similar groupthink exists among them as most arrived in Paris at different times, had different statuses in previous lives, perceive the future in drastically different ways, and represent a broad spectrum of beliefs and customs. The browns and blacks didn't have the hereditary defeatist conceit or shameful pride of the poor whites, at least not to the same level of *puissance*. Despite the fact that many were born in France, they assumed the role of the other, embracing the *banlieue* mentality and readily armed to play the foe. People of colour in the *banlieues* get blamed for all kinds of vandalism and acts of violence, but from what I noticed, they just had more kids more often with younger families as some had religions that restricted contraceptives or encouraged more offspring. Kids are mischievous by nature, more so when there are few activities to do, and even more so when there's minimal supervision. I never saw this as an ethnic problem. It's a poverty problem. Poorness and boredom.

The uniting thread that has yet to stitch common autonomy is that all the residents are fearful and distrustful of the institutions, the police, and each other, of course. There's a lot of poverty, and therefore, a lot of people, especially the elderly, who have little else to do but watch, and watch, and watch until someone does something fucked up. Even an angel's bound to pluck another's feather if they're left without anything to busy their little halos.

I'm able to converse with both sides, holding no inherited hates or predetermined prejudices. I just let dogs sniff my hand and assume they won't bite. People didn't ever necessarily warm up to me, but they eventually recognized me, and some younger adults even showed amiability. With time, I was shown a mild courtesy after I kept showing up to cafes, restaurants, and supermarkets regularly.

Another anecdote worth mentioning is the over-eager correction of my slightest deviation from Parisian pronunciation. It's a work that'll always be in progress for the non-native speaker, and I don't think that my pronunciation is bad at all. Veer slightly off the expected accent or stressing of a vowel, however, and Parisians will act befuddled as if you were speaking Ubuntu, have you repeat the word or words numerous times, and then say it how they want it heard. To date, a young, blond waitress with marble eyes and frank bangs has had the following conversation with me over a hundred times:

"Bonjour," she says as if pre-recorded.

"Bonjour. Un café crème, s'il vous plaît?" I ask her.

"Un quoi?" she replies, puzzled.

"Uh, un cafe crème?" I repeat for both of our sakes to make sure that I wasn't speaking in tongues.

"Pardon?" she sounds confused and shakes her head with ample bother.

"Je veux un café avec du crème chaud," e-nun-ci-at-ing with im-mac-u-late con-trol.

"Un *crème*," she says definitively with an all-knowing nod, waiting for my acquiescence before gliding off.

For the first few months, I just said '*café*,' but found that I was drinking the tiny espressos way too quickly. Once I asked for a *crème* and was just given frothed milk. This conversation had gone the same way for a year, almost daily, always maddening.

Annoying and patronizing as the waitress's daily corrections were, they weren't symptomatic of her individual brand of pedantry. This was a common phenomenon found in virtually every kind of Parisian, in no way relating to breeding, stature, age, race, or sex. The conversation with Marie-Claude, which I eventually learned was her name, is one that I had with all kinds of people in all kinds of scenarios. What's especially damning is that I can expertly roll guttural R's in the back of my throat. I've been able to copy the smarmy iambic pentameter of French men and learned to *vous* the shit out of authority figures and pretty girls as a way to disarm them with foreign charm. Still, the poor stressing of a vowel, whether it be not *aiguë* enough or the *grave* not being distinguishable from a regular E, was an unintelligible disaster to the French. I could have a thousand *good* conversations and prove my adroitness in French, but with *one* fuck up, they'd spite me by trying to speak an English so broken that I'd end up feeling bad. Each error I made was like a personal insult.

My French *was* terribly rusty when I arrived. Brownish-red flakes must've fallen from words when I first tried to speak, pausing to search for missing vocabulary and mismanaging onerous verb tenses. I didn't really have anyone to speak with regarding any impactful or overly technical subjects at that point, however. I merely stuttered to all those I interacted with, realizing there was a small verbal island around which I could move freely. Eventually, this island expanded and offered greater width between the coastlines, growing as I read the papers and kept a notebook of slang and turns of phrases. The island would shrivel into a peninsula, narrow enough to splash on both sides at the same time, if I didn't immerse myself in the culture to try and expand my vocabulary, or if I drank too much and began to slur.

There was little work to be found for an Anglophone with a French degree from an English university residing in France. My one strength, a diploma-worthy understanding and ability to read and write in the French language, wasn't ideal in a place where even the most moronic, irresponsible, or ugly person spoke the language from birth. For the moment, the world's language is money, followed closely by English. Soon, I have to guess it'll be Mandarin. However, the protectionism in France makes it difficult for a non-French person to secure a job, and even more difficult to land a good, well-paying job. Nevertheless, I can't argue with the *take care of our own* mentality. In fact, when I realized that the native inhabitants of France were white-skinned Caucasians, it blew my mind for some reason.

The landscape of the *banlieue* has changed very little over time. The white French blame the brown and black French for mischief and violence, while lamentation flows towards the extremists and Neo-Fascists in the other direction. Journalists are often seen trying to fraternize with the locals on park benches or develop some camaraderie at local hangouts, looking to get the scoop after a terrorist attack or some racially or religiously-motivated demonstration, protest, or riot. The large number of Muslims in the area tends to make it a hotbed of accusations; a breeding ground for terrorism, or at the very least some kind of mobile headquarters. Personally, I'd never seen any indication of plotting or scheming. I never really looked. Once you start looking, you tend to find the answer you wanted all along: taking the spurious as the genuine article. I'd seen some cars overturned and alighted, but had never been hassled by either side, white or non-white, coloured or melanin-deficient. In any case, I don't look for trouble. I make eye contact, either initiate or return salutations, answer random questions with direct courtesy, and look like I know how to take care of myself.

I didn't have any cast-iron plans about staying, leaving, or returning home. I didn't move to Paris with some starry-eyed intention to assimilate and replant my family tree in another garden. I just wanted to wake up to new sunrises with differently shaped horizons.

3.

Coffee and booze; that's how I drank Paris in. There was no pressing need for me to find employment, but I craved responsibility and some kind of structure. Even though I'd been beset by a lack of purpose back home, I appreciated the orderliness of routine that I'd been able to maintain through work.

You see, I *need* to operate within a framework to use my time most effectively. Busy feels good and keeps one's mitts off the Devil's jungle gym. I enjoy the hell out of free time. I enjoy spending it in palatial leisure with my feet on ice, reading, smoking, and being at home in blissful, silent retreat. I can't have an abundance of leisure time, however. It's a gift to be enjoyed when it's rare, and a curse when surfeit. I need a blueprint to make sure that all my critical activities are well-managed: work, masturbation, sex when lucky, eating, sleeping, masturbation again, and miscellanea. Although I really loathe a *recipe on the back of the box* way of life, I can't stand the thought of fumbling through life without meaning, even if that meaning is a career, and that career swallows me whole and leaves no time for personal investment. I create routines to quell any anxieties that arise from the cascading of intrinsic panics about wasting away in the ignominy of laziness.

The possibilities of schedule-making and not truncating all the digits in my savings account were entirely valid reasons to enter the workforce in my new home, but the social aspect couldn't be overlooked. During my time spent sitting in cafes and reading newspapers with a miniature LaRousse English-French dictionary nearby, I'd developed something of a social phobia.

I tried several *token-native-English-speaker* jobs: teaching English, tutoring English, one day as a tour guide, accidentally being hired as a nanny only to be chided and then sent home, and my mainstay as a French-English translator. There were also construction and light maintenance jobs available, similar to those that the crag-faced addicts line up for alongside the Central Americans behind hardware stores and shipyards, but I feared that I'd embarrass myself with my paucity of construction savvy, and I hate working in the rain.

The language institute where I became a translator was in *Centre-ville*. I travelled about an hour each way on a combination of train, bus, and outsole every day. It was the first time that I'd experienced that thing that commuters back home were so fond of, along with their living quarters being separated by a meter-wide strip of grass or gravel, with bushes and fences, a retractable-doored garage for twin sedans, and whatever else the suburbs tempt people with to resign them to hours of traffic. Upwards of a dozen per week in some metropolises! I'd lose my mind if I had to scramble to my car only to wait in a frozen rope of wheeled-sarcophaguses from my cubicle to the horizon. I took public transit and bought a membership at an overpriced fitness club downtown so I didn't have to clash antlers and breathe other people's stale flatulence during peak hours. I also didn't have children and hadn't thought about establishing a pride of my own. I can see how that might alter my perception, to give my cubs some grass to roll around on and a disputably better chance of not being kidnapped.

The travel time passed quickly. My fetishized routine-building allowed me to figure out which times the train became a full deck of *blondes* and which times it became a half-used bag of dried tobacco. Speaking of which, *blondes*, or cigarettes in a package of twenty, cost triple a bag of shredded tobacco in France, including the rolling papers and the little filters that help reduce the sour filaments of Nicotiana that squirm out. Most importantly, where rolled cigarettes are for sailors and vagabonds back home, they're a socially acceptable and chic alternative in France. Business men, gorgeous women, and university professors all roll and smoke their own snuff.

The job itself was very informal, laid back, and gave one the impression that employees could show up one morning and find the copper wiring ripped from the walls and ceiling with a note saying *'Gone Fishing'* left at the front door with a pickaxe propped against it. There was a loose system of *as long as it all gets done* management. The company handled all kinds of publishing. We're talking books, magazines, movies, commercials, pamphlets, textbooks, and individual projects sourced to us by some agency. There was always work, and the particular type of project helped draft one's itinerary for the following day, week, or month. A small project like a pamphlet or magazine advertisement could last an hour or a day for one employee, while a feature-length movie or novel could involve multiple translators, editors, and the management team, lasting weeks or months. The door was on an axis and swung both ways as new hires were often brought in, while exits were common enough to allow space for newcomers.

The English department was a mere sliver of the company and spanned several floors of a building in the *M-district*. It was of medium height and had an unchanging, anile odor. Its brick and stone would be a remarkable attraction in most non-European cities, but fell victim to being one of many on the block. As a result, it was saddled with suspicious mould and poor ventilation.

For a job that often required collaborative effort, I rarely saw or spoke to my co-workers, usually found diving deeply into one of several thesauruses or encyclopedia to find the exact word to detail the *sadness* of losing a horse who'd been both a vehicle and confidant to a *greedy* pond of *hungry* quicksand, or the *craziness* of a sale that didn't 'trigger' those with mental disorders. I could also work as much or as little as I desired. There was very little accountability to determine someone's illness or reasons for either showing up or staying at home. If an employee was in-between projects, they could take days or weeks off at a time to travel, raise children, or sit motionlessly. Concerns would only appear when there was a big project going on, especially a more prominent and therefore costly project.

The manager who I had the most contact with, Mr. Stewart, seemed to have a fantasy that he'd one day parlay a successful cinematic translation into an acting gig. He'd always get his *best men* on projects, trying to sneak face time in with someone connected to the film. I had little rapport with him beyond that. He was in his fifties with immaculate posture and elegant presentation. To thwart his balding head, he kept it shorn to the crane and lubricated to give the mirror-like effect of spit-shined chrome. He was in charge of passing out the dossiers that required attention, which were partially meted out according to merit and skill, partially according to employee requests. A new person couldn't hop onto Stewart's prized projects, starting with very simple rubrics and straight-forward translations. As time progressed and the new employee's work needed less secondary editing, more responsibility was allotted from there. A veteran or above-average translator could request easy, quota-eating projects at any time, though Stewart would notify the *best men* about upcoming movies and novels to collect volunteers as the receiving date approached. There was no real incentive to do one or the other, as bonuses for completing large-scale projects were comparable to a multitude of smaller ones. The hourly wage fine. The pay wasn't going to incentivize a newcomer into life-long employment, but could keep them as busy as they wished, and was nothing to complain about.

The company's systems were very different from the rigid functions of the financial industry and the cookie cutter models of corporate restaurants. I was used to a regimented system of accountability that relied on technology, statistics, and the diligence of superiors to make sure targets were met. In France, there were dull, gray metal box-cabinets containing paper files from last week to the last several presidencies. Perhaps the changeover from paper to electronic seemed like too tall a mountain to bother climbing. Computers weren't assigned, so new people like me were bounced from desk to desk due to seniority and employee preferences. People tended to decorate *their* cubicles on the inside, but trinkets and signage were often thieved by cleaners. The desks were built primarily for supporting numerous books at a time and the office was understandably silent.

Cigarette breaks and lunches were monitored with carelessness at best, and the chain of command was nothing but bastard links and sign-in sheets.

As one can imagine, there was little camaraderie, what with the focus on silence. I was on friendlier terms with some people. Ethnicity and age usually played the biggest roles in assigning affiliation, not unlike life in a penitentiary. The transient nature of the job meant that the drier and drabber people seemed to be the cotton-twilled lifers that were comfortably unambitious in their personalized workspaces. Young adults, travelling students, and those with gypsy spirits would come in for a spell or two and be off. Paris isn't a cheap place and people who lived without restraint were often financially gutted within weeks of pastry-centered diets and excursions. It was also a very boring job for people who liked to move around and engage with other human beings. The job suited me just fine. I usually snared a cubicle with no one to my rear so I could blaze through my tasks and then search the ads in the paper for jobs that posed different challenges.

4.

The one drawback to this new life was that I still had no social circle, or even people that I spoke to on a regular basis, if at all, outside of work. Work was a full deck of new faces and personalities, but due to the individualistic nature of our chores, there was little chatter or fraternizing. The workspace layout was a *Plan Voisin* that Le Corbusier charted for mankind's next step towards a bright cold day in April, where the clocks strike thirteen.

My trip home always shook off the dormancy that my body had collected from sitting in silent productivity all day. I rode the train, encapsulated in the bubble of a novel or news article that helped pass the hour-long commute. I usually heated up a plate and puttered around my little flat, walled and roofed in a cellular network of families, single people, lambs, wolves, and harbingers of things. Nothing was known of them beyond a nice word, agreeable glance, or at most, putting a face to an apartment number. I went for coffee and the odd kebab, making small talk if there was enough clay to make it with, all the while developing an anxious paranoia. I was irrationally scared and apprehensive to make any attempts to meet people. I was either fearing some kind of rejection or had spent so long in the service industry that I no longer knew how to be genuine.

It had also been a long time, feeling infinitely longer, since I'd been with a woman. A lack of sexual assuage and a reliance on onanism tends to erode the mind and soul, both becoming increasingly friable, as a man disintegrates into a weaker, more pathetic version of himself. He loses his authority, power, and control over his confidence. He becomes a craven and susceptible creature, vulnerable to manipulation and emotional pillory. He begins to question his instincts; his unseen feelers and antennae shrivel and become fossil-like. He doubts the functionality of his most basic senses: taste, touch, and the rest, as if they erratically deviate from their forms overnight like some kind of Kafka character's bewildered morning soliloquy. A dry spell is beyond physical. It causes a man to equate his drive with the characteristics of a drought. In particular, it occupies the image of a wrought, knotted, dying-dead tree in the desert, solemnly twisting its last wizened limb skyward to try and pierce a too-high, mirage-bred cloud to vainly slake its deathbed thirst.

Such is the spirit of a man who cannot will himself to intercourse, whose katana was once oft-indulged with the flesh of another, turns on himself. The warrior becomes a beggar. The most corrupting aspect was the void of opportunity to woo or coax a woman in my day-to-day life in Paris. From time to time, work would present an attractive woman, or at least a lady who elicited a second pass, but it was an uncomfortable environment within which to approach someone with romantic inclinations, like flirting with a woman in postnatal or palliative care. If I'm being honest, even in these Spartan times, I'd lost the confidence to smile at a woman or even hold eye contact.

The closest I got to intimacy was in the gym shower one day. There was a hulking middle-aged fellow with a De Boer orange tan and barrel-chest covered with thick, black hair and steroid acne. He seemed like the CEO type. He said that I had a '*belle bite*,' which he kindly translated for me after I must've looked at him mildly stunned, repeating in English that I had a '*pretty cock*.' I thanked him for the compliment and hurriedly finished soaping the neck and head of my adorable penis as non-sexually as possible, which seemed futile both in theory and in practice. I finished up quicker than either of us would've liked, not really knowing how, or caring to, build on his flattery. I didn't know if he required a compliment in return, or if that would be leading him on and earn me the reputation of *shower-room-cock-tease*. Socially and morally, the best option was to dismiss my lather with haste and excuse myself.

The lack of sex and imposition of solitude were making me feel unfamiliar with myself. Jackie and I had stopped talking altogether. She'd been an outlet that had previously inspired uncharacteristic optimism, as well as a chance to describe my sexual longings that had oftentimes graduated into playful back and forths. We used to speak about trivial or serious things, which had helped relieve tension. I should've noticed when the small talk outclassed the deeper entirely. I used to at least be able to practice-scrimmage my sex talk and flirting, and sometimes, although it was a poor substitute for the taste and smell of a woman, we'd had phone sex, which had sadly been the closest thing to a fuck I'd experienced since her real, organic vagina.

I had to explain to myself why I couldn't shake this misery off, using simple vocabulary and tenable examples as though I was a child. Jackie had become the alpha and myself the beta in the stratified hegemony of dominance that is *human relationships*. Her justifiable avoidance of me was akin the shedding of an old, tattered skin; how a gecko relinquishes its tail when trapped under a rock. After a couple months of silence, I gave up. Perhaps she'd discovered something previously unbeknownst to herself and was angry about my past fuck-ups and apathies. Perhaps she'd found a new partner and wanted no index of me and my memory. Our former friends and coworkers could've been providing her with shoulder, ear, or dick and doing little to defend my now faceless and fading name. Perhaps they'd never even liked me.

No matter what feelings of love I'd had for the girl, losing her had left me alienated and isolated to the point of sorrow. She'd got one over on me like few others had. She'd kicked the leg of the chair while I'd still been seated. What was damnable, was that it made me revere and crave her in an entirely self-denigrating way. I wanted to tell her that I loved her, but even saying it to myself didn't sound like the healthy, selfless love that poets squirt recklessly on charred-fringed parchment. I reminisced about the contours of her tiny waist and bubbled bum, which gave me implausibly hard, pathetically self-pitied erections. Sad masturbation is the worst masturbation. The grossest of chores.

If it exists, love that is, it must be extremely rare. How can it exist for any two individuals in the same capacity, with the same criteria, with the same patterns, and the same definition at the same time? How I define it is probably different than how any of my friends or coworkers define it, how my parents define it, or how *you* define it. That's right, I'm talking to you, *one-who-is-reading-this*. Yeah, I know you're reading this. Pretty weird so far, isn't it? You're probably like *'Where's he going with all this back story? Who talks like this?'* Me. Fuck you. Anyways, I can relate to the popularized notion of what most people think love is, but I don't know if I can accept that as *my* personal definition. Love is a word, clearly, but with such a range of definitions and interpretations, it's hard to pinpoint exactly what it means. What one person perceives as a monogamous, trusting, and coaxial love, may be suffocating and unnatural to another. Love can be equated to a deep fondness, reciprocal care, sexual rapport, intellectual stimulation, a sharing of obscure interests or values, a mutual desire to produce offspring, economic compatibility, physical safety, and financial security. Of course, there are even more occasions that are often perceived as love than those listed here. However, do any of them function as practical synonyms for love? Is it a combination, hodgepodge, or potion with adequate ingredients mixed in a cauldron over a fire of elk bones?

Is love more complex than being able to look someone in the eyes and feel as though everything under your top layer of skin is melting into a puddle of hot black treacle? I don't have an answer to that question. I'm waiting for it to evolve arms and legs and meander on all twos or fours into the conceptual realm. Anyways, *love* is one of those things that Alex could prattle on about *ad nauseam*. All I knew was that I was lonely. My perception of the world was becoming tainted with antipathy, poisoned by solitude and made morbid by a lack of human caress.

5.

The day was an unlabeled mason jar of spring. Not late spring with its aggressively lengthening days, nor early spring when the cold season doesn't loosen its icy fingers until peak daytime hours with flora and fauna still as shy as silhouettes. It was mid-spring: the umbrella, sniffle, almost-impossible-to-predict footwear season.

I'd finished work early that afternoon, having earned my first real office triumph. That is, I'd finished translating a significant collection of marketing materials. These translations consisted of all kinds of advertisements for a line of beauty products, complete with jargon and verbiage. The supplies were meant to keep women looking young and feeling the *je ne sais quoi* of the Bardots and Chanels. Truthfully, it was a random project that was accidentally given the same Manila envelope and beige folder as any other project in the to-do stack. I tended to grab packets at random, gauging their thickness to decide how hard and long I felt like working for.

Just trying to plan ahead, coach.

I suppose that the beauty product company must've carried a fair amount of prestige and notoriety, because while breaking topsoil on the project the previous Friday, coworkers approached my cubicle without prompting and engaged with me in a manner that I hadn't experienced before. My closest memory of a similar situation was seeing the male investment specialists at the credit union punch-arm and offer double-edged praise to one another, a toast to healthy competition.

"Wow, stepping into the big leagues," said one with drumlin excitement.

"Was wondering when you were going to get a *real* project," admired another.

"Look at you, Mr. Man."

I will never know what to make of that type of idiocy, but I took it as a compliment. I needed all that I could get.

"You're so lucky! I love their products! So jealous! Be careful, they're a big company. So jealous!" exclaimed a cute, brown-skinned co-worker with a healthy, promontory nose and a wide mouthful of pearls. I was appreciative and thanked them all for their words of encouragement, whether or not they even meant it.

I'd given extra care and attention to the marketing material, which mirrored the magnitude those around me were placing on the project. To me, it was just another packet of information that required translation, but the reactions of my cohorts certainly raised the profile of the pile of papers. Now, my good name and standing were linked with my effort.

Mr. Stewart came to me with great words of inspiration.

"Well, I'm glad you picked this project up," he uttered quickly, trying not to sound shaky. "Not sure how it slipped into the *random* heap... I'd intended to work on it myself, but you seem to be well underway. Yes... I trust you'll do a fine job. Who knows? This could be the beginning of bigger things for you. That's not so bad now, is it?"

Indeed, truly inspirational stuff from a man who was able to elicit such passion and excitement from his frontline of infantrymen, somewhere between George Patton and Raymond Domenech. The Desert Fox of the translation world.

I took the packet home with me for the weekend and put my head down. It felt rewarding to occupy my time with something that felt important, putting the idea that it could lead to better opportunities as far out of my conscience as possible. I even went as far as enlivening the homework with a glass of red wine, sipped from my finest coffee mug. I don't know why all glasses don't have handles, it just makes sense. I also don't understand why they carry so much stigma. If wide-mouth glass jars are now the trendy and hip way to imbibe Gatsby era cocktails, then there's a place for handled ceramic glasses as an equally swank and even more useful vessel.

I returned to work on Monday with much of the project completed. I worked through all breaks and ignored all offers of assistance, even staying late. With confidence, I quilled the final curlicues on Tuesday, just before lunch. Before passing it on to the editing department, I collated, proofread, and perfected that bitch. While printing it out on the deluxe, noisy, and therefore best printer, Mr. Stewart traipsed over and asked if I was finished. Then, if he could see the final copy. With previous projects, I'd either e-mailed the assignments or printed them off on regular sheets of cheap computer paper. Today, I was making the effort to gussy up the presentation, even though it was a transitory piece of work soon to be wrinkled, stretched, and carved with a red ink pen by multifarious departments and marketing specialists. I used the extra fancy, mid-gloss 8 ½ x 11 paper with coated resin for extra sheen. Mr. Stewart thumbed through the spiral-bound presentation booklet, complete with a title page, table of contents, and pointless stock graphics, all of which had taken me a few extra hours of trial and error.

"This looks very professional. A lot of hard work," Mr. Stewart said with his lips forming a manta-like downward curl of tacit approval.

"Yeah, you know, I kind of figured out how important this was. Wanted to make sure it started and ended strong," I responded in my best 'Coach, I'm really trying' voice.

"Can I take this to edits?" he asked, still thumbing through the booklet. Only the top of his shiny, bald head was visible.

"Sure, of course you can," I responded. This would happen no matter what I answered.

"I have a pretty big project coming our way… Wouldn't mind getting you on it as well. A motion picture that needs some subtitles… post-production…" he said slyly. He shoulder-checked as if he was passing me an offer on a facedown napkin at an unassuming diner.

"Oh, crazy. Yeah, that sounds awesome," I said like a bored trophy wife. I just wanted the interaction to end. "I'm good with whatever you want to throw at me, chief."

"*Chef*," he pronounced, with the satisfying lilt and smirk of a man who'd embraced his feminine side. "If you must. Perfect. Well, how about you kick out for the rest of the day? Enjoy the sun, and I'll see you tomorrow morning."

"Will do, *chef*," I glad-handed with an inner shudder that'd require a stiff pour of whisky to reconcile. I didn't dislike Mr. Stewart by any means. He was a bit of a twerp and kind of pretentious, especially with that *chef* shit, but a decent enough fellow. I supposed that I'd have to start trying to find the bright spots in him. A decent fellow, seems to care about things, is gainfully employed as my superior… wearer of pants and is sparklingly baldheaded? That would do for now.

Who cared? I'd been gifted a free afternoon with pay (I assumed). I walked around for an hour or so, thinking of nothing and everything all at once, unable to grasp any meaningful thoughts, yet incapable of not critiquing my interactions with cohorts, quality of work, future prospects, libido, and failed opportunities, as well as wondering whether my jacket was too heavy or too light for the mild breeze and soggy atmosphere in spite of noon's idealistic glow.

6.

I happened upon a little cafe with outward-facing chalkboards showing the specials *du jour* and favourites *du* more habitual consumption. The wood-paneled exterior was stained a dark, cherry-gut red. A lightly rippling maroon canopy spread itself atop the patio section. Sprigs and laurels of brass ornamented the entryway and framed the worn, wooden bar top. It appeared that the wicker furniture was making one of its first outings following a lengthy hibernation period, much to the appreciation of everyone except those who love skiing. I claimed a chair, had a coffee on the terrace, and began a fresh section of a book written by some angry, mostly-coherent 20th century writer while I waited for a *croque-madame* and side salad to be prepared.

In Paris, food preparation and bill times never failed to surprise me. There's an unspoken understanding, common sense if you will, of how long toasted cheese bread with ham and a fried egg on top with dressed field greens on the side takes to prepare. Anyone can ballpark a reasonably approximate time that it *should* take to master such an order. In Paris and against all logic, however, I'd received the same meal after anywhere from five minutes to an hour and half, with the number of guests at the establishment and its hustle or bustle having no bearing on this phenomenon. The servers never care, the food's delivered with the same detachment whether there's a considerable amount of time spent waiting or not. Globally speaking, being knighted in the American tradition of the food and beverage industry with its Fordist principles of production and efficiency does the American a disservice when abroad. With no tipping and apathy at its zenith in Paris, the wait times that were pathologized back home for inhibiting consumption and therefore reducing profit, are moot here. It took me a while to get used to the way things worked in France. And, to learn that I should never arrive at a restaurant on a fully empty stomach or in a hurry.

I'd finished rolling a nice *brun* when my coffee arrived. I light my cigarette and was just as quickly forced to blow out an opportunistic flame that was consuming a pocket of loosely rolled cigarette paper, threatening to undermine the entire operation. It was also threatening to ignite the hairs of my beard, which had begun to sprout while I'd been hard at work on the beauty project.

Just as I was digging into my novel, I was interrupted.

"You almost burnt your face off. I couldn't decide if it'd be better to let that thicket singe off and laugh, or throw a cup of water on you... and laugh," said a man's voice in English.

"I was hoping that no one saw that," I responded without taking my eyes off the page, speculating that I was being heckled by some random tourist or passer-by. Noticing that the character's shadow was remaining in my presence, I fanned the novel out and exhaled the way a huffing tycoon might straighten the daily newspaper out during his morning shoeshine.

"You must really like those Russian authors. Too long for me. But, that goes for most classic literature in general. Necessary evil, I guess," he said.

I nodded dismissively, but was suddenly arrested by his choice of words and the fact that yes, I did often read Russian authors, at least since moving to Paris.

"How the hell did you know that?" I screwed my eyes and head towards the anonymous speaker, only to realize that it was the beautiful man in black from the metro. "Good memory," I sounded. The words exited my mouth as though they'd been pushed out of an airplane.

"Thank you, kindly," he nodded with a smirk. "It was *Brother's Karamazov* on the train, if I recall. And now... Tolstoy? *Light reading*. I thought that you looked familiar as I was walking by. Don't know if I would've recognized you since your face was being swallowed by that book, and that beard. Luckily, you almost lit yourself on fire. Made me double take.

"Yeah, that happens sometimes with these stupid things... Can't roll them too loose or they fall apart, too tight and they won't smoke properly. If the tobacco's too dry they burn like it's a race to your fingers, too wet and you might lose a filling sucking on that mother fucker."

"Poor plight of *le petit prolo*," he said smarmily with deliberate francophone emphasis. "Can I offer you a *blonde*? It *probably* won't set you ablaze, but I can't make any promises. You might just be incompetent."

"Well, sure," I responded, weighing the prospect of human contact against the neurosis that stemmed from not completing a chapter. I piously accepted the cigarette that he was brandishing out of the pack, its brown filter pointing at me.

"Jesus Christ, what's a guy got to do to be offered a seat around here?" he joked.

He stepped over the railing that separated the street from the cafe. I apologized for not offering sooner and gestured at the seat across from mine. He set down a pack of Camels, a Zippo lighter, and a black, leather-bound notebook secured with a black band.

"Put that *thing* out already and have a good one. It smells of poverty. I'm going to grab a coffee," he said. He was speaking without boredom or excitement, just a frankness that I'd come to know as his default tone, devoid of any distinct emotion.

He rose from his seat hastily. "I'm Alex by the way," he said as he threw his right hand towards me as a Roman would salute a fellow soldier, shield in his left.

7.

So, that's how I met Alex. It was as simple as any indiscriminate, one-time encounter with a stranger during a confusing inaugural trip on the metro, where a scant conversation was briefly held while crammed into a brimming Parisian subway car, ineffectually trying to locate my unseen living quarters with only a faint idea of where I was headed, leading up to a chanceful encounter at a cafe that I'd never been to, chosen at random thanks to an early dismissal from work for the completion of a project for an esteemed client that I should've never been given, but hit it out of the park and warranted a victory lap in the surrounding area. Easy.

At first study, his hands, grasping his little mug and flicking the ashes of his cigarette, looked clean and well-cared-for. They weren't delicate like the fine fingers of a pharmacist, nor stocky like the stone fingers of a net-hauler on a fishing boat. He had an elegant masculinity. When I shook his hand, I was surprised by his grip strength, for a man of his svelteness. He was dressed entirely in black again: pants, shirt, coat, shoes, socks, and probably underwear. Now, I've seen him wear other colours, though not often. The all-black attire adhered so conformingly to the manner in which he viewed himself and how he preferred to be viewed by others: authoritative, elegant, sophisticated, powerful... and it didn't show dirt. A wolf in wolf's clothing.

"Much better, isn't it?" he asked.

"Indeed," I agreed. "Much smoother. Though really, I don't mind the other ones."

"Bullshit. No one *really* likes to roll their cigarettes," he said. "Maybe it's cool in that bohemian, *enfant terrible*, man of the people kind of way... But, tell me... what *king* really enjoys the playthings of peasants? It's the little things that show the divide between haves and have-nots."

"No, seriously," I said. "They aren't bad at all. They taste fine. And, I can assure you that I'm not poor." I threw in a chuckle to keep it light-hearted. "It's just easy and cheaper."

"Well, you may not be poor, but you're obviously not rich. You know what? It doesn't matter. We're both addicted to the same plant. It doesn't matter if you shoot smack with a hand-me-down needle in a crater where your elbow used to be, or between the toes like a pretty lady with a syringe created for astronauts. We're still both addicted to fucking heroin."

I took a big drag of the admittedly better filtered cigarette and exhaled its slate-coloured smoke.

"It's a lovely day," I said. Just like that, I'd betrayed my own scruples. I felt like I had to entertain this man, give him a reason to stay. He just stared out onto the street. "Yup... Little chilly still, but lots of people walking around outside again." I couldn't stop myself. I wanted to punch my drab self in the mug.

I wanted, no, needed a friend. Fuck it.

I tried thinking of an actual topic to discuss. I started mentally scanning the news, sports, cinema...

"All I see..." Alex started, "is that time of year when the sewers are beginning to wring their rags out onto the streets. Have you seen the number of homeless people moping around today? Trash all over the sidewalks? Dog shit everywhere? It wasn't like that last week. Did you know that the reason why they all have so many dogs is because they get a government stipend for each one, like a kind of meal allowance? The dogs are normally stolen from their masters, the ones that owned them, fed them, and paid for their shots. Dogs are imbeciles, you see. Their loyalty lies in their stomachs. These street-dwellers and trash-humans would do *anything* if it meant getting paid to do *nothing*. Another excuse to be lazy and useless. They treat them like shit… feed them food from jagged cans, so the dogs' snouts get all cut up. The bums use the money for booze or drugs."

"What? That sounds made up. Why would someone do that?"

"You think it's just the homeless that harm dogs? Listen. I'm no animal rights activist, but humans have doomed the canine race to need them for every little thing, even going for a piss or lapping up a few tablespoons of water. Well, except for those feral mutants in poor countries. They'll eat your face in an alleyway if they have the chance, the *good boys* that they are. Trust me, if there's ever any kind of extinction event, the cute little ones will be eaten; arguably better than being imprisoned in a cage for twenty-plus hours a day, only being taken out of their kennels so the owners can walk their egos. *If* there's an apocalyptic event, I'd love to see the dogs rise up against the humans and leave nothing but eyeless sockets staring at the moon… Anyways, the first sunny days. You can smell the syphilis as they start begging for money, trying to wash car windows at red lights, screaming obscenities, and clogging up the streets. Fucking useless creatures. As useless as the shelters and the work and learn programs that waste tax money. Sneak poison into the grain liquor. That'll help them a lot faster than the syphilis, which takes too long to turn the brain into one big ulcer. That'll help everybody. Bikes will stay lassoed to the racks, property insurance prices will go way down, and we'll have successfully eradicated the only garbage that we can't legally incinerate. Useless pieces of fucking shit."

I stared at Alex. I wasn't sure if he was done. He picked up his cigarette from the ashtray. "Not a dog person, I take it?" I said.

"Ha, no. I wouldn't call myself a *people person* either."

"You don't say," I said. "Maybe cats?"

"I know that look…" he said. "I hope you're not about to give me that *everyone is equal* shit," Alex said with unadorned candor.

"I wasn't…" I wasn't.

"On days like today, when everyone in the city takes up space and pretends to be doing something meaningful, you can really pick out the people who are barely living. Just surviving without the strength and will of someone who wants to live. Look!" he gestured at an elderly person on a scooter.

The lady wore a nasty scowl that seemed to have been permanently carved onto her face. She was obese, yet the scooter carried her with undeserving swiftness. She beeped sharply at the people in front her, speeding up and hitting the heels of the unsuspecting pedestrians who failed to move away quickly enough. I couldn't hear what she as barking, but there was a husky violence in her tone. I hated her.

"They prop up the old on those things with all sorts of tubes helping them piss and shit, forcing the wind in and out of their broken lungs and pumping the blood through their decrepit cells. It all costs money, and for what? They've lived so poorly that they can no longer move their own body parts, but are rewarded with inconvenient speed. They burden everybody, more than just their families who want to see them in a bronze vase."

"I mean... They're not that bad. Someone probably loves her, no?"

"I can see it in your eyes. You don't even believe what you're saying. You agree with me. And, I bet her family does too."

"I mean... Well... Don't people deserve..."

"*Deserve*? What does anyone deserve beyond equality? By that, I mean equal opportunities to live and die. Does that woman *deserve* to have her, what I'm assuming is a wretched life, to be prolonged? Because of what... Fear? Guilt? Blind duty? Does that look like someone who was a loving mother and economic powerhouse?"

"Maybe?"

"Why do people idealize the old? Do you think you live to be that age by being nice? All the good ones die early from work and stress. That... thing over there... could just as easily have been a Nazi."

"Okay. I agree."

"Good. She clearly has some kind of killer instinct to have made it this far. Some strength in her better days. A trail of good people, dead and gone, in her wake. It's time to put the old girl out of her misery."

"Only the strong should survive, Dr. Darwin?" I asked.

"In a way, yes. Everyone *should* be given the same opportunities to succeed and survive, but it's important to know when enough is enough. If the funds that you need to live cost more than what you make, or have ever made, then the burden of your existence is an easily calculated cost-benefit analysis."

This was the first conversation that I had with Alex. Maybe not word for word, but fairly close. It was quite the introduction. He really went for it and didn't care if he scared me off. He didn't, obviously. I also hadn't had a substantive conversation in a long time. It beat my attempt to discuss the fucking weather, at least. I also noticed the looks of female passers-by. I felt special, if only to be seen with him.

ALEX

Alex is an enigma. He talks a lot, mostly about his views and opinions, and rarely about himself or his personal history. I'm not sure if his lack of sharing is arcane or frustrating or rude. He's just slippery and fucking opinionated.

Alex's outlook on life combines an existentially nihilistic approach to the world with a haughty distaste for humans in general. Such a black and white nature *should* make him easy to read. Alas, no, tears-brimming-the-bucket sadly, no. More often than not those colours bleed together like paint mixed in that same bucket. The gray is thick, spills out, takes flight, and becomes a disorienting fog. A loose backstory allows Alex to have a shape without form; to be a perfect line with an infinite number of corners. He's a problem for non-Euclidian geometry and the world's greatest psychological minds.

Alex has no idea what his background is. *He doesn't care.* I was raised in America, where heritage is an obsession. Most people know their family history to the $1/32^{nd}$. People will tell you they're Dutch-French-English-Cherokee-Danish-Indian-ad infinitum. You're white. Somewhere along the line your grandfather was cucked by a Latino. So, what? Why is it that you're boiled down to wherever your family descends from in America, but you're nothing but American everywhere else in the world? That is, unless your family had slaves or you have a cleft chin. Then, you're

American as fuck. Land of the free… to dissect race and act like it ain't a thing, when it's the biggest goddamn issue that's ever existed.

I feel for the light-skinned dark girls and dark-skinned light girls who know this first hand. Those angels with butterscotch, caramel, or toffee colouring. Hell, even women with tapioca flesh and cat eye makeup are approached with frail and insulting attempts to kickstart a weak conversation centered on their ancestry. Beauty is beauty, leave it at that. Finding out what mix of Anglo-Saxon, Vietnamese, Bajan, or Tutsi produced the off-white, *exotic* skin tone of a woman seems to burn inside men. White men. Neo-cracker men. Needless to say, there are better ways to go about determining how purple or pink a flower is. Besides, who cares? Pussy is pussy. Anyways, my inborn, American attachment to racial identity and affiliation combined with Alex's lack of knowledge and concern about his own lineage was shocking at first.

"What's your background?" I asked him, noticing that he was seamlessly slipping between English and French without a perceptible accent in either one. His French had no butchery of verbs or gendered pronouns while his English was smooth and lexically banqueted.

He just shook his head at me, almost let down. "What does it matter?"

"Well," I started, feeling no better than those men asking girls at the bars if they were mixed-race, "What's your mother tongue? You have no accent… I mean, I can't tell…"

"I don't know," he leaned back with levity. "I've spoken lots of languages for as long as I can remember: English, French, German, Arabic, Russian, Chinese… Some more, I think, if I'm pressed. Languages are easy when you move around a lot."

There were dots of blue and gold in the brown of his iris. His nose apexed with subtle pointedness. Beyond some European descent, anything could've been smuggled into his DNA.

I let it slide and asked about his family.

"I never met my mother. She'd died during birth, or after. Anytime but before. I never really found out."

"That's sad. I'm sorry," I said.

"Why?" he shook his head. "No, you're not. You're just saying that. She could've been a monster. I'm here, that's all that matters."

"Where were you born?"

"New Zealand. That is, if my aunt and uncle were telling the truth."

"You don't remember?"

"Newborns don't have the best memories, you know."

"True. What about your father?"

"I didn't meet him until I was in school. Before that, I was raised by my aunt and uncle. My first real memories, assuming *they* can be trusted, were in the States being brought up by my mother's sister."

This sister, his aunt, was married to a military man who was continuously shuffled around, traversing the continental United States and also being stationed in Japan and Germany.

"They said that I demonstrated a high-level aptitude early on. My report cards from military school said that I was brilliant and needed to be challenged. I never tried. I developed a lackadaisical attitude and stopped caring when I discovered that I didn't need to try. Ever, in anything. I could master what took others a year in an hour."

"Did you like school? Were you a nerd? I bet they hated you for being so smart."

"I *hated* school. For the short time I was in it, at least. It was *so boring*. The kids were *so dumb*. It's nothing but a shrine to the maintenance of averageness and mediocrity. I was under-stimulated but over-performing. I got in trouble for being *disruptive*. I think the teachers were scared that I was smarter than them."

"Did you drop out?"

"Not exactly. I was trying to enjoy it. I was discovering that I was charming, good-looking, nimble-tongued, and could make people do what I wanted. I seduced a teacher and had the football team almost fight to the death."

"Jesus, what happened?"

"Well, I guess my father wanted to claim what was his…"

At some point during middle school, his father had demanded him back. His father, from what he told me throughout our relationship, was a rather tall man with strong-looking, wide-set shoulders and an ink-black, pencil-thin mustache that hugged his rosewood lip. He was built like an inverted isosceles triangle and looked like a late 19th century boxer minus the taped fists and jockey pants. He was a classically handsome, even striking man with prominent facial features. *'Like his face was a fist,'* Alex had once said. He was serious and unsympathetic. The place holders gave up young Alex after quickly abandoning their initial protest.

"My aunt and uncle were fine. They had rules. They weren't warm, but not unkind. They were just there." He paused. "My father, however, was something entirely different."

Alex's father was a man who required constant movement. "He had businesses. Illegal or legal, who knows. Who cares?" Alex said. He, and Alex, had bounced between countries and continents. Alex recalled being stationary long enough to complete a single semester at one high school, though he was never enrolled. Whether or not his dad had been aware of his prodigiousness was uncertain. Primarily, Alex had read and taught himself what he felt he needed to know.

"I don't know what my father did. I never asked him, and he never told me." Alex's father would *partner* with African dictatorships, South American *juntas*, Eastern European *cabals*, and wealthy Americans who donned camouflage and carried assault rifles on their massive, off-the-grid estates. Alex was never told where they were headed or what was going on. "A lot of my father's *clients* were on the cover of whatever-country-we-were-in's newspapers."

Alex's father hadn't had any friends, so Alex hadn't either. "I don't think we ever engaged jovially or shared anything close to a tender moment. No conversations about girls, love, feelings, or manhood. Movies and sports didn't exist to us." Attempts to start conversations would deflate like hopeful red balloons. "My father used to strike me for speaking. At times, he'd go off about random shit, a stream-of-consciousness where he presented statements of opinion as fact. That's probably where I get it from. That was the closest thing we had to an act of bonding: my father's diatribes with me mumbling and nodding. He wasn't soliciting feedback."

"What did he talk about?"

"Death. Capitalism. Governments destroying each other. The world being a craven orphanarium. Normal fare. He was a mysterious, laconic man who spoke morosely about earth and its unfortunate inhabitants. He was both a fatalist and opportunist, recognizing the future's hopelessness and firmly contending that we'd already passed some chimeric boiling point. His actions didn't matter because there was no future."

I never knew if Alex was full of shit or not. If he was, he believed his own shit. One day, while regaling about the best cup of coffee he'd ever had, noting that the one we were currently enjoying at the cafe was like hot garbage water strained through a gypsy's scalp, he made glancing reference to travelling from Cuba to Miami on a homemade raft. Since our conversation had been centered on the excellence of Cuban espresso, the whole *floating on a raft to America* part had merely been an aside. When pressed to describe the experience, his response was a flat: "Oh, you know, it's not an ideal way to travel. I'm relieved that I haven't had to do *that* in a while. But, I'm telling you, the coffee's so fresh and strong... it gives you a full body erection. That's why they had to invent cigars..."

There was also the simple but universally evaded question of what Alex did for work. His ability to elude telling me for as long as he did was preternatural and made Mengele seem easy to catch. Generally, when someone fails to reveal a piece of information, especially one so basic as what they do for work, you end up having to imagine an answer. My guess certainly didn't involve a corporate structure or a time card and punch clock. Alex never seemed to have a scarcity of bank notes and his hours could be best described as translucent. He was busy and left it at that. He had security, money, and opportunities. He said that I was just as obsessed with work as I was with heritage and that I'd learnt nothing since moving to France.

8.

"What do you do for work, then? Since you're either obsessed with it, or let it define you and are dying to tell me." Alex asked, listlessly. He must've picked up on the fact that I was invested in exchanging introductory information, even against his own predilection. "What requires you to don that two-piece suit day in and out?"

"I work for a company that translates one language into another, in a giant nutshell. Few blocks over that way," I indicated by pointing eastward down the avenue. "We do all kinds of written, verbal, and most anything that needs translating into French, English... all the way to Arabic, and I think even Swahili."

"Sounds awful. Do you enjoy it?"

"It's alright... Probably one of the more interesting jobs I've had. I don't know what that says about my occupational history, though. I've always worked with people, restaurants and banks, and was getting pretty jaded with feeling like a servant. In a way, it's what I went to school for. I did a French major in university..."

"French major? Ouch." Alex guffawed. "Four years well spent?"

"...Yeah," I wheezed.

"Oh well, look at it this way. It got you a job in another country and the opportunity to leave the States. *The new American dream.* I know lots of people are trying to get in there, but it's not the 20th century anymore. The worms are going to eat that place from the intestines out." Alex thought for a second and resumed. "I don't know how you could have a job with *people*, especially dealing with their needs. Conviviality and empathy have never been my strongest suits."

It didn't seem like it.

He continued: "How can you eat shit, wipe it off, and keep a big spearmint smile etched on your face? How can you suck up your pride and take *orders*, not requests, but *orders* from, well, *any-fucking-one?* Don't misunderstand me, I can be amenable... even downright cheerful. But to have a yoke around your neck that forces you to be nice to morons and assholes would be my personal hell."

"It's not *that* bad." I was somehow defending that which had led me to have numerous spiritual breakdowns, knowing that it was just as bad as he was describing. It was a strange notion, defending something that I hated for no reason other than the fact that I'd done it, and Alex clearly hadn't.

"Have you ever worked in one of those industries?" I asked. "Or have you always been some kind of one-man-show?"

He tightened his squint at me, ever so slightly. "Working for and with people made me want to work for myself. I've done a lot. Shitty jobs with shitty humans, lots of things I'm glad never to do again." He stopped, not abruptly, but rather seemed to choose not to continue.

"So... what *do* you do?" I asked.

"My businesses."

"Which are?"

"Mostly supplying the demands of my clients."

"In what capacity?"

"Products and services."

"That's vague."

"So is my line of work. Or was. I'm stepping away bit by bit. Years of swimming with sharks tires you out."

"You sound like a drug dealer. Or a banker."

He let out a wry laugh. "Is there a difference? Show me what *isn't* a drug these days. I'm more of a financier, let's say. I deal with stocks and secure deals for my partners. I create needs, establish dependencies, and watch the ballet unfold."

"So…"

"Like I said, I'm stepping back. The feedback loops that I've concretized do the work for me."

"You're retiring? So young?"

"No, no. I just have a better ability sit back with a glass of merlot and watch. At this point, though I'm very much active, I don't *have to* do anything. My businesses make money *for* me. I need to oversee certain things, but can choose not to get my hands dirty, if I so please."

"Fine. I get that. But… what are these *businesses* and what kinds of services do they provide?"

"A little of this and a little of that. I keep a lot of wicks in just as many candles."

"You don't look like a candle maker to me."

"I don't make candles. Those guys are called *chandlers*, former heads of chandlery in wealthy medieval households."

"So, as far as actual jobs go…"

"Nowadays…" he started, ignoring me, "That is to say contemporarily, a *chandler's* just someone who sells candles, and chandlery itself is more of a blanket term for the sale of nautical items, especially those designed to be carried on boats and ships. Pretty strange, eh? The Yanks, you guys, started calling them ship chandleries for some reason or another, probably relating to the fact that they sold lanterns, various oils, lards, and resins, or possibly because they were the first people off the boat and *lit* the way for the rest of the crew. And chandeliers, well, I think you know what chandeliers are and how they must've gotten their name."

"Yeah, I'd imagine that they used to have candles in them," I responded dumbly.

"Exactly, and the person who used to light the candles was…" he paused for effect, "…a chandelier!" Alex smiled triumphantly.

This was an early taste of how our conversations would tend to go. Alex swore that he didn't have Asperger's syndrome, which I inquired about several times. When I broached, he rescinded like a pound dog. He'd tell me things insofar as *he* felt like it. As frustrating as it was to be sidestepped whenever I posed a question meant to engender a more detailed and meaningful understanding of the man, it was equally aggravating to have the technique that I'd always used employed so formidably against me. I was having my throat slit by someone who could wield a sword better than I.

9.

I'd grown quiet. Alex seemed comfortable with the silence. I was about to make another vapid comment about the weather when he spoke first.

"What's your goal?" He looked at me, piercingly, the sun at his back.

"My goal?" I asked. "What do you mean?" I understood what he meant, but needed more time to avoid debasing myself with an unready and disjointed response.

"Well, we can start off with your career goals, as you seem rather fixated on employment and career. Typical Yank. Do you want to sell fruit on the side of the highway in Central America or be the President of that same Banana Republic? Or, more than likely, something between the two?" he spoke slowly, possibly in jest. "What I really meant was… what would you like to get out of life?"

There was no sardonic grin nor mockery in his tone.

"Life as a constellation of experiences that trace our overhead view of the universe, filling it with images and characters, individual but connected. Life as a game, the game that we're forced to play with a halberd poking us in the back, licking at the kidneys, making us roll the next turn, though at times tempting us to lay back for the big sleep."

"That's a good way of…"

"*Are you* one of those people for whom life is a scrapbook, a catalogue of reverie, full of clipped out images of things you desire? An endless collage of man-made objects that you crave and exotic paradises that you want to travel to? All endpoints, without a notion of how to achieve them?

"Is your life like a volcano? Chaste and bubbling beneath the surface? Oxford-shirted, buttoned-up-to-the-lip of the crater, seething with magma that extends for miles under the soil, that may one day turn oceans to gasoline and blot out the sun?

"Is your life like that of a hummingbird, buzzing and mincing around without a care for what happens twelve seconds from now, thinking only about dipping your beak into the nectar hole of a soft-lipped petunia until you're swollen with the sugar-rich liquid? Then, looking for a she-bird to mount and fuck at ten to fifteen strokes per second? Then, finishing, dismounting, and drinking more nectar? *Fuck, finish, nectar! Fuck, finish, nectar! Fuck, finish, nectar…*"

"I get it, I get it." I said. He was getting louder with each repetition and could've very well kept on and on forever and a day. "I don't know if any one of those scenarios describes me." I eventually responded, not entirely convinced myself.

He grinned at me. "Volcano. No. Hummingbird."

"Well, I mean, it's not like the hummingbird just eats, fucks, and sleeps. The hummingbird pollinates flowers as it drinks from them, just like bumble bees. Plus, it probably takes a lot of coal to run those little engines nonstop."

"Perhaps," Alex responded, squeezing his eyes ever so slightly at me once more. "But, so do bats and any other insect, and those contribute more than those tiny birds do. Did you know that hummingbirds have the world's fastest metabolism rates and have to make their bodies slow down to hibernation level when food's scarce? They're takers. They'd drain the earth of its juicy core if their little suckers were long enough." He paused. "I think we might've gotten a little off topic here. Look, there's nothing wrong with being a hummingbird, but humans need more than just nectar.

You should want to own the nectar and the tree that it comes from. If you're a hummingbird, then go full hummingbird and suck all the lilies you can before you die a quick death from a heart attack. All that wing flapping is hell on the ticker."

He studied me with intent, and mused once again. "What do you want to do? Who do you want to be? What's your objective in life?"

"Well, I guess my dream is…"

I was dismissed before any momentum could be gained.

"I didn't say *dream*," Alex said, almost irritated. "I said what is it that you want *to do*? What's your *mission*? Your *goal*? What's the *objective* in your life that you'd go to *war* to attain? What is it that you're striving to do? Not a dream or a fantasy, but in the *real* reality of your living *life*?" He continued with his hands folded in the most diplomatic of postures. "Dreams and fantasies are for children who still believe in fairy tales; poor little girls who dream of platinum-coloured unicorns and marrying charming princes, not of living in wretched poverty along the Danube in plywood shanties and being forced to fuck their uncles because their worthless fathers owe them money for a bum donkey."

I stared back at him. My caterpillars tightened, mouth slightly agape.

He continued. "Objectives, goals, those are for adults. Look at me. I decide what I want and figure out how to get it. Do you see this?" he asked while smoothing out his black-shirted chest, pinching the fine-looking fabric between his fingers. "This is the uniform of success, or success as I define and wish to present it. Cashmere. I love this shit. Comfortable as a shell is to a tortoise, and it makes almost anyone look cut. Like a wolf." He then moved his hand towards his face and rubbed his velvety jawline. "This presentation is how I feel I'll best succeed. Simple, stream-lined, elegant, and I leave the option for opulence open."

"Well, what are *your* objectives?" I asked, chewing my lips.

"Mine is simple…" he began with a terse reply and a new cigarette, "…to stay the course." He paused to reflect, nodding to himself.

"Cheap answer," I said.

"Perhaps, but…" he was searching internally as he withdrew his eyes down and to the left. "I find…" Alex began with an exhale that concluded with the second word, "…self-improvement to be indulgent and masturbatory. Self-exploration or whatever you want to call it. *Finding yourself* or some other broad term that overfed, spiritual fuckers use. It's just a sleight of hand for being selfish and replacing the sun with your own image." He continued before I could ask him to clarify. "People are selfish by nature. We have to be. We wouldn't have survived this long otherwise, which really isn't very long in the grand scheme of things, or even when compared to most other creatures. What I hate, what I just fucking hate to the creamy, nougaty marrow in the centre of my bones, is the tone-deaf insincerity that comes with lamenting about the disparities between the successful and unsuccessful. I hate the words *luck* and *chance* being mis-construed with the reality of most people being too lazy or weak or stupid to comply with the natural inclination of our species: to kill or die. Don't you see? We're stalling evolution. There's a primordial propensity within all of us. We're descendants of the same roots as baboons and orangutans, even bears and tigers if you go back far enough. We put on this façade of fulfillment-seeking over the basic tenets of our survival... On bullshit ideas like uncovering *the better you* and realizing your *hidden potential,* or whatever the fuck those people say. Be honest with yourself! How deep will you dig before you realize that you're digging for fool's gold? How deep can this treasure be buried? If you're too weak to survive or too arrogant to see the truth, then don't bother. It's the hollow pursuits of bored, non-essen-tial humans that are the cancer of society. They're the *spiritually homeless* tramps that hop from one fad to another. If you want to find your true self, you won't succeed through Buddha, meditation, or trying to patch a leak with some fabricated identity. You'll succeed by living in the real world and facing real questions with honesty. No one ever has the balls to answer for their own shortcomings. *'Why am I empty and unfulfilled?'* Simple. I'll save you time: Because *you aren't special.* No amount of religion or self-help books will ever tell you the truth. You aren't special, and worse, you can't will yourself from that pitiful normalcy."

"So," I began, "You don't believe in somebody investing in themselves? Going to school, taking classes, exercising, whatever the activity or practice may be? You can't rise from normal?"

"I wouldn't say that," he replied, once again ruminating on the ques-tion. "I mean...They don't just let you walk into an operating room and pick up a scalpel. Who'd want to watch regular, untrained people play sports, act in movies, or cook my pastoral *lamb pavé* with anise, lemon-sautéed fiddleheads, asparagus with saffron, and butter-mashed endives and fingerlings? I'm not a masochist."

"Then, I'm not sure what you mean," I said.

"Were all headed the same direction. Death. *The great equalizer,* as my father used to call it. Rich or poor, quick and painless or long and torturous, we're all promised the same conclusion. Life, though it seems excruciating sometimes, is a short spell. Call me a softy if you must, but I hate to see wasted, misallocated, or unused potential. I hate the complaining that follows and I hate to see people spend their short time on the earth spinning their tires with no purpose or design. Most are hopeless, designed to enjoy the charade. Some won't deign, and a few have the ability to know themselves and unearth a purpose. I actually admire those who haven't let their averageness hinder their existence."

"How do you find purpose, then? How did you determine what it is that you wanted to be and do? Did it just descend from the heavens and fall into your lap?" I tried to mimic his vacancy of emotion on the subject. It was hard. Clearly a skill. "Or... Do you just connect the pieces like some giant puzzle?"

"You're talking destiny? Now that's just as crazy," he chuckled. "I don't go searching for *purpose.* I might go insane if I tried to link everything I did to a grandiose chain of meaning and worth. The only destiny, the only thing that's for certain and exists as a constant, is that *I will die.* I've been keenly aware of this my whole life, the knowledge that life isn't meant to be forever and that there's no God to tuck me in at night. If you try something and it doesn't work, there's a strong chance that it was never going to work in the first place. It has nothing to do with kismet or predestination. Only you. Sure, you can keep trying. You can place it at the fore of your existence. If it fails, there's nothing lost and experience gained. You'll know what you were trying to accomplish wasn't meant for you and move on. If you keep failing and keep trying, you'll devolve to a madman, knowing the certainty of an outcome but trying in vain to corrupt the result. The idea that *anyone* can do *anything* is the credo of the disillusioned, played on a loop by the people who make profit."

"Are you a Marxist?"

"I'm not an anything, but if the most demented person is allowed to speak at length for a decade or more, than every few years he'll have what seems like a moment of clarity."

"Then, what makes you different?"

"I'm smart. I also have a terrible habit of always winning. I'm also well aware of the talents and skills that I possess, that the average human doesn't. I also know my limits, what I can do and what I probably shouldn't do."

"So for us average losers the objective is to not even try?"

"See?" he said. I didn't see. I didn't know what I was looking at. "That's the most fundamental aspect of life!" he exclaimed, verging on jubilant. "Having the *ability* to wake up in the morning to try and fail. Or succeed. The crux is in the choice. You don't have to be sarcastic about trying. If everyone stayed in bed, nurses would be billionaires. The smartest people, or maybe just the wisest, know when to try, to tap into their precious energy stores, and when to hang their hats. Without choice, we wouldn't have republicanism or toilet paper. If someone hadn't tried one day, there'd be no air conditioning, transatlantic trade, or the hangman's knot. There'd be no suicide bombers, saints, or runaway teens."

"You're an advocate for freedom of choice, then?"

"Of course! It's that which I hold most dear! I loathe the idea of law. *Sometimes* it helps in keeping people safe and providing a template for order and organization. The truest forms of law are those found in the wild, kill or die, nuanced to befit the human species, of course. We're not beasts. My conception of law and how to act in society exists as a social contract that we all sign without even knowing it. It's far from a new idea." Alex inhaled with an air of extreme self-satisfaction. "Most laws are like overbearing school headmasters, taxing the joy and existence of students because they had unfortunate childhoods. Laws related to what people choose to do with their bodies: selling them, filling them with poisons or mind-altering substances, doing harm to themselves in any way... simply shouldn't exist. Laws shouldn't forbid, especially what one does with their own body. They should instruct and guide people. Inform them, not handcuff them. If someone wants to commit suicide, they should be able to. More power to striking one more useless soul from the planet. Whether you want to be an

Olympian or a smackhead, you should have the same rights to do what you feel is necessary for your own well-being. Is it an equally grave offence to steal as it is to listen to music too loudly on the metro? To me, yes. Knives out for each offender, as each has violated the contract."

"That's not the same at all."

"Not the outcome. A runner's high and a cocaine high are polar opposites of each other, but each one makes the person feel good. It's like the Thai says: '*Same, same, but different.*'

"But, it's not the same. One's good and one's bad."

"Says who? Why is one good and why is one bad? Because someone said so? Ten people? Ten million? I stand by the *right*, and I mean the *right* for human beings, endowed with the supreme machinery of logic and reason, to decide whether or not they want to wipe themselves off the earth prematurely. They also have the right to do what they want with their body-temples more generally. They should be well-informed about things like the dangers of, let's say heroin in this case. What are the risks of exposure for the average consumer: overdosing, addiction, and transmitting diseases? Let them eat heroin. They can tax the hell out of it. Big money for playgrounds and public cemeteries."

"Heroin. Smack." I said, unsold. "You think that the average person has the ability to limit themselves with the most addictive substance in the world? Do you actually think that the average person is smart enough to use their common sense and not wind up a junkie or dead?"

"No, no. I don't. Call it a progressive selectivity. There are some individuals, very few of them, who are the sutures and stitches that keep the world we're accustomed to from breaking apart, bandaging with their red tape. Some won't be tempted. But, the majority of people offer as little as possible and take as much as their arms can carry: the lazy and unappreciative, the confused hordes of the directionless and talentless. For every spoiled Westerner wallowing in self-pity there's some wunderkind in Mumbai sifting through an ocean of garbage for a piece of tin to fix his shack with. What does that mean? Nothing. There are *way* too many people that are fighting for, or wasting, resources. Cities and towns are overrun with idiots who have stomachs without brains. Instead of trying to survive for as long as possible, we simply don't die for as long as we can. Scientists and doctors spend so much time healing the sick and the lame, who are sick and lame through their own machinations. As a result, we're moving at a fraction of the speed that we potentially could. It's like walking through a busy street. You're buoyed by the idiots that sway about slackly. Let's say we blink out just a few of them, half of half of half even. Imagine how much easier walking to the *tabac* at rush hour would be.

"Isn't that a little ruthless?" I asked. "Did you get that from your father?"

"With intelligence comes ruthlessness, among many other things, but *that* ruthlessness is the ancestor, and offspring, of directional certainty. He taught me that you *have* to be ruthless to understand that forward movement requires a brutal push. I want to live in a world where drugs aren't illegal and a hooker can be the next Warren Buffett. Where non-contributors perish from their own sloth. Where suicide is no longer stigmatized as being the bastion of the weak-hearted or cowardly, and is instead proffered as a reasonable and even charitable solution. A noble and civil act with a dedicated seat in a stadium or a notch on the plaque of a cenotaph... the hall of the brave... or something like that. With all that in mind, the least we owe to all those people are their natural rights: the right to water, clean air, *and* not to be limited with the choices they make pertaining to the edification or destruction of their own bodies."

To Alex, if the *Godheads of State* were shrewder, they'd levy a seismic taxation on prostitution, drugs, weaponry, and whatever else they could afford to decriminalize without fear of Fenian-style raids overthrowing the regime. He yearned to eradicate the lowest stratum of people from existence, which to Alex, was a big win for all those concerned with creating and achieving *the good life*. It's not that he cared if people were able to express themselves openly. In fact, the millennial point of view that each person was a snowflake, able to select their own gender, race, and how they identified their entire structure of being and self was ludicrous to Alex, but entirely acceptable. It fell under the same Personal Freedom to fuck, snort, shoot, punch, bite, run, kick, spit, bludgeon, sleep, and die, which was a two-way street. Because Alex believed that he was free to roam the yard without a leash, everyone else was given the same opportunity equally unburdened. A real Voltairian. A Renaissance man.

"Forget Marxism. You sound like a Libertarian."

"I don't care for labels," he said with indignation. "It's hard for me to rationalize fully agreeing with *any* ideology. My beliefs are my own and if they coincide with any school of thought, then that's a coincidence. I don't know if it's possible to have an original thought anymore, at least not an original thought that hasn't already been written down by someone else. I've read a lot of books, heard a lot of stories, and seen a lot of things in my life. Much like myself, I have no idea where my thoughts really come from, nor do I care."

"That's fair," I said. "Maybe it's university, or the way people use and value knowledge, but it always seems to have to come from *somewhere*. Be built on the foundation of someone else's opinion."

"You're living in a box, brother. It's a fine box, and you've decorated the walls with posters and motivational pictures. The ones that say *DETERMI-NATION* and show a cheetah chasing down a hare, with a quote on why you shouldn't give up on your ambitions."

"Yeah, I know the pictures. Pretty sure they've been present at almost every job I've had the pleasure of working at."

"And that's *your* choice. It may not seem like it, but your life rests entirely on your shoulders. *You* are what *you* see yourself as. It all comes down to what you want, if you have the means to get it and the ability to act at that crucial moment. *The trigger pull.* It's a wonderful thing. Wonderful or terrifying, depending who you are. I for one am enamoured with the fact that, if I or anyone else wakes up one morning with a crazy idea, it's not impossible to act on that crazy idea. You may get arrested, but that may be a pittance."

"I don't think everyone has the same capacity, though," I said. "I've been trying to get into something worthwhile and haven't been able to for years."

"Like what?" he responded.

"Like, jobs," I replied quickly.

"What kinds of jobs?"

"Lots of different kinds."

"You have no idea what you want," he boldly and correctly accused. "Have you ever really asked yourself?"

"The last time I did, I figured that I wanted to be in France."

"And what'd you do?"

"Moved here."

"Exactly, you did what you wanted. Do you question yourself much?"

"Question myself?" I repeated aloud as I questioned myself. "I guess so. I do spend a lot of time in my own head. I don't know many people here and have to focus on something. I tend to look back on what I might've done. I…"

"You just stay captive in your own head and make negative comments about the patterns on the wall paper. My guess is that you just piss and moan about how the landlord is a worthless crony and that the neighbourhood is run down. Do you ever try and figure out what you *really want*? If it's just about experiences and having fun, you don't seem to be doing it right. If it's about career and making money, you don't seem to be doing it right either."

"Well, I'm not… That is to say, I'm not like you…" I mumbled defensively.

"Stop it. Don't complain. Don't compare yourself to me, and don't whine. You don't even know me, and the more you do, the more you'll realize that comparing yourself to me is pointless. Don't compare yourself to anyone, for that matter. Look at the *success* of others as a model to, at most, emulate. I fucking hate complaining. I hate complaints and I hate fucking excuses. You make your own choices and you must realise that you're responsible for your own failures. You. Not me, not your boss, not your parents, not your partner, not the world, not the rich people or the poor people, not the celebrities, not the societal trends, not commercialism, not your face, not your clothes, you. Fucking you."

"I think I need to go back to school. Get a Master's or something. I need…"

"We're given all that we need from birth. If there's something to nurture, a gift or a strength, something exceptional, you have to use it. In most cases, who stops us besides ourselves? How many times have you defeated yourself before starting? Conversely, how often have you wasted your time and sanity on things that were never going to work? The connector is *you*. Front and centre."

He looked around the street. "Look at that big girl over there. She's weighs maybe... 220 pounds? At *least* 200 pounds. Look at her feet: red-bottomed, Christian Louboutin heels. Those pumps probably go for about 1000 euros per dog. Look at the way her plump sausage foot is wedged into that gorgeous shoe. Her calves are so chubby that they make her feet look like hooves. That can't be comfortable. The clerk at the store probably scoffed and snickered at our girl over there, but do you think she cared? She probably made the cheeky little rake of a woman squeeze her fat, little foot into that torture device. All things considered, she's extremely well dressed for a fat woman. That shirt and jacket probably had to be custom made, but they look stylish. That bun on her head says that she's thinking about business and sex, simultaneously." The woman noticed that we were checking her out and tossed a little smile our way. "See?" he said, winking at her. "Look at that confidence! Do you think anyone was ever kicking down that donkey's door? No, not for her looks. But for her confidence? Maybe."

She swaggered past us, wiggling her four-plus handfuls of ass cheeks.

"Did a wealthy, saggy-skinned Greek buy those heels for her? No. Does she have more confidence than a girl half her size? Yes. Would I fuck her? No." Alex paused. "Well, it might be fun. Who knows?" He thought to himself. "That lady isn't taking her weight lying down. She's probably tried to lose it at some point or another, and failed. Maybe she's a gourmand! I respect the hell out of her *fuck it* attitude, one thousand times more than a boozed-up wannabe-model that sucks off geezers in Mykonos for spending money."

"You're probably right," I admitted. "I get stuck inside my own head. I guess I'm not easy on myself and have probably spent a lot of energy getting nowhere. I don't even know if the choices I've made could be called good or bad. I just haven't had to make that many real, impactful decisions in my life. Not that I haven't wanted to, but I don't think that I've been at the crossroads of that many life-changing forks in the road."

"That's bullshit. Each day you're at the foot of an almost infinite number of crossroads with every decision you're forced to make. You can rely on your instincts and take the easiest path like a reflex, or try one of the other infinitesimal other directions. Fail, succeed, it doesn't matter as long as *you* choose..."

"I don't really question my reflexes."

"And when you did, where did it get you?"

"Here. But, even a broken clock is right twice a day, if you want to look at it that way. I'd rather be given more black and white, life or death type choices."

"Well, let's test those reflexes out. What do you want? Knee-jerk response. What do you want at this moment? Right now."

"Sex!" I almost shouted at him. I'd submitted to the most primary reduction of his original question. His philosophizing and demagoguery had been holding the conch for a long time. I didn't know whether he was prone to pontification or was using the lengthiness of his sermons to break down my character like a cult leader uses low-calorie mush and brainwashing propaganda.

"Oh… that's it?" he retorted, as if I was a merchant who'd just quoted him a laughably low price for a coveted item. His cheekbones raised with a slight wince.

"It's been a while… I haven't met anyone yet, whether at work or anywhere else. It's been lonely and I'm bottled up and bored with myself. There's much that I want, but sex seems by far the most important right now," I tried to defend my position and clearly underwhelming response.

"You need to take care of your basic needs: food, sleep, roof over your head, and I guess emotional satisfaction before you can move on to the bigger picture stuff," Alex rationalized for me in Maslowian terms.

"I wouldn't call it emotional," I snickered. "I just really need to get laid."

"So, your weakness finally appears. I was half right. My little Humming-cano."

"It's not a weakness…"

"Don't be embarrassed. Everybody needs to unload the clip now and then. Sex can be good for the mind and soul. Too much can make your brain turn to soup, though. When people lust, it makes them do all kinds of crazy shit. Not getting any sex, however, will make everything taste rotten and the world look ugly."

"Oh, exactly. I haven't been with a woman since I was back in the States, and I know she's probably getting poled…" I added, self-deprecatingly.

"Maybe as we speak. Right now. Getting hammered in the ass and loving it," he added with a little too much enjoyment.

"Fuck you," I roared.

"Look brother, no disrespect," Alex said softly. "You're here, and who-ever it is that you're thinking about, she's there. Forget her. She's dead to you now, or might as well be. I don't know who she is and I don't care about the story between you and her. The past is for the maggots. You're here at the moment, in Paris, at a cafe, with me! If that girl mattered to you, if you really thought she was that special, you'd be there, maybe at a cafe with her."

Solid logic.

"Also," he started anew. "If women are your thing, I know the perfect place to meet some classy, sexy women. *Parisienne* women are the best, my friend. Why do you think I stay here when there's a whole world of women out there? Whatever you want, it's here. Any fetish or type that you have, she's here. You can have a supermodel or a street mouse. Long legs and short hair or a curly mop-top with thighs made of thunder. Breasts shaped and sized like any fruit at the produce stand. It's all here."

"No girlfriend I take it?"

"Nope. No girlfriend, no boyfriend, no pets or car or loans or lines of credit." he said. "I bet you haven't even had yourself a night since you've been here. I'd go mad if my spirit was being slugged around in your carapace!"

Alex loves Paris. He said it was the most enjoyable city to be in at any time of the year. He said that it was *'the right kind of dirty'* with people that were quick to judge but quick to forget. In other words, French. He said you could get in the kind of trouble that you could only find in third world countries, but get stitched up and not worry about sepsis. I responded that I hadn't really explored that side of Paris. He told me that I hadn't seen anything until I'd seen *his* Paris and that it would either put me on a jet back to the *New World* or give me the kind of cravings that made cigarettes seem like licorice whips.

"I suppose I can do that," I concluded, as he snatched the cheque out of the server's hand.

"Perfect," he said slyly. "I'll take your number and we'll get you some *chatte, mon ami.*"

I scribbled my number on the back of the cheque and offered to give him some money for the bill. He dismissed my notes.

It would end up being a while before I saw Alex next, as I had no way of contacting him. At the very least, that was consistent with his mysterious nature.

I returned home and tried to make sense of the individual I'd just met, who in reality, was the first person with whom I'd had more than mere superficial exchanges with in Paris. He was fucked, an incessant and opinionated individual, though a handsome and somehow charming man. Above all, he was interesting and was saying a lot of things I'd been thinking.

Had I only hung out with him because he was handsome? Because he'd noticed me and had taken an interest? Were the two things intertwined? A small part of me wanted to be seen with him and swim in his wake.

Part of me wondered if he talked to everyone like that. He wasn't combative, but incisive. I couldn't tell if he was trying to be helpful or a dick. My balls outweighed my concerns. *A small tear in a massive bucket, but a tear nonetheless.*

10.

The week finished anti-climactically. I hadn't received any work-detail of exceptional importance, nor had I been summoned by Alex to try my luck at a drink or meeting some nice *classy* ladies. I wouldn't have normally held out any expectation for his call, but the fellow seemed to have some kind of interest in me. I suppose the interest could've mostly been that I hadn't cut him off or told him to take his crackpot theories about society and ethics to La Seine.

The promise of a new project soon rattled the hallways, and it was a behemoth. Our company had secured the rights to translate a massive Hollywood blockbuster, one of those films that had been worked over by the hype machine since its creative inception over dry-as-dust martinis and daintily chopped lines of blow at a hotel bar in Los Angeles at 2am.

Of course, the movie wasn't an original concept. It was based on a literary trope that had previously been adapted into a successful franchise and was much beloved as an influential hallmark of some prior generation's cultural identity. The idea was to aggrandize a drooping bottom line with a few capsules of nostalgic Viagra right in time for movie season. The dialogue would be sacrificed to bolster the lushly digitized special effects and innovative, tour-de-force green-screen vistas in post-production. It was about merchandising; toys and posters and collectible cups and beach towels and t-shirts and Halloween costumes and video games and dildos and pocket pussies and sex tape leaks featuring the star actors.

The story was a tawdry hero epic, ripped and vivisected and spat out over and over again. It was the kind of tale that proved that we as a species are more comfortable with the old than the new. Of course, the tastemakers are more than happy to prolong a steady stream of gruel-like drivel to keep us bathed in our cozy, sterile uterine pods of unchallenged obedience. Aside from making a character flamboyant, but not gay, or changing one to a woman and another to a minority, it ossified the reality that our czars of agency, culture, and entertainment are pussies. They fear blowback, like that they'd receive for making darling male crackers black or female, which would be too great a challenge for the passivity of the wider audience. They play it safe, having invested enormously and expecting a return. They ignore new ideas and rely on reviving corpses, hoping they shock enough pulse into the diminishingly vivified carcass to slop its way to the bank one more time.

To maximize exposure and recoup money spent, the film was to be translated. Not only the film, but all of its promotional material, which was to be made available in every language conceivable as part of a worldwide, guerilla campaign to shove the film down the throat of mother earth herself.

The production was bedevilled by controversy from the get go. A sexual harassment accusation was mounted against the director. Social justice organizations waved red flags over racism and a lack of minorities in the cast. Complementing the ethics debate and backstage grab-assing were the devastating leaks of footage and scandalous infighting between actors-actors, director-actors, producers-director, writers-producer, writers-actor... and *everybody-every-fucking-body-else*.

Needless to say, the translation process was to be expedited.

Our company was chosen, which should be obvious by now. It was an *all-hands-on-deck* situation, with the kind of mayhem that enlivens the senses and makes days fly by like falcons. Peregrine translators arrived in spades. Our office turned into the bullpens of New York's precincts after the 1977 blackout overnight. The film had to be released in time for the holidays, with the trailer for the second installment to be unveiled during the previews.

Mr. Stewart bounced restlessly between departments: peering into cubicles, nodding, clapping his hands, and saying *'Let's go!'* like Bobby Knight. All workspaces had to be shared with *at least* two chairs to one cubicle. Most people brought in laptops, so there usually weren't any issues over computers. However, personal calls, noisy chatter, pen clicking, and other annoying behaviours ignited hostility between co-workers with ease. It was the result of long days and close quarters. The normal, day-to-day workers like myself were creatures of habit; we'd come to expect a work experience built on a bedrock of consistency.

The influx of people meant that these expectations either had to be reset, or thrown completely asunder, depending on who your new workmate was. It was more like high school than work. It was also very entertaining to watch Spaniards and Italians interact with Brits and Germans. These rivalries always dissolved into either football or one of the World Wars. Soon the Mediterranean employees gathered in the clamorous west side of the office and left the Goths and Saxons to occupy its studious eastern corner.

I regarded the project with seriousness and allowed it to consume my days, including some early mornings and late nights, working harder than I ever had at school or any other job. I neglected to trim down my facial hair. After the shadow had thickened, I decided to let it become a fully ripened beard. It gave me an air of gravity; I only had to glance in the direction of someone making noise in my space and they'd vanish. Unfortunately, at times I'd simply wanted to engage in conversation with those people, becoming quite burdened with staring at words all day and my eyelids all night. There seemed to be some interesting people that'd been brought in, and I wouldn't have minded learning about Surinamese culture or the Arkhangelsk Oblast.

Many of the indentured staff were quick to ring bells when the newest additions were found in *their* seats. I never had that problem. I was *always* early to a fault, probably because I'd been late for my first day of grade school and had to be introduced to the class by the teacher at the front because my dad had left the car on E and my mom had had to siphon some gas from the house we'd stalled out in front of. You know, formative years.

There was a palpable excitement and metropolitanism that filled the office, for me at least. It was something like a world fair or multinational bazaar. The lunch room was in constant pandemonium with different languages and smells vying for position against one another, though the multi-coloured curries heated in the microwave always seemed to reign supreme. It was a United Nations summit for the working class; an expo with a singular purpose where everyone worked together towards an ultimately useless cause and were fittingly overpaid due to the nature of the project and the deep pockets of its shareholders. The tumult broke up the tedium that accrues when every day is the same and threatens to suffocate you with its monotony. I tried to enjoy the moment, to live in the percolating now, but found myself left without enough daylight to cut the outline of a whole shadow.

Mr. Stewart had given me the job of overseeing that the translation of the French screenplay was true to the original, an admitted massacre of the English language. I wasn't certain if he wanted me to drag French language version through the slaughterhouse as well. It was so poorly written that the French *might* last ten minutes in the cinema due to their intrinsic distaste for anything of inferior quality.

More obscure languages, on the other hand, received less attention and could be completed at the leisure of the employee, because who really knows how long it takes to translate a sci-fi movie script into Tahitian or Burmese? And who can say it's wrong? Mr. Stewart was administering his most potent style of micromanagement over the languages he was most familiar with, French and Spanish being his specialties and therefore the acmes of his concern. He pinned me near the coffee machine one day and told me that he wanted to provide one, or many, voices for the dubbed versions, thereby adding one of the biggest films of the decade to his resume. The residuals, the trickledown of future work, the chance to be flash-bulbed on the red carpet... the little man had worked himself up only to be let down. His style of over-management that balanced *his* hopes with *my* sense of duty like water buckets on my shoulders annoyed me. *Do it for the Gipper.*

I worried that I was missing the improving weather. The rain and clouds were slowly giving way to the sun and its comforting warmth, bit by bit, promising the shortening of skirts and the disavowing of bras beneath sheer cotton blouses. When possible, I took lunch or coffee and cigarette breaks at a cafe to fantasize about approaching the dark and soft-featured French women that maneuvered the streets like a breeze. I oftentimes ended up at the same cafe that I'd met Alex at, hoping that I might spot or be spotted by him. It was possible that he lived nearby, if not above in the brick-nestled windows that sat above the cafe's awnings. It was approaching the beginning of summer and I still hadn't crossed his path or received his *appel.* Anyways, I was determined to meet some new people and new women after this project was completed.

11.

It was late June when the translation of the film finally wound up. The office was exhausted and, though there were rumours of a wrap-party, no such fiesta was ever delivered once Mr. Stewart heard that he wouldn't be providing the voice for any of the film's characters. The office became a ghost town. Projects had stacked up that didn't carry any high profile cinematic value. Deadlines were adversarial. Many of the European-born employees took the opportunity to head south, east, west, or even north for their *first* vacations of the summer. Like democracy and lunch wine, the summer vacation is considered a *right* for the French, Spanish, and many other Europeans.

The office was desolate. I was left with some of the other die-hard translators to sweep the aisles of the asylum. The diminished energy was even more pronounced with most of the younger employees absent. Some floors went days without needing the lights on. Regardless of the pettish manager or the irresponsible staff, work needed to be completed, however unimportant. Stewart had taken off to Nice; in theory, one could've stapled the sign-out sheet to the front door, padlocked the entryway, and supped free for two weeks. It was hard to remain motivated without the buzzing of the printers and people. There were only the sounds of the street below: of the beauteous days, the smoking of cigarettes, and the drinking of bottle after bottle of inexpensive but delicious red wine... all being lapped up by carefree locals and tourists alike. It was torture.

I'd slowly fallen back into a shallow pit of spirit-addling self-enclosure, worsened now because the weather wasn't mirroring my temperament. It added a sense of squashed hopefulness, watching carefree women and confident men, seemingly younger in disposition than I ever remembered being, enjoying their lives in leisure, too resplendent to approach. I was an outsider, living in the prison of my own gloomy headspace, once a-fuck-ing-gain. *Why did this keep happening?* The circular pattern of talking myself up to try and accomplish the menial task of approaching another person for a conversation, only to fail, was draining my enthusiasm for life. I castigated myself with pity masturbation and chain smoking to fill the void when I wasn't working or keeping my brain and body busy. Even when I managed to do an activity that took my mind off the loneliness, my first idle thought brought me right back to self-loathing. What I couldn't figure out was *why*. Why couldn't I shake this sense of defeat and inescapable self-pity that I had no justifiable reason to feel? I was doing well at work. I was healthy and in the place I wanted to be. *The fuck was wrong with me?* I relied on the notion that it was only a matter of time before I was given some *temps-libre* to exorcize whatever devils had taken residence in my attic. Maybe a backpacking trip. Something to force me out there. I was growing aware that I *may* have been withdrawn and turning weird due to isolation, with aberrant behaviour that simply wasn't consistent with the person I'd always known myself to be. I couldn't have always been this way, this bad.

It wasn't until the office was starting to function normally again that it all made sense. The human resources woman, Olivia, was handing out paycheques one Friday afternoon. I had a crush on her. It was one of those far-fetched, impossible-to-act-on crushes. She was of Amazonian height and stature, and had amber skin with shiny black hair. She had a round face like a smiling Buddha statue with ultra-dark pharaoh eyes. She might've been part Asian, possibly Ural. It was hard to tell. She wasn't skinny, though not quite American-style thick (re: thicc [*sic*]). She was medium-set with strong, full legs and brawny shoulders and arms with noticeably small breasts. She looked like she used to play some ball, volley or basket, in school. She usually wore a low-cut, button-up blouse without a bra, always teasing the appearance of a cinnamon-coloured nipple but never quite parting the clouds for a clear view of her modest summits. Her hair was pulled back into a ponytail that led three-quarters of the way down her spine like a horse's tail, and she sported a big, thin-lipped smile. She had perfect white teeth and a perfectly triangular-shaped nose with semi-prominent nostrils, the left one orbited by a golden hoop.

"Congratulations!" she appeared with an electric air. "You officially work way too much," she said with a fuzzy giggle and shoulder touch that made my neck and jaw feel tight.

"It's not a big deal," the words struggled out of my cinched throat. I cleared it and smiled. She smiled back and offered some affectionate sympathies, saying that she understood how tired I must be and that my work was also greatly appreciated. I rubbed the back of my head and snickered humbly, the universal body language for an awkward, shy male. She then passed me my paycheck and gave me a hug.

I'll never be able to say for certain, but when Olivia embraced me I felt as though my spirit had been struck like a gong, vibrating with a complex and overwhelming onslaught of emotion. I'm sure she meant it to be a quick clutch, but I clasped her back with considerable force. I inhaled the light smell of her burnt caramel and teakwood perfume and the crisp freshness of her hair. My hands spread over her softer than expected shoulders and firmer than expected lower back. I squeezed. Her small chest pressed against mine. There was a stinging sensation in my jaw. My teeth reverberated against my tongue. Hot water rushed from my sinuses and filled my mouth. My neck stiffened and lost all power, unable to stop from slowly descending to the spot where Olivia's shoulder and chest met, like a child finding its lost mother. My eyes closed and filled with wet tears, threatening to fall from the corners down my cheeks.

I wanted to put all my weight into her arms, bury my head in her chest, and sleep until the next cheque day. I wanted her to take me off my tired legs, carry me to a cloud kingdom, sing me lullabies, and lay me in a basin (*bay-sin*) of clouds.

It was the first human contact I'd experienced since shaking hands with Alex, and the first feeling of affection I'd felt since I'd cradled Jackie the night before I left. I felt like I was going to burst into tears and blubber, right then and there, in front of all my *just-back-from-vacation* co-workers and the humbly adorned, black-flat-wearing-to-downplay-her-height Olivia. It was a hidden public spectacle of rich and intense emotion that I'd had no idea was living inside me and Olivia was hopefully unaware of.

She was easing off, preparing to disengage. *Not yet.* I hauled her in for one more cobra-clutch-hug, hoping it'd give me precious seconds to sniffle up any fugitive snot and tears trying to escape.

I thanked her for the kind words, which I imparted through a knotted and colourless mouth. I felt pale, as though all my blood was hiding behind my eyes and beneath my tonsils. And my dick, the rude boy, was pressing against my zipper. Olivia tilted her head and placed her hand on my shoulder, responding to my gratitude with gratitude. I hoped that I hadn't creeped her out. She proceeded to the next cubicle with her next bubbly introductory sentence that included something personal about the employee she was now engaging with. I remained standing, folded the paycheck in half, placed it in my wallet, and then proceeded to the bathroom on autopilot.

12.

I ran the water, curved my hand to feed my throat, dry and swollen, then splashed the rest of my pallid, vacant expression. I cupped two hands to catch more, I raised mitt-fulls of tap water to my face, erupting into a storm of sobs. I sprayed water at the judgemental mirror in front of me. I bowed my head and lowered it over the sink. This intense deluge of unprecedented emotion lost its vitality and tapered within moments; first to a whimper, then to a confused look that reflected my bewilderment back at me. I winced at myself with embarrassment, puzzlement, and fatigue. A ruddiness blossomed across my face, a deep blush settling longer on my cheeks. I was ashamed, like a man too meek to sing in the shower. I blinked my wet lashes and jammed my palms into my eyes. It transitioned into a deep, full-faced massage. My beard was wet and my cheeks were hot. I drew a fainthearted sigh, rested my hands on the sink, the archetypal pose for a living gargoyle such as myself, and contemplated what was going on in my head. I did feel better, though. Red eyes. Release. Almost orgasmic.

What happened was something that I couldn't, and still can't, define. It was as though all the hopelessness in the world, a phantasmagoria of all the negative spirits that circled my head, swarming me like evil planets, packed themselves into an orb as compact as the core of a diamond and detonated. Considering the immensity of the blast and the chemicals in the warhead, I'd say that I'd handled it well. Moments after another handful of water splashed against my face, I laughed. Hysterically. It all seemed funny. If that was the worst it could get, crying like a bitch in the washroom at work, then it was over and there was only onwards and upwards to go. It's now apparent to me that these could've been the thoughts of a renovated-optimism prisoner, finally deprived of his last strand of sanity, rambling towards lunacy.

I pressed paper towels against my face, patted my beard, and thought about Harlow's infant monkey studies of social deprivation. As different as I was from a *rhesus macaque,* I was human proof that a lack of contact-comfort can be psychologically undoing, manifesting reactions that defy logic.

I emerged from the bathroom and noticed that water was splashed on my shirt and crotch. It was due to the combination of an enthusiastic faucet and a shallow sink, which could very likely be interpreted as a lack of gentlemanly refinement that a man may unsuspectingly contrive at the urinal after a thoughtless piss and sloppy shake. For this reason alone, cotton-twilled khaki pants are the bane of man, principally the hydrated man. My pants were a light charcoal, so it was bad. I'd only become aware of my gracelessness on the way back to my desk, which was a fair distance away, with people to pass, sitting at hip level, no doubt invested in the state of my crotch and soon to scream *j'accuse* over tap water mistakenly identified as unhygienic slovenliness. I had no files or folders to shield myself with and no conveniently-placed plants to cover me the way older British films would imply nudity with clever and conspicuous cover-ups. I couldn't even manipulate the fabric of my pants with a hand in my pocket for fear of being labeled as a pervert.

I was, against all odds, doing it.

I'd moved soundlessly and ninja-like through the office, unseen with well-timed sidesteps and unobtrusive hand placement that adequately concealed my shame. I was close when the pretty Indian girl with the promontory nose, Priya, approached me with a fervent look in her eyes.

"Who's that guy that was just here?" she asked me hotly.

"What guy? I've been... filing." I was unsure of how long I'd been in the bathroom for.

Her eyes were burning holes through mine. "That beautiful, *beautiful* man. He asked reception where your desk was, and then left a note on your keyboard."

I'd mistaken her lust for anger. I had a feeling who it was.

"Well, why don't you let me check the note, darling?" I said calmly, keeping my slowly drying crotch aimed towards the partition of my cubicle. I unfolded the note with Priya's nose and inquiring eyes hanging over the cubicle wall.

The note read as such.

I lost your telephone number. Well, I didn't lose it. You wrote the number with a poor hand and the spring mists further ruined the ink and left the number unreadable. Please don't take this for rudeness. I meant to give you a ring to show you around town. I remembered that you said you worked in the area and it was easy to figure out the building based on your job description. I hope you don't mind me popping in. I'm surprised that you haven't returned yet. You're irresponsible, and I don't know if I'd hire you personally. I've been frequenting Wing Café near your arrondissement if you wish to meet me for a cuppa. I should be there tonight when you're done work. It's not a handsome location, but central and full of characters. If not, I'm sure I'll bump into you again. Get back to work. Alex.

"My friend, Alex," I finally responded to Priya, who was still nosing around my shoulders and watching me read the note.

"He was gorgeous," she sighed. "But, that looks like a ransom note."

I nodded at her, folded the note, and placed it on my desk.

"Hey…" she twisted her face, "Did you pee on your…" she began to ask.

"It's tap water," I immediately cut her off. She flicked her eyebrow at me. "The splash back got me."

She turned away, skeptical. I didn't buy it. And, I was the one explaining it. And, it was true.

13.

Before leaving work, I did a quick search to investigate the whereabouts of *Wing Café*, which I translated as *Café des ailes* in French. In his note, Alex had indicated that it was near my neighbourhood. Unlike the vast majority of cafes and bars, *Café des ailes* didn't have any online record of its menu, guest impressions, or even an address or contact number. *Strange*, I thought. It was generally impossible to escape the long, prying fingertips of social media in the information age. Staying off the grid was increasingly difficult, unless we're talking about a place with the exclusivity of Opus Dei or the mutual understanding of privacy of the Free Masons. Even then, the taxonomic attitude towards businesses of any kind had more resistance in Europe, but was slowly following American trends. Even dimly lit smoke and jazz filled speakeasies with 20-person maximum capacities, windowless and indiscernible from street level and requiring a special knock, were somehow becoming publicly subjected to qualitative analysis, exposing their entrances to the world. The hipsters and coolies then shift their moonless lairs and penumbral watering holes like vanishing opium dens in Shanghai, reappearing like intermittent oases, *only for those who knew.*

This cafe, however, had no internet presence or reputation with local Parisians at the office. The women at work curled their lips in and made their eyes larger and more innocent as they shook their heads in negation: *non.* The men elevated their shoulders towards their ears, shrugging their hands as though they were holding imaginary bowls of soup, slightly tilting their heads and smacking their lips as they exhaled through closed mouths with semi-closed eyes: *non, moi n'en plus.*

I was expertly familiar with my neighbourhood as I'd busied myself with long, cigarette-fueled strolls to explore the area, discovering amenities and options for amusement along the way. I couldn't recall having seen the cafe in question. In Paris, businesses seemed to cluster in similar areas, no matter which *banlieue.* There were the cafes and little pubs beside the *tabacs,* with laundromats and usually a barbershop or hair salon nearby, a pharmacy was never far off, a bakery and a grocery store, usually specializing in products from the area's most pronounced ethnic groups, and some kebabs and food counters open suspiciously late. I relied on the kebabs on lazy and unprepared Sundays when everything else was closed.

Being quite familiar with these little bunches of shops in my area, I was fairly stumped on the location of *Wing Café.*

I hadn't yet left the regional train station to walk home. The prospect of another anemic weekend alone wasn't ideal, even less because I'd more than likely resort to furnishing any down time with office work at home. I might even convince myself to take a trip to the office to get some files, which would simply to be something to do, wishing on a star to be swooned by some miraculous diversion on the way there. I feared that's what'd happen to me in old age, although I did welcome senility and dementia like children return to their loving yet criminally irresponsible parents after time apart at a foster home.

I began to ask newsstand owners, cafe workers, and random people if they'd heard of *Café des ailes.*

"*Café des ailes?*" I heard a man's voice, raspy and burnt, rattle out.

"Yes," I responded. I turned around to be met with the bulbous, red nose of a rummy with scraggly gray hair and a patchy beard glaring at me, unable to stand straight or still.

"Why the hell would you want to go there?" said the man, smelling of sour piss and sweet rum as he staggered closer to me. The couple who I was in the process of asking immediately traded condemnatory glances and made quick dust.

"Why?" I said. "Is it bad or something?"

"Bad?" he responded. "It's a goddamn shithole! The food's shit and there are a bunch of losers always hanging around that joint. Fuck them!" The man was slurring his words, which became harder to distinguish as he worked himself up.

"Well, where is it?" I asked, unsure whether or not to take the word of the ragged man with any measure of salt.

"If you insist on going, it's not far," he responded. "It'll cost you, though. 5 euros… and a baguette. And some cigarettes. And… rum bottle!" He finished reading his Christmas list. "A bottle of rum, thank you, please, kind sir."

I looked at the man, unimpressed, noting both the air of smugness that he'd developed from holding the upper hand and his compost-like odor.

I shrugged and put my hands in my pockets. "I'm not giving you shit, bum."

He tilted his head back as though his bid was outclassed at Sotheby's for something he didn't need.

"Well, how about just the 5 euros then, my boy?"

"I'm not paying you shit, old man," I responded to his renegotiated sum.

He studied me with bloodshot, barely-open eyes, little and dark, struggling to see over his broken-veined nose. "Do you have any cigarettes?" He tried to save face, still coming out with a profit like a merchant in a souk.

"Sure, I'll roll you a brown, but give me the address of the cafe," I agreed as I reached for my tobacco pouch.

"A *brown*?" he said dejectedly. "I prefe*r blondes*." He lifted his snout with an air of superiority, rolling his r's and hilling his vowels like a regent of noble birth.

The man started to describe the location of the cafe to me, pointing out informal landmarks that made little sense to someone without the street acumen possessed by the drift-about sort. "Make sure you include a filter in that cigarette, *boy*," he spoke chin first. "And, make sure you don't roll it too tight. I don't want to have to scrounge up another paper because you can't roll worth a damn," he continued with the same princely manner of speech.

"Are you going to give me some directions I can use, then?" My irritation increased. "The only directions you've given me are benches, statues, and fountains. Do you know how many fucking statues, benches, and fountains there are in Paris? What's the address? What goddamn street is it on?"

"I don't use street names or addresses," he responded haughtily. "Why would *I* have any need to remember addresses? All I need to know is where things are and how to get there. It's all about the journey, as they say. The metro isn't paid with food stamps or bottles... Make sure you use two pinches if you're going to pack the tobacco in like that! Christ! I'm going to smoke it all in one pull!" His eyes were fixed on my rolling, distracted by my inability to craft a rolled cigarette to *his* standards, standards that I'd find comedic if they hadn't been so impeding at that moment.

"What's near it?" I asked, completely abandoning the rolling procedure and letting the nearly-finished cigarette rest between my thumb and middle finger, my index holding the tobacco and filter in place.

"Let me see, there's a laundromat, though the name escapes me," he responded, cutely placing his hand at his chin to symbolize his safari into thought. "There's a video store. No, it might be a *tabac* that rents movies. Ah! There lies a soup kitchen, a mission with a little church, right next door to the place you're looking for. I received some food from them before. It was terrible. The soup was more water than broth, and the buns were too rubbery. Why would you want to go there? Stupid!" he said dismissively. "Saint something or other, M- or D-, one of the two. It's a man's name. That's the name of the mission. Full of filthy beggars. Ugh. Why go? Don't waste your time. People just take, they don't try to help themselves. Addicts and crazies of the worst sort."

"Too dangerous for you?" I asked.

"Well, no. They think I'm one of them, but I'm better. Far better than those savages. Animals," he said with sureness and pomp.

"Ok, thanks..."

"They're liars, cheaters, thieves, addicts, fornicators, disease mongers, and bringers of their own ill-fortunes! *I'm* only living this life transitionally," he said.

"How long has this transitional phase been going on?"

"Five, perhaps six years. I just need to get my business going again. Then, I'll get my wife back and my children will come back... little hell-raisers... buy a summer cottage..." he began to laugh, which degenerated quickly into a hacking cough, dry as a working-class steak. "Look! I just *earned* myself a cigarette; no stealing, no lying." His hands spread to punctuate his act like a magician.

By that logic, he was correct. I finished packing his cigarette and took care in the licking of the yellow adhesive strip and the final twisting of the paper. He accepted the cigarette with an elegant hand flourish and lifted it above his head, scrutinizing it triumphantly.

I had a better idea of where *Wing Café* was now. It was by no means close to my apartment, but walkable in this weather. The idea of closeness in big cities is highly subjective, depending on the person and their desire to travel. For a good enough reason, money being the most common, the centre of Paris fills and deflates with daily journeyers who make the trek to keep a roof over their heads and food on their plates. When their most imminent necessities are sated, individuals can choose to remain in their neighbourhoods or venture outbound for some excitement. Many move to trendy neighbourhoods for access to their presumably trendy establishments, foregoing the rigmarole of traveling from whatever corner they reside in to bask in a homogeneous environment that they helped create, or gentrify. In the *banlieue*, unless it's a trip to the football pitch, the next neighbourhood is too far outside the bubble; why would I go there when the same things are all here? Several city blocks are enough of a distance to yield the decay of friendships. For the average *banlieue* resident, the neighbourhood and its immediate vicinity often become the bricks that seal their invisible igloos. Sure, they must leave to hunt, but are quick to return with the kill to skin and devour. This also contributes to the malaise and boredom of someone who lives in a stolid, unremarkable neighbourhood with no friends in the area to speak of, living too far from any trendy or desirable spots, left with little time to explore because of long work and transit hours. In my case, *Wing Café* wasn't that close to my house, but not that far either, and no distance in the city's breathless count of blocks seemed too far for me to venture in order to shake my wretched *ennui* and maybe have some fun.

14.

The sky was graying over. Its blueness was being paved over by a trowel, pushing and spreading cement over its azure surface. The air remained balmy, sticky enough to glue one's shirt to one's back.

Walking through the suburban neighbourhoods of the *banlieue*, any *banlieue*, offers the same sights and sounds as every other. Other than the standard amenities, apartment blocks were the most common sight: omnipresent and immense. I wondered what would happen if a fire were to befall one of the more gargantuan tenement housing projects.

The usual sounds of French, heavily tempered with slang and Arabic, echoed all around. Language and wording aren't very important, however, as the sound of a mother berating a child or the unrestricted bravura of teenagers sounds the same in any language. Picking a shortcut through a *banlieue* is always an exercise of gall; the boys and men who are usually found occupying the benches, their little parcels of territory, know who lives there and who doesn't. There's no reason for an outsider to be cutting through *their* swaths of fiefdom, so it usually prompts a conversation, or at the very least, a chorus of brazen eyes staring with a combination of curiosity, animosity, protection, and potential opportunism.

The walk to *Café des ailes* was uneventful. Loops of recycled backgrounds made the journey feel all the longer due to their stock-footage sameness, Flintstone-like. I was cautious of the stares that fluttered like batwings from kids playing in the middle of the streets and the older generations posting up on stoops and staircases. A distinct smell of spices and seasonings hung in the thick air like a musty towel; a rich Maghreb couscous or tajine stew fanned the rich smells of cumin, ginger, paprika, and saffron that moved through the sultry air like a whale, with just the faintest hint of cinnamon to add some sweetness to the earthen, sweaty melange of spices. I heard the sizzle and crackle of fried plantains, cassava, and chilies on hot skillets from windows of creole-speaking Africans, as well as the particular smell of scotch bonnet peppers that strains the eyes when too close. When the air was at its heaviest, the cuisine fought with the smell of sewage, rotten sulfides, and grimy, odorous gases that reminded me that I was still technically in Paris, with its ancient sewer system and citywide toilet smell.

The closer I got to the cafe, the rougher the surrounding area became. The number of pedestrians dwindled and the number of staggering adult males, either drunk or stoned, increased quickly. As I neared my destination, I happened upon a little clearing in the sidewalk at the corner of a street, which appeared to be a makeshift park. Though it had no greenery, it had several pots that appeared as though they should contain some perennial flowers, a Chinese maple, or at least a miserable shrub. There were benches and a long, elevated slab, all made of concrete. The out-of-place slab angled perpendicular to one side of the street, tall and narrow, appearing to serve no functional purpose other than being a crash spot for junkies and tired hookers. I stepped over, probably on, dozens of needles and orange caps that had been carelessly littered on the ground. The pots were full of cigarette butts, more needles, and spent condoms, though in many cases, just the elastic ring; the tubular unrolled part dissolved by time and weather. There were men sleeping on a few of the benches, some younger with ratty beards and ash-coloured skin with crimson-scabbed sores. Others were older, darkened to a reddish-brown with distension in their fingers and exposed calves and facial features. Some had dogs that sat atop their nests of needles. They were trying to snap food out of poorly opened tin cans, scratching the dogs' snouts and leaving abrasions all the way around them like muzzles of shredded fur. There were women with legs and arms the size of children's wearing rags that were hanging from their bodies as though someone was trying to dress up a standing antique hat rack. They moved jerkily but were amazingly shrewd at the slightest stir or sound or eye contact. They were on sentry and propositioning anything that drove or stumbled close enough for long enough. The older ones were 30-going-on-full-blown-AIDS. The young ones were *young,* perceptibly underage and too young to do anything but play with dolls. They were so young that their more definitive characteristics hadn't yet been starched out by the drugs and street life. The older ones looked like life had taken everything personal and sacred from them and squeezed every last ounce of joy from their hair, skin, and hearts. They looked toughened, roughened, and ever-ready; each one was smoking a cigarette with bright shades of lipstick left gobbed on the filters and wearing heaps of cheap concealer to cover up the blemishes that had accumulated like spider webs in a crypt.

Grimy gang graffiti coated the brick walls of the surrounding buildings, along with the street signs, benches, and any other surface that would hold ink. The cheap hardware store paint scrawlings in the *banlieue* were thin and languidly lined, with clearly visible words and names that ate up wall space without the pulchritude of more aesthetically-minded street artists. Skinny, jagged letters dragged for meters to plant gang flags in the area. Many were crossed out with an 'X' and a different name was tagged beneath or above the previous claimant to the space. The odd political one or two-liners were left as they were. As it was France, political graffiti went in hand with wine and cheese.

There were three entrances to the building's street-facing façade. The middle entrance seemed to lead up to the second floor, where I spied at least two apartment suites. The entrance on the left side led to the mission. The front window was tinted and covered with thick, round bars. There was a wood sign above it that stated '*Mission St. Joseph*' in old English font with the sentence '*Sauvetage* à *l'interieur'* written below in the same characters. Numerous bulletins stating hours of operation, dates of the soup kitchen, bible studies, dependency and addict meetings, and words like *salvation, rescue, help,* and *God* peppered the weathered pieces of paper taped to the window. There was a blackened window on the right side, beyond tinted, without any light coming out. The heavy-looking door had equally darkened glass and criss-cross prison bars with a knee-high kick plate at the bottom, probably a relic from before the bars had been welded to the frame. I noted that there was an hours of business card that had yet to be filled in, though it looked well over a decade in appearance. The dark window had two features: a miniscule '*Open*' sign in the corner, only visible within two feet, and the cafe's name, which looked as though it'd been written in white liquid correction fluid: bumpy, uneven, free-handed, and perhaps even more poorly composed than the graffiti on the side of the building. *Wing Café.*

No one had known where it was because it wasn't a French name, but an English name: *Wing Café.* And, the name was only visible if your nose was nearly pressed against the tenebrous, feculent window.

Well, fuck.

15.

The little bells fastened to the bars on the inside of the door jingled dissonantly as I was forced to exert a considerable amount of strength to wretch it open *just enough* to slide my frame through. *The bars must be solid steel*, I thought. The smell was the first thing that hit me, wafting out and taking over my senses before I could take in a full visual of the place. Aside from the mingling of stale and fresh-smelling cigarette smoke, a sweet aroma and a sour odour were each grappling to be the strongest. The harshness of deep fryer and butter filled my lungs and coated my tongue with every breath. With the exception of a strong sizzling sound, it was dead silent. The entirety of the cafe was just a countertop with eight seats facing the menu and special-covered main wall, with another four seats set against the back wall where the bar curved around. The counter started a foot and a half from the window and ran the length of the eight seats towards a swiveled section with a hinge that allowed it to be raised up for passage, breaking up the bar, before curling against the wall and diminishing into a peninsular nothingness in the back corner. The seats at the far end had increasingly dwindled counter space, with the last seat, overly snug against the corner wall, only having enough room for a carefully placed, American-sized coffee mug. After the racket I'd kicked up by opening the door, the room returned to its dark, heads-forward drear with the quiet hum of coffee sips, utensils scraping on plates, sniffles, and coughs. I scanned the small room and spotted Alex lightly conversing with the man behind the counter. He was an interesting-looking Asian man. I couldn't distinguish the country of origin of the fellow, dressed in a thick, white cook's shirt and brimless hat. Not a beret, but similar to the seamed cap of a sous-chef. Neither of the two had looked up when I'd entered. As I approached them, I passed a man with his head on the counter, shabbily dressed in faded denim with his hand still clasped around a half-drunk beer bottle. Another was sitting silently, dazed and appearing as though he was about to say something, the dirty smell of malt liquor radiating from his husk.

Approaching Alex, I noticed that there was another man speaking with them as well: a little fellow, troll-sized with a nasty face and dark brow. He appeared to have short and thin arms and legs beneath a gaudy suit paired with an equally garish, loosely-buttoned, aquamarine-patterned shirt. His head was shaved and he seemed to be gripping his little glass tensely with his stubby fingers. The Asian man stood there with his arms folded, muttering something under his breath, while Alex sat upright with the posture of a viceroy, smoking the middle of a *blonde* and casually sipping his espresso, appearing to be listening calmly to the two gentlemen with a washed expression. With two steps, I was right across from the Asian man. He turned towards me without making eye contact, and returned to Alex and the other gentleman, never uncrossing his arms. The little man turned and looked contemptuously at me with his little facial features converging into a sinister jib and wrinkled mouth, then turning his head forward and staring down at his cup.

I sidestepped the little man and approached Alex, confusedly, offering greetings with an outstretched hand. He returned the salutations and congratulated me on finding the place. He said it was a *'piece of garbage, tucked away in the deepest part of the landfill, in the dirtiest city in Western Europe.'* He seemed surprised that I'd bothered to make it this far even though he'd invited me. I asked him if I was interrupting and he said that his friend was just leaving. He muttered something in what I took to be Arabic, and the little man jumped off the stool like a jockey would a horse, nodding and grunting, then marching bowlegged out the door. Alex asked the Asian man, whose name was Wing, for two coffees and a new ashtray. Wing sluggishly grabbed the ashtray and banged it on the garbage can before dropping it back on the table.

"Friends of yours?" I asked.

"No," he answered. "Just a little meeting. Nothing important. Hungry?" he asked me, not allowing for a follow up question.

"I could eat, yeah," I responded, noticing the emptiness in my stomach.

"We'll have a cup and then some sup. The food here isn't terrible, but I can't promise it won't make you sick," he answered. "First, have a cup. You've probably been looking for this place for a little bit, considering you get off work at 5pm and it's 8pm now… You've been hunting for this dirt hole for a while!"

I told him the Wing-*ailes* mix-up. He didn't even crack a smile.

Aside from the tall glass and chrome sugar dispensers and matching salt and pepper shakers, the plastic, faux-wood bar top, and the loose newspapers sitting randomly on the countertop, there was very little in the cafe. Certainly nothing that would elicit any continuity as far as décor or even a pattern would be concerned. A very plump, rotund Asian man could be seen in the back working over a flat grill with a metal scrub brush, wearing a white smock and paper cap. The walls displayed various clippings, signs, and revised menu items. The menu items included everything from sweet and sour pork and fried rice, to Belgian waffles, to English breakfast, to hamburgers. The signs had captions like *'We don't pay for bottles, nor do we allow the removal of bottles. Bottles are the property of the establishment,'* and, *'Prices are subject to change without warning or other indication.'* Some outdated pricing lists even used francs and indicated the exchange rates for pounds and deutschmarks. Curiously, there was a handsome, intricate-looking espresso machine in the corner. It was polished and sleek, the stainless steel was immaculate, the handles had a rich, mahogany finish, and it held a dozen spotless white espresso mugs on top. The countertop was laden with sticky drink rings, pieces of scrambled egg, and other unaccounted for food pieces. The floor was the exact colour of shoe dirt, none of the dishware or cutlery was clean or matched, but the espresso machine was pristine and made a hell of a delicious cuppa.

"You come here for the coffee?" I asked Alex after he offered me a cigarette.

"You could say that," he said as he lit my cigarette. "Still on the *bruns?*"

"Like I said, I don't mind them," I answered. "Do you live near here?"

He looked me up and down while taking a big drag of his cigarette, causing the paper to hiss and wheeze as the tubing was devoured by the fast-growing ember. "Are you calling me poor?"

He had a severe look with the eyes of a cottonmouth viper. He held this look for five Mississippi's while I stumbled over my own tongue trying to choose the right words.

"I'm just fucking with you," he broke into a dastardly smirk, his eyes retaining their serpentine staidness. "It's *mostly* for the coffee. You can't put a price on a really good cup. I've been coming here for years. At one point, I did live in the area. Not really by choice... Sometimes, you just need a place to lay your head. It's always been shit, but not the total shit you see now."

Wing, the owner, maintained his crossed arm stance and glower, standing in the exact spot he'd been occupying when I arrived.

"Wing here has been here even longer, *n'est-ce pas, Wing?*" The owner cleared his throat and licked his lips. I have no idea what they were talking about when I arrived, but it appeared as though Alex's toying was consternating Wing. "*Wing, les cafés? Sinon...*" Wing finally moved a few feet to begin the coffees. Alex's levity faded into intentness as he watched Wing begin making the espresso.

"So, what would you like to do?" Alex asked me as he turned away from Wing, again with calculated mirth. I knew exactly what I wanted to do, but asking someone you don't know very well to hunt trim isn't the easiest subject to broach.

"Well, I wouldn't mind... It would be nice to..."

"Don't tell me you still need to fuck?" Alex said with disbelief. "I was just in your office building today. That place is crawling with pussy: big, small, short, tall. I mean, you can't throw a stick and not hit a bitch in that place. How have you not fucked someone in the bathroom at work? Just to get your head right for the afternoon. No? How have you not at least gotten a number? I bet the standards are *low* there."

I didn't really have an answer. "Well, people don't always work there for long, and you know, working together..." Alex cut me off again.

"More excuses? Look, it might seem harsh that I'm coming at you, but you're a nice guy. Good-looking, but a pussy. A coward. Depression? Snake-bit? Fear of cunt?"

"No fucking way! Before I moved here I did alright. Back home, I mean. Maybe I cursed myself? I was a dick to some girls." In my defense, I believed what I was saying.

"First off, you're telling me that you did better back home than in France? In Paris? Whores and prostitution weren't invented here, but they damn near perfected it. And, no. I don't think you're cursed. I think you're probably lonely, which makes you confused, which makes you awkward, which makes you a bitch."

The coffees came and Wing placed them on the table. I nodded at him, but he just looked at Alex, who didn't return his gaze. Alex took a sip and I followed suit. Damn, it *was* a good roast. Clean, bitter without being acrid, and with an innate creaminess that was buttery and bouncy. Alex remained silent, looking out the window for a moment before resuming.

"I'll get you laid, and then you'll feel a lot better."

Sadly, his offer of charity was appealing. My drought was all too real, and hanging out with a guy who looked like him couldn't hurt, even if the women would mostly be interested in him.

"Ok," I said. "We can go out tonight. I don't have any plans and maybe I just need to knock the dust off."

"I'm not saying you have to get married," he grinned. "But, maybe a nice girl who'll suck the balls out of your shaft will do you some good. I know the perfect place. A friend of mine owns a club. There, you can talk to some ladies and get back into the swing of things. Trust me, after you unload a clip, you'll be a new man."

"Sounds great!"

"I personally don't understand *you people*, so preoccupied with getting your dick wet, chasing flesh, and needing that kind of verification to know you're alive, desirable, or whatever it is. It's foolish. Currency, that's the only chase. People are so easy with such simple motivators. Do you even know what your end game is? You get laid, then what? You meet a nice girl, plod along on dates until you move in together? Get married with a big ceremony? Have underachieving kids that'll continue to drain resources at a rate that can't be replenished and carry on the cycle infinitum? It's crazy to me. I guess that's how I describe people. *Crazy.* Illogical. I try not to empathize, otherwise I'd go crazy myself, and then what would happen?"

Alex took the final gulp of his coffee and put his cigarette out in the cup.

"I can't speak for the rest of humanity, but I have a void that requires sexual stimulation," I said.

"To validate your worth? To release stress? To what end? Unless you can control your thirst, you'll be miserable: digging wells, and never striking water. At the very best you'll spend your existence trying convince yourself that you can be satisfied with mediocrity, trying to make it feel like happiness, hoping there's something better, but knowing deep down that you don't deserve it." Alex paused to light another cigarette. "I'm not saying you have to deny yourself pleasures, but don't let pleasures, or rather the chase, define who you are. Guns or butter. Guess which one gets you castles, Ferraris, supermodels, and live-in chefs."

"Well," I started, "what's the point of living? Most live like that. That's the American dream, isn't it? I won't ever live the life of the lord you're describing. What should I chase, then? What keeps you going?"

"Well, you moved to a strange place to try and live out the *American dream*," Alex said. "The people who have those things… they took. Or they stole, or inherited. There are smart, ruthless people that live in this world. However, they aren't distracted by the castle, the women, the cars, or anything like that. They have those possessions in spite of themselves and I doubt they really enjoy them… I mean as much as you or someone like you could. As for me, I'm still trying to nail down what drives me. Guns or butter, as I said. I consider myself a business man." He leaned in. "But… my real interest is to have an impact on people's lives. I guess that's what really gets me off. Not everybody, and not in the most conventional ways, but every so often I see someone, someone like you, like a little dog in the pound, and I say to myself *'I bet I could help make a difference in that person's life,'* and I do it. I have some aspirations, objectives that I choose not to share because in the pit of my heart I'm superstitious. Silly, I know. But, short-term goals, right here and now, I want to help you unburden yourself so that you can stop your fucking complaining, get on with your life, and start living a little better, for your own sake and now mine since you are *my* responsibility. Talking to you, while you're full of promise yet crippled by your own misplaced ambition, is pathetic."

Alex crashed his cigarette into the already-full ashtray and said that we should be off. He told me not to pay. He didn't either. We left the area to catch a cab. They wouldn't come here, he said. Alex described the area as we walked: this building manufactures heroin, that one's where the dealers reside, that unassuming *tabac*'s a front for running firearms, counterfeit jeans, wallets, and purses are made in this tenement, and right there's a chop shop that also welcomes sex slaves from the former USSR.

As much as the overload of information about criminal activity in the neighbourhood was interesting, and terrifying, I was processing what Alex had said back in the cafe. I didn't know why he'd taken such an interest in me. He talked a lot of shit. He spoke with authority and said things that a stronger, more confident version of myself would likely say, if I didn't care whom I offended.

"Look," he said. "Life to me… it isn't roses. I look at life as being stranded in the middle of the ocean, holding onto a life preserver or being marooned on a small piece of rock that might've once been an island. You're waiting to die. You can wait for a boat, you can try to swim for it, but you can't afford to daydream while you're surrounded by a black and ferocious sea. The waters are always hungry and happy to eat. There will always be waves crashing and throwing you off. The only thing you can do is try and hold on while you still have enough blood flow to fill your fingers with strength. It's bleak. It's *real* bleak. You can harpoon enough fish to keep your body and mind strong until a ship passes by and picks you up. But… you'll more than likely die first."

He then let out a piercing, high-pitched whistle and threw his arm skyward: "Taxi!"

The cab slowed down to let us in.

"Alright," he opened the door and gestured for me to enter first. "Let's get you some fish to stab."

16.

We exited the taxi after some thankfully lighter-hearted banter about general nothingness. Alex, despite having what even he referred to as a *bleak* outlook, was a supremely charming conversationalist with much to say about everything when he felt like it. He could always turn it on when he needed to woo someone.

I had no idea where we were, but the streets were dim. It was dark with the exception of an empty restaurant and a chilly wind was cutting through the air. Alex told me that the club belonged to his friend Bruno. Though he wasn't much for clubs, he'd never left this one without a smile. I grabbed a quick kebab to neuter my stomach growls. Alex smoked at the door while the owner shaved meat with a long knife.

"Do you ever eat?" I asked him, wiping crumbs from my beard as we walked.

"Of course I do, Jewish grandmother. I ate just before you got to Wing's," he answered. "You know… with all this talk, you've got me in the mood to fuck."

Well, that was nice. I didn't feel like I was putting him out now.

I finished the kebab as we rounded the corner and came upon a vibrant street. The clothes and hair of people in the queues reflected the alternating colours from the neon marquees of clubs and bars.

The lines to enter weren't too long. The bouncer presence was heavy and many places were offering ambitious drink specials and free cover. Alex said that it was still early and that Parisian clubs tended to fill up later and become livelier after midnight. He also pointed out that this area used to be the gutter, now asserting itself as a *new* club district. I only then noticed a dozen or so junkies and hookers peregrinating like wandering ghouls. Just as I was about to ask myself why such a polished fellow would hang in such seedy, unsavoury areas, Alex turned sharply to the left.

We faced 6 to 8 giant, brown-skinned men. It wasn't near freezing, yet each man was wearing a sizeable, ankle-length coat. Alex was standing eye to eye with one bouncer.

The behemoth with short-cropped hair spoke first: "What do you want?"

"Is Bruno here? Just wanted to show my friend a good time. He's new to the city and wants to meet some people, some ladies," Alex retorted.

"Bruno ain't here right now. You and him cool?"

"Well, I can't imagine why we wouldn't be. We go back too far for something stupid like that come between us. Plus, the area needs people *like me* to visit fine establishments *like these*, or it'll never become anything."

The doorman grunted and looked around at his cohorts, uncertainty obvious on his rugged face.

"If you say so. It's busy, but no line up. Not a bad night. Good to see you."

Alex nodded, maintaining a businesslike demeanour.

I followed Alex through the doors. "So… you know these guys?" I asked.

"Oh sure," Alex responded as he nodded at the coat check girl. "We go way back. The owner, Bruno, Moroccan guy. Known him about as long as I've lived here."

Well, that was that.

17.

We passed through the first little room, which was thick with dark lighting.

Alex dropped some notes into a glass jar in front of the coat check girl. I handed off my blazer, suddenly feeling a little gawkish in my work clothes, and followed Alex down the narrow stairs exiting the foyer. The sounds of dance music began to boom with my first step and pulsed louder with every additional one down the tapering, swirled staircase. At the bottom, another large man in a heavy coat was standing by a door. Alex nodded to him and he nodded back. We emerged into another room, which was vast and full of men and women. To my surprise, many of the men were also wearing shirts and ties. I stopped feeling so out of place. It was a flurry of purple beams with pinks, blues, oranges, and greens; glasses, glowsticks, wristbands, and other merchandise helped to embellish the orgy of incandescence.

"Do you want to get yourself a drink?" Alex asked.

"Sure!" I responded, yelling in his ear in order to be heard.

"I'll meet you over on that side." Alex pointed to the opposite corner.

I shouldered my way to the bar amongst the men and scantily clad women. The men seemed to be mostly professional types: all ages, all sizes of pot bellies and degrees of hair-to-baldness. The women on the other hand, down to the last one, were stone-cold foxes.

I got the attention of the tall, blond bartender. Her height was accentuated by her long, ropey limbs, pedestalled by spiked stilettoes. She wore a black tube top with black cyclist shorts that exposed both breast and ass cheek. Her proportions were impeccable. She had the much-coveted appearance of looking exotic while still being Caucasian. She had plump lips and cheeks, a half-sharp nose, and almond-hooded, blue eyes. *Russian?* I thought

"What you want?" she asked me in a thick Russian accent.

Nailed it.

"Can I get a beer?" I shouted with my hand cupped to my mouth.

She grabbed a green bottle from the iced well, popped the cap off with her bottle opener, and placed it in front of me in one slick motion, then set to grabbing other orders.

"How much?" I asked her.

"What?" she snarled, squinted, and scowled. This was made all the more intimidating due to her eye shape and high cheekbones.

"I said how much, my dear?" I yelled back, trying to make my shouting voice as kind as possible.

What followed was a slap on the bar top and a diatribe in Russian. I'm not sure if the Cyrillic alphabet uses asterisks, octothorps, and ampersands, but I'm certain that's how you'd write the words she was screaming at me. I spun around confused and left a 20 euro note on the bar. I was hoping that no one would nick it, but was only too eager to leave the berating.

I slicked across the dancefloor. As I was moving the waist of a black chick to get by, as I'd always done while working in bars, she threw her hand around my neck and began to grind on my cock. She kissed me on the neck and up my jawline and bit my ear. I started to grow rigid against her muscular horse-hind. Her thick, dark waves smelled sweaty and sugary. The hand she'd flung around my neck was wading its fingers under the collar of my shirt. She placed my left hand on her big, supple breast. I'm pretty sure my eyes had begun to roll back into my skull. I felt the blood rushing from my brain directly into my dick as her waist undulated in tiny circles. My cock-head settled in the split of her ass, a valley saddled by two enormous peaks. I opened my eyes and saw Alex leaning on a pole, watching me, having a chuckle and smoking a cigarette. I snapped out of ecstasy and told the girl that I'd be back. She gave me a pouty look and then went back to dancing. I watched her ass move again, shaking wildly like it was trying to escape her body. I turned to meet up with Alex and almost walked into a pole. *Damn.*

"Don't let me stop you if you're having fun," he started off cheerfully. "I wouldn't have pegged you for having the fever. I bet she'd eat you up like a panther."

"Huh? Oh. I don't think I have a type. I guess I like to be taller? But that's more for the girl's sake. They're weird about that shit," I held my beer and adjusted my crotch while keeping eye contact with Alex.

"What about you? You see anyone special?"

"Ah, I usually let them come to me." He scanned the room. "I'm also waiting to see if someone I know is here tonight. It's been a while, but it'd be nice to see her."

"Hey," I started off, feeling my member begin to release its turgidity and my ability to think recover. "What's the deal with this place? The bartender yelled at me when I asked her how much the beer cost. I couldn't understand her. It's all suits and ties, but the girls are all dressed like…"

"What do women want?" Alex began. "Security? Dependence? Wealth? Let's face it, they aren't going to let any ugly women in here. These are tens, my friend. Tens bring in men who want to spend a lot of money. Money keeps the tens interested. Maybe a condom breaks? Maybe their lives get a little better? Aside from the bartenders, the girls who come to this club are the ultimate opportunists, don't get it confused. You think the men here are in charge? These guys?" Alex waved his arm, gesturing at the red-faced, horny, sweating men. "Not a chance! These girls have these guys by the balls. With all the drugs and booze, these guys are lucky to make it home!"

I asked him what the deal with the bartender was, again.

"Ah, her," he began. "Well, she was probably pissed off because you're with me, so you get to drink for free. One less chance to get a good tip."

I half nodded.

"Or, she thought you were asking how much *for the night*." He laughed. "The bartenders aren't whores," he laughed harder. "I didn't know you were so brash." He was nearly out of breath.

I looked towards the bartender with my mouth apologetically agape.

"Do you like fake tits?" he asked.

"I guess so? I mean, sometimes? It's hard to say," I responded. "It's kind of a case-by-case thing."

"How so?" he pressed.

I told him about my ex-girlfriend who had a boob job, offered a quick background as to how she changed, and then added, "If it gives them more confidence, you can't really argue with that. But, sometimes it's lily-gilding, or some kind of complex where nothing's ever enough. There's a personality type that usually gets *enhanced*, and they normally aren't my kind of girls," I surmised.

"But, sometimes they are though, right?" I juggled some thoughts around in my mind, and he continued.

"See, I love them. I think they're slapping God in the face and telling nature to suck it. Sure, it's vain and in some cases crass, but that's plastic surgery in a nutshell. You can go overboard with anything, but getting breast implants is the most feminist thing a woman can do. They're doing something for themselves, trying to achieve the apex of femininity while becoming an even more lethal apex predator. You can't will yourself, workout, or train your body to grow bigger or better-shaped tits. Sure, some women say they do it for men, but really… they do it for themselves. *They're* the ones who permit atheism. *They're* the ones who deny nature's stringent rules. Your ex-girlfriend, there. Don't you wish you'd met her after she'd had them done? So you wouldn't have to remember how she was before? You could've met the version of her who'd already outgrown you, before she had to outgrow you."

"Hey, fuck you, man," I said defensively. I liked her how she was before the surgery. "So, you like a woman like that?" I asked as I pointed to a blond woman with massive tits, the cheerleader archetype, taking a rail on the bar.

"No," he responded. "While I like the idea of fake tits, I prefer smaller breasts. In fact, I'm more attracted to women with very small breasts. Total flatness. They know they have a weakness, at least a handicap, and still thrive, circumventing the rulebook and its norms. They work harder, fuck harder, and know exactly who they are.

18.

The joint became even more energetic as the evening went on. Almost everyone but Alex and I were snorting cocaine off the bar or lounge tables.

Clones of my first beer respawned one after the other. The alcohol began to take its wonderfully aggressive effects. Alex continued to smoke, lighting new cigarettes off of used ones, and drink espresso, posted up at the far side of the wood. He smiled politely at the approaches of women, but nothing more. He didn't seem unfriendly, perhaps a bit cold, and the women didn't persist once rebuffed. I wanted to roam around and be social, but Alex refused to give up his lean on the periphery. I set off on a quick tour of pissing and mingling, returning to find Alex speaking intimately with a woman. The outsides of their fingers were touching beneath the bar. Their eyes looked like they were magnetized to each other.

I drew closer. The woman was gorgeous. She was thin, almost frail, with milky skin and shoulder length hair the colour of nightfall. She had thick, full eyebrows that roofed massive black eyes, like dark planets that had eaten up white-pitched galaxies. She had small features, aside from thick lips that weighed her little mouth down to her short, pointed chin like overripe tree fruit. She wore a black nightgown that was slit up the side with a tumbling neckline. If she had any breasts, they would've fallen out long ago.

"Who's your friend?" I glugged. I was getting clumsy from the booze.

"This is Mariana. I was hoping she'd be here. She's from Milan. We go back," he looked at me and then returned to her.

"Nice to meet you, Mariana," I said.

"Enchanted," she swept her long lashes towards me, blinking with charmed adagio, then shifted back to Alex. Eye contact with her was like taking a baseball bat to the head: bewildering and causing a loss of short-term memory.

I didn't want to cock-block. I tilted my green bottle to my lips and turned to survey the area. A tall, slanted-eyed, slender woman slinked towards me with infinite grace and asked how I knew the group.

"Yes, well, Alex yes. I don't really know Mariana. Just kind of met her right now," I stuttered.

"Yes," she spoke calmly. "I haven't seen him for a long time. Mariana misses him. Maybe we should give them some peace."

"What's your name?" I asked. Somehow.

"Adriana," she said.

Adriana and I walked towards the lounge area and sat down. Like Mariana, she was more elegantly costumed than the other women. She was *beautiful*. Not hot, not a smoke-show, but *beautiful*. She wore virtually no discernable makeup on her smooth, beige skin and had a thin mouth with nude-coloured lips. She had apprehending, jade eyes with tawny flecks squeezed by tight, sky-tugged eyelids, giving her the impression of hope in her physiognomy. She was skinny, not fragile-looking like Mariana, but svelte with streaks of lean muscle tone. She was demure, though not timid. Her eyes had a strength that made her folded hands seem poised rather than nervous.

"Are you from Milan as well?" I asked.

"As well?" Adriana started. "No… I am from Kazakhstan." I now remarked her accent.

"Oh," I said. "I figured because Mariana's from Milan…"

"No," Adriana cut in. "She is from Tirana. Albania. But, she was in Milan before she was here, so I guess that is true. I met her in Paris. We're like sisters."

Adriana wasn't striking me as the most charismatic, engaging, or even amiable woman I'd ever met, but she was one of the most beautiful women that I'd ever seen, in person or print. Alex was right about smaller-breasted women.

"I'm glad you decided to come here. You're extremely beautiful. What do you do for fun?" I asked, not knowing what the hell else to say. Next up: the weather.

In her perfect posture, Adriana outstretched her hand and placed it on my thigh. "I am sorry. I am really tired tonight and not myself. You are very cute," she touched my arm and smiled with her mouth only. "I…"

"Maybe a drink would make you feel better?" I interrupted. Her lips rolled into her teeth and her neck bent forward. Curtly, and only once.

I flagged over a cocktail waitress. Before I said anything, she nodded and went away.

"I work a lot. I work here, which is why I am a little bit… standoffish?" Adriana said. "Coming to your work for fun is a bit of a little… catch-22."

"Joseph Heller, right on." My dad-voice was making an appearance.

"Oh my, yes. I love that book," Adriana said.

"Me too!" That was my in. I did love that book. Even if I didn't, I would've started now.

We started discussing literature and our favourite books. Her favourite was Catcher in the Rye, which was my most hated. During the time it took for the waitress to return, we'd already been at it without pause for 45 minutes. My bottle was bone dry, but the stunning Kazakh had become more animated, which reddened her cheeks and made her nimble, serpentine body move in a hypnotizing rhythm as she spoke. Somehow, she was even more beautiful and entrancing.

The waitress set down a green bottle for me and a fruity cocktail for the lady. She ignored her drink completely. We continued to chat. I sipped my beer and embarrassingly pulled out my pouch of tobacco, fiending a smoke. She waved her hand and offered me a *blonde* from a chromium case with something written on the top. It was engraved in a lovely cursive, but I couldn't make out what it said. She lit my cigarette with a similarly adorned chrome lighter. We carried on about her passion for reading. She said that books were always her fall back, her way to escape the real world and all its ugliness. She'd lost her parents very young and sought solace in fantasy; imaginary characters whose lives were far better, or far worse, than hers. She didn't touch her drink much. I took that as a sign that she was interested in our conversation. I was in disbelief that I might be able to wheel her back to my place, or hers. At the very least, I could try to get her number and fight old fashioned-style.

"Maybe we can go someplace a little quieter?" she bowed her head, peering at me through her thick eyebrows.

I choked on my beer, sending frothy backwash up my throat. "Yeah… I mean… I was thinking the same thing. Crazy, huh? We can go to my place, though I have no idea where it is in relation to here." My voice had raised in both pitch and speed.

She paused. "No… I have a place that is much closer to here. Much more convenient," she said without blinking.

She stood, unfurling her long, slender body and stood fully erect, cobra-like, her slinky gown dropping down to the floor. She held out her hand for me to grab. She pulled me close, wrapping the fingers on her other hand around my head and kissing me. Without any real tongue or significant mouth opening, it was the most arousing kiss I'd ever had. She cooed as she isolated my top lip and submerged her ethereal frame into mine, with all its taught musculature and bony protrusions.

"Okay," I said, swimming in her tawny-speckled jades.

She led me through the club by my mitt. I saw nothing except her body's silhouette through her thin dress. The static pounding of bass and the blurry colours streamed around me unnoticed. I thought about telling Alex that I was leaving, but I was sure he was doing fine with his woman. I'd have to thank him the next time I saw him.

We weren't heading towards the spiral staircase we'd entered from. We headed to the furthest corner, passing some college-aged men, boys really, that were occupying a sectional couch with some women. One of the women was the black chick from earlier. One taller, brunette kid in glasses was waving his hand. A male server in tails with white gloves came and popped a bottle of champagne, proceeding to pour out a few glasses before placing it in a standalone chiller. I made eye contact with the black woman. She pouted as she had before.

Your loss, babe, I thought, seeing her with the college kids.

You still got it, I further mused to myself, spicing my saunter with more swagger.

We walked past a cutaway room where there was a chubby blond writhing against a pole. She was unattractive, drudging through the humdrum motions of her set. There were opposing lines of tables with white tablecloths at the flanks, most appearing to have wine or some other liquid stained on them. I was positive that one guy was getting a hand job while a man on the opposite side was getting throated. They winged extended thumbs at each other.

What weird fucking clubs you find in Europe.

Further down, we reached a larger metal door, guarded by a fellow who looked similar to those found out front and peppered throughout the club. Adriana and the man exchanged nods and words I couldn't hear. He opened the heavy door, stepping aside for us to pass. The next hallway looked like a hotel. The doors didn't have any markings and were spaced evenly. I felt Adriana's hand pulling me, which meant that I'd been slowing down.

"Just right here," she turned and said to me. She opened the door to a dark room and led me in. She turned on the light. As the room became visible under the harsh fluorescent lighting, my feet became cinderblocks. One bed, one nightstand, and the fading sound of distant bass. Adriana sat me on the bed. She unclipped her moon barrette and shook her lustrous, black hair down. It reached just past her shoulders.

"Can you give me one minute?" she asked, not waiting for me to answer. She backed out of the room and shut the door firmly. I thought the distant sound had been the bass, but my heart was bouncing savagely against my chest.

What the fuck is this, I thought frenetically. There were fliers on the nightstand for escorts and whores. I fiddled through them and found a drink menu. There was an intercom above my head, which probably connected to the bar service. I opened the drink menu.

Drinks:

Beers and Highballs, 5 euros.

Nothing out of the ordinary there. I guess Alex really did have my bill.

Initiation Cocktails:

200 euros.

What the hell was that? A bad feeling started to emerge within me.

Client Room Cocktails:

500 - 2,000 euros.

I have a very, very bad feeling about this.

Bottle of Champagne:

5,000 euros.

Oh, fuck. I wonder if those boys know what they're doing.

19.

All the pieces were dropping into place. In spite of being tipsy, I realized that Alex had taken me to a whorehouse. A classy brothel, but a brothel nonetheless. Adriana wasn't interested in *me*. I was already 200 euros deep, and now I was more than likely in the *Client Room*. I felt sweat trickle around my ears, forehead, and armpits. We'd passed a menacing-looking thug at the door, and listening more closely, I heard bedsprings and the moans of both men and women coming from the surrounding rooms. I stood up as if by reflex and decided that escape was the only solution.

The door opened quietly and Adriana floated in softly. I don't know what my face looked like, but I was feeling a strong urge to fling bile. My nuts, guts, and throat felt tight with fluid.

"What's the matter?'" she asked, laying her hands on my wetted chest.

Frozen in place and not knowing what to do, she moved in and started kissing my neck and nibbling my ear. The breath from her nose was giving me goosebumps.

"Why don't you have a seat?" she asked, listing me towards the bed. It was knee height and I couldn't help but land on my backside, springing gently onto the mattress. She mounted me, putting my face in her flat, smooth chest and my hands on her small ass, rounded perfection with punchy dimples.

"What's going on?" I tore back, swallowing whatever was trying to fight its way out of my intestines.

"What do you mean?" she said.

"I mean... what *is* this place? What are you? Where's Alex? Where has he taken me?"

"Are you on drugs?" she asked earnestly, grabbing my head and observing me like a medic with a penlight.

"No! Well, maybe a little buzzed," I responded. "But, what is this place?"

"I don't want to say it... you know... You've read enough Hemmingway to know what this is."

"I don't want to pay for sex. I didn't know that was the deal. I thought someone like you was *too good to be true*, but this is a little more than I was expecting."

"Listen..." she steadied my head. "Alex is taking care of you. I do not normally do this. I only take select clients. Alex said he thought I would like you, and he wanted you to meet me. He was right, you are cute, smart, and even funny. I am not a big laugher. Oh! And I think you like me," she ran her hands through my hair, feeling my stress begin to quell and my blood begin to flow again. She pushed me onto the bed.

"Umm, that happens sometimes," I grew fast and hard, poking her pussy. She started to grind, her long legs straddled over my waist, her lithe body moving like a wave.

"Just let yourself have some fun. Let me take care of you."

She began to kiss me again. I pushed away. "I can't now, knowing that you're being paid to fuck me. It's just not cool with me. Does that make sense?"

She slumped. Her dress had fallen below her shoulders and her tits, half mounds with pert nipples, were exposed. I could see her sharply-defined abdominal muscles hugged by pristine skin down to her black panties.

"Do you want someone else, better?" she mumbled, pulling her straps up.

"No, no! Definitely not!" I said. "I'd put you through the wall if this wasn't a transaction. Hell, I'd take you to dinner and introduce you to my mother if it wasn't for money, Adriana. You're amazing. The most beautiful woman I've ever seen."

"Really?" she said. "I do not get rejected... *especially* when it is like this," she wrapped her hand around my pant-covered dick.

"Ha... ha," I laughed nervously and moved her hand away. "Well, you have no idea how much this hurts me to do. Or, might hurt me if I don't get home soon. But, I have to. It's weird."

"I guess I understand," she said. "But, if a nice dinner is still on the table..."

Before she could finish, the door slammed open, almost tearing it off the hinges and putting the knob through the wall.

"You with Alex?" a big man asked.

"Yes?"

He grabbed me by the collar and lifted me up with one arm, sending Adriana to the ground. She yelled something at him. He said something back, swung me into an arm bar, and drove me out of the room.

He led me *further* down the corridor, through another door and into a back office. Alex was sitting in the office, his collar stretched, his jacket on his lap, facing a large wooden desk. Mariana was sitting on a couch behind Alex with mascara lines half-glistening on her ivory cheeks.

An old man in pink-tinted glasses and a chunky medallion was sitting behind the desk. He was about seventy and looked like evil put into a human frame: ridiculously tanned with a salt and pepper pompadour and a half-open, gaudily-patterned shirt. His face was all teeth and a pointy, needle nose. I was sat down beside Alex, facing the old man. Beside him were dozens of black-and-white monitors showing the club and the private rooms.

"So…" the old man began. "Alex. Welcome back. It's been a while. It should've been a longer while. Or, even longer still. Forever's a very long time. I told you never to come back here, to stay away. Yet, here you are. And, with a friend. With a friend who was with my Adri."

Jesus fuck, I thought. *What the hell has this bastard got me into?*

"Bruno," Alex started off. "I didn't come here with any motives. Well, one I suppose, but I just wanted to visit an old friend," he nodded over his shoulder at a whimpering Mariana. "I figured since we're both men of business, we could put our history behind us. Bury the hatchet, or the machete in your case…"

The door creaked open and Adriana was sat beside Mariana. She looked at me nervously.

"Look," Bruno said. "When you left, you left a big hole here. If I wasn't such a nice guy, I'd have had you cut up. Or, I'd have had you brought here so I could do it myself. But, I realized that you're an individual, a lone wolf, and you can't be in a pack. I get that. I knew your father and he was the same way. However, I can't allow you to sniff around here and get everyone worked up. Especially the girl."

Alex looked back at Mariana, and then back to Bruno.

"Alright, Bruno. Until the day comes, I'll stay away from Mariana, and I'll stay away from here. Shit, I'll stay away from the neighbourhood if you like. I have my own things going on and I'm just being greedy. I'm sure you can understand that."

Bruno laughed acidly. "Ha, you're right. Can't hate what I helped make, you orphan fuck. And, the girl will be fine." Bruno then looked at me. Any joviality I was carrying was instantly bankrupted. "I don't know you. I don't give a shit about you. I'd sooner wipe you off the map than waste words on a bitch-faggot like you. She, Adriana, is mine. Alex had no right to offer her up, and you had even less of a right talking to her, let alone looking at her, let alone fucking her!"

"Sir, I swear that I didn't…"

"Shut up!" Bruno barked. "The cost for her is more than you could imagine, let alone pay. Fuck your mother. I'll kill you if I see you again."

I was impotent to respond with anything beyond a *yes* and a *sir*.

"Good. I'm Bruno," he said while grabbing for something under the table. He pulled out a machete that looked more like a scimitar. It was scabbed with grime and battle-worn. "I see you again…"

"Understood," I said meekly.

"Good!" Bruno said with mild glee. "How's business, Alex?"

"Can't really complain. Busy but rewarding," Alex responded.

"That's good, son. I…" Bruno was cut off by one of his large henchmen whispering in his ear and pointing at one of the screens.

I peaked. It was the college students, arguing with the waiter, probably with the exorbitant champagne bottle bill. "Send them down here. I'm sure they'll settle their bill, with gratuity."

We were escorted out of another door from the same corridor. This one led out to an alleyway. The doorman said that Alex was very luck. *Stupid and lucky.* Alex shrugged it off, sarcastically thanking him for the hospitality and saying that he'd see them again, soon. There were no guards at the alley exit, just eeriness. Before the door slammed shut, Mariana slid out. Alex and Mariana exchanged a powerful, noisy kiss and whispered hurriedly to each other. She started crying and slapped Alex's face. He guffawed. She scampered back to the heavy metal door, barefoot. As she entered, Adriana, who'd been holding the door, poked her head out. She and I made eye contact, but said nothing. I saw pain and longing in her eyes, and she saw something similar in mine; similar, but not the same. Lost opportunity, animal lust, terror, I couldn't say. She was pulled back inside and the door closed with a hoarse bang. I turned around to see Alex walking gingerly towards the main street, fanning out his shirt.

"What the fuck, man!" I charged up to Alex and slammed him against the brick wall of a building with one arm. The other was ready to shatter his orbital bone.

"Hey, hey, take it easy. My brother, take it easy."

"Brother?" My teeth were fused together. "That's how you treat friends?! Lone wolf… No fucking kidding, you're bat shit. You could've got me *cut up*!"

"No, no," he began to play it off. "He wouldn't have laid a finger on you. Adri's not even *his*, he's just protective. She's a grown woman, she can do what she wants. *Trust me*, you were never in danger. I was in control. That's not the first time I've been back there."

"Motherfucker," I was no less incensed. "You take me to meet some women, and they're fucking hookers?!"

"Stop!" he exclaimed, drilling his finger into my chest. "Mari and Adri are *not* hookers. They're not even escorts. They are, however, perfect specimens, and under contract. I've known them since childhood. They're beautiful, intelligent, and excellent people. I'm not going to apologize for trying to stimulate your mind and body with the finest human women in Paris. You're just being rude now. You should show those goddesses amongst men, and me, some respect."

"You're insane. You're saying that I have to pay to get fucked?"

"You idiot," Alex said calmly. "I don't pay for pussy. I didn't pay those girls. No matter what I do, eat, drink, wear, or fuck: I like the finest. Mariana, she's the finest. Adriana, a close second. I told Mariana that I *might* pass by and asked if she had a friend that deserved to be shown a nice time by a stand-up gent. Working for Bruno, the girls don't meet down-to-earth men very often. They're playing a role, but are real women and need to connect with real men at the end of the day. Not just actors, footballers, stockbrokers, and archbishops. I'll admit, the venue might not have been the best, but it was last minute. Those girls don't just suck and fuck anyone, they're more selective than pandas. If they *choose* to fuck someone, *they* choose it. Take *her wanting to fuck you* as the highest compliment!"

"Can you hear yourself?" I said. "You took me to meet women at a bordello. That's fucked."

"Those two facts are mutually exclusive. *Yes*, I took you to meet some beautiful, wonderful women. *Yes*, I took you to a bordello. But those facts are not united, in this case. I didn't pay. You didn't pay. And even if you did have to pay, which you didn't, it would've been worth it. The money that those women make is astronomical. Mariana has one guy that she doesn't even have to fuck and makes 20,000 per month. To wear a maid outfit and clean his flat once every two weeks. *One* man."

"Doesn't it bother you that your girlfriend is fucking other men? For money?"

"She's not my girlfriend. I've known her for a long time and she provides me with companionship here and there. She's making more money than a doctor multiplied by a lawyer... all after barely surviving weeks on a refugee boat in the Mediterranean. She wants for nothing. Same with Adriana. She was a lumpy, Mongol-looking orphan from the Caspian Sea when I met her. Now, she's saving up to buy her life back. Mari told me that she genuinely liked you and is expecting you take her for dinner. How pathetically cute."

"Really?" I stopped a moment. I hated him for saying that, thinking about the planning that would be necessary to take Adriana out clandestinely. "No way man, that's suicide."

"Worth it," he said smugly.

"Not a chance," I shot back. I wasn't so sure. I *still* think about it.

"I do apologize for how it all ended. Bruno's protective. He's like... an uncle to me. He knew my father, as he said, and he gave my first real job. He wouldn't harm a hair on our heads. I'm sorry if that was a little alarming. He's theatrical and I thought he'd be gone. I wanted you to have the best."

"What did you do for work?" I asked.

"Waiter. I poured champagne for the high-rollers," he answered quickly.

"Hmm, interesting," I said, trying to picture Alex in tails and Mickey Mouse gloves. "You think Adriana actually dug me?"

"I know so. I could see it in her eyes. She probably doesn't get to have many good conversations with her insipid clients. You charmed her. Hopefully not too much, that might be bad... Wait for it to cool down, then I'll link you two up."

"Seems like a bad idea, plus she could just use me to..."

"If you think like that, why bother living? You attracted her in the first place. No one was paying her to do whatever you guys did. Give yourself more credit. Kudos."

As we exited the alley, the side door crashed open again and the three college kids were sent tumbling onto the concrete. Two friends rushed to the other, who was screaming and holding his wrist.

A barrel-chested monster with a husky voice belted at them: "It'll be more than a finger if you bitches come back without the money! Now, bring half tomorrow or it's the whole fucking hand. I'm keeping your passports."

Not a fucking hair, huh.

20.

Though Alex had nearly been the benefactor of my demise under the heavy blade of some lunatic pimp's machete at a bawdy house in the slums, it was the most entertaining time I'd had in Paris. Maybe in my life. It wasn't the ideal method of assuaging the monotony that had defined my life in the City of Light, but it felt invigorating. It was dangerous, sexy, roused my heartbeat so I felt it for the first time in a while, and let me sample a part of life that lay outside my self-constricting itinerary. I felt alive.

Alex made the episode seem… well, normal. As normal as standing pints with the lads at a pub watching the game. I swear, if he'd had a normal upbringing, he'd be a tobacco lobbyist or some kind of dog-wagging industrialist that was fine with dumping toxic waste in lakes.

Following the dust up at Bruno's brothel (the real name of the joint was *Minoux et Bijoux*), I worked steadily and continued to hang out with Alex whenever his schedule permitted. I was wary to commit to anything but coffee, but…

We sometimes met close to my work or apartment. The bulk of our meet-ups were at Wing Café. Wing never so much as uttered a word to me, nor did the rest of the clientele. Alex still never left so much as a *centime*. Why did we always meet in a shithole like Wing's? I couldn't say. We didn't resemble the vagrants and hookers who usually torched their guts with the greasy-spoon slop. Despite Alex's previous relationship with the area, he only seemed to know people who held a derisive-cum-inimical attitude towards him.

As always, I had more questions about Alex and his background than he proffered to answer. I wondered if he had ADD or was notched on the spectrum. I settled on the belief that he was a bizarre fellow, austere and opinionated, and was never told to shut up due to his charm and looks. A force field girdled him. It had the effect of making me want to know more about him, listen to the things he conceited, and to become almost intoxicated by the carefree, dispassionate spiritedness with which he spoke. The man was an enigma, a veritable white swirl and dark wave of dualism.

"Why do you work?"

"Money," I said.

"What I meant is… Why do you work for someone else? According to their hours and calendar?"

I hesitated. "Are… are you unfamiliar with the concept of work? It's quite an established norm…"

He shook his head.

"Look," he started. "I've lived a life that I could sell a hundred times over to make a book or movie. I've seen some of the worst things that you can imagine. Why would I, or you, work for someone else? Make their money? I have people to do that for me. They work for me, and I can't comprehend *why*. I'm thankful for their lack of drive and ambition. It keeps them shackled and bound to me by need, doing *my* work, but *why*?"

"Money," I said.

"Idiocy." He slapped the table. "You're a smart man… but you're no different from a slave or a fool because you chose slavery. You make money for men that would throw you from a helicopter without a second thought if it meant consolidating and conserving their wealth. You need to think of a good idea and go with it. Start a business, *write a book*, invent something. Hell, get yourself a gun and rob a bank. At least when you get caught by the *gendarmerie*, you'll be draining tax money from fools like you and giving back nothing to the people who were trying to fuck you until you die."

"But…"

"Nevermind that, prison's the worst. Too many rules. You can't do anything. The rules there are even stricter than the ones out here. If you go, hang yourself."

"I…"

"Listen, I'm sure that knowing you put in an honest day's work and feeling accomplished with the satisfaction of having made an honest buck is all fine. But, celebrating this hard and pointless work is only boastful consolation; it's a paltry crown for the lazy, the stupid, and those of unfortunate birth. Do you ever hear me complain? About work? No. If I fuck up, I'm responsible. I know that I work hard. I don't have to bore other people who work hard with the same story. Everybody knows it!"

"Why can't we all be as lucky as you…"

"What you call luck, I call well-aimed brilliance and calculated goal-striking. Fool-slave."

Alex never explained why he'd chosen me to be groomed as his sidekick. I suppose he enjoyed my company, naivety, and the cut of my fabric that he used as a sounding board for his reverb. I assumed that he also enjoyed the fact that I was neutral in most senses thanks to my averageness. I wasn't easily swayed, neither did I have a particularly dominant belief about anything. I might've be the only person who let him soliloquize to completion, not judging or acquiescing, just letting him finish his thought.

Most people only listen so they can talk, one-up your piece, or change the subject just to take the conch and speak about themselves. That's all we really want to talk about, our favourite or most hated, but always our most passionate and ruminated subject: ourselves. Few have the desire or patience to listen. This is how you get a partner above your class, by the way: just listen to their bullshit and let them tire themselves out. I was used to listening and playing the hands-in-the-cloak, statue-like bartender. Alex's sophism was white noise to me. At least I had a friend.

I snagged a promotion at work that allowed (forced) me to develop my leadership and people skills. Whatever. The offer was tendered with the usual 'This will look better on your CV, it's basically management tier, you help us and we'll help you,' kind of bullshit speech. I didn't care. This was the first promotion that I'd ever felt I earned. Soon, I could have business cards printed out and when meeting people, I'd tell them my full name followed by the business I worked for and the role I had. I guess that's what I wanted? I didn't know, but this would net me a bit more money and responsibility. The hours were longer and I couldn't just show up to get a paycheque, but it was an opportunity nonetheless. Stewart emphasized that I could follow in his footsteps. Whatever, but it was nice to have someone recognize my hard work. Upon telling Alex that I'd been given a role that meant more time at the office, some weekend shifts, and the chance to work with more people, his reaction was less than optimistic.

"So, you're trading your bronze shovel in for a golden one? You'll still be shoveling the same shit, maybe just more of it, for the same fruity boss. For a few more pennies on the hour? You know, if you work long enough, your salary zeroes out, hmm? You're *still* perpetuating someone else's dreams and goals. Of course, your manager was elated to have you step up. He's just downloading his most boring and trivial duties onto you. He's feeding you shit and you're asking for seconds. Congratulations on the new job though, I'm sure you deserve it."

He patted my shoulder. *Whatever.*

21.

My shit pile was now larger and my shovel, somehow smaller; made of fool's good and leaving green on my mitts. My translation duties were the same as before except now I had a large dose of clerical and file management work that was simultaneously tedious *and* unrewarding! Alex was right, the cunt. My new salariat coinage was levelling down the more time I spent alone at the office. And, it was boring. I couldn't give Alex the satisfaction, however. I kept saying that the new job was great and that my role was better.

He saw through it, had fun with my bullshit, pressed me about details, and gained momentum when my reticence was apparent. I felt stupid knowing that my answers were overly optimistic, and worse when his condescending tone was right. Luckily, Alex didn't really care all that much. He only smirked once he got a rise, and then changed the subject.

We weren't drifting apart, but I was busy and had less time. Soon, I'd have even less time.

One day, Stewart rushed to my cubicle in a panic while I was pouring through files. He asked me to follow him to his office. Before I had the chance to sit down, he said: "We're in trouble."

"What's wrong?" I asked.

"Remember the *big* project? The first of three movies? The sci-fi epic?" he said.

"Of course," I answered. "It's been in post-production all this time. You said that the son of a bitch would never be released… Good thing we got our cheque." I joked, chummily.

He squeezed his eyes at me. "Well, they started screening it to execs and test audiences. Meanwhile, the second movie is already wrapped. It turns out that one of the alien races, the ones with the noses and cheeks? They're being seen as antisemitic! The producers heard the backlash and ordered for a large portion of the film to be reshot. Such a scandal! And now, the translations for the re-shoots must be redone *post haste*. We need to get all the linguists, all the translators… everybody we can, back here immediately. We need to do this ASAP!" Stewart said in frantic, machine gun sentences. "You're my number two, and as my number two, I need you to make sure that this is handled swiftly. Professionally. We *must* send for all the translators we can. We need this started yesterday. What's tomorrow? Tuesday?"

Number two? Fuck. That was news to me. I felt a little gross inside, but sent an e-mail bomb to our rolodex and outsourcing agents. I prepped everyone: *The same as before but quicker and tighter.*

The following day was exciting in a chaotic, *'Where did you come from? Were you here all this time?'* kind of way. Not every person could be recalled, but all main languages were accounted for. There was a palpable buzz and frenetic pace in the air. The office exploded and damn near broke. Errors were made, people were yelling, and the flashing from the photocopier gave some kid a seizure. *Madness.* The everyday workers were once again put out by the theft of their usual work spaces, the thieving of lunches from the company fridge, and the commotion that accompanied a tenfold swelling of employees in the course of 24 hours.

I loved it.

If Stewart didn't model his look after Foucault, he'd have torn his hair out in clumps. There wasn't a massive amount to retranslate, but the material was vital and urgent. There were also insulting Asian and African stereotypes which I'd previously noticed, but somehow those were left in the film.

It took two weeks for everything to be lice-combed for any minor errors and stupid mistakes on our end. I helped oversee the English and French editing and rarely left my cubicle, which I had to share. The hard work was done with prior experience this time around, so we were quicker and more confident in our work. *Back pats and handshakes for everyone.*

However, the studio had bigger problems. They'd already nearly completed filming the second installment, assuring the stakeholders that the first would be a box office success, and ordered the following installment to begin filming so they could capitalize on the heat that the first movie was expected to generate.

There was heat, alright. Blockbuster? *More like blockblunder, amirite?* I'll see myself out.

All this meant that we'd finish the re-edits, and then immediately have to begin editing part two. Far be it from me to tell professionals how to work, but the old adage of eggs, chickens, and the counting of them before hatching seemed relevant here.

22.

I ended up dating the woman who I shared my workspace with after the two weeks concluded. Her name was Marta and she was from the Basque Country in Spain. She spoke Euskadi, Spanish, English, and French very well, and was primarily there to provide translation for Castilian Spanish. She insisted that the re-edits were done for the Basque language as well.

Marta was from Bilbao and had also taken French in university back in her country. Thanks to being born in the European Union, her move was not such a big leap as mine. I found her exceedingly rude at first. Our first exchange involved me asking her where she was from.

"Bilbao," she said with an accent.

"Oh, Spain! I hear it's very beautiful," I followed.

"No! *Pays-Basque* is not Spain, English," she struck back venomously.

I explained to her that I wasn't English, but American. She said that it was all the same to her. The Spanish don't have the same relish for irony as the French. Marta wasn't what I'd expected out of a Spaniard, at least not in my imagination. South Americans, *Indians* as she called them, were the Spanish speakers I was most accustomed to: bronze-skinned, almond-eyed, easy-going, and dancers. I didn't expect Spaniards to have the same features, but darker than the French with lithe, long frames. I wasn't incorrect, but was imagining the stereotype of people from Seville and southern Spain. Marta was light-skinned, though could tan, and had a dusting of milk-chocolate-coloured freckles on her nose and chest. She had thick, raven hair that she wore in a bun and stood no taller than five feet. She was busty, the polite form of saying not thin. She was squishy, but wore it well and had a wide, heart-shaped face, a round nose, and serrated chin and cheekbones. Her best feature was her bafflingly large posterior.

She initially came off as rude and bossy, but not without some charm. We generally worked back to back, but as her ass needed a lot of room, she routinely smacked her swiveling chair into mine.

"*Perdon*," she'd say once an hour, and once an hour I'd turn and look at her thickness jutting towards me under the formal clothing of a woman who preferred layers, even in summer, to conceal her girth. As time wore on, probably due to our proximity and the days spent inches away from each other under the hard office lights and the buzzing computer monitors, we started conversing.

I asked her how she was finding Paris.

"I find the people very cold," she said.

"I'm sure once you get to know them they're really nice. I mean, they're close with each other, that says something," I responded.

"Maybe, or maybe when this is done I should just go home. I came out here to improve my French, but I only ever speak to *facha* Spanish and I could do that from my mother's apartment."

"You live with your mother?"

"Yes," she said, like I should've already known. "All Spanish live with their parents until they get married."

"You're kidding, right? I've been living on my own for years, since college."

"Since high school? Oh my god, did your parents kick you out? Were they American drug addicts?"

"No… college like post-secondary school. University, if that helps."

"Ah… *claro. Vale vale.* I know you people like your drugs. I didn't know if you did drugs, too."

"No, just whiskey and cigarettes, ha-ha. But I haven't really met many people here either. I have one friend, kind of. I think he's a gypsy or something."

"Aish! *Un gitano*?!

"No, I was being facetious. I don't really know what he is. But, he's my only real pal. A weird, gypsy-like guy."

"Thank God. *Ugh.* No girlfriend?"

"Nope, no one seems to dig me out here."

"Yes, you are funny looking. Too big for here, and you walk like military."

"Okay… Do you have a boyfriend?"

"Aye no, the boys here are all too… scrawny, yes? I thought I would like them but they are cheesier and have less class than the boys back in my country. Besides, I am not skinny. I have big breasts, but I also have a big, big bum. They do not like big bums here."

"Well, that's unfortunate. I, myself, am a huge enthusiast of big bums."

"Ah, yes? Well maybe we should have some wine."

After the first glass of wine, we'd both realized that we were sex-starved creatures who'd come to Paris with expectations that'd gone sorely unfulfilled. I met Marta in her neighbourhood, near the very nice apartment her father was paying for in *Centre-ville,* at a little brasserie for some wine and tapas. It was clear what we were both interested in as we finished the bottle of Spanish red with haste.

Marta was new to sex. She'd been half-guilt-tripped by a lover who could've only had sex a couple times himself, and had half-wanted to get the virginity fucked out of her before she left Bilbao. As mentioned, she was more comfortable in layers: billowy dresses and loose-fitting clothing to conceal her paunchy mid-section. Her body, aside from her gut, was very well taken care of, as though she was waiting for a charming French man to sweep her off her feet and kiss the length of her smooth, off-white body. She had that rich girl dedication to grooming. She shaved and waxed and plucked for someone she couldn't find, or get. She'd just bought a shiny, new car, painfully longing for a passenger to tell them how smoothly it rode.

Her lack of sexual experience was evident. She liked the preamble and was passable with the mouth and hands, but the next step of penetration and releasing oneself to the ecstasies of mounting sensuousness confounded her. Like a nervous guy who finds himself without pockets, she didn't know what to grab, where to focus, where to kiss or bite or scratch, when to take it, when to thrust back, which degree to spread her legs, and became alarmed when I quickly switched positions. She proved to be a quick and able student, taking to the sport with the success of an amateur who only needed time with the racquet.

The *moment* I ejaculated into the slimy condom casing, tied the end, and dropped it into a bag-less, empty bedside dust bin with a *shlock*, a renewed take on life was bestowed upon my humble soul. The world and all its cares no longer balanced on the shoulders of poor, old Atlas. I cast the globe aside as I lengthened myself and yawned, half-covered by soft Egyptian cotton sheets, tugging my knee towards my abdomen and then crossing my arm over my chest for a post-game stretch. I was a mill grunt on a Friday: grabbing his hat, punching his card, and bidding farewell to the foundry, if only for the weekend.

I rolled onto my back and let my eyes sag with big, slow breaths. I started thinking about Adriana, and whether a blow from a machete would be worth a blow from a goddess. My mind wandered as I looked aimlessly around her dark room. I let out a sigh of pleasure and decided that no, I wasn't all that attracted to Marta. She cuddled into me and called me baby. Instantly, I was cognizant that this might've been a rash play.

"Hug me, now." She sucked her teeth and forced my arm to drape over her.

We were concluding our re-edits and I knew that she was on the fence about moving back home. I could start dropping more hints about the benefits of her returning to Spain. Or, I could be straight up with her. Or, still, we could be friends who fuck. Marta let out a groan that dripped with satisfaction, crawled onto me, and put her head on my chest. She pulled my arms around her.

Look at you. A famished hound who was thrown a steak, I thought to myself. *Too haughty to nibble on the bone? Weren't you the hound that was having hunger throes an hour ago?*

"Why are you on the edge of the bed?" Marta grumbled. I'd inched away, not thinking she'd notice. "Come here. That was amazing. We have to keep doing it."

With my balls drained, I wasn't seeing the positive aspects of Marta's thickness anymore. In the dark, it was all sweat and lumps and folds. I hate being mushy after sex with a relative random in general, even more so with someone who I didn't really like personality-wise. I suggested leaving, citing some vague excuse. That was met with vociferous protest. Marta said that I was treating her like a whore, that maybe they do that in the new world, but not in Spain.

Though he doth protest, I had a girlfriend.

23.

God bless the Spanish for their passion, as I sure as hell feared Marta's temper. That night I found myself sleeping at her place as a hostage trapped beneath chubby branches. Still a starving dog, we did it once more that night and twice the following day.

I was now anchored by an affectionate, overbearing girl who was making up for a life of being the heavy friend who witnessed her girlfriends' romances and pined enviously. She insisted that I sleep at her place, calling my apartment *the ghetto*, and provided me with symbols of love and possessiveness at every moment. By the next week, I was already in over my head, my fight subdued by consistent pussy. I don't know how, but Marta brought a temper out of me that I never knew I had. She *was* a caring and thoughtful individual, but codependency and jealousy were her major flaws. Even on the first day at work after we started having sex, she started calling me honey and sweetie, constantly feeling my arms and placing her hand on my thigh. I could feel the *he's-with-her* looks and comments raining down around me. My previous relationships had been relaxed and characterized by *sex-and-chill*, which was perfect for my noncommittal, blasé demeanour.

Within a week, I had an anniversary date to be attended monthly. Marta also forcibly gifted me a modern, avant-garde wardrobe to replace the t-shirt and jeans that may have been fine back home, but were low-class rags in Europe. I had to drink kalimotxos during the day and stay up until the sun rose every weekend listening to some Galician hippie with one long braid play guitar and sing about what a dick Franco was. Every time I wanted to do an activity that went against Marta's grain, or be by myself, a fight would ensue. I wasn't going to start a brawl every time we disagreed, and certainly not for something as trite as a movie; I watched the same flick about a scruffy Catalan and a tender-hearted Basque sharing an unrequited love more times than I'd seen Goodfellas, and spent many nights on the losing end of battles like that.

For all the squabbling and irritation, the fucking was surprisingly good, sometimes great, though a starving man would eat the pink out of a melon, as well as the seeds and the rind. Unfortunately, the sex didn't make me an amnesiac as I became a little more aggrieved with every tussle. The part that irritated me the most, and was in no way sexually arousing, was that although Marta made it clear that she *wasn't Spanish*, whenever she lashed out, she blamed it on her *Spanish temperament.*

How picky a person can become when they go from famine to feast. Worst of all, Marta began to say *'I love you,'* within a few weeks of our first time. *Love* wasn't a level I ever thought I'd achieve with her. I'd describe my feelings as a kind of morbid fascination mixed with guilty lust that needed its fix. She could've bought me all the homoerotic, V-neck shirts and made the best paella in the world, and I wouldn't ever have felt the word *love* for Marta.

On one lucky day, Marta had a spa appointment with one of her visiting Spanish friends, so I was given the whole afternoon off. I went home to wrangle a gym bag and was met by a familiar voice near my stoop.

"Long time, brother."

I turned around. "Alex!" I was genuinely happy to see the guy. "It's been a minute."

He was leaning against my building with his arms and legs crossed, accentuating his svelte build. "On your way up?" he asked. "May I follow?" I nodded and led him up to my apartment. As we entered, he looked around the room, largely unused in the past while. He nodded his head in neither approval nor disapproval.

"How have you been?" I asked.

"Good. Busy. You know how it is. Yourself?" he asked.

"I've been decent," I started. "Working on the old movie, new movie. You know, translator shit."

He looked at me suspiciously. "That's not all, is it? You've got yourself a little girlfriend. Well, not so little, ha-ha."

I froze, stark and surprised. "How…" I started to ask with a bent-up brow. "How did you know that? Wait, how'd you know where I live?"

He returned my puzzled look with a cold, dead-eyed stare. A moment later, he answered.

"I have business in the area. I noticed you and the girl once or twice, figured you must be spending all your spare time with her. As far as where you live? That's easy. You mentioned that you live in this area and you're the only American in the neighbourhood. These *banlieue* people, they're *my* people." He was jocular, and it was still uncanny. "It's good to see you, my friend," he patted me on the shoulder, then landed himself on the couch. "So, this is the castle, is it? I can see why a girl wouldn't want to spend her time in a place like this." He lit a cigarette.

"It's not that bad," I said. "The area isn't the prettiest, but the rent is manageable and it's close enough to the train. I don't subscribe to the whole '*make your house a home*' thing…"

"Sure," he said, underwhelmed. "When can I met your, little, ahem, lady?"

He'd definitely seen her. I crinkled with shallow embarrassment.

She *had* begun to put on weight, to the extent that she'd taken two pregnancy tests and visited the doctor to assure me and us that she wasn't carrying the seed of a life-ending child. No, it was just the comfortable laziness of a relationship.

"She's put on a bit of weight since we started dating. You know, ladies…" I started to trail off. "They get comfy and next thing you know, 5 or 10…"

"Kilos?!" he broke in with joy. "All good, brother. I don't care," he gestured for an ash tray. "Oh… I was with Mari and Adri the other day. Adri was asking about the handsome American man that promised to take her to dinner."

Son of a bitch.

"Any time," I sputtered. "I can meet her any time."

I gave him an ashtray. He nodded with smarm and satisfaction.

"You know I'm just fucking with you. I know you're a better man than I. *Inner beauty.* You're the kind of guy who doesn't care about looks. You see the Cinderella inside of the pumpkin… carriage, the pumpkin-carriage. I'm sure that you guys get along like a pumpkin and a pea inside of a pod. The Spaniards, they're a docile bunch, aren't they? Easy-going and care-free!

Early to bed and early to rise! Not like you can be very productive between twelve and three anyways!" Oh, he knew.

We went for coffee and cigarettes. I tried, very casually and carefully, to sugar-coat Marta. I told him about our bad luck in Paris, her family, where she was from, and all the other positives I could muster.

"Oh man," he started. "Not only is the bird a Spaniard, but she's *Basque*? Talk about not knowing how to take a loss. The war is over! You lost! Speak your weird elvish tongue and pay your taxes, cry-babies!"

"She'd murder me if I said that!"

"I don't know why you bother dating her. Or dating, period. I'm not going to sit here and preach to you about how monogamy is for strictly for penguins and Christians, but it's just an unneeded stress. Hell, man, it's borderline dangerous! Most people can't keep their own lives on track, and now they want to take on the life of another? For what? Lust? Desire? *Love*? All of it eventually fizzles away and leaves a dried-up lakebed of loss, pain, and time you can't get back."

"I'm not looking to get married here," I began. "But, it's not like I was hitting any home runs before Marta. I was having a serious dry spell, if you recall. I couldn't even bang a goddamn prostitute!"

Way too loud. Some people turned. I hunched over the table. I changed my phrasing, not wanting another homily about the benefits of whoring: "Sorry, a beautiful woman from the former USSR who was *not* paid to take my dick in the back of a brothel, but was on the cusp of it before an old man with a machete threatened to kill me." Alex mouthed 'Ah, Bruno,' and looked to be reminiscing on the moment with golden nostalgia. "Anyways," I carried on, "It's not great, and I wasn't looking for a girlfriend, just something fun. It was fun. And now, well, we just kind of have to see where this goes."

He curled one side of his lip up, as if feeling apologetic. "I'm sorry. I have opinions, some are hard to swallow… You're my friend. I just want to make sure that you're content and getting the best out of life. It's been a while, and you seem a little beaten down."

"Thanks," I replied, surprised at the apology. "I'm okay, man… Life's a struggle… Work is… She's bossy!" I blurted out. "She's demanding and jealous. Territorial to a fault. She's let herself go and wasn't petite when I met her. She's not negative… but something's always wrong with her, or her family, or co-workers, or her feet. Fuck, man. I can understand why you give me a hard time for complaining. Sorry for doing it now."

"Quite alright," Alex said, lighting a smoke and listening with his legs crossed, Freud-like. "Continue."

"There are positives, you know. She's passionate, caring, and wants what's best for me…"

"As long as it's best for her," Alex said.

"Yes…" I started again. "She, uh, takes good care of herself…"

"Not enough to keep her physique for the *one* guy who finds her attractive enough to throw her a bone," Alex fired in once again. Fuck.

"She…" I tried to turn over the engine one more time. "She's actually quite a phenomenal lay."

He looked at me sceptically, but didn't interrupt.

"Yeah, she's actually really experimental. Real engaging and outgoing. I guess it *is* good enough to keep me around," I laughed nervously.

"Hmm," he began. "This is your first vagina in a long time. While I don't doubt that you yourself are giving this woman a great time, are you sure that you're not squinting in order to make the sex *seem* great? I'm sure you're aware of what slop a starving tramp will cram down his gullet. I'm not calling her slop, but need I remind you that Adriana, who can put both legs behind her head and swallow a whole banana, is waiting on you. She's *not* a whore, before you imply it. But, it doesn't have to be her! There are millions of women, dozens of which are probably good for you. There are men, too, but you probably aren't there yet."

"Men? I'm not…"

"Listen, I'm not saying that you should break up with her, though the relationship probably never should've been given wings. It doesn't seem like you're getting anything out of this besides a comfier bed in a nicer neighbourhood and pussy that no one else wanted. Give it some thought, because I've heard your mobile buzzing without cessation since we arrived at your apartment, which means you're in for a fucking earful of *coños* and *maricóns* and *putas* when you answer. Season your life with diversity and change. I'm sure relationships have positives, but while you're young, they're like eating boiled chicken every day."

Yeah! What if I wanted lamb, steak, halibut, or even just a salad? I asked myself. *Boiled chicken every day? Even though I like chicken, it might get a little bland. What a way to ruin chicken. Fuck that bitch! I can do this!*

I pulled out my cell phone. Alex snatched it, and read the messages to me aloud. *'What are your plans? Where are you? What are you doing? Are you home for supper? Are you with woman or man? Why do you not pick up? The spa is over, give me call. What you want for supper? I am making Basque chicken soup, you no like it. Answer your SMS.'*

"Is that boiled chicken I smell?" he said. I let out a heavy sigh. Alex choked on his cigarette mid-pull.

"Nice shirt, by the way," he said. "It's busy." I pinched the shirt off my chest with the opposite of admiration. It was baby blue with white, navy blue, and gold boxes placed on it sporadically with cursive writing that I'd never bothered to read, segments of it in paragraph form. It had swirls of pointless colours in the background and a golden falcon near the collar splaying itself down the side stitching.

"It was a gift," I said meekly, hating it even more now.

Alex cackled like Satan at a suicide, a laugh unlike any of the chuckles I'd heard previously. "Oh my god," he began. "Do you *love* her? Has she made you say it? I have to meet her, that thing is hideous."

I paused at the word *love* and made a face.

"That's a firm no. She loves you, doesn't she?"

My face contorted.

"How sad," he said. "That poor girl. She wouldn't even pass the rape test."

"What the hell's *the rape test?*"

He looked at me with pitiable gravity. "It's just what it sounds like."

I looked at him. "I've never heard of it... Like we rape..." I said, thinking aloud. "Man, I have no idea what the fuck you're talking about."

He leaned in, blowing blue smoke out through his nostrils.

"The rape test is very simple, and the best part of all is that it doesn't require any *actual* rape!" he exclaimed with macabre animation. "Just close your eyes!" I did. "Closed?" Yes. "Good. There you go. Now, imagine that your Marta's been raped by 5, 10, or even just 1 man..."

I tried to interrupt. He told me to be quiet and close my eyes.

"She was savagely beaten and raped. Just so you know, most times, women, and men, actually enjoy the feeling of the rape, which is why it's so psychologically damaging to them. It's why they question themselves, sometimes kill themselves… it's the conflicting feeling of being violated and enjoying it. Anyways, Marta, or whoever you're dating, love, or think you love, was ravaged by a pack of men or a singular male. Evil men, dirty men, pirates; thorough as forensics when they forced themselves inside. They raped and tortured your beloved, but didn't kill her. They left her alive: a broken-boned, fleshy heap. A crumpled mess covered in and full of so much blood, spit, and semen that paramedics didn't know what they were pumping out. They picked her apart like crows do carrion. She's battered and torn-up. She's taken to emergency, put on life support, but thankfully, pulls through! It's such a happy scene! Her family's happy, you're happy, everyone's happy and relieved. The family respects you, the stand up, *good guy* that you are, for being by her side, keeping her company, and getting her back to feeling human again. You're at the hospital every day. You bring her magazines and books and wishes from all her friends. You feel a little dirty when you spoon feed her yogurt and some slips out on her chin and splashes on her gown, like her rapist's cum. You're forced to imagine what went down against your conscious will, but hey, you're a *good guy*, remember that! You might picture the scenario, you might get angry… you might get horny! Your cock hardens against your best efforts when you accidentally sexualize the scenario and haven't masturbated in x amount of time because of the overnight hospital stays. Don't worry! There are better days coming! The joyous day has finally arrived! She's discharged, you walk her out of the hospital, and now you two can finally get back to being lovey-dovey-loving lovers. You guys go home. She's quiet on the ride and keeps to herself for a while after. Eventually, she starts telling you some of the gruesome, horrific, and shocking details about the scene and the assailants. She confides in you because she feels she has to tell someone to move on. You listen to it all and try not to let anything affect you. You keep a stiff upper-lip. You die a thousand internal deaths. You can't twitch, frown, cry, or get angry, or she'll lose all the progress she's made. You might slip and wonder if his or their dicks were bigger than yours. *How much bigger?* She always said that yours was the biggest she'd ever had, but… Besides the detectives and maybe a nurse, you're the only person she feels comfortable spilling this disgusting episode with, and she needs someone to talk to about it. A *good guy*. Hey, like you! She can't bottle it up, but she can't relive it all at once, so she has to let it out in installments. She seems better. Depressed, but better. She's still not past the random, rage-filled episodes, though: breaking down like an old Dodge, crying and throwing violent fits, putting scissors to her wrists, trashing the house on a whim… You're her confidant, her best friend, and her *lover*. You're a *good guy*. You understand. You clean the messes, slowly take the blades from her hands, and listen to all the squirming, testicle-clenching, intestine-wrenching scenes you can't help but imagine. She goes through each choke, kick, and cock with bravery and precise detail. She's thankful to have a friend and *lover* like you who stands by her, carries her, and sustains her through this painful process that no woman should have to go through. She pre-emptively thanks you for understanding that she can't even think about having sexual intercourse until she seeks some therapy to address the traumatic crime that befell her. Plus, it still hurts. Telling you was a start, but not an end to her journey back to mental health. You know all this, or at least you understand it; you say you do anyways. You appreciate her strength and tell yourself to see her as a heroine. She was the victim of a crime that's worse than murder, because at least the murdered don't have to live with perpetual fear and misery towards men, dark alleys, deathly silences, being alone, and every little trigger that relapses your woman into a spiral of anguish and terror. People remind you how *good* you are. *Good boy*, like a dog. Obediently, you take her to her doctor and therapy sessions. You escort her everywhere she needs to be as she can't stand to be alone these days. From time-to-time, you catch her: the narrow glances and side eyes. Like you're one of *them*. You're a person she *thinks* she knows, but can't be sure. Can you really know anyone? You're a *good guy*, but you're still a guy. How can you help that? If you could change, you say, you would. You can't do anything to avoid reminding her of them. Something as simple as a word or a touch can be a trigger. The trust isn't where it was before, and despite your efforts to care for her like a bent sapling, you're rewarded with reminding her of the worst time of her life. You don't even know what you did to make her scream or cry. You just touched her arm, and that was fine last week. Sometimes she needs space and sleeps at her parents' house, somewhere safe. You're still a *good guy*, of course, but this *good guy* spends six of seven nights alone every week, lonely and clueless. The seventh night is at your place and you've waited days to lie next to your *lover* and see how she's progressed. You miss her. Do you miss her or the old her? You can't think like that, you know it. This is her now. However, on that night, when you try to pry some affection from her, you're met with tears and sobs, feeling like a villain and covered in dirt. You hug her and she cries more. You feel increasingly sad and confused. Confused, because no matter what you do, your *lover's* life was ruined by some faceless demons and you can't pull her out of the pit she's in. You empathize with this pit and don't want to force anything on her love. You're sad because you're a normal human being with needs, and at your core you're a selfish, biologically-driven animal. Now, you start feeling guilty because of the random thoughts that haphazardly dance around in your mind, such as *'How long is too long to wait to try and get back to where we were?'* and *'Sarah at work, she thinks I'm a good guy, too. She understands where I'm coming from and wants to come over and talk about it. She's so nice and pretty and smells good. I'm just so lonely.'* You *know* you're not the victim here, but begin to feel as though you are. You can't tell this to a soul. You're sickened by even having these thoughts. You're selfish and are losing love for yourself and everybody around you because you feel cornered by the situation. You just want to help her get back to where she was. *For you or for her?* Your *lover* lapses seven days later because you tried to turn spooning into sex, not even on purpose. It was your stupid body, you swear. That thing has a mind of its own. You were dreaming and didn't even want sex. No, it's not that she's unattractive to you now. She is. You tell her again and again, but add that you understand and are trying to be sympathetic to her ordeal, but are still very attracted to her. You tell her she's beautiful and that you still love her and find her sexy. No, please, she doesn't have to spend *seven* nights of *seven* at her folks' place. You can sleep back to back! Put the long pillow between the two of you. There's no more blue and brown around her cheekbones, and the stitches in both sets of her lips have dissolved. Life's rolling forward. You've learned which provoking words and actions to avoid, to stay away from her neck, and to refrain from using the word *cunt* in all its possible deployments, even about your cunt boss Mr. No-Neck being a complete cunt last Tuesday in the cunt meeting. You still haven't had so much as an open-mouthed kiss, and weird sibling-like hugs are the new-normal display of affection. You haven't felt like yourself in however long, but you can't discuss it with *your best friend*, because your best friend is also *your lover*. Who'd listen to a selfish monster like you sympathetically? Sarah does. She's such a sweet woman and a good listener. Boy, did Sarah ever look good yesterday in her pencil skirt and low-cut blouse with the red bra you can see when the sun hits just right from the southern window at 1pm. *Forget Sarah!* Please try and forget her, you scream inside your head. Life's motionless. You feel halved. Guiltier still. You've stuck around this far, though, and she says she's improving. You don't see it. Thigh pats still make her cringe, and she says that you sometimes hug her too aggressively, pushing you away with a caged tiger look in her weeping eyes. Did you decide that after the therapy ended and she started hanging out with left-wing feminists (and that one band-t-shirt-wearing guy with the hairdo that looks at her *that* way and trash talks you whenever you aren't around) that you'd invested enough time in her rehabilitation to walk away, still being a *good guy?* What's the acceptable timeframe to leave a raped woman in? you wonder. Others might've left right away, thinking it was all too much for them, for their egos, to take. You didn't, though. *Good guy* that you are. You're not like those guys. You stayed. You *will* stay. You'll see her and her recovery through until things can go back to how they were. Do you stay until *she* outgrows *you* for reasons that *you* were never in control of? She'll never not be the victim, you know. Just as you *never* can be. Even when she threatens to up and leave your stuck-in-the-past-ass because you aren't sensitive or supportive enough… 6 months, a year, or even more down the road? Are you still holding on? Every time she cries, her tears cut through you with an invisible knife, making you feel like *you* assaulted her, every time you touch her like a *lover*. Will that go away? The day may come that her tears mean nothing to you. Do you even still *love her?* Right now? The selfless, humbling, generous, sexual, lustrous, impeccable, benevolent, foundational, celestial, eternal, and outspoken *love* that you had before? Would you have even described your *love* with all those words, and more, before *it* happened? Have you been a *lover* just to be a *good guy* all this time? Have you been *lying?* To *her?* To *yourself?* You fraud. I ask again, as simple as the spikes on the sleeve of a rose, do you still *love her?* Can you still *love her?*"

"I... I..."

"You don't have to answer that because we both already know the answer. You'd better get cleaned up and ready for chow. I hear the Euskadi women boil a mean bird. I have to run myself, business never sleeps. I'll see you soon, hopefully with your *lover*, brother."

24.

I went home to throw some things into an overnight bag to take over to Marta's flat, noticing that much of my wardrobe, toiletries, and miscellanea were already at her place. I stuffed some flamboyant t-shirts and a pair of white capri pants into a maroon-leather flight bag. I paused to hate the hideousness of the clothes that I'd never normally wear, outweighed by not wanting to get bitched at. I thought about Alex's stupid rape test as I walked to the station, during the entire train ride to the centre, and up the lazy wind of Marta's staircase. For a man that hated the ordinary, regularity, and mundanity of how everyone except the rich and the deviants lived, he liked to weigh in on my life. I don't believe that having a partner limits a person, however, I didn't love or care much for Marta. There were many more factors that worked towards condemning a person to a life of abject normalcy. Alex's jabs had been low hanging fruit, even for him.

I slurped through supper nodding and agreeing with whatever Marta said. The soup was inoffensive. I was cuffed when I tried to add some salt and pepper, being told that the recipe was perfect and that my taste buds must be broken. I wanted to go for a walk around the *arrondissement* but was shot down as Marta cited a chilly wind and an increased sketchiness afflicting the area. She put on a very unenjoyable American sitcom dubbed over in Spanish as I sat on the balcony to roll a cigarette and enjoy a little pick-me-up from the moka pot. I'd poured a cup and turned off the burner. It wasn't too shabby of a system and removed all the grounds from the final cup. I'd have to steal it when I finally walked out.

I watched the street: gently kissed by the falling sun, still as busy as it was at midday. I admired the women floating ephemerally down the street. One woman wore a summer dress with tight brown curls that moved like little springs around her head. The outline of her plump backside shifted beneath her flowing dress with each step. A college-aged blond girl in large, gold-rimmed spectacles, probably not prescribed, wore no bra under a loose white shirt and high-waisted, light-wash jeans with a hole in the knee. A tall, important-looking, dark-skinned woman with a sleek glossiness on her poised face was dressed fashionably in a black shirt, black bralette, and black, cropped blazer, snapping at the concrete in black high heels and holding a black, leather clutch with peerless indifference to her admirers as though unable to see her own kind. I was hungry, and not for the soup in the fridge.

That night ended with a very poor and uninspired sexual performance on my behalf, though I deserved some credit for the successful use of a half-inflated cock. Marta asked me what was wrong, not in the most civil of ways, but out it came. I told her, save for my being attracted to every ass, tits, and smile that walked by, which seemed unnecessary and a tad gauche. She repeated that as long as we cared for each other and were willing to try, the relationship didn't have to disintegrate. I told her that we needed to spend more time apart, that spending all day at work and then all night at *her* place was devastating to both of us and didn't allow either person to be independent or do individual activities. She felt personally scathed and flew into a rage, citing her bad back, French cuisine, her sinful birth control, and her *Spanish temperament* as the culprits. She also said that she was passionate, cared for me deeply, and displayed her affection in a very normal way. Basically, I pussied out.

We spent the next few nights in our own beds, still working side-by-side during the day. Marta wasn't trying to control her *Spanish temperament,* which led to some fantastic, fiery sex that even occurred in the bathroom at work. *Au fur et à mesure,* one night of sleeping over led to two, then three, then a gift of a gaudy button-up shirt with a silken elephant print and out-of-place lamé crest on the breast that I was expected to wear in public. Marta was determined to wiggle her big bum back into my life. Being a slave to my greedy dick, I fell back into our old ways, trapped like steam in a gasket.

On one fine day off, while sitting at a cafe, the long-awaited blow up finally came. It was a banger.

We were enjoying some *bocadillos* and *horxata* on the terrace of a quaint Franco-Spanish eatery when Alex, the agent of change, happened by from behind me and placed his hand on my shoulder.

"Brother, how are you?" he twinkled beneath a fashionable pair of shiny, black-framed sunglasses.

Marta looked up at him with curiosity and contempt. She faked a smile before bending her neck down to sip at her chalky beverage.

"May I join?" he asked.

He hopped over the little fence and daintily pivoted an unused chair to sit before either of us answered. He lifted his index to the waitress, rotated it down, and pushed out his thumb to indicate that he wanted an espresso. He then flopped his packet of cigarettes onto the table. Marta grimaced at Alex. I grudgingly made the necessary introductions. Neither sought to shake the other's hand. Alex appeared to be full of more *joie de vivre* than I'd ever seen before. His movements were vivacious; his demeanour was chipper and carefree. He had the presence of man who was just happy to be there. Almost giddy.

"You must be *la Marta* that I've heard so much about?" Alex said with aggressive gaiety.

"Yes." Marta responded curtly. "It is I."

"I've heard so much about you. Much, much. It's nice that you two can be together on this beautiful day. The sun couldn't even face itself in a mirror today, it's so bright! It really brings out the gold weaving in that shirt, brother. Goddamn, that motherfucker is *bright*. What are those, tiger strips? What *is* that material? *Jesús*, you let this guy dress himself?" Alex snorted.

"No, but no," Marta stopped him with a raised palm. "I picked out his shirt. I like it, it is a Spanish designer and he always uses golden threads. It makes his muscles look nice and him more tanned. Are you not hot dressed in black? What was your name again?"

"I'm Alex," he said. "And no, this cashmere is so thin and the thread count is so high that I'd be freezing if it was any chillier. Hasn't your boyfriend told you about me? That seems strange. We've had some adventures together. Haven't we, brother? But, as far as I can tell, both your white asses need tans."

"I don't need a *tan*. I'm *Spanish*!" Marta fumed.

"I thought you were from *Euskal Herria*. Strange thing to say for one of a proud people like the Euskadi," he grinned, Chelsea-like.

"Ugh," she said with disgust. "Why are you here?"

"Thank you, darling," he said to the waitress who'd brought him his *petit café*. He lit a smoke and offered me one. "I haven't seen my good friend here for a bit… almost never, actually. You're stealing my best mate," he smile-fucked. "I was passing by and thought: 'Why not meet the lady who's been absorbing all his time?' And, wouldn't you know? I did what I wanted!" Marta grunted. Alex continued, "You don't mind me joining, do you? A quick cup and goodbye. You're *nearly finished*."

Marta shot Alex a steely eye. "*He* does not smoke around me anymore. I do not like the smell, and you should not smoke around people who do not like the smell." I pulled my hand back from the cigarette that Alex was offering me and put it on my lap.

"You know that's crazy, right?" Alex said. "You're on the terrace! You can take our buses, planes, markets, hospitals… Hell, we'll give you all indoors, but leave us the outside! I feel like I'm in an Orwell novel!" I couldn't help but snicker.

"*Oof!*" exclaimed Marta. "What's wrong with you?"

Alex began to speak to Marta in Spanish. They conversed, one coolly and one with fire. I'll let you figure out which was which. I sat sheepishly: nervous, excited, confused, intrigued, and entertained all at once. I felt like a child defying his teacher, prophesizing a strapping at home but ignoring the punishment and living in the moment.

"Your friend…" Marta broke off. "He is not kind! You should not hang out with him, you know."

"You were right," Alex said. "That Spanish temperament *is* a handful. You're a stronger man than I. I pray she fucks as good as you told me."

Marta gaped at me, appalled. "What did you tell him?"

"H'okay, h'okay," I raised my mitts, bubbling with the uncomfortable laugh that those who fake humility attempt to manufacture. "You can see why I never introduced you two…"

I was interrupted by the two speaking in Spanish once more. Marta was straining with lengthy tirades and finger-pointing, sweat coruscated on the black-brown hair of her temples and upper lip. Alex was reclined, fanning out his shirt, feigning blithe smiles, and speaking calmly.

"I'm just saying that *maybe*..." Alex switched to English, "*Maybe*, you guys rushed into things. *Maybe*, just *maybe*, had you taken it slower, there could be more happiness. For everyone, not just you."

"Do you believe this?" Marta turned to me. "What have you told him? You are happy, no? Now, yes? We are back to being happy?"

"I..."

Alex interceded. "He won't tell you the truth. He lets you walk all over him. I'm sure you're fine, but not fine enough for him."

"But I love him!" Marta interrupted. "And he loves me! He has to! We work together! I can tell our boss that he made sex with me in the WC!"

I was quiet. So was Alex. My eyebrows were above my hairline.

"Blackmail, huh?" Alex patted down his shirt, tapped his cigarette into the ashtray, and nodded vaingloriously. I observed Marta's flaring nostrils, clenched little fists, and bulldog posture leaning on the table.

The tables surrounding us were laughing and talking. The mellow Sunday energy in the air was hanging static around our triumvirate.

The tension could've been cut with a stick of warm butter. Marta was on the verge of turning over the table. Alex was on the cusp of ejaculating. I was... just kind of chilling and checking out the round-seated girl in yoga pants that had bopped into my field of vision.

"Anyways..." Alex said, "I ran into Mari and Adri the other day. Adri, in particular, wanted me to tell you that she says hi. She wants to know when she can see you again."

That did it.

Up went Marta from her spot. Her big ol' *derrière* made the patio chair squelch backwards, causing all the passers-by and patrons to turn and face us. To my surprise, she didn't make a peep. This was more than likely because she'd nicked her baby toe on the table as she'd shot up, lacerating between her ring and pinky. In the same motion, she'd knocked her white sundress against a knife covered in ketchup, leaving a carnelian smear. She limped off. I stayed seated with no control over what I wasn't even sure had happened. Alex lit a cigarette and watched Marta huff her way off the terrace, leaving little droplets of blood down the street like Hansel's breadcrumbs.

He turned to face me, chortling at my expression. It must've been hovering between amazement and fear. He passed me his lit cigarette and I screwed it between my lips.

"You're welcome," he said.

I smoked silently.

"On the plus-sized, I mean, on the plus side, she may be average, but she's far from normal." He was pleased.

The cigarette disappeared with a couple audacious drags. I had another. The ashtray was filling up quickly, like a free clinic at lunchtime.

"You should probably go do what you have to do."

I quietly excused myself, reaching for my wallet. He said it was his treat.

"You're welcome, by the way," he said heroically.

Thanks.

25.

Time to face the strap: a bombardment of screaming, silence, and random objects being thrown with furious rebuke at my head and body.

I slowed my pace to a windless drift. I didn't want to overtake Marta on my way home for fear of public wrath. Little vermillion dots were drying on the pavement, occasionally streaked as if they were brush strokes, leading a trail all the way back to the steps of Marta's apartment. They puddled at the entrance. Marta must have lost her motor skills and fumbled with her keys in her fury. I paused on the stoop before entering. I rolled, lit, and inhaled one more cigarette for good measure. Even when expecting a certain outcome, it's hard to be fully prepared for a difficult moment.

I unlocked the door with the delicacy needed to tie a knot with a piece of human hair. Marta was at the sink. She had one foot in a sandal and the other one wrapped in *my* towel like a cast. She was standing in her bra and panties with *my* toothbrush in her hand, violently scrubbing the stain on her dress.

The sun was seeping in from the half-open window in front of her. The light was bright and vivified her every bump and ridge, making every additional pound she'd gained since we'd met visible. As I looked at her body and how it'd changed, I felt guilty. I wasn't only not attracted to her, I was repulsed. Was I being vain? Shallow? It didn't matter. If I loved her, it wouldn't matter. I'd stay.

I definitely didn't. With the exception of sex and the two-sided blade of companionship, our relationship wasn't ideal for either of us. Especially not for me.

Soup was bubbling in a big pot on the stove.

"Well?!" she said without turning. "What do you have to say for yourself, asshole?"

I remained ten feet behind her, scratching the back of my head.

"Your friend, what is his name? Alex? He is the real asshole, hmm?" *Why couldn't she shut the fuck up?* "Imagine him, not knowing me, or us? Saying we are not good? Saying all that bad stuff? What an asshole."

I tried to put together a cohesive strand of words, but the likes of '*yeah,*' '*well,*' and '*I mean,*' seemed to be all I could find.

"Excuse me?" Marta snapped. She dropped her dress and pointed my toothbrush at me like a bayonet. "What are you trying to say? You agree with that *cabrón*?"

"I don't *disagree* with him… for all intents and purposes," I tapped my fingertips together.

Here we go…

"He said some things I've been thinking about." *A good start.* "I have no idea what you guys were rattling off about in Spanish, but… we fight… and fighting's something I've never really done. I know you'll say it's your '*Spanish temperament,*' but come the fuck on! That's just an excuse for someone who can't control their crazy ass when they don't get their way! You never asked me if I wanted to be with you. You guilt-tripped me into spending every night here because of the rules and status quo back in your land. We aren't there! We aren't in America either! We don't have to do anything we don't want to do! It's always your way or you start a fight. That's like abuse. I'm forced to cater to your ego, but what about me? Do you realize that you threatened to accuse me of being a sexual predator or some kind of goddamn philanderer to our boss? Are you nuts? The fact that we never really had time to get to know each other before we started fucking, and then went straight to virtually living together, is fucked up! It's not what I wanted. I like you and the sex, but I can't keep doing this."

Marta listened to my speech patiently enough, with one hand on her hip and the other leaning against the sink, still holding my toothbrush. She'd only tried to sneak in a couple times, but I'd been able to hold off her attempts like a well-guarded citadel.

"I never forced you into a relationship. It was love at first sight, like a fairy tale. My parents fight all the time. It is normal. We are both passionate people, passionate lovers, and we are both in this new place trying to be happy. I do not believe all these words you are saying. I think your friend is a bad influence! I forbid you to see him!" She paused and flipped her demeanour: "No, don't be a silly, I did not mean to threaten you. I was just saying because I was so shocked that your asshole friend would say all those things about *us*. Maybe we should start over, take it slow, and then we will be new and better. I want to be with you forever. I love you! I want to take you to Bilbao and introduce you to my friends and family." She wasn't irate or showing the anger that I'd anticipated. She was either maturing, or I wasn't conveying something properly.

"I don't know if you get it," I said. "You can't make decisions *for* me. You can't go around making these long-term plans for us when you aren't aware or don't care how I feel. You can't tell me what to do. You're fucking bossy, man."

I saw some sparks flickering in her eyes. The soup was belching. It smelled of garlic, onions, celery, and thyme. It made the stifling apartment stuffier and breathing harder.

"We can work through this." She was on the cusp of tears. "I love you!"

Then, something happened. The look in her eyes was like that of myself trying to remember the names of obscure state capitals.

"I... I don't think you have ever said that you love me."

Bismarck. Montgomery.

"You always say 'me too,' 'back at you,' 'same,' or 'thank you,' but you never say it to me first!"

Juneau. Carson City. Topeka.

"In fact, I want to hear it. Now!"

Augusta. Helena. Olympia. Lansing.

"I can't do it," I said.

"What?" she said.

Dover.

"I never loved you. Ever."

The soup broth was frothing: rattling the lidded pot, crashing against the bright red coil underneath, making a sound like a glowing iron blade being submerged into a barrel of water. My toothbrush, a towel, a tea cup, a Kafka novel, and a dinner plate were all flung at me one after the other. I dodged everything. The poor book, it deserved so much better.

I retreated out of the apartment as Marta yelled '*vaya*' mixed with other foreign language insults. A thud came from above, which I assumed was the heavy soup pot being overturned. I missed a few stairs and put too much faith in the shaky handrail mounted on ancient screws.

In the lobby, I realized that I'd left my belongings there. Could I get them? Would they survive the night? Doubtful. I couldn't remember having left anything of value. I didn't own anything of value anyway.

I pushed the door open and nearly hit someone standing on the stoop. It was Alex. He was smoking a cigarette. He held his pack towards me and edged one out with his thumb. "Have a tasty one, brother. Sounds like you could use it."

I took the salient *blonde* and lifted my face up to make eye contact with him. He lit the cigarette for me. "Pretty girls don't light their own."

"How did you know where Marta lived?" I asked.

"Your lady sprang a leak," he said. "I finished up at the cafe and had nothing pressing going on, so I wanted to see how far she'd bled for. I just arrived. I'm surprised she had enough energy to throw you out! I'd be on the couch drinking orange juice."

"Yeah." I replied. "That makes sense. She's pretty hot right now."

There were sounds of glass breaking and plates crashing overhead.

"Hey…" Alex said in a conciliatory tone. "I apologize if I was a little… strong. I didn't mean to push her that far. I wanted to say what you're a little too nice to say. When I saw you, you had the hangdog look of a man mutilated by marriage."

"It's… it's fine, actually," I said. "I didn't love the means, but the ends were honestly what I'd been wanting."

"You weren't kidding," Alex said. "She really had her hooks in. You just wanted to swim free, little minnow. It's a big ocean. You *are* welcome, by the way. Again."

"Let's move," I said. I could hear Marta sobbing from the open window above.

I suggested grabbing some beers, as it was still a splendid day despite the circumstances. Alex suggested that we head to my neighbourhood, specifically to change my clothes, or: *'The bile that Euro-trash vomits after eating too many knock-off Versace rags.'*

On the way to the metro, I stopped him and made something clear.

"I appreciate you throwing me out of the airplane, but you've got to remember that I do care about Marta and I don't want her to do anything rash. We still have to work together and maintain some kind of conviviality. I'm relieved that I'm free, and I owe you that. But, if this somehow happens again, maybe a softer approach would be in order."

"Brother. Friend. Listen to me. You had a one-way ticket to a miserable, despicably average life. You would've been stewing, resentful, and worst of all, complaining to *me*. You'd have just sat there with your dick in a vice. Marta would've overpowered you whenever you even thought about leaving and beaten you to a pulp. I did you a favour, and you should be thankful. I *will* take you up on that beer because I saved you from a penny-candy woman."

"I've learned my lesson."

"You seem to believe that you're destined for a middle-of-the-road existence: the regrettable, loathsome, and harmful state of pitiful averageness. I disagree! You're better than that. You're a decent man, but you're too soft and weak to make the right decisions. You care about the feelings of *others* when you should care about your *own* success and the outcome of *your* life. You want to settle for the mundane? Be my guest. I think you can do better. I can *help* you do better. The chains of normalcy hurt you. It's why you're so tormented. You don't understand, but it's the struggle to break them that led you to France and to me. You refuse to settle for less and you, deep down, know your worth. I know a lot of people, but I wouldn't call many of them friends. Why? Because they're hopeless. They're weak, soft like you, but too stupid, impatient, or just plain and average to be anything but hope-filled yet hope-less. You are who you are. You're a *good guy*. But, I know you could be better. When I look at you, I see promise. I see an overlooked man with a special flame in his eyes that yearns for an exciting and rewarding life. I can't stand by and watch you make choices that undermine the potential I know resides inside you. As your *friend,* I couldn't sleep if I didn't try to help you.

"Thank Alex, I…"

He still wasn't done.

"I see you adhering to principles that you've forced upon yourself, I know they aren't yours by choice. To settle, to accept instead of challenging… Why? Laws! Invisible fucking laws! Why coexist with others when you fail to do so with yourself! Where's the KGB that forces your hand to accept life as it seems? Fuck the imaginary councils and moral police who enforce their short-sighted ideals with slander and defamation. Fear no man but God, and realize that you're your own Jehovah! No man or woman can control your fate but you! Who said that you must stay with a partner out of kindness or pity? If they die of sadness, they die, but you live! Equality exists in the mind, but not in the wild! Why do we coddle the weak instead of allowing them to sink or swim?"

"You've gone a little off topic, Alex…"

"Fine. Why do you, a university graduate, a clever and handsome man, have no career opportunities and struggle to find a meaning that will never reveal itself in today's world? Why are you so frustrated that you assumed the role of steadfast partner to a fat, moody bitch of a woman? You don't think I couldn't see you eye fucking every slightly above average female that passed by?

"Did you rehearse that?" I asked. I was sure that he was done.

He tilted my head to make sure that I was looking into his eyes.

"Yes. But am I wrong?"

I wanted nothing more than to refute his claims. "Shit," I said. "No."

He reached out to shake my hand and turned it into a partial hug, like a Vikings' embrace.

"I'm proud of you," he said with a firm grasp where my shoulder and arm met. "You owe me a beer."

26.

The flow of work doesn't change based on disintegrating personal relationships and failed workplace romances. Marta's notorious temperament fluctuated between an overly sweet, clingy tenderness and ornate dismissiveness, promulgated with abrupt responses and an irregular pattern of workspace migration.

On a normal day, she started off by bringing me coffee or asking how my morning was going. If my answer wasn't to her liking, she immediately showed her discontent and became unbearably gruff, pouring the coffee into the garbage and storming off.

She adopted the sobriquet *Hurricane Marta* around the office, as she wasn't only concentrating her lack of grace and impoliteness on me and was allowing it to affect her attitude and ability to get on with fellow staff. She even snipped at Stewart on numerous occasions, brazen enough to the point that he asked me to have a word with her about her 'negative energy.'

Whenever I tried to be amicable, she petitioned for us to try again. I was using every iota of my strength not to react with flames to her fire. No matter how lightly, logically, or aloofly I responded, she persisted with the same pattern of pathetic pleading. It hardened my heart instead of allowing it to grow softer. It seemed unlikely that I'd ever reflect on our relationship and decide that the positives outweighed the negatives, but her chirping and erratic displays didn't even make me wistful when I could've be tempted to give her a late-night fuck-call.

Alex found the stories of her behaviour amusing. He said he should be my *consiglieri* from now on. He jokingly suggested ways that I could get her fired or exiled from France, if I was so inclined, and out of my life forever. I told him that she was still smart, a good worker, and a relatively nice person. I also joked that I'd let him know if the situation came to that. I was 80% sure he was joking.

Much to the staff's surprise and approval, the higher-ups decided that our morale could use a shot in the arm and we were thrown a party one Friday night after work. It was legitimately pleasurable to formally meet the various, oftentimes faceless and nameless people that surrounded me every day. Everybody spoke French and most also spoke English. Everyone had their own story; some were sending the powerful euro currency home to their poor families in tropical countries, others wished to pursue careers in translation, copyediting, and writing. They'd brought in a massive assortment of wines and spirits, some beers, and a selection of sodas and bags of potato chips for the Muslims.

Marta was being a mega-bitch before I took her aside and reminded her that we were all being rewarded for our good work. I suggested that if alcohol was exacerbating her capriciousness, maybe she should abstain or remove herself from the scene for the sake of myself and our cohorts. I was really hoping to get into the cups. It was free and there were a lot of interesting people from all over the world; an Erasmus program for the vocationally transient. I also wasn't against planting seeds for other office romances. The booze was talking. Some people never learn.

Perhaps it happened because the liquor was free and I was nowhere near the drinker that I once was back home. It could've even happened due to the fact that I'd created a quota for sex that was now backordered. In any case, I woke up in Marta's bed with a head splitter and immediate panic. Her bare buttocks were partially covered by the sheets as she lay facing away from me. My tummy was sticky and my balls were slick.

It had been unthinkable only 24, fuck, 12 hours ago.

I tried to stand up, thwarted to my ass with a bulldozing headache. I didn't even feel Marta stir. She began to kiss my bare shoulder and ask me if I wanted some water and aspirin.

"What the fuck happened?" I asked in a shaky tone, not unlike a concussed boxer still lying on the canvas.

"You were *borracho*, silly," she said. "I needed to take care of you so I brought you back here. It was late, so I started to undress you and…"

"Stop!" I broke in. "I must've been wasted. Fuck. Were you drunk, too?"

I felt her back away from my shoulders and coil defensively like a cobra. "No," she sprayed. "I stopped drinking when you said I was being *difficult*. You kept drinking and when everybody went to the club, I took you back here."

I opened my eyes and reached for my boxers with my foot. The movement of my hips made the fluids in my gut swish and swirl around. I dressed amid stumbles and nearly vomited as I bent down to draw my pants up. I threw on my shirt, unbuttoned, and tossed my socks into my pocket. Marta motioned me back to the bed. It was a comfortable, kitten-soft bed with pillows like puffy, summer clouds. She begged me to rest until I was in a more suitable condition to be in public. The acids were rising into my throat, so I swallowed both pride and bile. I declined and blurted that we'd made a mistake. Marta was on her knees with her blanket wrapped around her like a beach towel, looking at me with the contrariness of a child whose gentler parent was assenting after the stricter one had said no.

"It is destiny, you know," she said matter-of-factly. "This was no accident. People are their true selves when they drink."

"*In vino veritas*," I hiccupped and laughed. I realized how very un-sober I was. "I'm pretty sure you took advantage of me in a drunken state… I *think* women can do that to men." Give the girl a gold star for resilience.

"Where are you going?" she asked. "You are still drunk… You can stay here as long as you want. We can watch a movie and get kebab."

'No," I said. "I can't. This was bad. This didn't happen. I have to get out of here."

I fled the scene as Marta was getting worked up to launch a howitzer or two. A paperweight and a jewelry box were the two items closest to her. When dating a Spanish woman, you must make a mental catalogue of any weapons and hand-sized objects that could become projectiles. I was so acquainted with the practice that I could do it in a stupor.

I pilfered my late library book from the little circular table beside the door and fled as quickly as my rust-stiffened joints and broken computer of a brain could. I heard a faint string of foreign curse words rattle off like Kalashnikov rounds while I lumbered down the stairs, almost pulling off the handrail and taking the quick way down via summersault.

I arrived at my building two hours later after falling asleep and missing my connecting stop. I had to circle back and nearly missed my stop again, a product of my parents driving around to get me to sleep as a child, I'm sure. I checked my phone and discovered missed calls and texts from co-workers the night before. I guess I'd been frivolous in giving out my number. *Such a friendly guy.* There was also a missed call from Alex, to whom I responded on the walk back to my apartment. I embarrassingly told him what'd happened. He just responded with a brief, *I'm-not-mad-but-disappointed* message. I asked him for coffee. He declined and said that he was working.

I got home and began the process of recovering from what would be a nearly three-day hangover. I threw the book I retrieved from Marta's table on the couch and found that it wasn't my book, but a copy of *Love in the Time of Cholera* written in Marquez's native tongue.

On Monday, my co-workers were surprisingly receptive and told me that I was a fun drunk, less tense and serious than usual. They also said that they couldn't understand how I'd dated a woman like *Hurricane Marta*. I shrugged it off, not feeling any closer to my cohorts, but appreciative that my drunken self wasn't boorish nor that Marta's impertinence had been imposed on my character.

I took my late-morning cigarette break and noticed that Marta wasn't in the office yet. She was always punctual, usually early. She didn't nec- essarily *need* to be at the office so I let it slide, figuring that she might be embarrassed, angry, or wanting a few days to compose herself and organize whatever thoughts or emotions she might be dealing with. One day turned into two, three, and finally a whole week of absence. Stewart finally asked me where *my little friend* was hiding and if she was working remotely. It was out of the ordinary not to receive any texts from her. Even at her most volatile, she still catapulted insults, apologies, and sexual or emotional- ly-reminiscent texts. In any case, I was enjoying the silence. I let fire a couple of quick, work-related messages and got no response. At home, I tried a more tender-hearted approach. Still, no response.

I met up with Alex on Saturday. I explained the situation and asked if he had any idea what I should do. I did have a key for Marta's place, fig- uring that I could pop by to check in on her. Marta could still be molten, but I worried about her safety and career. Alex told me that my heart was too big and that things would sort themselves out. Perhaps she'd gone back home for a few days to clear her head.

He also asked me if I could help him move some boxes the following day. He hoped that my muscles weren't just for show, because he needed them for functional purposes. I agreed.

I returned home. I felt uneasy about how things had gone down with Marta. What if I'd broken her? I also realized that I'd finally get to see where Alex lived, one of the many questions that I'd pocketed while knowing the guy.

27.

We met at a picturesque, some might even say majestic, apartment downtown. Alex was moving some big boxes, bags, and a couple of large lamps. The décor of the apartment was bare bones. There were no pictures on the wall. The paint and possibly original Victorian wallpaper were old and yellowed owing to decades of cigarettes. There was a grandmotherly sofa wrapped in plastic. Some minor furnishings including an empty bookcase covered with dust. An expensive espresso machine sat on the kitchen counter with one cup and saucer beside it. Alex sure loved his coffee.

He thanked me graciously for my help, citing soreness as the reason he couldn't do it alone. I noticed that he was a little banged up with scratches and bite marks, but didn't say anything. That's what friends do.

The bedroom door was closed and Alex said that the plumbing was inoperative, again. This was one of many problems with old places, and the reason he was getting rid of it, preferring *one of his more comfortable lofts.*

The guy must have some kind of loot, I thought. Places like these, in the centre, were unable to be purchased or rented easily as a rule. And, they were fucking pricey. This gorgeous, multi-roomed apartment with a balcony that overlooked a park was only *one* of Alex's residences, and it appeared as if it'd never been decorated.

"Why bother having… things?" he said. "Remove the kitchen junk, the bathroom junk, the junk that you sit and sleep on… what's left? Objects of isolation that create hermits. Why stare at pictures or portraits when there are real, interesting things beyond the walls? I don't cook, and without any junk collecting dust, I don't need to clean. Minimalism is key for a man such as I. There's more to life than the things that keep you from truly enjoying it, brother."

"Yeah," I said. I huffed another solid, crammed box, using my knee to get it onto my chest and arching my back to stop from falling. "Alex, you wrapped these things like old people's suitcases… the fuck you moving?"

"Listen," he followed me with a few tripods and lights, "I call you brother because that's how I see you. I trust you. My interests… that is to say businesses, are aplenty. I never show my cards to anyone, not fully at least, and that's because one of my interests isn't exactly *legal*."

"You don't say…"

"The lights? They're hydroponic lamps. The bags and boxes are drugs and growing equipment. That's the bedrock of my wealth and reason for secrecy. I'm sorry if this seems dishonest and downright illegal to you, but people will always do drugs and it's easy money. Shit, in another country not far from here it's as legal as coffee and croissants. You know the corners, but you can't know the shape. It's best for you if we keep it that way. Trust me. You're not in any trouble. You've met my friend and silent partner, Bruno. He wouldn't allow anyone to try anything cute."

"Uh-huh," I said. "Can't say I'm shocked."

His involvement in the drug trade didn't surprise me. It was one of my theories. Alex worked weird hours, always had a lumpy bankroll and designer everything, and was on a first-name basis with scumbags and villains.

"Does it bother you?" he asked.

"I don't care. Your stance on drugs makes sense, I guess. I'm pretty liberal. If someone wants to poison themselves, who am I to say no? I'm not anyone's daddy."

He smiled. I nodded. It was nice to know something of substance about the guy.

We finished loading the snub-nosed moving truck. I declined a ride home. I wanted to stop by Marta's apartment and see if she was alright. It was Sunday and I hadn't heard from her in over a week.

"I wouldn't," he said. "Stop tormenting the poor girl."

"I'm not and I have to. I feel guilty."

"Your heart's far too large," he said. "I don't understand you, but I cherish you, like a mongoloid child handling shells on a beach."

"Thanks?"

"Wait, I have a little present for you, brother!" Alex reached into the cab and opened up a black leather messenger bag. He took a smaller bag out of it, which contained a Dopp kit: tan leather with a bronze zipper.

"Shaving cup, bar, and brush, just add water…" he said as he held each item. "Aftershave to seal any cuts and starch away any wrinkles. Some pomade to hold down those *alfalfas*. A comb, and this…"

He removed a sleek, wood and metal, banana-shaped object.

"What's that?" I asked. It was the same shape as a pocket knife. Smooth and polished.

"This…" he said, "will be the key to you transforming into an *even better* version of yourself." The object went *snikt* and divulged a stunning blade. "They've tried and tried but never ameliorated the original design," he stared at it like a beaker full of mercury. "I'll bring over a leather strap and teach you how to shave, how to *really* shave, like your papa should have. You can unburden yourself of that scraggly cheek fur and even out those dreadful sideburns *if* you insist on keeping them. We'll also clean up those brows before they decide to get married."

I thanked him and kept the razor out. I withdrew and sheathed it several times with my thumb. *Snikt, snikt.*

I arrived at Marta's as the sky was beginning to mutate from azure into charcoal. It was humid but pleasant. Marta's neighbourhood was buzzing with affable chatter and the clinking of glasses. The damp glow of patio lights blended with the drowsy sun. I tried texting her again and rang the buzzer before letting myself in.

"Marta?" I spoke in a docile tone in case she was cutting vegetables or sharpening a mop handle into an arrowhead. Nothing. I fully dunked myself into the breezy, open room, only to find it vacant. I said Marta's name again and crept cat-like around the apartment. Nothing. The bed wasn't made and all the windows were wide open. Nary a Basque woman in sight. I leafed through some papers to find my novel and left as I'd entered.

As I walked towards the metro, I received a text from Marta. She thanked me for my concern and said that all was well. She'd returned to Bilbao hastily because her grandfather was dying of cancer. He'd been terminally ill for the entire time that I'd known her, but her family had sensed that his final days were upon him. She was needed. She apologized for not letting work know, but had been swept up in a current of emotions related to her grandfather, and me, hitting her like one big tidal wave. She was angry and processing everything. I wished her solace and let her know that I was here if she needed anything. She thanked me curtly, then later responded with an upswing of tenderness. We kept in contact throughout the week. I explained the situation to Stewart, who now had to find a replacement. He was cross, but nothing a bottle of Chablis couldn't mend. A week or two later, Marta told me that she wouldn't be returning and would get in touch with her landlord. She said that there wasn't anything for her in Paris other than sadness. She'd also met a boy, and explained he'd been a source of stability and love that I hadn't had the *cojones* to provide her with. It was all very fair. By the time we stopped messaging each other, I was almost sorrowful, a state she'd refused to let me earn while she was still here. Technically, I'd been gifted the easy way out that I'd desired, but the result was that there was one less person who loved me in the lonely world that I'd created for myself.

28.

Now that I understood why Alex was often tied up with secretive engagements, I understood why he'd always had me meet him at Wing Café. That shithole never grew on me. However, he made good on his promise; he came over every day before 7am to teach me how to shave with a straight razor. He cleaned up my neck and jawline and slapped me with searing aftershave alcohols, nasal-clearing quinine powders, and soothing balms. He found it amusing when I held the blade too acutely and spilled my blood in the sink. He also brought me other gifts like clothes and cologne. He was softening, less automaton. *He might be human after all.*

Back at the translation quarry, there was still much stone to break. The sounds of hammers and chains refused to yield. The Spanish-language replacement for Marta was a gazelle-like creature from the southern province of Malaga named Enrique, or *Riqui*. He was willowy and windswept with a work ethic tantamount to a cactus and happened to be sleeping with the boss. He was Stewart's adrenalized hire, quickly becoming his boyfriend after he spent the first week dazedly revelling at Riqui's lissome equinity and glossy, Moorish-black mane. By his second week, Stewart requested that Riqui work *directly under him*. By the third week, he was saying shit like '*Two of a kind, you and me. What is it about these Spaniards?*' and, '*I love the Iberian's peninsula.*' Winks were abound with every unctuous, suggestive phrase.

Towards the end of the summer, I asked Alex to take me out again. We always met up at my place, Wing's, or some other cafe. The summer was now walking alongside its horse, each night darkening quicker than the last. Enough time had passed since Bruno's and 'we' had become a daily ritual. My condition was that there were to be no whores, pimps, pushers, or hoodlums. No grimy or violent souls, just nice people. Alex said that there was no way to magically determine who was a criminal, lowlife, junkie, or even murderer and who wasn't, but that he'd do his best to keep it *classy*. He also said that he'd just wanted to show me the grittier side of Paris on our previous excursion and that our trip to Bruno's shouldn't represent his tastes overall.

"Maybe you invite Adriana?" I asked.

"It might not be the best time… for you or her…" he responded quickly.

I organized our *rendez-vous* at a harmless location. Somewhere close to work that I was certain was hooker-free. It seemed baffling that that was our *sine qua non*, but alas…

I chose a cocktail bar that I'd walked by countless times, always saying I'd try it someday. I arrived early and sat at the bar.

The bartender was a toothsome woman: blonde, green eyes, and a sleeve of tattoos on her right arm. She was slender, but not without curves. She wore a tight, midriff-baring shirt with no bra that accentuated her flat stomach and handful-sized breasts. Her golden hair was pulled back into a functional ponytail and her smooth forehead was delimited by her well-plucked, medium-sized, darker-than-her-hair, soft-angled eyebrows. She had giant, deep emeralds on each side of her powerful, long-bridged nose, prominent cheekbones, and a wide mouth shaded with matte red lipstick. The corners of her lips met perfect, symmetrical dimples. She was good-natured and nimble-spirited, but I was nervous to sit in front of her idly. I didn't want to stare, but couldn't look away. She began to disarm me with conversation: where I was from, where I was going, what I did for work.

Obviously a skilled bartender and charmer. I returned each question with one of my own.

Her name was Emiliana, and she'd moved to Paris from Berlin.

I tried to make a joke about which side of the fence she'd been born on, but quickly changed my half-cocked attempt to ask what had brought her to Paris.

"I came here to practice French. I fell in love with the place. My father always said that France was full of cowards and liars, but he didn't say that it was so exciting. There are enough Germans here to start another country, so the French part isn't coming along so great... I took hospitality in university and would like to open a restaurant, maybe a hotel. I don't know yet... maybe back home, or somewhere else." She was sultry and spoke with velvet bubbles. I froze every time she flickered her long lashes, drowning me with her piercing eyes.

"The adventurous type?" I asked. "Have you travelled much?" I was nailing the perfect first date questions. We suffered constant interruptions from rushes of new orders as the bar was filling up. She glanced at me as I watched her receiving chits and preparing drinks. The cocktails required a variety of tinctures, apothecary bottles, and even an old, Oscar de la Renta-styled *eau de toilette* atomizer. I was hoping to be stood up by Alex. I was currently finding everything good in the world in Emiliana's widely-set eyes. They gave the impression that she cared about whatever boring thing I said or shitty pun I made.

Alex *did* come, wearing black with a black leather courier bag over his shoulder. He *did* tear me away from the stool that I could've sat on for the rest of my life. He also noticed my ardent gazing.

"You don't want a bartender, man. Sure, she's kind of cute, in a Russian way, but don't fuck the help."

We had another drink in the corner of the bar. Alex said that he had his sights set on a *boite* a few lengths away. I told him I just needed to settle the bill, wanting one more chance to admire the beauty of the bartender. I approached the *frau* and asked for the bill.

"The drinks are on me tonight." She paused, biting her bottom lip and nearly taking me out. "That is, if you come back another day. It got busy and I wanted to spend more time talking to you."

I played it off like she was just building up her clientele, but it worked. I agreed and laid down a 20 euro note. I turned to walk away, then laid another 20.

"No, you don't have to," she contested.

I refused to take the money back.

"You said that you work just down the street. I'll be insulted if you don't come back. Maybe I'll hunt you down."

I blushed.

Germans. I could never truly tell if they were the most serious or the most dryly funny people on the planet.

"I promise, next week after work," I said, forcing the words out of my nerve-constricted oesophagus, also trying not to go too far the other way and scream in her face. "I'll see you in a few days, Emiliana."

I drew out my hand.

"Emi,' she said smiling.

I blushed and turned to meet Alex outside.

29.

"Are you wearing that?" Alex asked me with condescending venom as we strode onto the street.

"This?" I asked, looking down at my harmless button-up shirt and dark-wash jean ensemble.

"Yeah." He grunted. "*That.*"

I paused with a look of incertitude.

"Well, I didn't bring a change of clothes, and these aren't from the Marta summer collection. I thought…"

"It's okay, brother. I came prepared for this," he said. He unshouldered his bag. "Step into the alleyway."

We made a quick turn into a darkened alleyway. Charming.

"Strip," he said, pulling some clothes, still with their price tags, from his bag. "Put these on. They should be your size." He had shoes in his tote as well. "Shoes and boxers too!" He flung a microfiber, European cut pair of black underwear at me.

"Boxers too?" I moaned.

"Of course," he said resolutely.

I turned to expose my bare ass to the street, starting with the boxers, one sock, the other sock, pants, shirt, and then shoes.

"What about my stuff?" I asked with a pleading tone.

"It goes in the bag," he replied. "And, the bag goes in the trash. There might be a bum with a mildly better get-up tomorrow morning."

I was surprised that he actually tossed the bag. It was a lovely composition of leather and buckles. I had to admit, however, that the clothes were an upgrade and fit perfectly.

"You paid 300 euros for a shirt?!" I exclaimed.

He snatched the tag off. "On the cheaper side."

"Jesus."

"You're welcome," he said.

Alex didn't like sitting at the bar and hated overly-crowded communal areas. At the door, he flashed bank notes to grant us preferential treatment, like royalty, and offered bottles of whatever flat or bubbly elixirs that we wanted.

The irony was that we detached ourselves from women, but ended up inviting their curiosity at a greater rate than I'd ever done mingling with them on the dancefloor or offering to buy them drinks amidst the throng.

Alex could pick up a girl outside the club, queued for the washroom, or with a finger from across the room. *Even the staff.* It was so easy for him. A quick squinting of his eyes, a slight purse of his lips, and a perfunctory head nod had a girl tugging at his arm. He'd pick up one girl and drop another. He'd pick up three girls, add a fourth, and then drop them all. He'd insult women to their faces to see how much they could stand, then let them walk. He'd apologize to them, get them back, and do it all over again. You can only squander the gifts you have, I suppose. I was constantly embarrassed and confused by the tragicomedy happening around me.

Alex said that he had high standards and that people were beyond replaceable at discos. He continued to buy women drinks, send them away, bring them back, berate them, kiss them, touch them, and send them away again. He was like a woman himself.

To say that we bounced around was an understatement. We moved to so many different locales that I struggled to maintain a buzz and not get drowsy. Alex had a flask that seemed to energize him after each secretive pull. I was getting unnerved with him and his consistent disrespect and dismissiveness. I just wanted to get laid and he was wrenching the gears something fierce. We wouldn't have to relocate so often if he could stop his teasing, like an eight-year-old with more money and malice. Wherever we went, be it a dance music club, a moodier chamber setting, or a sophisticated lounge, Alex garnered attention.

At a quieter location, the second to last, he was buried in the cups.

"Women," he said, "are below objects."

He was wasted.

Two women sitting beside us had been gradually inching closer for the past half-hour. They made a repulsed look, then inched a little closer.

"It's just so easy for me, you know?"

"No," I said.

"They fall for me so quickly. They fall for pointless reasons, money, and looks. It's so immature... How can I respect that?"

"How sad for you," I said.

I wasn't sad. The girls beside us leaned in to listen.

"They're nothing but leaflets from those annoying flier kids. Do you know where fliers accumulate? The trash. Little colourful squares announcing some bar's specials, heaped around garbage cans like moths that never reached the light."

"Oh, you're a poet now?" I said. I took a big gulp of my drink and smiled nervously at the girls beside me.

"Hello, garbage," Alex said to the girls.

They left.

"Why?" I said with utter bewilderment.

"I... I'm sorry. I don't know why. I don't *hate* women. No more than men or anything else, I guess. Person-to-person basis."

"It's fine."

"No... I'm letting my prejudice get in the way of your dick. I'm a drunk light-weight because I rarely get to enjoy the drink. Must be the company I keep."

"Really, it's fine. You're funding the night... Just try to keep it chill, you know?"

"You got it," he said as he finished a glass of champagne.

The flute exploded into crystal shards against the brick wall beside us after it suddenly left Alex's fingers. He flopped a few of those ridiculously-sized 500 euro notes onto the table and we made our exit. I apologized profusely to the server. The older, tuxedo-wearing barman shook his portly, bald head behind the lacquer-finished wood.

30.

I didn't speak to Alex on the way to our final destination other than snidely telling him to slow down on grandpa's cough medicine. I also asked how he was able to bring an outside container into every place we visited.

"You give the doormen enough money and you can walk in with flip-flops and a fucking bazooka, brother," was his response. "I'm putting their Algerian, half-breed bastards through football camp."

Despite my concerns, Alex pulled it together for the duration of our visit to a loud, boisterous disco full of tall, statuesque people with outfits the price of mortgages. Perhaps he finally felt like he was around his equals. Perhaps he knew the owners and respected them. Either way, I finally got drunk.

Soon, he and I were on the dancefloor with some model-types whose legs started at my chest. Cocaine was the currency at *this* bar. Everyone was sniffling and sweating their makeup and hair products onto their greasy shoulder blades. Alex disappeared periodically. I didn't have to ask where he was going. He came back with his eyes more blood shot and his dancing more aggressive each time. He was recklessly spinning girls around, biting their necks, lighting cigarettes on the dance floor, burning hair and exposed skin around him, and knocking people off balance. The bouncers said '*put that out!*' and '*settle down, sir,*' but made no moves to abrogate his savagery.

We eventually stole away to a booth with four women. Alex ordered two magnums of gold-bottled champagne, two bottles of steeply-priced vodka, two tins of caviar served on ice with an overlapping, circular spread of blinis, and a box of Cuban cigars. I had no idea that nightclubs even carried that shit. I also couldn't tell the difference between a 500 euro bottle of vodka and a 15 euro bottle of vodka. It all tasted like hairspray.

"Careful of caviar stains!" Alex roared in the booth, a girl under each arm. We had four female guests: two Americans, one Brazilian, and one Lithuanian. They were models who travelled together and had been shooting in Ibiza, Malta, Dalmatia, Oludeniz, and most recently in the south of France. Paris was their headquarters, with frequent sojourns to London and Milan.

The Brazilian was the biggest partier. She was unable to sit still, going from glass to cocaine to caviar to dancefloor, then back to the booth to restart the cycle. The Americans didn't seem to like one another, though both were nearly-identical copies in dress and appearance. One was from California and used words like *woke* and *wanderlust* to describe herself. The second, originally from Connecticut and now calling Manhattan her home, was a feminist who was *only* modeling to earn money for philanthropic purposes. I couldn't tell what their rivalry was based on, but it seemed that each one thought that the other was pretentious, hollow, and did too many drugs. Each would wing criticisms when the other one left the table while placing a rolled bill to a line of powder, fine as ground ivory.

The Lithuanian was either coked-out or overwhelmed by the experience. Maybe both. She had a pointy face softened with satiny skin. Her timidity made her seem much younger than her friends, who themselves couldn't have been older than 21. She fiddled with her hands, crossed and uncrossed her legs, tousled her hair, and flicked at her nose compulsively. She'd reach for a blini, smear it with caviar, and then put it down with a look of melancholy. She said that back home in her village this would all be unheard of. Rabbit and eel over rye bread were the finest dishes she'd previously known. Alex sat between the two Americans, amused by their proliferating snippiness, trying to push the passive aggression beyond its simmer to a full boil, and accidentally burning their shoulders with a stogie hanging from his mouth, Castro-like. I was listening to the Lithuanian's ramblings about her homeland: growing up in a tin-roofed shack in some village, how she'd been discovered, and why she *had* to become a famous model to make sure the kids in her village could all learn to read and write. The American women interjected that they *hoped to also* use *their* platform to change the world and *also* 'learn kids to read.' The Brazilian was deep in the powder. She had a cigar burn on her short, blue dress and was grinding her teeth so hard, I swear, she was trying to get rid of them. She imposed herself beside the Lithuanian, forced the booth to shuffle, and poured herself a glass of champagne. It was all foam due to her shaking hands, also spilling a glass-worth on the table.

"What's that?" asked the Lithuanian, touching the Brazilian's thigh with two fingers. She brought them up to the light and rubbed some substance between her fingers.

"Probably cum," the Brazilian responded without thinking, focusing on the oversized champagne bottle. "I gave some guy a hand job on the dancefloor. He couldn't hold it in. Probably got some on me."

The Lithuanian's horrified expression, Alex's head-thrown-back, riotous laughter, and the Americans' dismayed head shaking left me looking rather indifferent. The Lithuanian pushed herself over the Brazilian to go to the bathroom, closely followed by the Americans. After slamming the glass and the rest of the champagne out of the bottle, snorting a line of caviar and a line of coke, then lapping up some of the spilled champagne, the Brazilian trailed after them.

"Which one do you want?" Alex looked at me.

"Do I want…?" I looked at Alex's unchanging face under the alternating pink, purple, and blue stage lights. "I wasn't getting a vibe from any of them really, if I'm being honest."

Alex puffed at his cigar, removed it, and leaned in. "Vibe? Nonsense, brother. These girls created a debt for themselves that they already know how they'll pay. *This* is how it works." Alex placed his cigar back into his mouth. "Just pick the ripest, lowest-hanging peach…"

I frowned, gripping my rocks glass of premium vodka that was glowing bluish in the dancing lights.

"What is it?" Alex stared at me. "You *don't* like beautiful models. You *don't* like the highest class of escorts. You prefer Soviet barmaids and bossy, fat wogs? Here's a pearl for you: this is what it's really like! This is how it's supposed to be. That organic, boy-meets-girl bullshit? It's a fairy tale. It's nonsense that's spoon-fed to regular people, like Jesus fables and meritocracy. The world's give and take… dollars and cents. *Sex is always a transaction.* To get the right woman, whether a model, hooker, doctor, or whatever, you always pay. Maybe money, maybe cocaine, maybe dinner and a movie… it all leads to the same thing in the end. If the roles were reversed, they'd be inviting us to a table to eat salty fish eggs and drink gaseous, fermented grape juice. These are just the roles we were born into. It's nature. Don't fight it and don't be a faggot."

The girls returned with their clutches and handbags. Alex turned and smiled, biting on his stogie. The Americans slid back in as the Californian was finishing a conversation with the New Yorker.

"I don't know why! I wear glasses! Not prescribed, but I have frames. I like to play video games sometimes. I'm such a *nerd*, ha-ha. I can't ever find a guy who gets how complex I am, you know? I just want a nice guy who's the *same* way and has the *same* interests as me!"

The Brazilian looked even more disheveled, somehow. Lipstick was streaked across her mocha-coloured cheek like a Nike check. There was a wet spot on her dress where she must've tried to scrub off the semen. She hopped in the booth beside me and started to suck on my neck, full-power. I pushed her off and laughed forcedly. I looked into her vacant, unfocused eyes. Her nose hairs were a salt mine.

The Lithuanian remained standing at the front of the table shyly, her arms shaping the number four with her right hand innocuously rubbing her left forearm. Alex said something to the Lithuanian in what must've been Russian. She nodded meekly.

He turned to me. "I know a little after-hours place… We should take the girls there. Aside from that Brazilian who seems pretty keen on sleeping in a dumpster, we could start to wind down a bit."

He whispered to the Americans. I looked at the dazed Brazilian, her head rollicking in a circular pattern. She was moving her hand up the inside of her remarkably taut, striated thigh to her panties. Alex leaned over to address the Americans, who seemed to be in agreement with him.

'Sounds exclusive!' said the New Yorker.

'I hope they have Molly,' went the Californian.

I popped myself over the Brazilian like an airplane seat, batted her hand from my crotch, and spoke into the ear of the Lithuanian. I asked if she was having a good time and if she was coming.

"Kind of. I'm a little tired and it's a bit much, all of this… It'll be nice to find some place quieter," she peeped.

We exited the club and lost the Brazilian within a block.

"Fucking Carol," said the Manhattanite. "She always fucking does this. She gives *women* a bad name."

"At least she didn't ask you to take her panties this time," joked the Californian as she rubbed her reddened nose, sniffled, and accepted a cigarette from Alex. "I swear that when I go back home, I'm done with cigarettes. Ugh, I'm so *French* right now." She laughed twice in two identical, rounded tones.

The New Yorker also took a cigarette and echoed her sentiments, saying that Manhattan was so health-obsessed and that she'd be ostracized from her gym if she smoked. The American girls, who Alex was now calling the *Yanks,* walked with their arms laced around his. All three were tall, angular, and well-built specimens. They were talking about how difficult it was being fettered with the titles of influencer, model, *and* enlightenment-seeker, not being understood by most people outside of their sphere, what they'd do when they were done with this phase of their lives, and which photographers they'd fucked.

"It's *totally* feminist," the model from Manhattan said about modeling. "We're expressing our femininity! We're like Tubman or Parks, who are both serious role-models to me. My dad said that he'd pay for me to have an article in the *New Yorker* when I get back home."

"Oh, amazing," Alex said. "I *love* reading opinion pieces by rich white kids funded by their rich white fathers. It's always *such* a refreshing take."

I sensed his patience drying up as his responses became increasingly belittling, like he'd done earlier in the night with other women.

The Americans started speaking about people's rights to label and define themselves. One of them said something about transgender people.

"Choosing your gender, is like, a right. A human right. Everyone should get to be whatever they want," the Manhattanite said.

"I agree," Alex said. "I have no problem with men wanting to be women and vice versa. I don't give a shit. It doesn't affect me. It's very much a class and race specific issue, anyways. Poor people and coloured folk can't afford those thoughts. They have to focus on surviving. Anyways, if you can remain productive and participate within the social climate, cool. If you want to try and change the climate because it's stuck in the past, great. Whatever. Fuck whoever you want with whatever set of genitals you want."

"Wow!" the Californian said, "You're, like, so woke..."

"But!" Alex cut in. "Where do you draw the line? An elf? A watercress? A Polack? Come the fuck on. That's insulting."

"*You* can be whatever *you* want," the Manhattanite said.

"Maybe I'm a wolf! A motherfucking alpha wolf. *That's* how I see myself. So, you're telling me that's okay with you? If I decide to go *all teeth* and pick off the weakest of the herd, feed on the blood of lost children, and howl breathlessly at the moon? What if it's dangerous to others, or myself? Isn't eating people illegal?"

"What...? N-...That's... just... no... sex changes..." the Californian started.

"It *might* be a sign of mental illness! *Maybe* God just made a few mistakes. I don't know, or care. Who gives a fuck? Do with your body what you will; hack it and sew it up until you look like a ragdoll. Be my guest, it's your property. But if you're telling me that it's okay to let people who can't face life head-on make believe that they're frogs or goblins? Let them preach about it, shoehorning their narcissism and what might be a phase into the public's concern and demand respect and attention? That's fucking asinine. Why do *I* have to believe something because you, or anyone, says so? They're not me and I'm not them. We don't know each other's stories, and neither of us gives a fuck beyond our own cause. I don't have to recognize your sickness and you don't have to recognize my alpha-syndrome. Be sick, just don't beg for my pity. Do whatever you want and don't blame anyone else for it. First off, why not figure out *why* you're trying to be something you're not? Think of it, define it, and then repeat it back. Ask yourself: Am I insane? Or, am I too weak or sheltered or immature or mentally underequipped to deal with life like an adult?"

One of the Americans responded. "Well, I don't know about that... but all I was trying to say was..."

They were loud, but easy enough to ignore. I was a few paces ahead with the Lithuanian, Lina, who I was beginning to feel pity for. Her maximum 95-pound frame was addling from the drug and drink, producing a timbre of desperation and paranoia in her tone and comportment. She told me that she'd been recruited to model very young as she'd hit puberty very early. Since being taken from her village, she'd been tutored in English, French, and Spanish and learned mathematics and some minor science lessons, but mostly had been trained how to pose and look beautiful. She *was* very beautiful. Her complexion was milky with astonishing bone structure. She had arresting features: almond-shaped, tear-coloured eyes and oversized lips that looked like they'd explode with cherry cordial if pricked. She had near perfect teeth with a slight gap in the middle, lending a touch of uniqueness to enhance her beauty. She was as compact as a gymnast, slender and pert. She stood out from the Americans, identical yet constantly insisting how individualistic they were.

"That sounds like a pretty tough life," I said to Lina with a tone that showcased my inability to decide whether or not I was telling the truth. "Though, it sounds like you won the lottery in some respects."

She paused and thought. "In some ways, yes. My family, my village, and much of my country is very poor. The other girls have rich parents in their countries. They can go back to their homelands, go to school, and rely on their families for help. They don't need to worry about money, ever. I can't do that. So, I smile and look nice and pose and drink champagne and do cocaine and have sex with people so that I can keep making money." She paused again. "I guess I'm lucky, but what happens when I turn 20? Maybe I'll start getting less attractive..."

I responded gallantly. "There's no way you'll ever not be attractive, and you've already got a work ethic and the desire to be something better. You can do anything you want. The doors are open for you, just make sure that you take advantage of your situation and work for what's really important. And save your money."

She cuddled up closer to my shoulder and I heard her exhalations, deep and steady. Her little ribcage was like a swallow's when in song. She was calming down. I realized that she was looking at *20 years old* as a far-off age and point of decline. I had to ask...

"Lina, how old are..."

"Really!" Alex's voice boomed with bellicosity. "You think THAT is cute?"

My attention was commandeered by the truculence in Alex's growl.

"It is! Look at them, they're in *love*," the Californian retorted dreamily, hand on her heart.

"Brother, are you getting this shit? *This* fucking hippie thinks that *this* puddle of filth, this homeless man and woman spooning in the middle of the goddamn sidewalk, is *romantic!*" Alex yelled at me from fifteen yards down the street.

"You don't have to fucking embarrass her, you asshole," said the New Yorker with indignation.

"Easy there, girl. Wipe your nose off," Alex oozed smugly.

"We're all God's creatures, and these two have found each other. It's beautiful," the Californian reasoned with conviction.

"Beautiful?" Alex asked. "What does that make you? Garbage? Or just an Idiot?"

"Uh-oh," I said. I dragged Lina back towards the conflict. The American girls were standing with their arms crossed, facing Alex.

"You're right and I'm wrong," Alex mocked. "It's a *beautiful* thing that two pieces of garbage are making one heap of refuse that the trash men can take to the incinerator in the morning."

Lina was confused. The Americans were irate. The Brazilian, Carol, suddenly strode up to the group: "Where'd you guys go? I met some cute guys that want to take our picture," she disgorged sloppily. Alex laughed and I felt numb with bewilderment.

"Goddamn it, Carol. Every fucking time," said the New Yorker with vexation. "I can't *fucking* even."

Alex looked over his shoulder and shot a malignant grin at me, a grin with evil sown deeper than the juvenile rings of an ancient redwood. "Ha-ha, this *bitch* can't even." I could tell that he'd chosen his words to cut, to slice deep into the Americans, especially the uppity Manhattanite.

"Excuse me?" said the New Yorker. "You didn't just use the word I thought you did, did you?"

Alex curled his lips and nodded. "You know I did, and I can say it again if you'd like. You sun-bleached, opportunities-for-no-reason *bitch*."

Alex always contended that the word *bitch* was this generation's *nigger*, a word that's now socially anachronistic and a relic of a less conscious time. If you were entangled with anyone who identified as the least bit as a feminist, that was the word with which to start a fracas. Of course, the same woman who despises the hegemony and the history behind the word calls her friends *bitch* as a term of endearment, and allows *bitch* and other terms to be employed during rough sexual melees. *Nigger* was still the worst. You don't use that during sex.

The Americans, especially the girl from New York, took fantastic offence to the remark and began to scream in Alex's face. Alex, ever the humane character, laughed and offered them a cigarette. He said that they should wipe their noses lest they look more like strung out crack whores in nicer clothes.

He then turned and laid a soccer-style kick into the spine of the sleeping homeless man, who hadn't stirred during the commotion. The girls shrieked, so he did it again. And again. After the third or fourth leather shoe hit the squirming homeless man's back, I relinquished Lina's stiff grasp and swung Alex 180 degrees. The Brazilian was laughing and the Americans were gasping profanities and attempting to impart boney fists and hardy manicures onto Alex. Lina remained in her shy pose with her face pointed down. Alex relaxed, so I let him go. He reached into his pocket and shed a number of 100 euro notes onto the sleeping homeless couple.

"There," he said. "That fucking better?"

"Fuck the both of you!" said the New Yorker. The Californian stood with a traumatized expression by her side. "You fucking psychopath! To think, we were going to go with you… Come on Lina, let's go."

Lina looked up at me for an answer. I didn't have much in the way of consolation or alternatives, having been quite surprised by Alex's actions myself.

"Don't look at him, Lina. You're *our* responsibility. Did you even tell him how old you are?" I had a bad feeling, but she couldn't have been that young or she wouldn't have been allowed into the club, right?

"She's 16, you fucking pervert," said the New Yorker with enmity.

I felt disemboweled.

"You judge? You bring a child to get coked out at a nightclub?" Alex said lasciviously as he tried to punt the homeless man again. I quickly grabbed him by the shoulder. He didn't connect.

"Animal," snarled the Californian as she pulled Lina away, nearly snapping her heel from the strength she had to use. Lina kept eye contact with me as she left.

"Nice to meet you, *Yanks!*" Alex hollered jovially. "You still want to party?" he asked the Brazilian, who was still there.

"Let's go!" Carol pointed down the street.

I swung Alex around. "What the fuck, man? Again? What's wrong with you?"

Alex shrugged me off. "Brother, those women, girls rather, were idiots. And it looks like I saved you from yourself. 16, though not illegal, might be too young for a *sensitive* man like yourself."

Carol snickered.

"Why'd you kick that guy?" I demanded.

"To prove a point," he responded.

"Which is?"

"That those girls were pathetic… *'Oh, look at me, I'm beautiful and have strong opinions and want to be taken seriously and have no idea how things really work and don't pay for shit ever and have a rich family that'll make sure that I'm never wanting and could very well end up a diplomat because that's the way the world is going and would take a handout from the Devil himself if it meant having more people like me and recognize me for my brain as well as my beauty and…'"*

"Kill it, man. You're just making assumptions and you sound like a fucking… I don't even know what."

"No," interjected a messy Carol. "He's absolutely, one hundred percent, nail the hammer on the head, bang on…"

I shook my head as she lost steam. "I just wanted a chill night and to meet some nice women." I was tired and exasperated.

"And we did. Well, you met a middle-schooler, technically speaking," Alex smirked.

"You're a psychopath, man… You're insane," I sighed.

"Whoa, brother, whoa," Alex said with his hands up. "I won't ask you to take that back, but let it be known that looks aren't everything. *They're a lot*, but not the whole package. I'm not insane… I'm irrevocably, sometimes inconveniently, and maybe even reprehensibly, *sane*. I'm worse, the worst thing for these snowflakes: I'm honest. I see through the bullshit and don't bite my tongue, no matter how beautiful or famous or important the person is or thinks they are. I was going to fuck both of those women, and we could've gone straight to a place to do just that, but, they were just so..."

"Pretentious!" belched Carol defiantly.

"Exactly, my dear. Nailed the hammer on the head, as you say," Alex said as he pinched her chin as though he was her grandfather. "*You* can't judge character. Don't blame me, brother."

I was tired, drunk, and way past the point of wishing to argue discursively with a coked-up Alex whose blood was lava and jaw was a bear trap.

"The wonderful thing about Paris..." Alex began, "is that if one was so inclined, he'd never have to stop partying. It might outclass or outprice the average proletariat, but we can continue in this vein for days. Let's move!"

The homeless man wriggled and shifted uncomfortably.

"This piece of shit is lucky I didn't stomp him and his bitch to death," Alex said with diminishing rancor.

"We're human, too," the homeless man trembled beneath a wool blanket.

Alex turned. He crouched down and whispered to the man: "You're *barely* human. You smell like shit. See you in hell, motherfucker."

Carol grinned. "We have many people like this in Rio. They have whole cities, *favelas*. Millions of people live there. They are disgusting, filthy places." Alex shuddered with antipathy.

The booze was leaving my system at an incredible rate as we walked, causing me to question my motives, the hour, and if I really wanted to be out at these profitable sleeping hours.

"Take a sip! It'll put some shark back in you" Alex unscrewed his flask. I tilted my head back. "Hey, hey, just a little one! This shit could put down an elephant! Don't want *too* much shark in you."

It tasted bitter and salty. Its oily texture left my mouth dry and mealy. It slicked through my organs like quicksilver. I could've thrown it right back up, but kept swallowing it minutes after my sip.

I began to wobble and stumble. I watched my feet scrape beneath me, barely lifting from the pavement. Blocks of nondescript, brick buildings panned by in a darkish brown blur. Barely a soul was lurking on the streets. There was sparse lamp light, patches of pitch-black... *Kids with stones,* I thought, or Alex said. I burped, a taste worse than fish oil, but couldn't throw up. Carol and Alex were tripping over each other clumsily, grabbing cock and fingering pussy, kissing and sucking mouths. Alex whipped Carol's tit out and clamped his teeth around the areola to her giddy cachinnation.

The last solid thing I remember was a group of men, probably younger, outnumbering us by at least double. They demanded our wallets, cell phones, jewelry, and even clothes.

"Strip!" yelled one, brandishing something in his hand.

"Don't make us fuck you up!" yelled another one with a black hoodie and shadowed face.

Carol screamed and clopped off out of sight. Her heel tapping became soundless, either from her losing her footwear or having fallen down.

"No," Alex said firmly.

They whispered amongst themselves before one emerged, saying: *"Don't make us stick you, pretty boy."*

My fragmented senses were squirming, but somehow pooling into a voice that was telling me to give up my cash and plead for safety.

Alex took a step forward. He put his hand to the small of his back under his sport coat.

"Turn around," he said glacially.

I turned around. I was fucked up.

"I'm not the pussy you're going to fuck tonight. Go back to your *maman's* or get a bullet in the head. Do it. Now. Go."

Still turned away, I heard silence. Then, the shuffling of the gang's feet. Alex patted me on the back.

"Do you have a gun?" I asked. He was a few paces ahead of me.

"Ha!" he turned, "No. But I called their bluff, didn't I?"

"Yeah, I guess you did."

"That fucking Brazilian's out of her mind. The spot's just around the corner. We could've sprinted." He lit a cigarette. He passed it to me and it fell out of my hands. "I knew those kids weren't thugs. I can smell a pussy a mile away. They must've taken their little rap records too seriously tonight."

I tried to pick up the cigarette from the ground but staggered, and possibly fell over.

"Brother, you look drowsy. Take one more sip of this stuff and... we'll... get..."

He pressed the flask to my lips as he spoke. It was no more than a touch of wetness, like communion wine and...

Black.

1.

I came to as though I'd died. A newborn, inexperienced with the sharp edges and harsh, ultra-realism of life. My eyes snapped open; an imperfect, stale-white ceiling with bumps and pocks and cracks and stains with no pattern was above me. My mind was blanketed by a solid fog. My brain had concretized with my skull: a solid mass, void and incapable of thought. I was hypnotized by translucent squiggles and out-of-focus, hair-like strings floating in front of me. I couldn't get up. Anxiety surged every time I fell asleep and woke again. Nervousness. Moist spine. Dread. I was weak. A thousand-pound head on the axis of a petrified neck.

From a single glance, I knew that I wasn't staring at my ceiling. I needed to find out where the fuck I was.

I was sore. It wasn't the tenderness that resulted from a fight, but something more transcendent. A religious experience. My circulatory system had been picked apart by crows, my nerves endings clamped down and bludgeoned, my brain removed and slammed repeatedly in a car door, and fire irons quenched in my eye sockets.

The light pulsated terrifically with every overwrought heart-bang, desperately coercing blood into my graying organs. I craned my head right and left repeatedly, to build momentum, to get onto my side, to get a better view, to get the fuck out.

I wiggled my toes, rotated my ankles, bent my knees, and clenched my glutes. I wasn't paralyzed. My hands worked. I roused my arms, shoulders, and trunk. I was naked; half-covered with a sheet that left everything east of my dick exposed. Goosebumps scurried up my legs and down my arms like ants on a branch. I felt my stomach for stickiness, wetness, dryness, or crusting. I smelled my fingers.

As I pulled my hand up, it touched someone else's. The universe rushed towards its centre. My lungs shrank. My head expanded and imploded. Sound and sight returned.

The hand belonged to a naked woman; a frail-looking, red-haired woman with a round ass. Her face was buried in a pillow. I looked under the covers, saw my body as I remembered it, and looked at the pale woman's buttocks. Her pink lips blew me a kiss as she shifted.

The room looked like a by-the-hour motel. The ones that ethnic teenagers and chaste young adults with strict home rules use to fuck in when they tire of the backseat. There was a desk with a flimsy wooden chair, a tall standing lamp without a cover, and a closet with one half-broken door.

Fuck this, was my first thought. I refused to even try summoning memories of the prior evening, maybe multiple evenings, that had passed. I didn't recognize the ass or the room. I rotated my body with maximum effort and dropped my feet onto the floor.

A silent Alex was lying under the comforter with the girl's other arm on his chest. On the nightstand beside him were two cell phones, a wad of cash, a flask on its side with sticky residuum pooled under the mouthpiece, an expensive watch… *and a pistol.*

My neck stiffened. *Something about a standoff with some thugs.* I didn't remember gunfire. I tip-toed past the sleepers and picked up the piece. It was heavy. I didn't know much about firearms. I'd shot bottles a couple of times in the field with my friend's parent's gun, the same one that used to steal his folks' smokes.

I pressed a button and the clip ejected. I caught it, bobbled it, held it, and pressed on the cartridge. There was no recoil or bounce. *Full clip.*

I jammed the clip back into the handgun. Alex groaned and the redhaired women stirred. He brushed her hand off him and resumed breathing steadily. I placed the gun back on the table.

I found the all-black apparel that Alex had gifted me the night before and my keys, wallet, and a dead mobile. It was small victory that did wonders to ease my anxiety and disarray. I couldn't find any boxers, though. I hustled into my pants and shirt. The covers slid off the red-haired woman as she turned over. She snorted, rubbed her nose, and then kept snoring with her mouth agape. I looked at her face and naked body. I was struck with anxiety, nastier than before.

She had a small tuft of brownish-red pubic hair and non-existent breasts with nipples the colour of a newborn kitten's paw. She had a nubile face, a round, Gaelic nose, and pink lips speckled with juvenile acne. Her lips matched her pussy, thin and open. *The difference?* Teeth with braces.

If Lina had only been 16 years old, this unnamed red-haired girl…

Still-frame images darted like spectres behind my eyes; drive-in theatre projectors against the backs of my lids, trying to make me remember. *Not here and not now*, I thought with my head sluicing around like a half-full aquarium. The window lacked shutters and blinds. I didn't recognize the area, just vagrants, addicts, heaps of litter, dilapidated buildings, and aggregated destitution in the neighbourhood. *Alex's choice.*

I had to piss and found the Brazilian naked in the bathtub. Her eyes were rolled to the back of her head, her tongue was drooped to one side, and her hands were outstretched over the sides of the tub. Her bronzed skin looked mucky and worn. There was white powder scattered in her hair and caked on her nose and dry, broken lips. She was breathing. Her ribcage lifted and collapsed with every breath her lungs pulled off. I started pissing, and the trickling noise woke her up.

"You want to fuck?" She didn't open her eyes and hawked to clear her throat.

"No," I replied.

"Fine," she responded surly.

I finished and zipped.

"You have blow?" she asked.

"No."

One heavy step after another, through the abrupt hallway to the stairs. The bottom came quickly and I was spilled onto the street. It was an unknown hour on a torturously bright day that I *hoped* was Saturday.

A few disorienting steps. I looked around. The colours were offset like an old television with busted tubes. Everything was real, but not. I rubbed my face. I brushed the crumbs and mucus from my eyes, wiping my hands on my leg. I looked around again and the area started to look familiar. The smells and sounds weren't alien. There was a park of some kind. I turned to see where I'd come from. I looked up and saw a shoddily-painted chunk of particle board that said *'Salvation Inside,'* and to the right, the somberly tinted window of *Wing Café*.

2.

The following days of recovery were spotty, cigar-burned patches of inaction. I tossed in bed with intervals of intense heat and chills, toasted bread on the stovetop, urinated sporadically, and drank gallons of water to combat the efflorescence that was making me feel like a mummified insect.

I got home at 10am and set an alarm for Monday, waking up to periodic memory flashes and startling fits of cosmic depression. Scenes darted in and out of my mind.

Alex's head down, welcoming rails of white powder into his nostrils with wild child models. A German bartender who made my heart sink the first moment she returned my eye contact. A gun on the nightstand. A callow-looking redhead. Changing my clothes in the alleyway.

I was coming down like an anvil from a rooftop. I'd come down from drugs before, but this stabbed with such profound sorrow and confusion that I felt tears in my sleep.

"Hey… hey. Wake up." A voice snapped me out of absolute darkness. "Pretty sure you have work today, and you haven't shaved in a couple. You look like a bum. Need a kick in the spine?" I recognized the questioning lilt. Alex was half massaging my shoulder, half shaking me awake. He lightly slapped my thigh, the way a jockey would a thoroughbred after a tough day at the track.

"Give me a minute," I said.

I was naked. Alex had somehow eased himself into my abode. I didn't know what to address first. He rose to his feet as I sat upright and yawned. I was stunned by the morning's rays, toning my apartment a faint sepia.

"What the fuck are you doing here?" I squinted at the blearing aurora.

"Your door was unlocked," Alex answered. "I popped in yesterday but you were out cold. I figured that you needed some rest, but also figured that you didn't want to miss a day of sitting quietly."

I thanked him ironically.

"What the fuck did you do to me?" I asked. "What the fuck happened?"

I could hear him grin.

"You let yourself go, brother! It seemed like you were having a lot of fun." Alex recounted the night in a favourable, almost nostalgic light. "We met at some cocktail bar and I wrenched you away from a barmaid. I had you change your clothes to better suit our adventure. We then proceeded to hit a few *boîtes*, discos, classy bars… all over really. Too many to count. We met some Yanks, a sloppy Brazilian, and jailbait from the Baltic Sea!

You and her got on *really* well before the American *princesses* had a fit. Coked-out prisses. Then, we went to an afterhours haunt, chilled there for a bit, met some girls, and took them home. When I woke up, you were gone and I figured you'd gone home to sleep it off. Nothing *too* crazy, just a good ol' lads night out!"

"Lads night out?" I said. "That's what you call it?"

"That's right," he said, "good ol'…"

"That's what you call attacking a homeless man? That's what you call pulling out a gun? That's what you call waking up next to a *jeune*?" I wrapped the sheet around my waist and stood up. "What the fuck was in that flask?"

Alex stepped back, out of swinging range. "I told you already. I don't have a gun, brother. I'll admit that I let my prejudices overrun me for an instant when I laid a boot on that decrepit, filthy waste of sperm… I blame the alcohol. You know I'm not a big…"

"What about the… *child*?" I whispered.

"The red-head? You picked her up. Don't remember? Want to see the video?"

I was stiff with *angoisse*, but was too worried to be hostile. I needed answers. "What was in the flask, Alex?"

"A sort of tea," Alex said simply. "An all-natural, organic, psychoactive tea. A little scotch, a little water, some of this, some of that. And, a healthy dose of Ayuhasca, if the guy who sold it to me was telling the truth. Or some other…"

"Like vision quest shit?" I asked.

"Yes… if it was genuine. Otherwise, it was some other psychoactive. I don't know, bath salts or…"

"No wonder I've been feeling like someone tore the soul from my body and beat it…" I slumped onto my bed.

"Of course! We partied, my brother! Alex style! Even a veteran such as myself needed a good recovery sleep. I mean, we were chock-full of powder, booze, and the like. You did very well, though. I'm not surprised that you don't remember anything. A night with me will break you down into fibres."

I exhaled with resignation. "What about the piece? And the red-head girl?" I put my chin in my hand. "I thought the Brazilian was dead in the bathtub."

"The Brazilian was out of her mind. She kept begging for dick and dope so I told her to cool off in the shower after she threw her guts out all over the floor. The ginger girl? I don't know… We met her, sorry, you met her, at the afterhours and she wanted to have some fun. What do you remember from that?"

"I remember waking up and seeing a young, *young* girl lying naked in between you and me, unconscious. I also remember seeing a gun on the dresser."

"Ah…" Alex pondered. "She was just a tag along. If you want to see the action, it's all on my phone."

"Fuck you! I saw the gun! What about the gun?"

"Unloaded," he said airily. "We burned out a clip shooting streetlights on the walk back to the room. It was *your* idea. Something about beer bottles in a field… I can't remember. You're a pretty good shot. The girls were impressed by your brawn, *dead eye*. If you'd have picked it up, you would've seen that it was just an empty Glock 19 with the safety on."

Liar. I tried to conjure the memory of blasting out streetlights, but couldn't remember anything after the second sip and waking up.

I was mortified by the existence of the video he was talking about.

"Why were we in the rooms above Wing's?" I asked.

"If we're being honest here," Alex said, "I own that building. I own a couple buildings in that neighbourhood, *hence* why I'm always there, *hence* why I have a room, and *hence* why Wing comports himself like a sullen, little toad. He doesn't like what's happened to the area. Fuck him. That's the price of doing business. Besides he's no one to…"

Alex pointing out all the illegal activity in the area rushed back to me. He hadn't just been recounting illicit activities, he'd been bragging about them. My comfort level was slipping, but I couldn't take too long to react. I felt like I should play off what he was telling me like any other piece of information.

"Did I fuck the… How old was the…" I trailed off, thinking about the red-haired girl again.

"Well… I did, Carol did, you, well, you can see for yourself exactly what you did if you want. It's actually kind of funny to watch. Here." He reached for his phone.

"No!" I dropped my head into my hands.

"Hey, listen, the youngest and cutest-looking ones have the worst imaginations and want to prove that they aren't so young and cute. Don't be a pussy. You're fine, she's fine, I'm fine, and Carol's a fucking train wreck of a human being who's on her way to a tropical photoshoot to blow a photographer right now." He noticed my curled-in-a-ball forlornness. "Look, if she was at the club, she wasn't a minor. You're bringing an umbrella for a blue sky. More importantly, *you got your night.* You got a night out where you got to see what it's like not being a normal, everyday worker and experience how the better people in society spend their Fridays. You didn't do anything wrong. Now, hop in the shower and let's get rid of that face moss, brother."

"Nah. I'm good and I think you should go."

"What are you saying?" Alex said looking pained.

"I'm saying that I need you to go. Let me figure out all this shit in my head. Let me give my poor brain some time. Let me get back into a routine where I'm not waking up feeling like Poe."

"I'm telling you, there's nothing to worry about. There's no way she was your cousin."

"I'll talk to you in a bit, Alex," I said as I led him to the door.

"Yeah," he said dejectedly. "In a bit."

3.

A week of monotony at work helped to allay my dry sweat, enduring feeling of greasiness, and sporadic bouts of panic that occasionally flared up. It took at least a week until I stopped feeling a slight, apprehensive grogginess and a psychosomatic, oily film on my skin. Like a tree frog. I felt like I was going cold turkey, albeit on a smaller level. I had withdrawal symptoms from something I had no interest in tormenting myself with ever again. I didn't even know what it was. I'd never been so happy to be an average, boring cunt in my life.

The German bartender, Emiliana, was on my mind. I wanted to go sit at the bar and stare at her longingly as she measured liquids and stirred Nergonis, but felt emotionally low. I wanted to allow the effects of Alex's *lads night* to drain out of my system and get back into full form before I went to see her.

Speaking of Alex, I hadn't made an effort to reach out to him. He'd left me alone to enjoy the night's after effects. I probably would've ignored him anyways. Whenever I tried to untangle the night with my smashed-vase memories, I began to sweat thick, heavy drops. I couldn't piece together anything that'd happened after my second sip of tea. I didn't remember the club, supposedly shooting lights out, fucking, or anything else until I'd woken up. I was sure I'd caught Alex in a lie about the bullets, the fact that he'd had a full clip at his disposal that night, and who knows what else. Alex only said *just* as much as he needed to when he'd been caught in a lie. He was committed to his bullshit.

I needed solitude. *I know!* Look at Mr. Lonely & Isolated needing time to himself. I'd grown comfortable having at least one constant string of dialogue with another person. Marta had been there before. After she'd left, I'd seen Alex every morning, often multiple times a day. I'd *still* been messaging Marta out of politeness and habit. And, I was horny. Following my night out, I didn't receive any more texts. That road had now been closed off for good. Good for her. She'd found someone. It was for the best.

No tears, no bucket.

4.

The long limbs of an Indian summer and the memory of how gray and wet Paris got in the darker seasons dragooned me into spending pointless hours outside. In a way, being around people, even strangers you'll never know, connects you to the world. Just being out there and taking it all in some-how manufactures serenity. Blades of grass and grains of sand must never feel alone.

"Well, well, well," an English voice said as I was sitting on a park bench near my office. I was reading a book and enjoying the breeze before taking the long train back to the *banlieue*.

I turned. "*Emiliana?*" I faced the ropy, slender woman with her hands on her noticeable hipbones. The sun was being partially blocked by her long sandy hair. I squinted up from her sneakers to her black, calf-length, low-waist skirt to her concave midriff to her angelic face. Her posture was imposing with no hint of anger. A smirk softly dimpled her cheek. "I've had a pretty weird couple of weeks," I said.

"It's okay," she said. "I thought I noticed your friend see the number I left you on the drink napkin, but when you didn't come in last week, I figured that was that." There was no hint of German in her accent.

"Your number? No, I didn't even..." I was nervous to blink lest she disappear. "I don't know if he did. I think he was already deep in the cups by that point. I'd rather have stayed with you all night. After... I... The office... I've been... slammed."

"It's fine." She glanced away as though I was lying. "I don't ever do that anyways."

"No, wait!" I barked, maybe a little too impetuously. "Sorry! Please. Sit with me... if you have time," I rose to my feet, sending my jacket and book to the pavement. "Please."

"Well," she said, "*only* if you call me Emi."

Emi sat down. I just stared at her, unable to look away. I was untroubled by the gauntness of my face, the glow of sweat on my forehead, and the likelihood that I was staring creepily.

"How are you?" she giggled.

"I'm feeling a lot better," I said, relieved. "Like I said, I swear that my friend didn't give me your number. I was going to come in anyways. Rough week... I had to kick the sauce for a few."

"Silly boy," she smiled. "We have some excellent coffee, or sweet, *virgin* lemonade if you want. What did you get up to?"

"Uh..." I started. The truth was... dodgy. "My friend... he's a wild-card. He has too much money, is too attractive, and is a lot to handle.

"I didn't see him. My friend said that he was a babe and pointed him out. I only saw his back. Tall, wearing black... He looked like the angel of death." She smiled. I thought I heard a flower break soil.

Hours must have passed, as it started to get cold. I offered her my coat.

"Can I be honest with you?" I asked. Too seriously. She nodded, probably unsure of what I'd say. "I'd like to take you out and get to know you."

I worried I was being forward or would get shot down, but a greater sense of *fuck it* was overriding every impulse.

"That's the big secret? I thought you were going to say that you were a serial killer or a ghost." She touched my hand. "What is it that you think we're doing right now?"

Our harmless encounter suddenly gained weight and felt like an audition. "What I mean is… when I saw you… I thought you were beautiful, but more… like you were everything I'm attracted to moulded into one person. I wanted to stay more than anything in the world, but my friend wanted to go." I let my stammers fly free and wild. My face could've cooked ore. "I was a bartender, so I know the courtesy, the chatter, the client building…" I was stuttering, mumbling, fidgeting, and my stomach hurt. I was dizzy, I could feel my hair and nails, my teeth burned, and my feet were scraping against the ground noisily. "I didn't want to be too forward, but…" I paused. *Fuck it.* I leaned in and kissed her.

She didn't pull away. She kissed me back and the tiny men in the control room in my head high-fived and flung their headsets off. It was a simple kiss, nothing fancy. I moved my hand gently, *doucement*, under her chin. Our noses touched tips and then cheeks. I rested my forehead against hers, pecked her top lip twice, and drifted back. I was too shocked to feel aplomb.

"I'm glad you did that," she mumbled, looking down at my hand timidly.

She stared at me like I'd stared at her. I was drowned in the depth of her ultra-green eyes, dark from the night but flickering like emerald flames in the muted light. Like a cat's.

"Would you like to go for a walk?" I asked. She quickly nodded and we set about the area. We walked a great distance, following the clamor of *La Seine* and providing each other with more detailed life stories.

EMI

Emi was born in New York City, Brooklyn to be exact, to a Russian Jew mother and a German Jew father. They'd both moved to America, met, fell in love, and then had their only child in the unofficial world's capital. Her father had later taken her to Germany after her mother's death. Her last name was Blum, although her beautiful, salient nose betrayed the suffix that her father had dropped when he immigrated.

She was immensely spiritual; not religious, but open to chakras, auras, and the types of Eastern healing shit that I feigned appreciation for and refuted politely as not being *my source of guidance or inspiration*. She had a full sleeve tattoo: half Mandala, half geometric design. She was still German, after all.

At 31 years old, she'd already traveled all over. She'd absorbed all those experiences deeply and developed an organic relationship with her soul, as well as the souls of others. She was the kind of person who was powerfully touched by nature's brush strokes, the emotional latency of music, and the electricity of human rapport. She allowed herself to adapt and change in tune with the influential events of her life. She was a feminist and a hippie, though not in the shallow way that the *Yanks* had been, nor with the holier-than-thou militancy that my university girlfriend had adopted. She was unpretentious, humble, and her concern and affection for others was authentic. She knew every event that was happening around the city, passionately supporting amateur artists and bands. She painted canvases and took artistic photographs in her spare time. She was a hard worker and a perfectionist; every task she undertook consumed her like a Swiss watchmaker. She was a knockout when she dressed for a gala or a nice dinner but was more endearing wearing oversized glasses, sneakers, high-waisted shorts, and her trademark midriff-baring shirt. She was fit due to genetics but danced and did yoga daily. She'd been a ballerina most of her life, which left her body with boa-like strength and sinew. She was dreamy but determined. The best? Her sense of humour. She had comedic timing and wit that only a German-American-Russian Jew could have, with a coquettish laugh that broke into a riotous, teeth-baring bellow and softened the sharpness of her Slavic features.

Love is like winter. You remember your first harsh winter and your record-breaking winter, with all the other cold seasons freezing together into an anthology. Every year the fangs of winter close around you, forcing your boots and parkas out of your closet, you shiver and shake, your teeth rattle, and your extremities prickle. When the summer arrives, melting the dirty snow and ice away, you're glad to finally see winter's hindquarters and hope it never returns. A truly cold, aggressive winter, a winter that makes you shudder to think about, a winter that you compare with all other winters like a poker hand, *that's* the winter that defines the season. Some people define love based on their first love, and some based on their last. Either way, the love you remember is the most powerful and influential love you've experienced.

After Emi and I parted ways, I knew that I was in love. She knew that she was in love. We'd been lucky enough to be in the same place at the same time. We'd planted a bulb, which would push out its little stem, break through the topsoil, and unfurl itself to bathe its petals under the nurturing sun and nourishing rains, forever.

The first time we had sex, not long after our chance meeting on the bench, it was as if we'd rehearsed it like an opera. We undressed each other slowly, embracing and handling one another like one of us might soon disappear. We rolled playfully, teasing entry and denying ingress as excitement and impatience wove together in jubilant restlessness. I used my strength to put her in a position of submission, feeling her entire body become charged, athirst, and soon quivering without penetration. I examined and traced her arms and legs, the sizeable mounds of her dark pink-crested breasts, and the smooth, taught seamlessness that dipped from her stomach, between her hips, and down to her knees. She hopelessly thrusted and tried to capture me, but to no avail. She shook her head playfully as I tried to kiss her again, cooing and moaning, softly whispering small utterances as I pulled away when she tried to kiss me back. I finally began to sink in, fighting off orgasm with the first wet, squeezing entrance and watching as she became soundless. I relinquished her, so she pulled my head down and kissed and bit me voraciously as her legs snugged around my lower back. Her ankles locked. She gasped as she accidentally thrusted me deeper.

"You're in my tummy," she choked out, breathing stiflingly as I pressed my toes into the mattress and drove in further still. I felt her breasts against my chest flattening as she squeezed harder, as though she'd otherwise fall to her death.

We'd entered my apartment on Friday night and Emi finally left on Sunday evening. She gave me a long kiss at the door and left to catch a cab back to her place.

"I'll see you tomorrow," she said confidently as she walked slowly down the hall in tight, black leggings and a long, white shirt. She had bruises on her triceps. The shirt was bunched up in the back, leaving her quite exposed in the sheer fabric that was wedged into the crevice of her bum.

She'd folded her black thong into my hand and turned to see if I was looking as she billowed her shirt over her backside, smiling with nude lips. I was. She watched me smell her panties.

5.

A blissful solace permeated my demeanour. I lay down in drowsy comfort after a long but rewarding day, somnolent without anxiety. I drifted away content, without apprehension; the peaceful resignation that comes only after the filthiest of wars. This feeling of serenity and *joie de vivre* came entirely as a result of sharing my days and nights with Emi. She insisted that I make up for lost time, squeezing in all the cliché touristic activities that Paris had to offer while the weather was still favourable. She always had a show or exhibit to attend, a new fusion restaurant to sample, or a tantric sexual activity that could eat up an entire weekend day. Most of the women in my life had either adopted the laid back, impassive ways in which I spent my *temps libre*, or in Marta's case, demanded my begrudging participation in the recreational activities only she enjoyed. Not Emi. Emi could effortlessly pique my interest in what she found interesting and entertaining, perhaps due to her gift of innate positivity or her ability to disarm and charm me. She had a skill for finding activities that appealed to me, taking my interests into consideration. Above all else, I loved her and loved being around her. I would've sat through a four-hour silent movie or picked apples in a Provencal orchard just to be with her and watch her engrossed. Her big, round eyes gave her a curious innocence, but they also showed the sharpness of a clever, intelligent human being who was unremittingly breaking down the world around her.

I'd pushed our dear friend Alex out of my mind, only occasionally wondering what schemes and malfeasances he was undertaking from his stronghold of grime at Wing's. It was strange that I hadn't heard from the lad, but was disinclined to reach out. I didn't need another episode like the one he'd contrived with Marta, though it probably wouldn't go down the same way. I'd sooner flip him where he sat than allow him to utter a disrespectful syllable to Emi, but why invite such potential unpleasantness?

Bizarrely, Marta had started to reach out. I gave her no inclination that I wished to continue a relationship with her. I didn't need her friendship. She talked about returning to Paris and my responses were lukewarm at best. Why would I care? I told her that I was with another woman, that I was sorry about her grandfather, and that I hoped she was in good health.

As autumn rolled around with its crispness and clarity, Emi invited me to go to Berlin with her for Christmas. I was pleased that I had something to do for the holidays, as the office gave us a mandatory extended vacation. I was also happy that I was a part of Emi's plans months in advance. It seemed premature, but I guess I shouldn't have been surprised. For all her spiritual dreaminess and optimism, the strength of her Deutsch pedigree was stereotypical. Dali for her dreams, Courbet for the rest. Emi's obsession with strategizing and scheduling her life dovetailed with her outwardly laid-back persona; sometimes frustratingly, sometimes comically, but it proved to be one of her most endearing qualities. On one occasion, we were elbows into the wine skin and hashish and heading to bed for a marathon session. Suddenly, as if pierced by lightning, Emi realized that there was a radio broadcast of a Banksy-type street artist who was being interviewed in Tokyo on satellite radio. She'd wanted to listen to the broadcast and take notes. She apologized and excused herself to scribble down a loose transcript while listening to the interview with savantic attention. At 3am. I couldn't help but laugh with affection as her naked bum hung gently over the seat of my little wooden stool while she scratched a pen against her lineless sketch book. I watched her for an hour. That was my personal definition of love that no words or philosophers could define.

I started receiving little texts from Alex. Some cryptic greetings and pleasantries, all of which I couldn't picture him saying in person. I eventually responded in a casual tone, limiting the information I shared. I don't know why. Something in my head was telling me to subdue my actuated cheeriness and dampen the perhaps uncharacteristic happiness I was feeling. I'd already shoveled the weightiest slabs of doom from our last excursion from my mind and heeled the rest into the deepest cellar-corner of my psyche.

I met him for quick cups here and there. He seemed apathetic to my dating 'the help,' which was perfectly fine by me. He didn't ask to meet her and I didn't volunteer a time they could exchange handshakes. I told Emi little about him. I didn't know a whole lot anyways, so I only published parts of our adventures. Saving my own reputation involved protecting his, after all. Basically, I told her that he was an inimitably handsome albeit shady entrepreneur who was intelligent, capable, and perhaps a little unhinged. I subtly tried to convey Emi's perfection to him, but he kept referring to her as 'the Soviet barmaid with the long beak,' then quickly resuming his lectures on social and cultural angsts and how ordinary my life sounded. One noticeable difference regarding our meetings was that we no longer went to Wing Café. I didn't ask why. I didn't mind going without visiting that part of the city. I saw him once or twice a week and we messaged infrequently. He was busy, I was dutiful. And happy.

Emi often ran her hands across my jaw and kissed it. *'You'd look good with a beard,'* she said. She teased the scruff that had accumulated after a weekend in Normandy to look at the cliffs in the maturing fall. It was a wet, misty, *hike-and-stare* vacation with each wink exhaustedly earned. We were cozily kept in a bed and breakfast that Emi squealed at adorably upon arrival. I missed having facial hair to fill in my facial lines and contour my profile. I agreed to grow my moss if she did the same beneath her underwear.

Alex confronted me about my beard inside a little hole-in-the-wall cafe during my lunch hour.

"Did you lose your razor?"

"No." I pawed my stubble. "Emi wanted to see what I looked like with a beard. I forgot how much fuller it makes my mug look."

"You look like a boxcar hobo," he said. "Much more handsome clean-shaven. I can't take you seriously with that… thing."

"Agree to disagree," I posited. I welcomed the insulation for the upcoming colder season and wanted to please my woman. Her bush was growing fast and thick, too.

"You *love* having your balls in a vice, brother," he said.

I shrugged. I felt confident like I never had before. Impregnable.

Bulletproof. Alex must've noticed that his needling was ineffective, so he kept on. And on. And on.

"Look man," I said. "I really care about this girl. I *love* her."

For an instant, Alex seemed genuinely disfigured by my words. Then, bemused.

"*Love*? Jesus fucking Christ on the cross, brother. How long has it been?" He reeled back in his seat. "A vacation, an art show, and then you love her? Seems fast… Good show, old boy. You discovered the wisdom of the ancients. You're *human*."

"Thanks," I said. I changed the subject and he remained sullen like a teenager losing his friend to a girl. That old play.

"You're changing," he said. "You're going backwards after making some real progress."

"Like you?" I broke in.

"Well, no," he shot back, running his hand through his hair. "You could never be me. But, someone who was breaking their lifelong template of complacency and obedience. Someone who was becoming the author and architect behind their own destiny. Developing ambition…"

"I *do* have ambition," I interrupted. "It's always been in there, like a shook can of soda." I hand-combed my fuzz. "The difference is… I'm *happy* and not bothered by the little things. Emi turns my bad into good. She makes me feel accomplished *just* by holding her hand and kissing her cheek. It might sound lame to you, but even if I was a fish monger or trash collector, I'd be fulfilled with Emiliana."

Alex looked like he was about to vomit. "Ugh. You… *pussy*. You're right. I can't understand that… but I'm *happy* for you. I hope you guys have kids that mong fish and collect trash. Cheers to you, brother. *Salut.*"

"You're jealous," I said.

"Me? Of you? I've never been jealous of anyone in my life! Ha!"

I didn't mean of me, I meant of her.

I went to crash at Emi's. Alex had been his usually harsh and critical self. And, he was wrong. He usually said what I felt but was too afraid to say aloud. This time, he was galaxies away. Maybe I was finally outgrowing him and his scathing views.

I got home and Emi slithered her arms around me, kissing the area between my eye and ear and rubbing her cheek against mine. I turned and kissed the bridge of her strong nose sideways, which had become my greatest demonstration of affection and tenderness. I held my lips on the bridge of her nose for a few seconds.

She leaped up and wrapped her legs around me. "You're my favourite person in the world," she said.

"Thanks, baby. I love you."

6.

Sometime before winter started, I was relaxing at home. Emi was working a rare closing shift at the cocktail bar, having given up her lucrative evening shifts for Monday to Friday day shifts so that we could spend more time together. However, some of her cohorts had reduced their schedules for the slow season and the money was better at night, so she was picking up the slack. As a result, we'd be spending a few nights apart each week until we could move in together.

I was drifting off when my phone rang. *Emi.* She never called this late. I fumbled for my mobile. As soon as I answered, her voice frantically whispered: "Baby, I think I'm being followed."

I sprang up and matched her panic with half-sentences. I tried to calm down and asked her to tell me what was going on.

"I'm walking home, and there's a man with a hoodie on. I noticed him following all my turns. I took a few corners and ran. He keeps disappearing, but then he's behind me again… closer every time. There's no one else on the street. I don't know where he keeps coming from."

She was whispering. Her trenchant consonant letters were double-crossing her attempts to maintain a calm and quiet voice.

"Get onto a busy street. Find somewhere well-lit." I offered the obvious with distressing impotence.

"Can you stay on the phone?" she whimpered.

"Of course." And, I did.

Emi made it home safely. She was jittered and kept me on the phone another hour, frozen with fright.

This was first of a series of strange occurrences that developed over the next several weeks. Emi felt like she was being watched. I stayed at her place every night, walking her to and from work whenever I could. The late nights were taking a toll on me, however. I offered to pay for taxis, but she insisted on walking and not being conquered by fear. I abided.

Emi was certain that there were *ominous spirits* in the air. I vehemently disbelieved in apparitions and the significance of mystical energies, but she was adamant. Something was making her spirit-based feelers tingle.

She made a list of people who might be stalking her. It ranged from swarthy man down her hall to a dejected bar fly to a psychotic lesbian crush. She said that in most stalking cases, the assailants were people that the victim was acquainted to, if not familiar with. They also almost always had a schizoid component, which scared her the most. Even during the bright daytime, Emi was often arrested by mercurial neuroticism and paranoia. Had she been dominated by her spiritual side, she would've shut herself in her house with talismans, amulets, and wreathes of burning sage. Her stalwart pride and resolution pushed her on, however, though she requested only dayshifts.

We discussed her anxieties and borderline complex, addressing her fears head on. I suggested she see a psychologist (a kahuna or soothsayer, if she preferred), or simply leaving Paris. She was becoming miserable; grounded by paranoia like a butterfly with broken wings. Her effervescence, zeal, and thirst for life were being sucked out. I couldn't wrench her from this phobic agony. I told her that I'd be her lemming for life, following her wherever she went. It comforted her and I meant it. I would've followed her to Berlin, Beirut, Bangalore, Boston, Baghdad, or Bangkok. I felt *actual* empathy for the first time in my life. Until now, I'd simulated a synthetic sympathy for others' sadness and losses. I'd consoled family members and even lovers out of chivalry but had always felt disconnected from their feelings. When Emi hurt, I felt a shiv rip my belly apart. I felt the hemorrhage of her torment leak as though my own soul had been sliced open. I felt the strain of her terror and was consumed by the shadowy dread of her demons.

I felt uneasy letting Emi out of my sight, but put on a valiant front and said that everything was alright. I hugged her, kissed her nose, and cuddled her with otherworldly strength and unabashed temerity. When she quavered, I squeezed her harder. When she sobbed, I licked her salty tears.

I felt the whitecaps of her anxiety and tried to damn and internalize them. I hoped to absorb and replace them with my care and tenderness. I wished that my affection might imbue her with the courage to walk confidently the way religious people prayed. I told her that she was brave and special.

Then, I was gutted by a phone call. Not from Emi, but from the hospital.

7.

The hospital told me that Emi had been attacked that evening after attending a friend's show. I'd taken some work home to finish in order to have the weekend free. She'd left the flat with a group of friends. The attacker was dust when she was found with a predatory drug in her system. The pre-toxicologist report pronounced the substance as a date-rape drug. She'd been beaten and violated. She had a massive gash above her eyebrow from a blunt object, ballooning her cheeks and jaw. She also had a few broken ribs, a broken scapula, chipped nails, and bruises all over her arms and legs.

She'd been found in torn clothes, wrapped in a skirt as opposed to wearing it, by a café owner who was locking up his shop. He took her for a smack head at first, but remarked the evident savagery upon closer scrutiny. She had no cell phone and her handbag was located a block away. She'd collapsed at the man's feet croaking some indistinct words in German and English. The medics who'd arrived on the spot instantly knew that she wasn't a user and stretchered her into the ambulance. They'd stitched, sewed, sutured, wrapped, and when the purse had finally been found by the officers, her identity had been ascertained. The officials had contacted her work, who'd given them my name.

Emi was out cold for two days. They said she wasn't in a coma, but resting. The doctors had stopped the internal bleeding and collapsed lung that could've been her demise. They presumed that her skull fracture wouldn't affect her mental capabilities, at least in the long-term, and despite the volatility of her heart rate and episodic *beep-beeps* from the monitor, I was assured that she'd pull through. I stayed with her and slept in a plastic chair with a little airplane pillow for the days that followed. I wasn't letting her out of my sight.

I was there when she broke through the barrier of consciousness on the third day. She suddenly began to stir and groan. Every movement seemed to send a shockwave of pain through her body that in her delirium, she still couldn't fathom. I took her by her hand and lightly touched her lumpy, bandaged head. She opened her eyes. They were glassy from the morphine; doped up and groggy. She smiled at me before the pull of her stitches made her wince. Thick tears slid down her bruised cheeks, flooding and overflowing from her long lashes.

"I'm sorry, baby," she moaned weakly.

I wiped the tears from her cheeks. Each globule exploded with tenfold the saline it appeared to contain.

"Shh," I whispered. Euphoria and sadness were commingling in a daze that made me numb with a mixture of relief and anxiety. "You don't have to be sorry, Emi. I should've listened."

She seemed to be having a moment of lucidity, though the painkillers were exhibiting their effects clearly. "No, I thought I was crazy," she coughed. Dry and difficult. It was hurting her. A pain shot from my toes to my urethra to my navel as she flinched.

"No, please. Don't be sorry. I should've listened... I should've been there... I shouldn't have left you alone for a second." Stinging heat behind my eyes and nose. "Do you remember anything? I know the police will... Emi?"

Emi's face began to twist and turn red. "I remember getting sleepy. All of a sudden. Feeling sick. I had to go. It wasn't late... I was walking... I was texting you." She groaned. "I remember a man... asked me a question... I was listening to my headphones..." She tried to control her breathing and closed her eyes. Reflective lines ran down her purpled face. "He wasn't dangerous-looking... dressed normally. He was holding... a map?" She made herself carry on. "A tourist... He tapped me... He had a question. I turned, taking a headphone out to hear him... He hit me..." I held her hand. The monitor showed her heartbeat quickening. There was sweat on both of our palms. She was fighting the morphine drowse. "It goes black... I woke up and... he was doing... things... I can't..." She cried and convulsed painfully.

"You don't have to," I said softly. "You don't have to say anything. Please, rest."

"I think... I started scratching and punching him," she said. "I did. He screamed, and then he hit me again, and..."

She ran out of consciousness. I hammered my thumb repeatedly on the nurse call button. I was lost. As Emi slipped away, my heart was pounding its cage into splinters. I was inundated with emotions: giant letters in all caps, in strobing colours, flying and swooping around my head, each one trying to imbed itself in my mind. They couldn't permeate. It was too much. Too intense. It left me devoid. Empty.

Emi was in and out of consciousness after that. I hesitated to ask more questions whenever she surfaced for air but couldn't prevent myself from imagining what'd happened to her. I gained a little information here and there, but her ability to bridge clear sentences wavered mightily. I cursed the nurses for being conveniently missing each time she was roused. I barked at the doctors for not doing enough. I'm sure they were, but it wasn't enough to assuage my guilt.

Time was passing independently from us. I didn't know how much of it was actually going by. Emi woke up groggy again and managed to stay awake.

"Did you see him?" I eventually asked blankly; a self-fulfilling prophet.

Emi was consumed with fatigue and painkillers. She was fighting her head from slumping to her shoulder. "He was a very attractive man," she said, as if dreaming. "He was yelling in English and Russian, I think." She then resigned back into soothing unconsciousness.

That motherfucker. Isn't foreshadowing a toothy device?

Kill. Dead. Death. Dying. Kill. Mangle. Eat. Destroy. Annihilate. Decapitate. Massacre. Obliterate. Kill. Kill. Murder. Kill. Sharp. Fire. Burn. Ashes. Kill. Bludgeon. Tear. Kill.

Words of destruction and a crimson anger cloaked me in a desensitized, radioactive trance. The heat in my face dispersed and pulsed throughout my entire body. Slivers of sharp bone were forcing themselves through my skin like porcupine quills. My restless desire for vengeance manifested itself as mechanized hatred. My hunger and fatigue were burned to ash alongside any other thought I could've had.

I watched Emi lie in momentary peace, which would be disturbed for good when she recovered enough to coherently articulate all the details of the attack to the investigators.

The nurses came in and asked me why I'd buzzed them again. I responded without hearing my own words, dulled murmurs from the external world. My inner voice was a washed-out mess of static feedback and high-pitched humming, like a mosquito flapping at the precipice of an eardrum. The humming magnified, becoming a gnarly distortion. I was removed from the room. The nurses would use my absence to sponge-bathe and spot clean her, rewrapping her bandages and emptying her dialysis bag.

I'd barely slept in days. My meals had been little trays of food that the nursing crew compassionately offered me at Emi's bedside. I picked at cabbage rolls, fragrant meat dishes with offensive gravy, grainy mashed potatoes, and fruit cups. I was still in the same clothes that I'd been wearing when I rushed to the hospital. I hadn't checked my phone and it was surely now out of battery. I was finally leaving the old, sterile smell of the hospital, being greeted by the brisk autumn breeze that jolted my senses into gear.

I caught a glimpse of my face in the lobby's full-mirrored wall. A mauve hue spiralled beneath my eyes, sunken cheeks, and drawn out cheek bones. Unkempt and wiry beard hairs corkscrewed from my *guele*. My dehydration emaciated body was that of a rescued miner, the sole survivor. The receptionist stopped me and asked if I was alright. I responded with words. More than likely, those words formed a sentence that indicated a need for a wash or a nap. She made me down a cup of powdered orange drink with electrolytes and a tough oatmeal biscuit, then offered me a cot. I guzzled the slimy drink and crunched through the cookie as I left, carving through the parking lot towards the bus loop on auto-pilot, like a cyborg programmed by an unknown master. *Kill. Murder. Cut. Break. Destroy.*

8.

I jumped from bus to train to bus on my way to Wing Café with no purposive knowledge of why I was heading there. I didn't know what I'd do if I found Alex propped on a stool with goons and cronies at a cry's reach. The high-pitched noise was still hanging around me like brume, straining my face and repressing my faculties. I was barely able to discern if my inner voices were trying to dissuade me from such foolhardy redress or not. When I tried to jerk myself into the self-evident facticity of the situation, an enveloping fuzziness and tenor of crackling noises drowned out any attempts to seize control of my mind with rationality or pry it back from its primordial, survivalist automation. This clamour resulted in nothing. The *fight* had trounced the *flight* option.

I emerged from the final bus to a sky that I didn't see and gusts that I didn't feel. I turned down the boulevard that put me kitty corner from Wing's. I finally felt my heart thrumming terrifically. Each beat vibrated behind my ears and shrunk my eyesight. The scope of my tunnel vision was narrowed to a pin-prick of light. I could hear my blood, a droning river, clawing its way through my veins and blocking everything out. Even panic.

My head was down, my shoulders were squared and hunched forward, and my fists were tight. I was the somatotype of a thoughtless ogre.

I readied to cross the street, sinking my nails into the flesh of my palms. Something felt off. My vision cleared. Something quite serious was happening in the vicinity.

Police car lights were spinning noiselessly. I spotted at least three cruisers and a wagon meant for hauling off suspects. I didn't notice the dozens of people standing around or the closure of the intersection until I was already in the center of the street. I slowed my gait. The cloudiness and screeching in my ears began to diminish. I felt naked. Exposed.

Officers were questioning junkies, whores, Wing, and his cook. I also saw some men who didn't fit into any of those categories. They were in handcuffs: standing around, leaning against cars, or being shoveled into the police van. One character was the little, angry Arab from my first visit. He grimaced at me while a cop ducked him into the backseat of a car.

Wing and his mate were standing with some other Asians, all frail and emaciated-looking. The gangster types were being separated into piles like quarters and dimes. The junkies were being investigated by disgruntled officers who seemed to know that their stories were going to be bullshit. The prostitutes were scattered into little subgroups, smoking and shivering. One such group stood underneath a scaffold 30 metres from Wing's. I noticed a very young, red-headed girl with a group of garishly-dressed, bone-thin women. I stared at her and almost threw up. Her expression didn't change as her eyes met mine and then moved away quickly. She was *young*. Her mouth was pocked with red sores. *Not quite acne.*

Wing saw me. He yelled and pointed at me, alone in the middle of the street.

"Him! Get over to him! He knows the man. Ask him!" Wing's eyes met mine as he spoke to the officer in heavily Chinese-accented French. His expression was hard and full of malice. The officer said something to another officer, who raised the palm on his left hand while hovering his right over his holster.

"Stop where you are!" he cried. He motioned for me to come towards him. I was confused by his directions and moved towards him slowly. He walked swiftly towards me with a militaristic stride. People turned in my direction. He grabbed me and pulled me towards the centre of the action.

One policeman asked for my name, address, and where I was from due to my accent. I gave him all the answers. The two officers whispered to each other. Wing shot vicious arrows into my perplexed eyes. I scanned the area to try and get a handle on what was happening, now that I was in the thick of the ruckus. There were police questioning and detaining people everywhere. Suited detectives emerged, scratching pens onto pocket books. Fiends were leaning against walls and crouching like back-catchers.

"What do you know?" barked the officer.

"Know about what?" I answered, moronic and clueless.

"Don't play stupid. Wing says that *you* know the guy we're looking for. Are you his customer? A worker? A friend? You're dressed like you could be one of those junkie-fucks that pulls his knives." I looked at him like he'd sucker punched me.

"I honestly have no idea what you're talking about."

"You're being a real piece of shit right now. You know that?" asserted the officer. Wing was seething behind him. "We're talking about a real sinister individual here, and you're withholding information. Have you ever been to prison?"

"If by *sinister individual* you mean a man named Alex, then yes, I know who you're talking about. No, I don't work for him. No, I'm not a customer. I *was* his friend." The officer began to whir with interest. He told me to stay put and another officer to watch me. He darted off.

The policeman returned with another man, this one in a suit. He began me with a placatory tone. "So... Alex, you say his name is? Last name?"

I thought for a moment and shook my head. "I don't know."

The detective grumbled. "What can you tell me about this *Alex*?"

I recounted how we'd met with a petty description, withholding any background information and my knowledge of his criminal activity. The detective moved us into the cafe. We sat down at the countertop away from Wing's dirty leers, the other cops, and the men being shuffled about in handcuffs.

"So, you don't really know much about him, do you?" the detective concluded, despondently.

"No, not really. I don't know why I really hung out with him in the first place. He's meddled with my life and made me lose a girlfriend. He's secretive and often busy. I don't know why he always had me meet him in this shithole of a dive. I figured he was a joker, had a weird sense of humour, and was just trying to get a rise."

"Why did you come here today?" asked the detective gravely. I had to think of an alternative to caving his skull in.

"He... talked shit about me to a lady... I wanted to *engueule* him for gossiping."

Nice.

"Well, it's a good thing you didn't," the detective said. "He's known to be quite dangerous and is suspected of some pretty vile, evil things. We figure that he felt the heat and hightailed it to another country, but we can't be sure."

"What did he do?" asked the most naïve man in France.

The detective sighed. "He, or a man fitting his description, set up a number of criminal enterprises in this neighbourhood. Weapon sales, extortion, prostitution, drugs, *activities involving minors*, human smuggling... the list goes on. We're positive that there's more still and want to pin him for all of that and murder conspiracy on top. He's a disease, a cancer, and not only to this area. Wing there, he'd had enough of being an accomplice, albeit under extreme duress, and blew the whistle. He was holed up in one of the rooms above the bar with a woman for a couple days. We only found a body, dead from a suspected overdose, and no other DNA."

Jesus fuck.

"A Brazilian woman?" I asked.

"…yes," the officer squinted, appearing to be thinking. "Did you know her?"

"I believe her name was Carol. I was there when they met. She was…"

The officer cut in. "A model of some sort?"

I nodded. "Yeah. A model. Of some sort."

"Well…" the detective said grimly, "she didn't look like her photos when we found her."

"Jesus Christ, man," I said. "Look, detective. If I find out… anything… that can help you catch Alex… I'll let you know."

I was lying. I wanted him for myself.

"Thank you," he said as he gave me his card. "Remember, he's armed and dangerous. All these people…" he waved his hand around the area in front of Wing's, "have had their lives destroyed. They've all been ushered down the same road by this sociopath. It sounds like he wanted to lead you down the same one."

We exited the cafe one after the other. He told me that he'd shared sensitive information with me, perhaps too much, and asked that I not disclose the particulars of our conversation to anyone.

I agreed.

Alex had been trying to lead me down a dark path, but compared to all the other souls, he'd wanted me to follow *his* lead. *His* path. I didn't feel guilty that I'd withheld information. I didn't give them any misinformation, at the very least. Who knew if Alex was even his real name or if the stories he'd crafted were genuine.

I kept the detective's card. *Paul Laurent.* He was a potentially viable option if I ended up getting in over my head. I ultimately decided that if Alex had any clue that I was putting a sting on him, he'd be a phantom at best.

9.

All my basic needs came flooding back to me like the sudden chop of a guillotine blade. I felt dazed due to hunger, lack of sleep, a crash from my altitudinous, adrenalized anger, and the chilly air. I needed to get back to the hospital but also needed to go home. Eat, shower, change, nap, and charge my phone. A taxi was the best solution.

I weaved through the mania of cops, hookers, and vulnerable types of all walks. I felt eyes on me. That wasn't good, but my emotional fatigue made me indifferent.

Detective Laurent waved me through the police tape and I dragged my feet, leaving the mayhem behind me. It was now dark and the inconsistency of poor neighbourhood street lights left my walk only patchily effulgent.

"Hey! Wait up!" said a voice behind me.

I turned to see a parched and beaten-down Adriana clapping her heels up the street. "Have you seen Alex recently?" she whispered with glassy, unfocused eyes.

"No… not for a bit," I responded warily. There were still traces of beauty in Adriana, but she was skeletal and her long hair was dried out like seaweed on a sunny dockside. "Are you okay?" I asked. Her skin tone was ash and her flesh looked like it was melting from her skull. She wore heavy makeup to fill in the lines and swells on her face. She had dried, white spittle on the sides of her lips.

"No," she said curtly. Her voice and posture quavered. I brought her into my arms out of compassion. Her small frame was frail and delicate. I could feel where her bones connected, even her veins.

"What happened to you?" I asked, concerned.

Adriana filled in what Detective Laurent had outlined with colour.

Alex was a pimp, human trafficker, drug dealer, arms dealer, and batshit sociopath. She and Mariana had both been 'recruited' by Alex and then 'sold' to Bruno. She didn't know the details of the transaction, but that's how she described it. They'd been devastatingly young when it'd happened. Each of the girls was vulnerable, poor, and dashed from their family. Alex had struck them as alluring, rich, and debonair. He'd promised them a better life full of the luxuries that they could've only watch other people enjoy previously. Mariana had been purchased from another 'bad man' in Milan, while Adriana had been seduced away from her troubled family after tramping their way across Europe. The tales and exploits of each girl were horrific, similar, and sadly common throughout the continent. Bruno was the tough authority figure and Alex was the princely, gift-buying older brother type. When Alex couldn't convince the girls of something, Bruno forced them. As they grew into teenagers, they were pulled from street work and became *'high-roller pussy'* due to their budding beauty and still-young age. They were presented as nubile, virgin sprites to wealthier men throughout their teenage years. They then aged, developed, and became even more beautiful. Less than 1% of the world population beautiful. Too old to extort the illegal fantasies of rich, old pedophiles, they transitioned into being escorts for celebrities and businessmen at exorbitant prices. Alex had wanted to split from Bruno's operations to start his own, but had also needed his blessing. They made a deal that Alex would continue to recruit and allow Bruno to pick from the pool of candidates to ensure the maintenance his roster of disenfranchised and orphaned youths. Alex had already set up his own prostitution and quasi-criminal ring, though lacking the pseudo-legal marquee of the strip club front that Bruno had created to legitimize his exploits. Alex had clandestinely set up various endeavours with his connections, some of which he'd apparently inherited from his father, starting with the sector he knew best: prostitution. He'd then moved on to the lucrative world of drugs, followed by the rest of his *'businesses.'* He'd chosen the neighbourhood as simply as he'd chosen which young girls and boys he'd transform into sex slave *'workers.'* It was already ruined and nobody would miss it or notice it getting worse. Why was Wing Café the nucleus? Adri didn't know. The neighbourhood had dirt cheap rent with slum lords that could normally be paid off or threatened.

Adriana spoke her piece in a quick-breathing, fact-firing way that was made all the more thumb-chewing by her anxiousness and shoulder checks.

She carried on that Mariana and Alex had always had a strange, erotic, brother-and-sister bond that was at times cute, but more master-and-slave in nature overall. Mariana looked up to Alex as a saviour, supposing that her life in Milan had been even worse. She was also helplessly attracted to her gallant chevalier. Alex treated Mariana with dominion that he guised as affected pity. She was the ultimate submissive, someone who he'd saved from the threshold of a nightmare. That made him feel knightly and noble.

Adriana contended that Mari loved Alex and Alex loved Alex, which in turn made him love himself even more. He'd been forbidden to 'take' Mari and Adri by Bruno. They made him more money than anyone else combined. However, Alex liked the way Mariana made him feel, often luring her to come with him and teasing that he'd keep her for himself by buying her out. Mariana would leave. Mariana would be found. Mariana would get beaten. Mariana would resume work. The cycle repeated itself. Mariana and Adriana were so close that Mariana wouldn't leave without Adriana, who'd figured out the unfavourable circle and had pleaded with her to give it up. She'd insisted that Alex was a snake without a spine. Sure, Adriana didn't want to be an escort, but she'd settled into her lifestyle and would one day be cut loose when she was no longer of use to Bruno.

"A couple of weeks ago, Alex came to Bruno's. We hadn't seen him since he came with you. He met with Bruno and when he came out, he said that Mariana could come with him. She was ecstatic but demanded that I be allowed to come, too. Finally, Alex said that we could both come. He said that he'd bought us, but of course he was lying. He brought us *here* and we had to stay in one of those disgusting rooms above that disgusting cafe. We weren't allowed to leave and he told us we had to fuck a couple people, just for a bit because he needed money. He didn't need the money at all, he just wanted us to do what he wanted. He made us do drugs and put things in our drinks. We slept for days at a time, and once I woke up with an ugly man on top of me without a condom on. We could hear him with men and women in the next room over. When he left, he had someone wait outside the door to make sure that we stayed in the room. I begged Mari to leave with me, but she said that she was happy, that Alex loved her, and that this was part of his bigger plan. She doesn't even know what happiness is. Never has. I escaped and was beaten by Bruno very badly, locked in a closet, and then thrown out onto the street. Bruno said that I was garbage, that I'd grown old and ugly, and was diseased like all of Alex's whores. Now, I'm living in a shelter. I don't know what I'll do."

I was unequivocally stunned and unable to fully digest the story, which I believed dogmatically. "Why are you here now? What about Mariana?" I asked her softly.

"I'm here because I heard the police came to arrest that evil man for everything he's done. I spoke to the cops. I don't know if they'll believe me. I don't even look human anymore. But, I told them everything."

I looked at her for a moment. "And… Mariana?"

Adriana spilled molten tears.

"I think…" She broke off and put herself back in my arms.

10.

Only the pharaohs were as still as I was that night. I woke up and pecked at whatever crumbs weren't mouldy in my fridge, then showered, dressed, and slumped onto the couch to check my charged phone. I responded to Stewart, letting him know what'd happened and that I'd be away indefinitely.

My only other messages were from Marta and Alex. I tepidly responded to both of them saying that work was busy and that I had a lot going on.

I set out for the hospital to see if Emi had improved. I hoped that she hadn't woken up before my arrival, then rebuked myself for such selfishness. I just hoped that she was getting better.

Alex kept texting me in a friendly manner and asking how my lady was. He pointed out that we must've been spending some quality time as a pair because it wasn't like me to not respond to him.

On the bus, I ruminated the situation at hand. I *knew* what the bastard had done. Bastard wasn't a strong enough term. He was too conceited and arrogant to fathom that someone on the median, someone average like myself, would be able to figure out his obvious machinations.

I arrived at Emiliana's bedside, passing some detectives who were on their way out. The nurse had informed them that I was her boyfriend and they quickly asked why I hadn't been there when she'd woken up. I felt like an asshole telling them that I'd slipped out for a bit to clean up. They said that victimizations of this nature, sexual assaults and near fatal attacks, can be hard for significant others to deal with as well. The victim needs unyielding support. They need familiarity and the assurance of safety and care. Their partner, then, needs a level head. They said that there were counsellors available for the partners of victims, assisting them on the survivor's long road to recovery. Victim and survivor. I focused on those words. Alex made a victim of Emi and forced her to become a fucking survivor.

Emi was weary, but responsive enough to break down into tears as soon as I walked in the room. I hugged her for an eternity plus a day, releasing, then swooping back in for another eternity. She was tender and banged up, but trying not to use the drugs as they kept her in a daze.

Some time passed before we actually shared a word amidst her crying, which broke my heart. I was too focused to shed any tears. My body and mind were on different planes. We both kept apologizing until we agreed that neither of us were at fault. I chose to shield her from the fact it was solely *my* responsibility that a demon had descended upon her life, which I vowed to remedy. Traveling back in time would've been the only real way I could've fixed the situation, and even then...

Time travel's a bitch. We may never have met. If we'd never met, we never would've fallen in love, but Emi wouldn't have been attacked either.

She told me that her father was coming to pack up her apartment and that she was returning to Germany. I asked to come with her. I had no idea whether she'd be receptive to or repulsed by the idea.

She was delighted and told me that she loved me. *I love you, too.* I offered to help her father pack her stuff. I'd finalize all my involvements in Paris before packing my suitcases and heading to Berlin. I'd stay with her as long as she was in the hospital and watch her like a hawk. She said that that was kind but entirely unnecessary. The hospital had their own *gendarmerie* and the police had said the assault seemed to be random rather than targeted.

Days passed and Emi recovered her spirit at an astonishing pace as her body struggled to keep up. I stayed at the hospital for many hours. I met her father, watched the little box television set, and had cute, harmless discussions to try and pry laughter out of her. She had good moments: when we shared earbuds and listened to her music and when I lightly moved my fingers down the bridge of her nose and cheeks. There were also moments when the quiet set in, the darkness fell, and she caught a glimpse of her reflection, becoming aware of her wounds.

"Baby..." she started. "I love you and I love how you're trying to make me forget about what happened, but we need to get it out."

"Get what out?" I waxed naivety.

"Baby... I was raped," her voice was sad and cold.

I looked straight ahead and nodded with a stiff upper lip. "I know."

She wasn't crying, just staring down at her mitts. Two fingers on her right hand were taped from having her nails torn out while trying to fend off the attacker. "Will you think of me differently?"

"No!" I said reflexively. "Of course not! Why would I?"

Her lips turned up slightly, easing her strained expression. "I just wanted to hear it. I love you."

I took her by the hand and kissed it and her deflating cheek. "I love you so much. I'll stand by you no matter what happens. I'm going to come to Berlin and start a new life with you. We can continue this one, or we can build a new castle, with spires and moats and…"

"And a pet dragon to keep an eye on all our gold?" she broke in, smiling.

"And a family of dragons! That's how much gold they'll have to protect," I said, smiling back.

I loved her so much at that moment. The hate in my soul momentarily melted and was replaced with reverence and respect for Emi's durability and strength. A psychologist that worked for the hospital came in from time to time over the next week and we talked about the attack, albeit in brief. I was entirely focused on Emi. We were talking about what life would be like in Germany, all the places she wanted to take me and the people she wanted me to meet. This galvanized her with something to look forward to. Upon her discharge, I was Berlin bound to support my lover's continued recovery.

She left the hospital with her father. He'd only spoken to me occasionally while we were boxing her things. He wasn't gruff, but understandably deep in his thoughts. Upon leaving, he shook my hand and told me that he'd see me in Berlin. He said that I was a *good guy*, that his daughter was fortunate to have me, and that he understood why she spoke of me with esteem. I thanked him and bid them both Godspeed on their journey. *Auf wiedersehen, my dear.*

11.

During Emi's recuperation in the hospital and until she was safely aboard the

Lufthansa aircraft travelling skyward from De Gaulle to Tegel, I'd kept Alex on the line by telling him that Emi had been attacked and that the police didn't have any suspects or leads. She'd been in a coma for almost two weeks before nearly succumbing to her injuries and giving up the ghost. I'd been allowed to sit in a room outside hers, which I'd done for the duration of her unconsciousness, only leaving to go home and pop into work periodically. When she woke up, she'd been immediately whisked away to the homeland by her father. I didn't even get to say goodbye. *A good touch*, I thought.

He blithely offered his sympathies, clay shoved through a keyhole, and asked me if I'd been by Wing's recently. Somebody must've ratted on me; word had travelled back to him and he needed to fish any information that he could out of me. His lack of genuine concern and hastiness to protect his neck was distasteful, though unsurprising.

I said that I'd been at Wing's. I'd been stunned by the events and had needed a friend. My phone had been dead and my auto-navigation had lead me to a familiar, *friendly* place. Alex suggested that we meet up so that I could tell him what I'd told the police. I suggested a cafe but he insisted on my apartment.

He arrived a prompt hour after the call and requested that I make some coffee, even if it was the shitty canned coffee that I loutishly dripped for my own consumption. He sat on the couch and ran his hands over his face.

"Seriously, brother," he exasperated. "Do I have to teach you how to shave? At least you smell great."

I was spooning dry granules into a crimped, white coffee filter. "The fuck? I've been a little tied up, huh."

He dropped his hands. After a moment of strict motionlessness, he arose and came to hug me. "Yes, yes, brother. Your Russian waitress, back in Moscow or wherever after such a tragedy. I'm sorry. I'm here for you if there's anything I can do."

As he hugged me, my whole body tensed with repulsion. *Russian?* I saw my opening.

"Yeah, back to Saint Pete's actually. How'd you know?"

He rubbed my shoulders with an affected look, too confident to be compassionate. "I was there when you met her, remember? The bartender with the overtly Slavic name and hard-bone face? Probably a Jew…? Am I right on that?"

I smirked. "Yeah, man. Very good guess. Accurate as an archer."

"I'm good with faces and names, brother." He released me. "You know that I'm here for you, hell, you even went to find me when you needed support. You must really respect and care about me. I can only imagine that she was beaten badly, maybe even put on life support."

It felt like he was masturbating right in front of me. "Yeah. Hell of a beating. They're surprised she lived. Raped and pummeled to the brink."

"Did you get to talk to her at all?" he inquired, probably fighting off a smile.

"Nah," I grunted. "Almost as soon as she was awake, her father, a rich Pinko oil man, took her from the city by chopper and then flew her back home on his private jet. I probably won't even speak to her again if her daddy has his way."

Alex shook his head and made a spiteful face. "Fucking Russians," he uttered. "All that mafia and oil money, still can't buy manners."

"I sure hope I do get to talk to her. I mean, I love her," I said with ostentatious hope. Alex made a pondering noise without moving his lips. He accepted a cup of coffee and walked to the couch. "She won't answer me."

"So…" he started after making a deformed face and grunt at the taste of the coffee. "You ran into the cops while you were looking for me. Tell."

I told him the bullshit he wanted to hear. I omitted that I'd found out that the red-head was a teenage prostitute, that the police had a good idea of what he'd been doing, that he'd abetted the Brazilian in crossing the river, and the entire encounter with Adriana. I maintained that I didn't know anything about him, to which he smiled widely and executed a prolonged wink, and that I didn't know what he did. I said that he was just a casual acquaintance in a city where I had no real friends. He was pleased.

"Just a bit of lying, I see. My name isn't important," he said ponderously. "There are thousands of Alexs and many of my associates don't even know my name… or haven't seen my face."

I inquired about what was happening and he was quick to feed me some lines. "Jealousy, largely. I have competitors and they get up in arms about my success. It's the dirtiest tactic, dropping dime and such, but all stratagems are in play when you're in this type of profession."

After I'd succored his fears about the police using me as bait to ensnare him and allowed him to covertly gloat about nearly destroying the woman I loved, Alex needed to return to one of his holes in the ground.

"Brother," he started as he got up to leave, "I'm sorry this visit was quick, but I'm doing some damage control. I'll be tied up this week, as I'm sure you'll be too… with work and all that normal people stuff. I'll be in touch."

He pulled me in for another hug. I quarter-heartedly returned the embrace. I locked the door behind him and sat quietly as the light disappeared from the room. Emi got a new cell phone in Berlin and her first text was a big heart. I missed her already. I was thinking that if I did something extreme, if I was able to exact some cold, ruthless vengeance upon Alex, would I ever see her again? Would avenging her sacrifice wrapping my arms around her waist and kissing the bridge of her nose?

Should I let the crocodiles sleep?

12.

I went to the office and spoke with Stewart. I told him about some of the unlucky events that had benchmarked my stay in Paris. While I loved the city, I felt it would be the death of me and had decided to leave. As an emotionally guided man, he understood and allowed me to work on pointless side projects for my pay '…as long as he got to play me, should they ever make a movie about my life.' That loveably deluded little fucker.

Then, something very bizarre happened, which unearthed yet another terrifying revelation about Alex. I'd been speaking with Emi on her new German phone number from the moment she'd unboxed it, her previous phone having been lost during the assault. Shivers and prickles shot up and down my spine as Emi's French number sent me a message asking me how I'd been one afternoon. Even more shocking than receiving a message from Emi's phone was the grisly epiphany of what actually might've happened to Marta. I played along with the French number. I asked her how home was, which she said was already cold. She said that she missed France but also felt at ease and safe, *in Russia.*

A chill carved through me.

Emi's French number carried on conversation. Marta's number texted me. Alex texted me. None of them ever wavered, deviated, or otherwise showed the slightest trace of anything irregular.

I was riddled with indecision about what I'd actually do to him, given the opportunity. The detective's business card was burning a hole in my wallet. I could call in a more capable squad in to take control of the situation, but what if they failed? What if he was able to escape by some degree of sloppiness or poor handling? Would he come after me? I felt sobered by my compelling lack of options. Each day I decided to *'sleep on it'* in order to find the appropriate vehicle to bring Alex to some form of justice. Each day I awoke without an answer.

I'd seen enough shit go down to doubt the reliability of the court system to have him incarcerated, the American court system at least. Lawyers and juries could always be bought. I didn't know how deep Alex's connections and wealth ran. Plus, was jail a good enough punishment? Was it too nice? I wished him hell, but a 1000 times worse.

The French number asked me what was new in my life. It asked if I'd found someone new and whether I'd moved on. I scrambled and answered that each day was a new one and that I was lucky to have a friend like Alex. I reminded the number that Alex was my best friend and the closest person in my life. *The number said that he sounded like a great guy.* I agreed. I said that he was intelligent, charming, and attractive. Very beautiful, in fact, adding that I was secretly attracted to him. The French number pushed a bit and I played along to make it sound like I had deeper sexual feelings. I said that I was confused about things, but that the one constant in my life was Alex and that perhaps I was *falling* for him. The number responded that maybe I should act on those feelings and that while we were together, *'she'd'* always sensed that there was someone else.

Well, well, well. That was interesting.

Alex messaged shortly after I finished the conversation with the French number. He'd freed up some time on Saturday night and wanted to get a drink.

One has to admire the shrewdness and self-serving craftiness of the amoral; using the fraudulent voice of my *'Russian'* lover, whom he'd plundered, to further his own desires and Machiavellian intentions. Such a scheme would only occur to a true villain. The purest fiend. Devoid of conscience and compunction. Blinded by his own narcissism.

Sometimes the deaf man writes a symphony while the virtuoso plays the fool. The rhinoceros gets trapped in the quicksand and watches the finch fly away.

13.

Packing for a move has a humbling effect on people. The realization that one may have too many objects, clothes, and knick knacks. In a word, *things*. Once special and unique, the things find their way into the most inconspicuous chasms and receded drawer-abysses in people's homes. There's a stress in parting with nostalgia, be it in the form of an out-of-style frock, figurines from relatives, or unused china.

The opposite experience is equally humbling. It took me less than an hour to suitcase what I couldn't be without. My entire tenement could've been razed to the ground and I would've only been mildly perturbed by having to dedicate an hour to replace those necessities. I didn't own anything sentimental or irreplaceable. My possessions were a mixture of dollar store wares, the cheapest versions of various kitchen items, some second, third, or possibly fourth-hand furniture, and clothing that I'd purchased or had been gifted to me by Marta and Alex. I had a computer that was nothing special, though I liked to keep my files for research that I'd never do. And porn. Last, there were my extensive grooming and hygiene products, which were the costliest and also my favourite items in the apartment, in spite of where they'd come from.

Emi had had all the necessary cooking utensils and machinery, cleaning supplies, and bedroom and living room paraphernalia. They were German-made: quality and long-lasting appliances. I'd have to ask her what they called *German-made* items in Germany. Did their domestic brands have the same appeal at home as they did elsewhere? Probably.

I was able to fit my life into two easily-zipped suitcases and a carry-on duffle. It was sobering to know that I'd amassed nothing of value in all my time spent living abroad. It wasn't my style to be attached to objects. *Sad, the tear-bucket overrunneth.*

As for the rest of my stuff, I could either leave it in the apartment or on the street. I was checked out, and the landlord, while not necessarily a person I wished to make life more difficult for, wasn't owed any favours either. He could probably use the junk that I was planning to leave to advertise the apartment as *partially furnished,* a common tactic used by slumlords trying to squeeze every red cent out from potential renters.

I purchased a ticket to jet me to Berlin on Monday morning, the first of December. The end of the rent cycle, very convenient. I only had to lock the apartment's deadbolt and slide the keys under the gap at the bottom of the door. I was eager to rejoin the woman I loved, who was feeling the comfort and security of being back home. The ugliness of Paris would never fade away for her. Emi was doing what she could to realign her spirit and heal from her physical wounds. It would be an understandably long process. I was proud and lifted by her strength, will, and determination not to sink into a void of helplessness. I was ready to be reunited with the thing that I cherished, that was almost destroyed, that almost destroyed me.

Alex was still in hiding from whatever forces were trying to suss him out. His braggadocio gave the impression that he didn't fear the police or Bruno's reprisal, which I'm sure he really did or he wouldn't be lying low. He was gasconade, bombastically deriding the ability of the police's inquiries and prating the ineptitude of his rivals.

"No one has anything on me. Do you know how long I've been doing this? I'm smarter than them. They might as well reopen the Dominici affair. Again."

I took his magniloquence as the cries of someone becoming unglued: gradually fracturing and unable to admit their failure. He couldn't recognize his abnormal feeling of distress brought on by the circling of vultures.

I assumed that the collapse of his network of whores and lackeys was what was making him seem more anxious than usual. He was a man who despised people, but who needed to despise them to prop himself up. Now, he needed something else to take the edge off his own declining self-image. By cutting the leash with which he'd previously bound his sphere of abused, weak-minded cohorts, he was left alone with only his depravity to keep him company.

"I smacked the phone out of a woman's hand yesterday," he texted me. "I told her that if she wanted to be a part of this world, then she should be concerned with what's happening around her and get the fuck out of my way."

I responded that such a maneuver seemed very unkind.

"It wasn't! It was necessary. You know the type of idiots that ruin your thoughts and day with their self-centeredness... Maybe it was unkind that I stepped on her phone and broke it. That might've been overkill," he responded.

I couldn't imagine that Alex would ever be able to reflect on his actions in any kind of meaningful way. You know, how life-sentenced prisoners meditate on their offenses and achieve a sense of woeful regret, even if only because they'd been caught and stripped of their most basic human rights. A normal person might repent or hang himself with a bedsheet. Alex probably wouldn't bother dissecting his behaviour, always guided by a law-like practice of what only he considered to be truthful and correct. To him, he was doing fine. Even now, Alex was incapable of identifying the repercussions that other people had suffered because of him. He could only identify his own successes within a flawed valuation system.

14.

By Saturday morning, I'd deviated from my plan to exact any revenge on Alex. I was focused on the reality that in two days, I'd be boarding an aircraft. Under two hours later, I'd be reuniting with Emiliana. I wasn't thinking about a job. I wasn't concerned about money. I was only fantasizing about how hard I wanted to squeeze her.

Thinking of revenge was stressing me out. I was sleeping very little and eating only when vital. I deliberated on just blowing off Alex until I left, leaving his fate to the multiple camps that were after him. I could abet either one, though I didn't fancy going anywhere near Bruno's station and Alex was smart enough to potentially spot a police ambush. I found faults in every new hatchling that I tried to devise. Time hadn't subsided my anger, but it'd stymied the brainless apparatuses of my rage. I could be with Emi again, and very soon, if I folded my hands on the table and sat quietly.

Alex shot me a message in the morning and asked me if we were still on for later. He said that he was excited to see me and wondered how I'd been holding up. Since dropping the hint to Emi's former French number that I had certain potential feelings for Alex, he'd begun to fawn me with questions about how I was feeling and what I was thinking. His tone was disingenuously considerate. When I tried to imagine the bits of text in his voice, it felt creepily manufactured, like the vacant, humanlike nature of a soulless mannequin with the unsettlingly realistic eyes of a marionette.

I responded with an overarching sense of despair, layers of sub-textual confusion, and a melancholy that was ripe for his exploitation. Doing it made me feel muddy, but not because of the lying. I was comfortable with the idea of lying to a liar. The muddiness came from the buildup of frustratingly unrealized fury that I had to keep buried in an already teeming reserve. This demoralizing feeling of dicklessness was made more dispiriting by the charade.

Alex had invited himself over around nine 'o clock. He said that despite everything, he still had access to some of the finest bottles of French wine ever made. I didn't give a fuck about his stupid wine and accompanying pontification. I responded pleasantly, insisting that it sounded great and that my plebeian taste buds probably wouldn't even know what to make of the tannins and minute hints of sophisticated citrus fruits. He agreed, the pompous prick.

After we'd made our plan, I paced, smoked, paced, and then smoked some more. I stopped occasionally to boil a fresh pot of acrid brown water before lighting another cigarette. I was on the *blondes*; it was a big day. At certain points in my deliberation, I repeated the words *'think, think, think,'* aloud, hoping to activate a secret portal in my brain that might contain all the answers. Instead, I focused on the word *'think'* and vocalized it to no end.

It was getting late. I had a shower to wake myself up. I was in the middle of massaging soapy lather onto my skin when the door clacked with a mirthful *'shave and a haircut'* meter. My heart bottomed out and the lump in my throat made me gag as the shower water hit my face. He was early.

Destabilizing, smart. I hollered that I'd be a minute, scraped the soap from my skin, and washed the shampoo from my hair. Glistening, I wrapped a towel around my sopping waist. I emerged from the steam-filled bathroom and found Alex in the kitchen opening and closing drawers.

"Where's your corkscrew?" he asked, mere moments before locating it. "Found it!" He cut through the foil capsule of a dark wine bottle, removing it and turning the device into the cork. "Corks!" he started with a pleasant tone. "They're the mark of a quality, old world wine. I'm willing to admit that the new world produces some prestigious collections, but screw-topped wine? Blasphemy."

I looked at him, nonplussed. "How'd you get in?"

He slowed his turning of the corkscrew, then sped up again. "Credit card in the dead bolt. Figured you wouldn't mind. I didn't know if you heard me knock."

"You're early," I said.

"A bit," he said. "I saw no reason to wait. I haven't seen you in a while. *I missed you.*"

I shuddered. Those words sounded so strange coming from him. "I need to get dressed."

"Well!" he said slyly. "You can stay like that, if you prefer. I can change into a towel, too." His smirk faded while he searched, unimpressed, through my cupboard for wine glasses. He found two, relics of Marta's insistence that I had glasses for when we drank wine at my place. We did once.

He frowned as he held them to the dim kitchen light. He used his sleeve to polish them. Still not speaking, he poured two glasses and swirled them, eyeing the legs making their descent. Seemingly satisfied, he took a cultured sip and closed his eyes. "It's disrespectful to the winemakers of Bordeaux to imbibe from these goblets, but they'll have to do." He held a glass of dark red wine towards me.

"After I finish getting dressed," I said.

Alex slinked through the small kitchen and brushed off a spot on the couch, motioning for me to sit.

"Sit... Have a glass first. It's stuffy and smells like cheap heating in here. Come." I was holding my towel, though it was knotted quite securely around my waist. I sat and accepted the glass, looking into it. He laughed.

"I wouldn't ruin *this* wine by spiking it." He'd read my mind. "The only thing in that wine beyond the tireless perfection of southern Frenchmen is whatever debris you failed to wash out of your vulgar stemware."

He looked at me earnestly. I wet my top lip with the wine.

"It's hard to enjoy wine when you can't drink it properly, no thanks to that unbecoming moustache," he said.

I placed the wine on the table.

"How have you been holding up?" he asked, placing a hand on my naked shoulder.

I contrived a look of wistfulness, trying to assume the character that he'd be expecting due to his espionage. "I've been... okay," I started. "It's been a tough adjustment, though we weren't together all that long, so I don't know what I'm so conflicted about."

He nodded smugly.

"I guess I've just been confused. I don't feel like myself. I would've loved to say goodbye and find out what happened to Emiliana, but that wasn't in her father's plans."

"Have you guys been in contact?" he asked knowingly.

"A bit, on more of a *friend* basis. I don't have many friends, so I kind of take what I can get. Except for you, I suppose. And you've been there for me, even though I haven't seen you much lately. You've got a lot going on."

A flicker of satiety and hunger danced across his face. "Yes, *I have*. I've always been by your side. I've always been your closest confidant. I've wanted you to follow me as I am. I see great potential in you." He reached for his wine. "I've been... preoccupied, but that preoccupation will dissipate and blow away, as it always does. Time is an important factor here. Time and love," he concluded. He left a hand on my knee.

"Alex," I started. "When the officers asked me about you...I would've lied to keep you safe, but I didn't have to. I don't know much about you. You've told me things about your father, your travels, and your childhood, but very little. I think that with the current state of things, you shouldn't feel scared to tell me a bit more. I'd love to hear."

Still rubbing my thigh, Alex grinned elegantly. He released his hand and my intestines instantly felt less constricted. He leaned over and placed his wine glass down.

"About little old me?" he asked as he lounged comfortably on the couch, facing me. "There's quite a bit to unpack. I've already told you more than most. However, I suppose I can share a bit more. And I will, but I want something in return."

The ground below was falling away from me. A forced reality check. My situation suddenly felt very lucid. "What," I stated, not in the form of a question.

"I want to watch how great you've become at shaving. You are my pupil, after all," he said with unabashed coyness. He tilted his head down and stared up at me, trying to look endearing.

"Fine," I said shortly. "Let's go to the bathroom. I'm feeling quite exposed in this towel."

"Perfect."

He filled his glass and plucked it from the table.

15.

Alex followed me into the bathroom. The room was still sultry with the smell of the suds that I'd been using in the shower. I grabbed the razor. He snatched it from my mitts and flicked the blade. *Snikt.* He stroked the edge of the razor against his thumbnail, gingerly wiping away the little flakes of nail dust that had collected on the blade. He paused.

"Not sharp enough," he said. He reached for the strop. It was hanging from a mounted bracket beside some cheap hand and face towels, the kinds that were sprayed with preservative plastics and made water bead on the surface instead of drying the skin. Testing the durability of the bracket, Alex extended the strop and began to drag the blade across it.

"You've kept this baby in fine condition," he said. "But, you can hurt yourself and your pretty face if it's not sharp enough."

I cleared my throat and nodded silently. I was trying to control my mounting anxiety and renewing rage.

"Nervous, huh?" he said, sitting on the lidded toilet and momentarily glancing at my grimace. I wondered whether the thudding in my chest was as sonorous in the little bathroom as it was in my ears.

Alex tested the blade again, this time against the flesh side of his thumb.

"*Magnifique*," he said. "Where's your lather?" I opened the mirrored cabinet and removed a small, porcelain bowl and a wooden-handled, horsehair shaving brush. He placed the folded razor on the basin and snatched the cup that contained a slightly rounded bar of soap. "My god, brother," he said. He decanted a stream of water from the faucet and began to froth the soap. "The bar's still so big. Do you ever shave?"

I palmed the razor into my right hand, trembling slightly at the knees and even more violently within. Alex closed the cabinet and turned my face towards his, lathering the bar of soap and empowering the earthy scent as the lather became richer and creamier. He began to whip the brush quickly and gently against my chin, moving from my cheek to my ears using circular movements. Intermittently, he looked straight into my eyes. I was concentrating on the swooshing noise of the lathered soap. It was normally a calming sound, but at that moment it was agitating my already over-extended nerves.

"There," Alex brushed a final dollop of soap onto my nose, trying to be cute. "Let's see how far you've come." I wiped the foam from my nose and rubbed it onto my toweled hamstring. "Oh, wait a moment," he said. He sneered after grabbing a face towel, wincing with a lemon-sucking expression as he felt the tawdry fabric between his fingers. He folded it with the ends meeting the middle and laid it over the edge of the sink. "This will have to do," he said. "I hope this piece of shit doesn't scratch *my* blade." I looked at him. I could've used some wine to steady my hand.

"Tell me about yourself while I do this," I suggested. "It makes me nervous being watched."

He placed his hand on my shoulder. "Hey. Listen, hey…" he started, "don't be nervous. I'm here, and I'd never judge you. Well, not totally true, but I *am* here."

I know you are, I thought. He was being a cryptic and overly-sweet; a smitten version of someone else. Gliding his hand down my spine before reaching for his glass of wine, he watched me.

For some reason, I started to feel a little more comfortable. I'd realized that I alone had given breath to my mind's creation of Alex as more than a man, almost superhuman. He didn't seem to take my apprehensiveness and nerve-jarred behaviour as anything more than the high-strung jitters of suppressed, forbidden love. Confidence billowed from him like factory smoke. He wasn't aware that he was mistaking my repressed rage and emotional militancy as coquettish submissiveness, curious willingness, and closeted sexual desire. It felt easier and easier to play along when I realized that his overconfidence wasn't only a character weakness, but a fatal flaw.

Snikt. I blossomed the blade from the handle and moved it near my jawline, pausing. "Alex, tell me how you met Bruno."

He nearly choked on a generous sip of red and swallowed hard.

"Well… I guess you could probably tell that we were more than just partners…"

I scraped the razor across my cheek, feeling the keenness of its tongue. I wiped the foam and hair on the towel and nodded.

"You seemed quite friendly. How did the relationship begin?"

He looked back at me and sighed.

"Much of what I've told you up until now is somewhat accurate, I don't like to disclose my past as I only know pieces myself. I'm pretty sure that I was born in New Zealand. My father was a man of arms and I never met my mother."

I scraped the razor again, removing more hair and more lather.

"My father said that my mother was a whore. He hated her and the fact that she'd betrayed him by leaving him with an offspring. I always sensed that he hated me, but I looked very much like him. I don't know why he tortured himself by keeping me around. Taking me, lugging me from country to country like a trunk. He always said that my mother was dead, and for all I know it's true. I wasn't lying when I said I'd never known her."

I gave him a look of compassion and he shook his head. "No. It's nothing to pity. I had too many gifts to be sad: my looks, my charm, and the ability to learn a language just by hearing it. I knew that I was smart from a young age. I was also bored. You know what intelligent, bored children do? They get into mischief, start gangs, and procure all kinds of trouble. I also knew that I was charismatic and handsome. I wiggled my way out of any detention or expulsion. Instead of being put in a class for troubled kids, I was in honour roll classes."

I nodded in agreement, continuing to glide the razor along the contours of my jaw, purposely taking tiny strips of soap at a time.

"My father, the Lord himself, may have become lonely. One day, he decided that he wanted a lackey to tote around. He used to smuggle things in my asshole, have me lie to customs... whatever he needed. I wasn't fond of the pistol whips and backhands. He taught me a lot, however... how to be a man, take care of myself, and read people like easily digestible pamphlets. He taught me how to shoot, stab... when to run and where to hide. I saw him kill and fuck in the same rooms that I'd been beaten in for speaking out of turn. He taught me how to shave, actually."

"So," I started, disinclined to burrow towards the deeper psychological meaning of this fucked up father-son relationship, "he taught you a lot. I mean, not traditional learning, but you got some education here and there. Even being on the move so often.

"We travelled around so much that my upbringing was mostly made up of second-hand care from my father's whores, which he'd later beat them for. And reading. He didn't want his son to be a soft, doughy creature. Keep in mind, this was all before I was 13... or maybe 14? I'm not sure how old I am. In my thirties for sure, but I have no idea when my birthday is. I never celebrate it. My aunt and uncle in America usually bought me a cake, a pair of khakis, and a polo shirt around my birthday during the years I was with them, so maybe I was a summer baby made in drab, gray winter. Although, that'd be summer in New Zealand..."

He trailed off and I picked up his train of thought as I wiped the blade again. "I recall that you guys went to all kinds of... governments?"

He resumed. "Ah, yes. My father was a gun runner with a taste for human trafficking. He was a black and white person with very little appreciation for the lighter sides of things. Everything to him was, well, business. Everything was available to sell, buy, or be negotiated for. You're certainly taking your time with that razor."

I chuckled '*hmpf*' and continued, as did he.

"We'd been in Europe for a while, mostly Russia and the East. I felt like my father was getting tired, perhaps feeling old. I have no idea how old he was. He mused, in one of his infrequent moments of outward deliberation, that he really wanted to do business in France. He thought it'd be a nice place to remain sedentary and hold fortress, as opposed to the nomadic lifestyle he'd been living for however long.

"I see…" I mused, continuing to pry.

"Anyways, he wanted to put his feet up on leather and operate from a centralized location. Paris, as you've learned, has a *wonderful* crime scene. And, it's central! My father had pissed on and pissed off a lot of people in his time. Some stabs in the back, some infringement on his rivals' territories… and he was a fucking dick to everyone, especially me. When we arrived in France, he was a lifelong veteran of smuggling, running, and organizing various criminal enterprises, but his luck expired. Within months, maybe a year, of setting up shop in Paris, he was murdered."

"I'm sorry," I said.

He carried on without responding. "Now that I've been around the block a few times myself, I realize that his murder was probably justified. I didn't care then, and I don't care now. He meant nothing to me. Beatings and stuffing heroin up my ass were his hugs and kisses. One time, the balloon burst. I had to get my stomach pumped and an epinephrine needle stabbed into my heart. He beat me bad for that. Totally my fault, *obviously*. Anyways, he was assassinated directly in front of me, inside a little cabin outside of the city. It was quick. Quicker than I would've done, which I'm sure I would've eventually grown the mangoes to do, had the hitmen not."

"My father's murder left me in the hands of said assassins. They took me, had some fun, but ultimately had no use for me. They sold me to a Chinese gang. A man had me fill bags with powder all day and offer myself to his cronies all night. This didn't continue for very long, as shitty as it was. The place was busted and I was freed! Free to be tossed into the streets with nothing. Alone, dirty, and not yet a man. That was when I met Bruno. He was younger, sprier, and more attractive back then. He offered me money for doing what I'd already been doing for little money, or for free. I was too attractive to be a street kid with no pimp. I took him up on his offer and started whoring myself out under his hand as hair finally started to grow hair on my balls. Not too long after that, Bruno realized that his female whores were genuinely attracted to me. He offered me a situation in which I didn't need to suck and fuck. Instead, under much easier conditions, I was to use my *effortless* charm and *stunning* smile to woo and wow vulnerable men and women to work for Bruno. I was able to make him lots of money and, because I refused to numb myself with drugs, stole that money away and began planning my own ventures. *My own empire.*

I said *Jesus,* or something, and he carried on without idling.

"I was a *vedette* at spotting and serenading the young to come away with me and work for Bruno. I even occasionally succeeded at winning over girls that had families with decent parents that *actually* cared for them. To me, those were moral victories. As I grew older and stronger, I became more of a partner to Bruno. He knew I was smart and we were on equal terms. I strengthened both my connections and ability to bring people over to my side. While Bruno focused solely on prostitution, I realized the same thing that my father had while running guns: *Why pigeonhole yourself?* I'd been consorting with many gangs, using the gifts of my indiscernible ethnicity, multilingualism, and mastery of concealing my hand. Despite the fact that I was great at keeping my face hidden, Bruno heard whispers of his boy testing the waters elsewhere, which instantly smelled of treachery. I calmed him down by insisting that I was still his boy, and he told me that he considered me his son. A son that he'd pimped out ruthlessly until he proved himself more valuable, but a son nevertheless. I continued to recruit because I said that I would, and I enjoyed it. I still enjoy it. It's one of the few things I truly enjoy doing. I love nothing more than starting with a pure, damaged, and impressionable young recruit, breaking them down, and then building them back up again in whatever way I desire. *Love.* My God. The number of lives I've changed. Give me an award. I'm like Jane Addams, no?"

As his voice inflected in the form of a question, I snapped out of the stupor I'd been engulfed by while listening to his story. The picture Alex was painting was terrible, but the candor he was using to describe being beaten, raped, sold, and bought was akin to that of a man sharing his mundane workday at the plant to his wife of 30 years over the same nuked tuna casserole as last night.

I felt nothing, however. His story seemed quasi-believable. The autobiographical timeline was sound and his account had been delivered with cold sincerity. There was no remorse; not a moment of humanity that earned him any compassion or mercy.

I took one final swipe at my chin, nicking the bone and causing a tiny cut.

"Silly boy," Alex said. He placed his glass down and grabbed the towel. "Hold this here."

He reached into the cabinet and grabbed some Italian aftershave, untwisting the cap and filling the room with its aroma. Licorice and alcohol. "Move the towel," he said, splashing some aftershave into his palm. "This might sting." I winced as he slapped his hands against my face, immediately stopping the blood flow of the tiny cut. "You're *almost* a pro," he encouraged. He closed the mirror and I caught my reflection. My face was now as smooth as a calm lake at sunset. I was gaunter than I recalled, almost ghostly. "You can stay in the towel. I recommend it!" he said while backing out of the bathroom. "Feel free to put on some comfortable clothes if you wish, however."

I went to my bedroom and slid on some jeans and a light shirt. I dropped my cell phone into my pocket, followed by the folded razor.

16.

Alex was on the couch, sitting with the facial expression and one-leg-folded-over-the-other posture of a tipsy woman who was moments away from becoming aggressive without instigation. I sat on the other corner of the couch and picked up the wine. I then placed it down on the table before getting up again.

"What's wrong?" I heard Alex say from behind me.

"Just want something stronger," I said without turning around. I grabbed a bottle of single malt scotch and poured two carpenter's fingers into a rocks glass.

"Where were we?" I asked.

"Can't remember," he responded lazily, looking at me under low-lidded eyes.

"You wanted to leave Bruno and start your own…" I began. That made him remember.

"Ah, yes," he said nonchalantly. "That was around the time I met Mari and Adri…"

"How are those two beauties, by the way?" I asked.

"Good! Still saving money to buy their way out. Saw them not too long ago. Adri told me to say hello!"

The fuck she did.

"I met the girls separately and took them to Bruno. I wanted Adri for my business; she was going to be a killer. I wanted Mari for myself, however. There was something special about her. She wasn't unique, but had so much potential… like you! She was a personal best. That always caused conflict between Bruno and I. He fancied her a lot, too. Anyways, little by little, I was able to build up my businesses. I started renting flats and running other enterprises from separate locations. I spread them out so that no one knew they were working for the same man. I had to get my hands dirty. I even had things done to me for the sake of business. I enjoy the gritty stuff. You have to love what you do."

He laughed, but I couldn't even manage a chuckle.

"Anyways, I'd come across a shitty little area, one of the most over-looked and forgotten about areas in the greater Paris region, and thought: *Where better to plant my flag?* The area already had copious amounts of whores with two-bit pimps. There were drug houses and addicted dealers that could be controlled or taken care of. There was also a little cafe owned by a Chinese man. You've met him."

"Wing?" I asked.

"Yes, that man," Alex stated. "He looked older, but I recognized him from my youth. Even better, he owned some buildings I wanted, so I threatened to kill his family if he didn't sell them to me for a very, *very* low asking price. So, he did."

"And, his family?"

"La Seine."

I'd always thought of myself as an atheist. Who was this *God* people were always fighting over?

Being an atheist denies the existence of the Devil, however. At that point, I knew I'd met the Devil, so there had to be a God. He was some coward scientist hiding under his bed, afraid of what he'd created.

"Are you surprised by this?" Alex touched my chin.

"No," I whispered. I must've been quiet for a shade too long. "Having the life and upbringing that you've had, it doesn't surprise me that you've been forced to do awful things. Enjoying it is something else..."

He reached for the bottle and turned another large dose of wine into his glass.

"It is what it is," he said calmly. "I don't do anything without a reason. I trust and really do care about you, and I know you didn't or wouldn't go to the cops. Why would you? You care for me as well." He narrowed his eyes. "You care about me *a lot.*"

"Of course I do," I affirmed, reaching to take a sip of my scotch. Alex tried to slow my hand, but I forced through and took at least an ounce into my mouth and swallowed with audible force.

"Do you ever wonder why you either never closed the deal with any girls, or settled for women that were beneath you?" Alex asked.

"Because..." I was thinking about how to respond, "I was lying to myself?" I said with affected uncertainty. "Maybe I always knew what I wanted." I finished definitively, at least.

He nodded and moved closer, placing both my scotch and his wine on the table. He moved to climb on top of me. One leg, then the other. He straddled me and paused for a moment. "This is it, right?" he asked with sly surety.

"It might be," I said as I ran my hand down his back. I suddenly felt a protrusion near his belt. "What the fuck?" I recognized the outline of a pistol.

"Shh," he whispered while reaching back and withdrawing the piece. "I need to be protected, to protect you, if something should happen." He tossed it onto a cushioned chair. "All the way over there, brother. *Lover,*" he said softly in my ear. He put his hand on my chest. "Your heart's beating out of control. I knew why you were acting so strange. This is new to you. You've been acting nervous all evening,"

"Are you gay?" I asked.

He scoffed. "I told you, I'm not anything. When I like something, I take it," he moved in to kiss me.

My pocket began to vibrate. I stopped him to address it.

Alex sat up, vexed. "Kind of rude to answer your phone." He watched me as the screen lit up my face. "Well, is it important?" he asked. Annoyed. Sarcastic.

"It's Emi." I turned the phone towards him to show him what he'd been craning his neck to snoop.

He snatched the phone and quickly scanned the screen, taking note of the name, number, and conversation boxes. He looked confused. Perhaps he thought that this was a message he didn't mean to send or had released unknowingly. Then, his look mutated into something I'd never seen him express before. *Fear.* He lowered the phone. His face was mortified. I popped the razor open.

Snikt.

Before he had the chance to move, I summoned every ounce of anger and sadness that he or anyone else had caused me. I felt my life of nervousness and anxiety transform into a precise, rampaging strength, swinging the recently-sharpened blade at Alex's face.

He must've seen the moment where my timidity melted into a gorgeously twisted vision of hate and scorn. I slashed at his head with the overhanded zeal of a tennis serve. A battle-axe hurled at a war bonnet. An Angolan slave swinging a scythe to draw the first blood of the rebellion. But harder.

The thin blade fidgeted as it tore. It scraped against the impenetrability of skull and bone beneath Alex's skin. A sudden gushing erupted as the edge entered his eye socket and lifted a part of his nose from its cartilage foundation. He pulled away with a bellicose groan and fell through the cheap coffee table.

I walked over to Alex's pistol and stuffed it into my pants. I trampled his hand and then kicked his chest and groin with my bare feet. I stomped on his leg and arm joints, hard enough to feel his muscles and veins give way to my heels. He wailed and shrieked as he tried to collect himself, backing up to the wall beside the bathroom door, unsure of which wound to tend to first. He leaked a thick, red trail to the spot where he stopped. It pooled.

Alex's blood was falling from the razor. Its blade was still secure and sharp. I approached him and saw myself in the bathroom mirror. His wounds had sprayed blood at my face and spattered all over my shirt.

White had been an unfortunate colour choice. I stared into my own frozen eyes momentarily, almost frightened by the image. I didn't see a glimmer of regret.

"I guess," Alex said while fiddling with his flapping nose, "she passed my little test." I swung another barefoot kick into his ribs and felt them concede. His eyes were like a peeled moon, but his voice never wavered. It was calm and cool. "The other one didn't, but then again, she couldn't survive. Pity. *She* wasn't supposed to die. I took no joy in that one. I knew she wouldn't have passed, but I think I got carried away. God. That nattering, bitchy voice. Had to shut it up. She was too weak to survive."

I threw my shin towards his face, which hit hard against his temple and sent him down. I bent down to check him out. His eyes were pinched closed and he was massaging his head where I'd just planted a right kick, groaning and grunting through his facial flap. "Fucking Russians," he said.

"She's German, you fucking idiot."

I walked towards the bathroom.

Alex scoffed painfully. "Then, you knew. You played along and didn't let on. Good job. You've learned well. Feel free to howl, little wolf man. You're there." His smirk made his face a Picasso.

"You didn't *teach* me shit!" I yelled. "You tried to use me for some weird, sick fantasy while hurting the women I cared about. Killing! Killing people I cared about!"

"Did you, though?" he started. "Care, I mean."

"You killed Marta, the Brazilian, Mariana… and tried to kill Emiliana. You probably had me raped in my unconscious state and who knows what else. You ruined my fucking life!"

"I never hurt you. I never did anything to bring you pain. I lied, maybe, but that was for a greater purpose." He reached into his pocket, one hand on his face wounds. "Look at this," he said as he passed me his phone.

It was a video of him, myself, Carol, and the redhead. I was passed out on one side of the bed. Carol was trying to wake me, undressing me and performing fellatio to no avail. She mounted me as the redhead grabbed my flaccid penis and tried to jam it into Carol's pussy. I was out cold. My dick flopped over onto my leg. They started messing with each other and the camera man.

"See?" Alex began. "Just a practical joke. Pranks that friends do."

"You're fucked up. You're so beyond fucked up. You're insane, you psychotic fucking murderer!"

"No!" he screamed back. "I'm neither crazy nor a psychopath." Alex was showing the signs of a reptile heating its blood for the first time. "You *still* can't comprehend what I am and what I do! You're a weak, ineffective, and average human being. You're painfully unimportant. You're prepared to simply settle into a boring, average existence and wait out the remaining doldrums of your meek, pedestrian life, blaming everyone and everything but your own lack of motivation and strength. You piss and moan about not being anything, but what you really are is stupid. A powerless pussy. You lack the courage and agency to try and make a difference. Or at least the intelligence and entrepreneurial spirit. There's promise in there, but you lack guidance. I knew it from the first moment I saw you. You were ripe with potential, spinning about pointlessly and needing a shepherd."

I listened to Alex while red syrup lurched steadily from his wounds. Half of me wanted to finish his throat with the razor, but the other half wanted to crouch down and listen.

"I figured you and your *infinite genius* out. I resolved to leave you looking like this," I pointed at him with the razor.

"Ha! I let my guard down, got sloppy, and didn't cover my tracks. Otherwise, you'd be oblivious that I ruined your women. I was also only a short time away from owning you like I do my whores. You probably didn't even plan this."

Alex smeared his wounds, his face dyed red.

"You." He pointed at me. "You are *fragile,*" he slowly eased his words out with bitter vindication and luxurious intent. "Fragile and weak! You're no different from those impressionable teens that I lure on the street. A wink and smile here, and gift or two there… If I hadn't been careless, you would've been holding my pocket, doing whatever I asked of you. What do you think you helped me move that day I gave you the razor? Drugs? In broad daylight? No… just the casual relocation of some hacked up Spanish bitch and the lights and tools I used to clean up the mess. You were idiotic enough to carry…"

I kicked him in the sternum. Something snapped. He doubled over.

"This is looking a lot more like a beating than self defense," he rasped.

I briefly imagined someone entering my place. Perhaps the neighbours would summon the police, though that was uncommon in a poor area like this. He hadn't damaged the lock and my fingerprints had likely obscured his on the pistol. I shrugged and caught the sight of my dead eyes in the bathroom mirror once again.

"Yup... I guess she passed the test," Alex coughed a blood clot out onto the wooden floor. He was pale and mumbling. "That Russian or German bitch, whatever the fuck she is." Alex seemed to be floating between different planes of consciousness now. He was grumbling in shrapnel thoughts, trying to prop himself back into a seated position against the wall.

"I tried. You could've been just like me... I saw it in you. You couldn't cut it, maybe? Maybe, it was weakness. Maybe, I tried to move too fast?" He was talking to himself, then looking up at me. "You and I aren't *that* different. If you'd had one more bad day in your life, we could've been the same. I wasn't greedy, was I? Can you honestly keep living without my influence? Can you go back and look at your entire life without the perspective I've given you? Will you be the same after this? I've changed you. I know it. You know it. I'm inside you like a worm. Like a sea serpent chewing at your organs. Can you still believe in things like hope and love? Have you ever really had or felt either? You and I both know that I opened a door for you. Make me proud, brother. Howl."

He held his arm out.

I walked past Alex's hand, his eyes trailing me. I stood at the bathroom sink. I washed the blood from my hands and the still-sharp, still-formidable razor. *Snikt.* Goddamn, that thing was well-made. Still sharp. *Snikt.* American craftsmanship. Land of the free. Fuck yeah. *Snikt, snikt.* Get it all off. Get the blood off my face. Take my shirt off and scrub my chest a bit. Watch the blood bypass the toothpaste and random white blotchiness in the sink and swirl down the drain. Lots of thinking to do.

I looked at myself in the mirror.

Am I insane? Or am I too weak or sheltered or immature or mentally underequipped to deal with life like an adult?

How should I end this?

EPILOGUE

Shake the cobwebs off, man. How long have you been zoning out for? Look at that motherfucker, still alive. Those eyes. Like a cartoon chipmunk. Is he still alive? Did he give up the ghost just like that? Kind of anti-climactic. Was that a breath? I should probably check. The son of a bitch got what was coming to him, motherless piece of shit. As angry as those words sound, I'm not angry. His demise, or imminent demise, is logical. I know he understands it; I couldn't have done it without his help.

'You taught me well, brother. Santé!'

What a weird way to smile. I've never really liked my smile. It looks too fake or too big. Too many worry lines. High-ass cheekbones. I guess that's what happens when you grow up more afraid of atom bombs than knee scrapes. Every time it rained, I felt a little on edge, worried that we'd have to pack up two of each animal. But, you all know that. God save the platypus! And, my mouth is too big and bottom teeth too crooked.

I miss Emi. I miss her so bad.

She rang. I should probably let her know that I might not make my flight. I have to clean this up. Maybe a maid? I have enough ducats. Should I unpack? Make it look like I wasn't about to flee? The best option might be to ring Detective Laurent. He'll get this. Fuck, I wasn't totally honest, but I feared for my life? No, I didn't. Hey! Stop smiling. That shit won't fly with the street-sharpened flat foots and their good-cop-bad-coppery.

I hope Emi's alright. In Berlin with her loved ones. I passed the test, or she did. We did, I suppose? What do we win? Or is this some kind of training exercise where there's no winning or losing? Only a metaphysical test? Take some time to get in touch with your inner existentialist, brother. I wish it was like The Price Is Right, I could use a fine German sedan. Good on gas.

He wanted me to be like him? Could I? How does one squire a Morning-star? How did Sancho not aim the lance on the knight errant himself? Does a normal person have the capability to emulate someone who's abnormal? Maybe not a person? Can someone learn sociopathy? It feels like converting a person with no religious experience into the Pope. Is this fumata blanca or fumata nera?

Me. Fragile... Skin and bone are fragile, but the spirit's bulletproof. The soul's a liquid state. God's alive and playing chess with his most decorated pupil. The conversation is always pertinent between moves.

Ow-oww-owwwwwwww. Hear me howl?

This entire situation is inconvenient and might take a while to resolve. I can't remember if I bought insurance. I probably didn't. I don't know if they have renter's insurance in France, so I probably didn't. I sure as fuck didn't buy flight insurance. Thanks, Captain Foresight.

What's that? My stomach! I'm famished. I wonder if ordering a pizza would be in bad taste. I could meet the delivery guy at the bottom, hand him the cash, and come back up. I don't feel like pizza. It's too greasy, and I want the ol' abdominals popping for when Emi wants to touch them. I wonder what she thinks about sex now. I know it's too soon, but I wonder how long that will take. Sandwich! But more like a wrap. Kebab meat with no bread, for old times' sake. That's what I feel like. And a glass of Orangina. I usually hate it, but really have a craving for it now. There's a tabac twenty feet from my door downstairs.

It's fucking stuffy in here...

ACKNOWLEDGMENTS

I'd like to thank those that were directly involved with the process of making the book. Young Boy Al for the photography. Spencer Motherfucking Croft for catering to my Every Little Tiny Trivial request with the art and shit. The Homie Syd: if it wasn't for you and our trustworthy friendship this would have never seen the light of day. Mama Bear Christina Cottell for being my first reader and getting through the original version *and* not calling the cops. To everyone that supports me, thank you, I love you.

To those that don't, you know what to do.
-Papa Croft